DAWN ATTACK

The mad minute was close at hand. Lieutenant Colonel Curt Carson checked his deployment of detachments. What he saw on his helmet display looked good. A silence settled on his tacomm channel. In the Yemeni desert command post, only the sounds of dawn were heard. Until…

Commence firing! came the call according to plan.

The ridge erupted with the sounds of rapid fire Saucy Cans. Carson riveted his attention on the road ten kilometers to the northeast where fifty warbots were rolling along against a backdrop of sharply rising bluff.

Suddenly, his tacomm came alive with the cry *Incoming!* and the explosions of 53-millimeter enemy shells burst on the scene. They were firing at maximum range, and the small caliber shells wouldn't pack much punch by the time they reached their targets.

Just as Carson had planned. He had them now!

I0627591

#10 GUTS AND GLORY

WARBOTS

G. HARRY STINE

Imholt Press

Originally published by Pinnacle Books

Copyright © 1991 by G. Harry Stine

Currently Published by Imholt Press, LLC

ISBN: **978-1-951810-03-0**

For more information contact **tim@timothyimholt.com**

TO:

Bryant A. Thompson, Captain, USAF (Ret.)

"The love of glory, the ardent desire for honorable distinction by honorable deeds, is among the most potent and elevating of military motives."

- Alfred Thayer Mahan, *Life of Nelson* (1897)

"There may they dig each other's graves, and call the sad work glory."

- Percy Bysshe Shelley, *Queen Mab* (1813)

Forward

In this tenth installment of Warbots, G. Harry Stine takes us further into the world of robotic warfare that G. Harry saw as the future, we see it as the present. The technology we use for this task improves every day. G. Harry reminds us that no good weapon or tactic development program goes unnoticed.

Some things seem to change at an ever-increasing pace, while other things stay the same. One of the never changing things is the situation in Yemen. This time G. Harry Stine puts our Warbot troops in the middle of that centuries old regional conflict as a "guard" force. That guard force that is always there just to take incoming and never make progress.

Will this time be different? After all this is Curt Carson we are talking about, and this time he brought his friends.

This is a topic we struggle with today. Can the United States be the world police force?

Can we do this policing when we can't seem to deal with our own internal struggles.

Is this sort of mission something we should do?

Us being a police force is certainly something we should continually do? Or in the middle of us finally turning the tide will the President of the United States call it quits and pull troops home?

I hope you enjoy this installment into Warbots, I give you Warbots Book 10: Guts and Glory.

Timothy Imholt PhD

Chapter One

"Don't touch that warbot!"

Sergeant Major Edwina Sampson yelled at the top of her voice, but it was too late. Technical Sergeant Bob Vickers' hand was already within centimeters of reaching out to punch the test button on the side of the recovered M33A3 General Purpose Warbot.

She had time only to spin on her heel and hit Lieutenant Colonel Curt Carson across the chest with a blow strong enough to knock him down. This wasn't an easy thing to do. Carson was a big man. But he wasn't expecting it and Sampson knew precisely how to take down a man in a hurry without injury.

The blow knocked the wind out of Curt, but as he hit the ground he knew why Sampson had done it.

The warbot exploded.

He heard something go over his head. Several things. One of them warbled. Fortunately, because Sampson had knocked the wind from him, his mouth had been open. That had equalized the effect of the concussion on his ear drums. But his ears rang nonetheless.

Vickers screamed in agony.

"What the hell?" was the cry from Sergeant Max Moody who was standing next to Vickers.

Gasping for breath, Curt rolled on his side and looked.

The warbot was still standing there, but it had a curtain of dust and sand around its barrel-like base and it had been moved about half a meter by the force of the explosion. Curt quickly surmised that the explosion had taken place beneath it.

Vickers was on the ground, rolling in pain and screaming. He was trying to grasp the bloody masses that had been his booted feet.

Moody was still standing, but blood was running from his nose as a result of the concussion. And he was staring stupidly in shock at the blood now covering his lower legs and ankles.

Sampson continued to react because Curt couldn't. He was still gasping to regain his breath. She whipped a hand tacomm unit from her equipment harness. "Medic! Medic! Injuries at the BOTECO recovery site! Hump it over here! Move it!"

Then she quickly asked Curt, "Sorry, Colonel! You okay?"

Curt managed to nod his head as his lungs slowly began to fill again and his breathing became regular. But he couldn't speak yet.

Seeing that. her regimental commander was in no serious trouble, Sampson gave her attention to the injured platoon sergeant and warbot technical repair sergeant. She stepped up to. Moody first and told him in a drill sergeant voice, "Max! Lie down! Lie down right now! You've been hurt. You'll be all right. The medics will be here soon."

"Uh...uh...It blew up. It shouldn't have done that," Moody replied in slurred tones, his voice betraying that he was in shock - hurt very badly but not fully realizing it yet.

"Damned right!" She wanted to kill the pain before he realized he was hurt, so she ripped the medikit from her equipment harness, tore open a syringe, and gave him a shot of painkiller. "Now, do as I told you. Lie down. And shut up."

Sergeant Max Moody was a disciplined professional non-com with seven years' service in the 3rd Robot Infantry (Special Combat) Regiment, the Washington Greys. He'd been through six combat operations, all of them deadly and all of them demanding of both the discipline and initiative of a twenty-first century American high-tech soldier. Even in his shocked condition, he knew that something was wrong, that another Washington Grey was looking out for him, and that he'd better do what he was told. So, he sat down, then flopped over on his back. The painkiller just began its work when the realization of pain hit him, and he began to moan.

Vickers was already down and still screaming. Sampson also gave him a painkilling injection. It took a few seconds for it to have some effect.

"Jesus!" Edie Sampson muttered as she got a good look at Vickers' legs. He'd been standing closest to the M33A3 Jeep when something underneath it went off. His feet, ankles, and calves were a bleeding mass of shrapnel-like wounds.

Curt had regained enough of his breathing control to join her. He saw why she'd vented that irreligious epithet. The two sergeants were a mess. Because it was something he could use quickly, he whipped the blue and yellow scarf from around his neck and began wrapping it tightly around Moody's left knee. "Edie! Tourniquet," he rasped as he sucked air. "Get that bleeding under control. The back of the knees. Popliteal pressure point..." He ripped the seal from his medikit to get at a bandage that could be used as a second tourniquet.

"Gotcha, Colonel," the redheaded Number Two regimental NCO fired back without looking at him. Then into the tacomm, she called, "Ferret Leader! Cavalier Leader! Get me some security cover in the BOTECO recovery area! Damned if I want those fucking Yemenis shooting at me while I'm tending to wounded..."

Biotech Juanita Gomez was suddenly there, all business as she unslung her backpack to get at biotech supplies. She took one look, then grabbed her tacomm unit. "Biotech Leader, this is Ferret Biotech. On that medicall that just came in from Grey Techie, get another biotech over here stat! And get me a quick picker-upper. Stand by to receive wounded."

Curt didn't hear the reply. He was too busy wrapping tourniquets around Moody's knees to staunch the flow of blood.

"Easy! Easy!" Edie tried to comfort Vickers. "The medics are on the way. Where did the Jeep blow, Bob?"

Vickers was incoherent.

"Colonel," Moody remarked thickly to Curt as the painkiller really took hold of his brain's pain centers, "it came from the bottom of the bot. I don't think there was any shrapnel. I think the explosion just kicked out a lot of rocks and gravel from underneath the Jeep.

That's what got me. I think."

"Okay, Max," Curt told him calmly, "we'll check it out…"

"Be damned careful, Colonel! First time I've ever run up against a bot that was booby-trapped like that…"

"First time for everything," Curt told him.

Within minutes, Biotech Sergeants Wally Izard and Nellie Miles showed up in an M660E Biotech Support Vehicle. They were accompanied by Major Russ Frazier and the personnel of his second platoon, Pagan's Pumas. Curt was happy to turn over the task of tending wounded to people who knew what they were doing. But he hadn't been about to just stand around until they showed up; in his mind, the first principle of leadership was the welfare of his personnel.

When he stood up, he saw that Pagan's Pumas had the area well under control with M60A Airborne Mobile Assault Warbots - Mary Anns - stationed at critical points over the surrounding hills of the Yemen Royal Republic. He turned to Edie Sampson and complimented her, "Quick thinking, Edie."

"Thank you, sir."

"What the hell did you see that led you to the conclusion the bot was about to blow?" he wanted to know.

Sergeant Major Edwina Sampson was the chief NCO tech wizard. She had a way with warbots and with the all-important regimental C3I gear that brought the battlefield to Curt and kept him in touch with the rest of the Regiment and the world. She shook her head in bewilderment. "I don't really know, sir. The damned Yemarks must have booby-trapped that Jeep when they discovered they couldn't use it," Sampson guessed. "Something told me it wasn't right. Call it a hunch, sir. I can't explain it any more than that."

Curt knew that Edie Sampson was one of those people who had an empathy or sixth sense with hardware. She was like Major Cal Worsham and some of the flyboys of the Regiment's tacair support squadron, people who could put themselves into intimate contact with machinery even without the technical help of neuroelectronics.

Regular warbots were operated as electronic extensions to human soldiers, the warbot brainies who lay on control couches well to the rear of the FEBA and fought their machines by the ultimate in remote control: neuroelectronic linkage. Sampson had been a warbot brainy once when the Washington Greys were still a regular Robot Infantry unit. But for the past eight years the Greys had developed the new Special Combat or Sierra Charlie doctrine where human soldiers had had to go back onto the battlefield alongside their warbots.

War robots couldn't do it all. People fight wars. Not robots. A robot doesn't care whether it wins or loses; it just does what it's been told to do and uses artificial intelligence to modify its original orders to fit the circumstances as much as possible. But it couldn't take the place of the human soldier when the opponent was a lot of other human soldiers. The Washington Greys had learned that lesson the hard way in the brutal school of combat and they had paid their tuition in blood.

"Thanks for getting me out of the way," he told her. "But I think you overdid it a little bit..." His comment wasn't a reprimand. Edie Sampson had been one of the two NCOs who'd come up the ladder with him in the Washington Greys. She and Regimental Sergeant Major Henry Kester had been part of Curt's team since he'd joined the Greys fifteen years before as a raw second lieutenant fresh out of West Point. When the regiment had transitioned from a pure remotely operated warbot outfit to the first Sierra Charlie unit, Edie Sampson had turned out to be a mean and nasty fighter. So Curt knew her very well. And Edie Sampson knew her Colonel, too.

"Honestly, sir, I didn't know what was going to happen," Edie admitted. "But I figgered you and I would make smaller targets if we were flat on the ground instead of standing with everything bared to the breeze."

"And damned lucky the crap went over our heads," Curt added.

"But not by much. I was trying to get lower, but my belt buckle was in the way."

"Well, what the hell blew? Where was it located? How was it

triggered?" Curt asked, not really expecting an answer. He was simply vocalizing his own thoughts as he tried to make sense out of what had just happened.

"Hard to tell, Colonel. But it sure as hell wasn't a primitive booby trap," Edie observed. "It went off before Vickers touched the Jeep. That sort of triggering isn't done with tape and string."

Curt watched while Vickers and Moody were lifted gently into the Biotech Support Vehicle for transportation to the regiment's headquarters area where Major Ruth Gydesen had her BIOTECO unit. Unfortunately, the regimental medical officer and her staff already had their hands full with injured and wounded Greys, far more so than in any previous overseas operation.

"So it's a semi high tech bot mine," Curt went on. Then he asked. "How would you build it?"

"Hell, Colonel, I ain't no engineer or ordnance expert!" Edie objected.

"You're a practical technologist, Sergeant," the regimental commander reminded her. "So how would you build such a mine? Electrostatic trigger?"

Edie Sampson thought about this for a moment while the Biotech Support vehicle lumbered off. She looked at the Jeep, then said, "No, sir. Not exactly. The mine itself was just plain H-E. The mass of the bot concentrated the explosive shock wave at the ground underneath it. What caught Vickers and Moody were rocks that the explosion threw out from the bot's skirt. No frag casing on it at all, I'll bet. I'll know when we find another one and look at it before it blows. But the trigger's something else. I dunno about that. Maybe electrostatic. But probably not. This damned dry Yemeni climate allows you to build up one hell of an electrostatic charge and throw a twenty-centimeter spark just thinking about it. Such a trigger would blow the mine when you didn't want it to. So I figger mebbe a combination of body capacitance..."

"What do you mean? Specify."

Again, Edie thought for a moment then mused to herself aloud,

"No, that won't work, either. Not if the mine is mounted on the bottom of the warbot...And this Jeep was picked up by the jib-crane on one of BOTECO's ACVs, and it didn't go off then...Sure as hell ain't any kind of a switch or trigger that I know of." She finally sighed. "Colonel, I can't figure out exactly how such an explosive device on a warbot's pan would be triggered by a techie laying a hand on the bot. But I'll tell you this: It ain't no simple gadget dreamed up by some Yemark and boiled up in his own kitchen. Someone somewhere else supplied the Yemarks with it."

"I can always count on you to give me an honest answer, Edie...even when you don't know the answer," Curt remarked and looked again at the Jeep. "I want you to instruct all the troops that they are *not* to touch any warbot that's recovered. I want them to consider that the bot will blow if they touch it. So, they're ordered to make a complete and thorough visual and IR scan before touching it. And then when they start to work on it, they're ordered to wear body armor. I can't afford to lose more people. We've got seven Greys wounded thus far."

"Colonel, that's going to slow down our warbot maintenance and repair activities," Sampson pointed out. "Our gear is taking such a beating here in Yemen that our bot techs are pulling Level Two repair just to keep us from getting short-botted. We're not only losing people; we're losing warbots at a rate we can't sustain for long...not unless Captain Dearborn can get replacement gear faster than the Aerospace Farce has been able to deliver it thus far..."

Curt stepped back and looked the barrel-shaped warbot over with a practiced eye. Its mottled tan and brown desert camouflage paint was scratched. It had several dings in the unarmored parts of its skin and evidence of bullet impacts in several places on its layered high-tech composite armor plate. To him, the Jeep didn't look any more dangerous than the rest of the M33s in the regiment. And all the equipment of the Washington Greys was beginning to take on a well-worn look.

So were the personnel of the Washington Greys.

Four months in the Yemen Royal Republic had taken their toll on both people and machines.

Curt was trying to hold together a regiment now operating at about 90 percent of its full strength in a situation where 150 percent was called for.

Being in Yemen was a logistical, medical, and technical nightmare.

Things might have been better if the Washington Greys and the other regiments of the 17th Iron Fist Division had been configured and trained to guard a 250-kilometer unmanned robot railroad, the Amran and Red Sea Railroad. It wound through some of the most desolate, rugged, and inhospitable terrain in the world from an altitude more than 3,000 meters above sea level down to the Red Sea.

The big problem was that no one in the twenty-first century United States Army had ever stood guard on a railroad. Not since the Civil War had a railroad played such a central role in a military operation.

Furthermore, this robot railroad was being subjected to an increasingly lethal series of attacks, sabotage, and general terrorist harassment by some of the most practiced guerrillas and terrorists the world had ever seen. Some of them were ordinary native Yemenis who had a centuries-old tradition of guerrilla warfare from their high mountain retreats and forts. But G-2 had reported that the Royal Yemen Army had been interrogating some Yemeni Marxists - Yemarks.

Someone outside the Yemen Royal Republic was trying to stop the Amran and Red Sea Railroad from running. If that happened, it would cut off nearly one-fifth of the world's high-grade iron ore in a world-wide economy and civilization that, in spite of modern composite materials, still depended mostly on iron and steel.

The Yemen Royal Republic - formerly the Yemen Arab Republic before another coup put the royal family of the imam back on the throne in the capital city of Sana'a - had officially asked the United States for help under the terms of a mutual aid treaty many years old. The administration had responded with the overt rationale that Yemen was one of the poorest nations in the world and needed the royalty revenues from the export of more than seven million metric tons of iron ore every year. So Uncle Sam would be a helpful world neighbor and protect their assets while the Yemeni army routed the guerrillas and hunted down the terrorists.

It wasn't working out that way in Yemen, of course.

And, unknown to the world at large and to the personnel of the 17th Iron Fist Division that had been deployed to do the job, the real reason American troops were there had very little to do with a piece of treaty paper. Curt suspected what it was, but he didn't want to contribute to the scuttlebutt making the rounds in Rumor Control.

So the 17th Iron Fist was in Yemen with four regiments-including the newly activated 7th RI (SC), the Regulars - strung out over 250 kilometers of the most rugged terrain this side of the Kofa Mountains of Arizona where the Greys had trained for three weeks before coming over.

It was a nightmare. Curt knew that the Greys weren't equipped to handle it.

When the Greys had been in Iraq a few years before as a temporary relief regiment in the Persian Gulf Command, at least Curt had had the opportunity to work out strategies and tactics that made the most of the maneuverability and shock power of a Sierra Charlie outfit. Here, under direct orders from General Hettrick, who was getting micromanaged from the Pentagon with even more restrictive orders, they could only patrol the railroad, take incoming, take casualties, suffer warbot losses, and continually react to an increasing level of terrorism and guerrilla attacks day and night.

"Okay, Edie, you've just lit my fuse," Curt muttered darkly. "If this goes on, we'll be fragged down to uselessness in a month or less. The answer is to change our mode of operation."

"You've got it, Colonel!" Edie Sampson agreed. "It's high time we used our recce capability to do more than just try to spot where we'll get clobbered next. Time to take the fight to the bastards!"

"If they'll let us, Sergeant Major. If they'll let us."

"Colonel, I haven't known that to stop you before."

"I'll see if I can't wrangle something through Battleaxe."

"General Hettrick can figger out a way if you can't, Colonel," Sergeant Major Edie Sampson predicted.

Chapter Two

Grey Head, this is Grey Chief! came the sudden call to Curt from his regimental chief of staff, Major Joan Ward, via the neuroelectronic tacomm unit in his battle helmet. It was a "voice" in his head because the NE helmet pads transferred the message electronically to his nervous system through his skin, and his brain "heard" it as "sound." It was ultrafast and super-secure.

Curt knew that such a call meant trouble.

He was right.

Grey Chief, Grey Head here, he brain-waved back. The neuroelectronic pads picked up the nervous system impulses that were his subvocalized thoughts. The circuitry in his helmet translated those into a comm signal that went to Ward. *What's up this time?*

The reply came swiftly. *Fusileer Leader is under attack at Rayda. Guerrilla forces mounted the afternoon down ore train and are using the loaded ore cars as protection. They're firing directly into the Fusileer position as the train carries them past.*

Shit! Curt thought to himself, careful to keep that thought out of the tacomm circuitry by thinking it at a lower level than his tacomm was set to pick up. It didn't diminish the emotional level of that expletive. This guerrilla tactic was a new one.

His GUNCO company had been deployed at two fortified positions along the A&RSRR where the range of the 75-millimeter Saucy Cans guns would overlap the artillery coverage of both platoons and the GUNCO of Colonel Fred Salley's 27th Robot Infantry (Special Combat) Regiment, the Wolfhounds, based at the main railway electric power station near Huth. The plan was to use the Saucy Cans to harass assaulting guerilla bands and keep them pinned down while assault companies deployed in quick airlift to the trouble site.

In Curt's opinion, it was a miserable tactical plan. It was the latest in a cut-and-try series of ops plans designed to carry out the mission. Curt had agreed to it because he didn't have a better plan at the time.

The Yemen Expeditionary Force was saddled with some highly restrictive rules of engagement. The YEF - the 17th Iron F1st Division - was tasked to protect the railroad. Period.

They could take no offensive action.

They could engage in no seek-and-destroy missions.

Their job was to keep the robotic ore trains rolling by defensive tactics only.

Given the very rugged terrain of the Al-Hijaz Mountains of Yemen, the highest terrain on the Arabian Peninsula, that was about all that could be done with such a defensive doctrine.

Curt was not a defensive officer. He had been taught that the offensive was the quickest way to victory if you had to fight. His extensive combat experience had merely honed that teaching. Curt believed and knew that an outfit had to strike, strike hard, follow through, and keep striking until the enemy capitulated.

He wasn't allowed to do that here in Yemen. The United States Army had a distinctly defined and severely limited role here. Retaliation, search-and-destroy, and other offensive missions were the sole responsibilities of the Royal Yemen Army.

Curt didn't think very highly of the RYA. Nor of its commander, General Qahtan ash-Shaabi. Curt and the other regimental commanders of the 17th Iron Fist had pegged Qahtan as a potential coup leader. Once the opportune moment presented itself for overthrowing the royal family, Curt believed Qahtan would be leading the attempt.

Curt responded quickly. *Okay. Joan, change in plans. Patch in the staff. Get me a link to all the company and platoon commanders. I'll be at the OCV in a minute or so. Then I want to hold an Oscar brief. If any officers can get there in person, great. Otherwise. I want them on the tacomm net.*

Yes, sir! We're patching up the network now! Joan replied in a serious but unhurried tone. She was a rock-solid officer, one who had never quavered when the crunch hit. That's the way she was running things now.

Curt had a plan in his mind, but he always linked his officers and senior NCOs into the procedure of tactical planning and operational orders. The Washington Greys were a professional and experienced outfit. The people were smart and combat-wise. They had to be. The Washington Greys were perhaps the most experienced field combat soldiers in the warbotized United States Army. They were one of four regiments who enjoyed the title of "Special Combat" or Sierra Charlie outfits. They fought in the field alongside the warbots.

But good reconnaissance information was going to be important for what he had in mind. So, he asked, *Has Motega got any birdbots up on recce missions?*

Yes. sir. Dale Brown has three birdbots aloft above the down train at this time. He reports full sensor contact, and his downlink data stream appears to be good. Motega has channeled Brown's data into Grady. Grady is accepting and storing.

Curt knew that Captain Dyani Motega would be on it right away. He had not been wrong in giving her the Reconnaissance Company, RECONCO, and appointing her as his S-2 intelligence staffer. Recon and scouting were in her Crow Indian genes. So was a total commitment to professionalism, second only to that of Curt. Which was perhaps one reason the two of them were a strong pair in off-duty hours. But only one reason, Curt reflected.

Grady, the regimental megacomputer housed in one equipment rack bay of Curt's OCV, had been upgraded by the tech-weenies only a few months ago. Curt was normally very antsy about the tech-weenies screwing around with the Greys' equipment, especially the master tactical computer.

Grady, of course, was an off-handed reference to Rudyard Kipling's "Judy O'Grady" which the ladies of the Greys had shortened to simply "Grady" because the computer had to be given some sort of a name. "Grady" turned out to be male to them and, because of the name's origin, female to the other Greys.

Grady had shown some moments of spiteful stubbornness and reluctance to follow programming. Edie Sampson maintained some of this was due to program bugs. Curt didn't like such program bugs. He didn't like any computer or robot he couldn't count on when his own pink body and those of his people were on the line taking incoming.

Get me a status report on all Grey units. I want to know who goes into the barrel on this one, Curt added.

Yes sir. That's done. Colonel.

Curt should have known Joan would take care of that as a matter of course. She was his second in command, his Number One staffer. Curt counted on Joan Ward. He'd always done so since West Point. Graduates in the same class, they'd entered the Greys together. Joan had been an out-standing, solid, reliable, and predictable platoon and company commander. But Curt also knew that for some inexplicable reason, Joan Ward would serve the remainder of her military career as a loyal, dependable staffer. She lacked that certain something, perhaps the charisma, to lead a regiment. She'd reached her leadership crest running a battalion. This saddened Curt somewhat. He had a brother-sister relationship with Joan, but he couldn't consider recommending her as his eventual replacement. Curt had to look elsewhere within the regiment for that. And he had two people in mind.

On the run here, Curt told her and toggled off. "Edie, tag that Jeep as unexploded ordnance. I don't want any more of our warbot techs getting hurt messing with it."

"I think it's shot its wad, Colonel," Sampson told him. "At, least, I'd be very surprised if the Yemarks had booby-trapped this bot in two places."

"Be careful. You could be more than surprised. You could be killed. These idiotic Yemeni are fanatics," Curt warned her. "Tell BOTECO to leave it be. We've got work to do. Let's go!"

Edie followed him as he lit out double-time for the gates of the Greys' casern perched atop the hill in an incredibly ancient Yemeni complex of buildings that served them as headquarters. The buildings looked like fragile gingerbread, but that was only their decorative facade. They were staunchly constructed of stone and mud bricks with walls thick enough to protect against anything up to a 25-millimeter round.

That was plenty of protection. Fortunately, the Yemark guerrillas hadn't revealed they had guns any more powerful than some ancient 12.7-millimeter Soviet and American heavy machineguns - and damned few of those along with a helpful shortage of the old ammo. Curt knew that the Yemeni picked up every scrap of brass from expended cased ammo, reloaded the ancient casings using either black powder or smokeless, and capped them either with cast lead bullets or reloads they were getting from somewhere. Thus, the Yemeni small arms - while ubiquitous among the Yemeni hill tribesmen – weren't very reliable or accurate. Some of the brass casings were so damned old and had been used so many times that they ruptured and split when fired. Which is why the Greys had tagged the reloaded Yemeni ammo as the Sierra Charlie's Friend.

The commanders of the combat batts and companies of the Greys were gathering when he got to his OCV. Lieutenant Larry Hall and his GUNCO weren't there, of course; they were deployed out along the railway taking incoming from guerrillas on the passing ore trains. Neither were Major Russ Frazier and his Ferrets who were with Hall's Hellcats, providing them with defensive fire. Major Cal Worsham was there, although his air batt was on the ground waiting to lift off and lay ordnance while the Chippewas stood by to provide instant airlift.

So, enough room existed in the regimental OCV for all thirteen of them. But it was a bit crowded. Regimental Sergeant Major Henry Kester had gotten Grady to lay down the holographic projection of the Grey's area of responsibility high in the Al-Hijaz Mountains of Yemen. Edie Sampson quickly patched up the tacomm net to the rest of the noncombat batt and company commanders. So, when Curt looked down at the three-dimensional map, he saw where his Saucy Cans guns were located, where the down ore train was, and where other units of the Royal Yemeni Army were deployed. The possible beaten zones of the 75-millimeter Saucy Cans guns on

Larry Hall's LAMVAs were also shown.

"Okay, this is going to be short and sweet, I hope," Curt announced to his officers. "We've got Yemarks riding on that ore train. We can't shoot up that train, but we can shoot the bastards off its side if we're real surgical about it. Kitsy, I propose to put your Cougars on both sides of the railway line a few klicks downhill. You can shoot them off the sides of the train as they come past. Any comments? Suggestions?"

"Yeah," was the loud and caustic comment from Major Cal Worsham who was never at a loss for words. He ran his hand over his shaved head while the tips of his black handle-bar moustache quivered in anger. "Hands's Harpies can do the fucking job *better*. We'll blast their balls *off* the god-damned train and *harry* them into an ambush. The Tigers can get Clinton's Cougars into position in time." That was just normal Cal Worsham speaking. Even though ladies were present, it didn't make any difference. The ladies were just as mean and nasty as Cal Worsham tried to project his image by means of coarse gutter talk. The ladies, however, typically preferred deeds to words in nearly everything they did.

Captain Kitsy Clinton looked about sixteen years old and was far smaller than Worsham. In her pixie manner, she asked, "Major, suppose they jump off the train before it gets to a spot where we can ambush them? Seems to me, Colonel, that we should let Captain Motega's recce people watch these bastards while we put the Cougars into a good ambush position along the railway. Then we'll try to get the railroad people to stop the train there. When we shoot 'em off the cars, they'll try to run. Hands's Harpies can then make their lives miserable by hassling them back into the hills."

"I'm not sure we can get the train stopped," Major Joan Ward admitted in a small voice that was out of character with her appearance. Joan was a big woman, and she wore the mantle of chief of staff by getting respectful compliance to orders, not by parade ground bellowing. "It's on its way down, loaded with ore. Its electric motors are acting like generators and feeding juice back into the overhead catenary. The empty up-train is being partly powered by that 'dynamic braking.' It's likely to put a real sudden load on the Huth power station if the down-train stops."

"We haven't got time for a big debate," Curt snapped. "I asked for comment, criticism, and critique. I got it. Okay, you've caused me to change the plan. We'll try this. Cal, get the Cougars airlifted ASAP to this point here in the canyon northwest of Dih Bin. Get the Harpies aloft and ready to chase Yemarks when they jump off the train and try to evade the ambush fire. Major Allen, coordinate between your ASSAULTCOs and GUNCO. Major Ward, I'll need the support of the Wolfhounds Saucy Cans at Huth because this ambush will take place near where our fields of Saucy Cans fire overlap. Major Atkinson, ring up the railroad office and see if you can get them to stop the down-train where we want and the up-train. I'll raise Battleaxe and see if she can get the Yemenis to do what we can't: Chase those Yemarks back into the hills."

"*Hell*, Colonel, our Harpies can *hassle* them to the ground," Worsham complained. "Why call in those frigging *stupid* Yemen Army bastards? *They'll* stick their tails between their legs and run for home the *first time* one of them takes incoming from the Yemarks..."

"Because we can't do that, Major!" Curt snapped back. "And you know it! We've got ROEs to follow."

"*Screw* the ROEs!"

"I agree. But that doesn't mean I can do it!" Curt fired at him, irritated, because Cal Worsham knew the restrictive rules under which they were operating here in Yemen. "Want to get General Hettrick's ass in a sling?"

"Better than getting' *our* asses shot off, Colonel!"

"We follow the orders we've been given, Major!" Curt told him forcefully, then turned to the others. "Any ideas on the revised ops plan? If so, make it quick. We haven't got a hell of a lot of time to move here...and no time for further debate."

Captain Dyani Motega spoke up without hesitation. "Colonel, Timm's Tigers can put me and Captain Lufkin's Leopards on the train itself. We can drive them off when the train stops."

"Not a chance!" Curt told her. "Complicates an already complicated mission."

Captain Patrick Lufkin, the Canadian Army exchange officer who'd been put in command of Dyani's SCOUT platoon, commented, "Colonel, it seems to me that Captain Motega's suggestion is about the best I've heard for employing the SCOUT Platoon." There was no question that Lufkin was Canadian; his pronunciation of the word "about" came out as "aboot."

"No," was Curt's response, and everyone knew it was final. "But if the Leopards can be stuffed into a Chippie somewhere, I'd like to use them as the reserves. I don't know which direction the Yemarks will choose to go when they get shot off the train. Major Allen, use Motega and her SCOUT outfit as your reserve to reinforce the Stilettos or Assassins."

Major Jerry Allen, who as head of TACBATT, would be the on-the-spot commander, snapped, "Yessir!"

Curt looked at him. "Major, I'm surprised you had no inputs to this."

Jerry looked his Colonel straight in the eye and said, "Colonel, given the circumstances, the lack of time, and the lousy defensive posture we've got to maintain here, there wasn't anything valuable or important that I could add. What I really want to do is maintain contact with these Yemark bastards after we bushwhack them, then follow them back into the hills where we can lay a hell of a lot of ordnance on them without worrying about screwing up the railroad."

"I'd like nothing better myself, Major. But you know damned well what our ROEs are. I don't have to like them, but I have to obey them," Curt admitted with a lot of frustration showing in his voice.

"This is not the kind of combat the Washington Greys were trained for, Colonel," was the quiet observation of Captain Adonica Sweet, the wholesome little blonde officer who was absolutely vicious on the battlefield.

"I know. Our doctrine has always been an offensive one: Hold 'em by the nose with fire and kick 'em in the ass with maneuver. I'm doing my best to employ that doctrine within our current rules of engagement," Curt admitted. Then he got off the philosophical subject of doctrine and got back to the discussion of mission details. "We haven't got time for further debate. If we can't take the offensive, at least we can attack from defensive positions. *L'audace. L'audace! Toujours l'audace!* Major Atkinson, you and Sergeant Sampson make sure that tacomm is maintained. C3I is vital. Any further questions? Comments? Okay, everyone watch your minus-x. These Yemarks are guerrillas, and they're everywhere. They can whang you when and where you least expect. it. Move out!"

Chapter Three

Goddammit, Kitsy, quit bugging me! Major Jerry Allen snapped via the NE tacomm command channel. It was easier to use the neuroelectronic feature of the tactical communications system in his helmet, especially with the high noise level inside the UCA-21C Chippewa assault transport aerodyne.

Sorry, Jerry, but I think I see some data on the tac link that might mean trouble, Captain Kitsy Clinton fired back.

She was, along with Jerry, maintaining strict professional protocol. Although she'd bypassed tacomm protocol, The Washington Greys knew one another personally and on a social level. They liked one another. With the sort of close-knit team that the Washington Greys represented, things wouldn't work any other way. But in a deadly shooting situation, professional cool kept everyone reminded that this wasn't just a war game or a bit of social gaming at the Club. It was potentially hazardous to their health. It was a situation in which every one of them had to behave as anticipated, as they'd trained, and with a minimum of ambiguity.

Everyone on the command channel that linked Jerry Allen with his company and platoon commanders knew damned good and well, however, what was really going on. Ever since Kitsy Clinton had returned to the regiment from a year-long sojourn at Walter Reed Army Hospital where she and the biotechs there repaired her broken neck, it was obvious that a professional rivalry had grown between the two of them.

Like a good commander, Lieutenant Colonel Curt Carson was training his replacement. In fact, he was quietly training two replacements so they'd be in competition with one another.

It wasn't necessary to be a genius to know that Major Joan Ward wasn't in the running; she'd said as much when she remarked that she really enjoyed her staff position. Joan had had her days in the trenches leading a platoon, then a company, and the TACBATT. Like many long-termers, she'd had her fill of being shot at.

Not that being chief of staff didn't mean also finding yourself in a battle situation where you couldn't get shot at and have to shoot back. In the 3rd Robot Infantry (Special Combat) Regiment, everyone except the biotechs was expected to be able to fight if necessary, even the support people in SERVBATT. Everyone was armed with a personal weapon, the M33A2 "Ranger" assault rifle which the Greys perversely called by its original Mexican name, "Novia" or "sweetheart."

The matter of Curt's replacement wasn't time critical. No one expected Curt to give up the Greys and pop for twenty-and-out; he was too young and too good. In spite of the very close personal relationship that had developed between Curt and Captain Dyani Motega, everyone knew that the two of them had no intention of resigning their commissions to get married and raise a family. At least, not right away. Nor did either of them anticipate requesting reassignments to divisional staff positions, although both were highly qualified for such a thing. Along with the rest of the Greys, they were warriors. They weren't ready to hang up their guns yet.

So it was more a matter of who could assume temporary regimental command if something happened to Curt or if he went on leave. Recently, Jerry Allen had taken over in Curt's absence on furloughs and leaves. But Kitsy had done so when both Curt and Jerry were gone.

Curt had established a competition, and everyone knew it. But it was a decidedly low-level competition. However, Kitsy rarely looked upon anything as a low-level affair. She tackled everything with gusto and with the intention of either winning or enjoying the hell out of it while it was happening. As Curt often pointed out, "Kitsy believes that anything worth doing is worth overdoing." Which explained the petite officer perfectly.

On the other hand, Jerry Allen had served under Curt ever since graduating from West Point and joining the Washington Greys as a raw second looie. Jerry had learned a lot from Curt. He worshipped Curt, but not openly or slavishly. No one could ever accuse Jerry of bootlicking. Curt was his role model. Others often found him saying the same things that Curt would say or had said in similar circumstances. As a result, Jerry had learned some of Curt's tactical brilliance and expertise. And a lot about how Curt handled both subordinates and superiors. The big difference between the two men was something more than a few years' difference in age, however. Jerry was deeply involved with Adonica Sweet. They were a pair to the exclusion of others and always had been in spite of occasional and expected (by others) lovers' spats. Curt and Dyani treated one another as first among equals. No one else existed in the situation between Major Jerry Allen and Captain Adonica Sweet.

Less than a minute from touchdown, and you think you see something new and different in the situation? Hell of a time to do it, Clinton! Jerry told her, then realized that his quick remark, made in the heat of the precombat jitters, might be misunderstood. It could be inferred that he was both chastising her and refusing to listen to subordinates' inputs. So, he went on, *What do you see?*

Birdbot sensors are picking up fewer targets on the train and additional targets along the right of way.

So?

So maybe the Yemarks have been slowly bailing out now that they've passed the Saucy Cans outpost.

Captain, that train is cooking along at fifty klicks per hour or better. Have you ever jumped off a train moving that fast?

No, sir but those damned Yemarks are crazy enough to do it. I think they have. So, we may not have as many targets as anticipated on the train. And, as a result, we may have to watch minus-x for any nasties who've gotten off and may hit us from the flanks or rear, Kitsy pointed out.

Sensor data can be misleading, Captain.

That it can, Major. But if you don't mind, I'd like to have Motega and Lufkin's Leopards on the ground with us ready to take the edge off any attack from those train jumpers.

I agree with Clinton, was Dyani Motega's quick but typically laconic response.

Hell, Dyani, you just don't want to be forced in sit in reserve while the real fighting's going on! Lieutenant Hassan Mahmud of Hassan's Assassins told her lightly. He was just as mean and vicious as any Grey, a heritage from his early years as a poor hill boy from eastern Iran where he'd fought both nature and other people for scarce resources.

Jerry let the breach of tacomm protocol slip past. He recognized it as precombat anti-jitters humor, an attempt by Hassan to lighten the tension they all felt in their guts.

Major, I want to be where I'm useful when the time comes. And it could come quickly. Put us on the ground. We'll scout out any potential Yemark approach and cover your minus-x, the young Crow Indian woman replied coolly. She'd do just that, too. She'd trained the SCOUT platoon in stealthy field operations. Her first sergeant, Tracy Dillon, was a westerner himself, and the two of them often joked about playing "cowboys and Indians" as children…but on different sides. Captain Pat Lufkin, the Canadian exchange officer from Calgary, Alberta, also understood the sort of tactics Dyani had taught her scouting and recce troops. The Canadians always kept a small, taut standing army to serve as a core group should something big come along, and an officer exchange between the USA and other countries allowed them to both learn from and teach American troops. In Lufkin's case, the match between his capabilities and leading the scouting platoon was perfect.

Very well. Make it so, Jerry said in a cool Curt Carson voice. It would compromise some flexibility of operations, but he knew enough to pay close attention to what Dyani had to say about scouting. In some ways, her reconnaissance company was like a light cavalry screen in its ability to search for the enemy, move quickly and stealthily around and through the terrain, and then provide a diversionary fire base while the main body reconfigured itself to ward off the new attack.

The approach of the eight Chippewa transport aerodynes was made using nap-of-the-earth procedures and terrain obscuration, the Chippie drivers hugging the rugged hillsides and taking advantage of every possible chance to remain in defilade. Nothing would

31

compromise the surprise of the mission more than to have the Yemarks spot the huge Chippies coming in to disgorge their troops and warbots. Timing was critical. They had to be on the ground and in position to ambush the train before the train got there. And far enough ahead of the train so that the incoming Chippies wouldn't give anything away.

It was tight. When the Chippies squatted on their landing gear and opened their cavernous loading doors, the Jeep and Mary Ann warbots were the first out so that they would draw fire if any Yemarks happened to be in the vicinity. They were quickly followed by the Sierra Charlies of Clinton's Cougars and Lufkin's Leopards who were lightly loaded with only lots of ammo, M100A "Smart Fart" anti-tank/antiair tube rockets, lots of water, and one MRE. The Greys didn't expect to stay there very long. This was not a war of field operations but of rapid response and rapid deployment.

It was also a defensive war, and the Washington Greys didn't like that one little bit.

Stilettos on the north, Assassins on the south, Jerry snapped via tacomm as they hit ground. *Train is two klicks uphill at the moment. It will be here in about two minutes. Motega, divide your forces as you see fit.*

Roger, Alleycat Leader, Dyani replied, then began to give orders to her troops. *Cole, I want you to join Dillon and me; we'll cover the north approaches. Lufkin, take Saunders and Esteban; do your thing to the south in those hills. Williams, stay with Alleycat Leader as additional biotech support.*

Grey Head, this is Alleycat Leader. We're on the ground and deploying as planned. No opposition, Jerry reported back to Curt.

In his OCV, Curt could see that on Grady's tactical display. He was chomping at the bit. The one thing he didn't like about regimental command was his inability to be in the thick of the fight. He was used to being up front. He wasn't used to managing tactical operations from afar. *Roger, Alleycat Leader. Be advised that the railroad moguls declined to stop the train. Here's where you get the chance to practice on moving targets.*

Roger. Should be easy. No windage corrections. Calm as all hell out here this morning. Wish we had a breeze. Would make things cooler, Jerry replied.

We never get our choice of weather in which to fight. Take what you've got and make it work, Curt advised him unnecessarily. He noticed the movement of individual beacons on the tactical display. *What the hell are the Leopards doing?*

Scouting to cover my minus-x, Grey Head.

What happened to the plan to keep them as a reserve force?

I shit-canned it. Sensor data shows some Yemarks leaving the train. I want to make sure they don't mount an attack on my rear while we're running the ambush.

What do you intend to do about a mobile reserve?

I intend to operate without one. No other choice. I wasn't about to leave my ass bared to the boonies here, so I deployed the Mustangs.

Curt didn't like it. But he wasn't about to micromanage Jerry's show. It was tough not to do that. But in view of what Jerry had decided to do, Curt began thinking about deploying additional forces as a mobile reserve to cover Jerry. *Do what you can. I'll try to find some backup for you.*

He couldn't do it. He had no reserves. All his combat forces were deployed.

So, he told Edie Sampson, "Get me a line to Colonel Salley."

Edie did her magic things with the comm gear in the OCV, then announced, "Wolf Head standing by, sir."

Curt didn't use NE tacomm for this. "Rick, we're about to engage some Yemarks riding the down-train north of Dih Bin. They shot up Dih Bin as they went past. We're squirting you our tac data bus at the moment, so you'll get the big picture."

"Roger, Curt, I see it. What do you need?" was the reply from the regimental commander of the 27th Robot Infantry (Special Combat)

Regiment, the Wolfhounds, based at Huth immediately down the hill from Curt's position.

"Loan me an assault platoon ASAP. I need a reserve force."

"No can do. My troops are either committed or in reserve themselves. Could you use some tacair?" Colonel Rick Salley wanted to know.

"Only if your aerodyne drivers can work with Cal Worsham."

"They will if I tell them to. I can loan you two Harpies."

"What the hell, Rick? Only two?"

"Curt, this operation is cutting me to ribbons just like you," Rick Salley admitted. "We're short of everything except Yemarks, and those bastards haven't kicked off their usual morning nastiness around here yet."

"I'll take the Harpies! And thanks! Have their drivers come up on frequency Alpha Four Tango. My tech sergeant will give your technie the skip codes," Curt told his compatriot. Two Harpies were better than nothing. Toggling off, he turned to Henry Kester. "Tell the Warhawks they've got two more Harpies coming. That's all I could get. The Wolfers are short of everything, too."

"Like I said, Colonel, when you're short of everything except the enemy, you're in combat," Henry Kester muttered darkly.

"Henry, you don't need to remind me of the basic truths of your code of combat," Curt told him. Then he toggled tacomm to Jerry and told him.

I'm not counting real hard on tacair support, Grey Head, Jerry announced when Curt told him. *This terrain is too damned rugged for good tacair operations. Yemarks can hide behind a hell of a lot of rocks. Worsham and Hands will have to go after them one at a time when they spot them. Takes a lot of time and uses a lot of Harpies. Good thing the Yemarks don't have baby SAMS. Okay, Grey Head, we're going to get busy here. The train she's a-comin' 'round the bend!*

It was an impressive sight, Jerry had to admit to himself.

The Amran and Red Sea Railroad was built for one thing and one thing only: to haul twenty thousand tons of very rich iron ore out of the Jebel Miswar mine every day and down to al-Luhaya on the Red Sea. There the ore was loaded into ore ships and carried to Madagascar where a large coal mine supplied the necessary final element to turn the iron ore into steel. Because it takes more coal than ore to make steel, the ore is always sent to the coal source.

With its two-meter gauge and no necessity to conform to an established loading gauge along the route because it was built for a single purpose, the A&RSRR rolling stock was huge. The lead electric locomotive came into view around the bend and headed into the cut where the Greys were deployed. It was rolling downhill loaded, so it wasn't drawing current from the 50,000-volt overhead catenary; its electric motors, being driven by the downhill momentum of the train, acted like generators and fed power back into the catenary. An empty up-train was already on its way up the hill from the Red Sea and picking up down-train generated current from the catenary lines. The power plant at Huth was designed to handle a loaded up-train if necessary, but additional economy was realized by letting the energy of the down-train provide juice for the up-train.

And, of course, the A&RSRR was automatic, a robot railroad. No human being sat in the high cab of the boxy electric locomotive.

Many Yemeni didn't like the robotic A&RSRR. Lots of sheep, lots of cows, many dogs, and a few Yemeni had been killed because the trains simply didn't stop for them on the right of way. The A&RSRR management felt that their obligation was discharged by issuing a warning to stay the hell off the tracks and posting signs along the right of way. Their attempts to fence the railway hadn't worked; the fences were quickly ripped down by Yemeni who appropriated the fencing material for their own uses. So those Yemeni who paid no attention to the announcement or forgot about the signs - most of which had been stolen, too - were killed along with the livestock which was allowed to foul the right of way.

If it hadn't been for the enormous boost to the Yemeni economy that came from the iron ore mines and the railroad, more Yemeni would probably have opposed it.

Jerry didn't know whether or not this was the basic reason behind the nastiness. The railway had been under increasing attack from Yemeni guerrillas over the last three months. Yemen was a rough and rugged land inhabited by rough and rugged people. Most Yemeni outside the cities were individualistic tribesmen. They were armed with a variety of firearms, ancient and modern. Every Yemeni male carried a curved tribesman's dagger, a *jambiya*, in a highly decorated scabbard or *dhuma* at the waist. The Yemeni had a long history of piracy, brigandage, and outright looting.

But Jerry didn't have a lot of time to reflect on such things. The 6,000-horsepower lead locomotive whined past his position, blocking his view of the other side of the defile. He kicked himself mentally. In his eagerness to get the ambush battalion into position, he'd chosen a position on the side of the rocky cut where the passing train blocked his vision.

Cougar Leader has targets!

Stiletto Leader has targets!

Commence firing! Jerry snapped into his NE tacomm unit then called to Paul Hands who was leading the tacair squadron. *Harrier Leader, we have made contact with the target. You are free to break stealth and expend ordnance on any targets you see leaving the train for the hills.*

Roger, Alleycat Leader! We have your beacons on our displays, and we're popping up now. We'll have targets as soon as we get line-of-sight on them!

But Jerry quickly sensed that something was wrong with the ambush.

Although the Washington Greys and their warbots had learned to conserve ammo in this faraway land out at the end of a tenuous logistical pipeline provided by airlift, they weren't reticent to expend ammo against targets. But instead of a rattle of fire from Novias, 7.62-millimeter automatics on the Jeeps, and 25-millimeter autocannons on the Mary Anns, only sporadic bursts came to his ears.

A 7.62-millimeter bullet whanged the rock next to his head and warbled off into the distance.

Alleycat, this is Stiletto Leader! was the quick call from Adonica Sweet. *Damned few targets on the train! And the targeting sensors are confused by the Assassins on the other side of the cut!*

Yeah, I know! You're putting fire into us! Knock it off! Jerry snapped back.

Another round glanced off the armor of his Jeep.

Hold it! Hold it! Fire only on targets that are moving with the train! Jerry fired off a general order.

What targets? We've seen only three! What the hell happened to our train riders? was the question from Hassan.

Mustang Leader, have your birdbot people been keeping track of the Yemarks who've jumped off the train? Jerry asked Dyani Motega.

In the melee, Dyani had indeed followed the information gathered by the recce birdbots under command of Lieutenant Dale Brown back in Amran. *Affirmative, Alleycat Leader. Thirty-one Yemarks have left the train in the past five minutes. I don't know how many got off after they ambushed Dih Bin. They're hard to track against this terrain. The ground is at about body heat, which makes infrared discrimination difficult.*

How many were on the train to begin with?

Unknown, Alleycat Leader.

Jerry made a quick decision. The situation now had too many unknowns. Very few targets were left on the train itself. He had more than thirty armed Yemarks out there, possible in his rear, and in unknown positions going in unknown directions. The mission was already a failure. Time to cut any future losses. *Grey Head, this is Alleycat. I'm aborting the mission. Most of the targets have left the train. Too few left aboard to justify having our ass bared to the breeze out here. And we're having trouble making IR sensor contact on the ones who've jumped already. I don't know where they are. And I don't know how many of them are out there doing what.*

Curt had been watching the tactical display in his OCV back at the

Amran headquarters casern. He, too, saw that the mission wasn't cost-justified. And that Jerry now had his neck out a mile. *Roger, Alleycat. Have no pride when it comes time to get the hell out of Whiskey Creek,* he replied with a time-worn aphorism of the Washington Greys - appropriated from West Point - which meant, "Get the hell out of that sticky no-win situation and save your ass to fight another day, mister!"

Alleycat Leader, Mustang Leader here. We've got targets coming down the rail line and out the hills behind you on both sides of the tracks, was the sudden report from Dyani.

Dammit, I should have known it! Jerry exploded, recalling Henry Kester's maxim of combat, "When your attack seems to be going well, you're probably being ambushed."

And they were.

Chapter Four

On Grady's tactical display in the regimental OCV, Curt saw at once what was happening out in the railway cut between Dih Bin and Huth.

"Goddammit, Henry, we ought to be out there leading that sheep screw!" he complained to his regimental sergeant major.

"With all due respects, Colonel, we can't," Henry reminded him quietly, although he felt the same way himself. "You're the regimental commander. And field manual six hundred dash fifteen sez we've gotta 'manage the battle,' not fight it."

"Fighting according to the book isn't the way I like to do it," Curt muttered in disgust, knowing that what Henry said was correct because they'd been given orders to that effect. "The people who wrote the book in the safe sanctuary of their Pentagon and Fort Benning offices weren't being shot at or watching friends and comrades take incoming. If it wouldn't get Battleaxe into deep slime, I'd shit-can the damned book!"

General Belinda Hettrick had ordered him to follow the book, although she felt the same as Curt about the formalized army field manuals. What was in the books wasn't her way of leading and fighting, either. She was being hassled from higher up in the chain of command to "follow approved policies, procedures, and doctrines."

"Well, Colonel, you know as well as I do that there's three ways of doing something: (a) the right way, (b) the wrong way, and (c) the army way."

"And we're in the army, so we don't have much of a choice unless 'c' doesn't work and the only thing left to do is uncover our anatomy and try 'a'," Curt muttered darkly as he watched the progress of the mission on the tactical display. He felt that perhaps he'd made a mistake this time trying not to micromanage Jerry's mission. He should have warned Jerry earlier to cover his minus-x a hell of a lot better. Maybe he'd gone too far in letting his subordinate get into deep slime before giving him a direct order to bug out.

Grey Head, Alleycat is taking some incoming from minus-x in all directions. We're on it, but it's going to be ammo-intensive! a tacomm report from Jerry interrupted his black study.

The Alleycats needed some support or Jerry wouldn't have transmitted that report that way. *Alleycat, Grey Head will try to get some help to you,* Curt told him.

Grey Head. I can pull this one out of the slime. I haven't got everything I think I'd like to have, but sometimes you don't know what you can do without until you try. Jerry replied. Curt could tell from the nuances in his projected tacomm thought message that Jerry was scared shitless, but like a good leader he was trying to project the image of a confident field commander just as Curt had done in many, many operations. *We caught this budding sheep screw early, thanks to Clinton and Motega. So, we aren't totally surprised. But we haven't got firm targets because of the inability to get good IR contrast. That will improve as they close on us. But in the meantime, I've got good enough data to call in Saucy Cans airbursts over them. Which I'm doing.*

Make sure you get your tacair support out of the way, Curt warned him unnecessarily.

Yessir. I may need the Harriers real bad real quick, so I won't let them get far. But area artillery support may be more effective than surgical tacair strikes with these indefinite target coordinates.

Goddammit, Allen, give me a fucking break! was the raucous call from Major Cal Worsham. *I've got Harpies airborne and ready to roll in on the goddamned Yemarks all over the fucking rocks down there. We can hassle the shit out of those unorganized guerrilla forces that jumped off the train!*

Jerry's reply was surprisingly firm and steady. Worsham was senior to him only in date of rank. But Jerry told him formally, *Warhawk Leader, thanks, but I don't want to just hassle those bastards. I want to kick the shit out of them with overhead AP Saucy Cans bursts. You know what that did to the Turks at Caldiran. I can't afford to lose personnel or bots to the Yemarks out there. I want to discourage them from continuing their advance and possibly an assault. So please stay the hell out of the way of my incoming artillery support and stand by. You'll have plenty of opportunity to lay ordnance later if the Yemarks don't call it a day. Which I think they will.*

Allen, those bastards out there are the kind of jerks who make a hell out of this world so they can enjoy paradise in the next! They don't give a shit if they get wasted.

Good! The more of them that are wasted, the fewer are left to try to waste Alleycats.

Do you know something I don't know?

Yes. I ran out of tiger juice a while back. Furthermore. I'm the guy on the ground running this show. So, see me later at the Club if you want to continue this discussion. In the meantime, I request that you stand off, keep your gun switches hot, and cover the Chippies. So quit sniveling or get off my freak. I've got to head off this sheep screw from a defensive position...and I'd rather be attacking.

Curt just sat there and listened to the rapid-fire tacomm exchange between his assault battalion commander and his air battalion leader. It took only seconds because thought-speed tacomm was many times faster than verbalized audio communications. Curt didn't step in. Not yet. He would if Worsham persisted. But he knew that Cal Worsham was just a gung-ho aerodyne driver who was slightly mad and decidedly uncouth. That was his way. Worsham, Curt believed, was probably the best air support commander in the army. He was glad that Worsham's Warhawks were part of the Washington Greys.

And he was proud of the way Jerry had handled the situation.

So he just listened for then. He noticed that Henry was sitting there with a hint of a smile playing on his well-used face.

Hellcat Leader, this is Alleycat Leader, Jerry called to Lieutenant Larry Hall, commander of the Gunnery Company. *I need artillery support. Please give me area airburst AP coverage on the targets that I designate.*

Alleycat, I see the targets you've designated, but they're smeary and some of them are out at extreme range for the Saucy Cans, was the quick reply from Hall. *And I see the beacons of your scouts. I'll try to aim so they don't get bursts on top of them, but we're operating at extreme Saucy Cans range. The first rounds may have too much dispersion and break close to the scouts. So get them under cover. I'll use the Fusileers for those targets because they're closer. They'll be more accurate than the Terrors.*

I don't care who you assign to shoot at what. But I want support right now!

Yessir! I'll put the Fusileers on targets to the north of my location. Terrors target on those to the south. But I repeat: the first salvo won't be right on target at this range.

Fire a smoke round salvo for effect, and I'll have observers feed you information to correct your aim.

Jesus, Major, I haven't got any smoke rounds left! Been on requisition for eight days. And no one has done visual artillery spotting like that for umpteen years!

True, but you were taught how to do it at the Citadel, weren't you? Sure as hell taught it to us at West Point.

Uh, yessir, I was. Anything taught at the Point was taught at the Citadel, except better, sir. You want to withdraw your scouts from the area?

Roger, will do! Jerry snapped and acted to toggle the tacomm to talk to Motega. *Mustang Leader, get your people back to the tracks. Hellcat airburst area barrage incoming.*

Alleycat, Mustang Leader, came the reply from Dyani Motega, and Jerry knew he was in deep slime. *We've Just come under intense Yemark small arms fire up here in the rocks! I can't break off without turning tail and possibly taking casualties!*

Why not? What's the sit? Report! Jerry suddenly realized that the situation had gone to slime.

Approximately ten Yemarks are up the hill from us in excellent positions. The incoming small arms fire isn't from the usual Yemark antiques using unreliable reloaded ammo. Sounds like Chinese A-99 stuff. We're returning fire with warbots. I need some fire support from Cougar Mary Anns.

Over sporadic small arms and Mary Ann fire, Jerry heard the unmistakable sound of incoming 75-millimeter rounds from the Saucy Cans.

Mustang Leader, take cover! Take cover! Now! Jerry called quickly. *Hellcat Leader, Alleycat! Hellcat Leader, cease fire! I say again: Fusileers cease fire! You're possibly laying ordnance on my scouts!*

Alleycat, the first Fusileer salvo is already on its way! I can't stop it now! The first salvo will have wide dispersion at that range, so maybe the rounds won't burst near them.

Up among the rocks and boulders of the mountain slope to the north of the railway, Dyani was taking cover. She had to. The Yemark incoming was intense and accurate. She had to put her Jeeps to work because their armored hulls weren't as vulnerable as her Sierra Charlie scouts in their body armor. *Leopards! Program your Jeeps to maintain fire on targets! Then make a ball! Incoming airbursts!*

Dyani wanted to wait until the last possible moment before going totally passive and defensive. She had her Novia snuggled against her shoulder and was firing single rounds whenever she saw a Yemark head appear over or alongside a rock. She wanted to continue firing so that the Yemarks wouldn't be tipped off to the incoming Saucy Cans and take cover themselves. *Crazy Horse, continue firing program! Fire at will against any nonbeacon target you detect!* she passed the order along to her M33A2 Jeep warbot.

Roger, Deer Arrow! Crazy Horse will comply, the warbot replied in English language audio mode through her helmet NE contacts.

At her side, First Sergeant Tracy Dillon sensed her hesitation to take cover. But when he heard the sound of the incoming Saucy Cans rounds, he decided he'd better take action to keep her from being hurt. "Get it down, Dyani!" he called to her verbally, breaking all protocol by using her first name. He'd been her platoon sergeant when she'd joined the Greys as a mere two-stripe corporal, and in the heat of the moment Dillon simply forgot their present difference in rank. He also reached out and pulled her to the ground. His cry was cut off by the blast of 75-millimeter shells airbursting overhead near their position.

The two of them did the only thing they could do. The Washington Greys had developed a make-do means of protection when caught in a situation where they could find no overhead cover during an incoming airburst artillery barrage. Both Dyani and Dillon made as small a target as they could. They dropped to their knees and rolled into a ball, their armored backs to the sky. With the armored warbots providing fire cover for them, this was the best defense.

Technically, they offered a smaller target to shrapnel from overhead airbursts if they remained standing; a human being seen from above has a very small cross section. But since airbursts may occur off-vertical and not directly overhead, a standing person presents a much bigger target to a burst that's even 30 degrees off vertical.

It was suddenly like being underneath a monstrous and very deadly fireworks display. Even in the bright high altitude sunlight of the Al-Hijaz Mountains, the airbursts of the incoming four shells produced brilliant flashes.

At first, Dyani heard only the rattle of deadly pieces of steel hitting the rocks and sand around her. A sharp clang told her that Crazy Horse had been hit.

But then she heard a scream next to her. The scream came over the neuroelectronic tacomm circuits, too; it was a cry of agony and pain.

The detonations of the first four-round salvo of Saucy Cans fire was followed by silence except for the continued muzzle blasts from the precision 7.62-millimeter shots from Crazy Horse. The armored warbot obviously hadn't been harmed by being hit by a piece of shrapnel from an airburst.

The screams continued to come from First Sergeant Tracy Dillon who was lying curled up on the ground beside her, his crimson blood soaking into the sandy soil.

At first, Dyani didn't understand why Dillon was screaming. Then she suddenly realized that her side hurt. Terribly. Dyani didn't know if she was bleeding. She only hurt badly. The first thing she did was act to turn off the pain. It seemed most second nature to her. She didn't realize that others couldn't do it. But she'd learned from her father and mother, and she'd gotten plenty of practice in childhood when she'd scraped her knees or otherwise gotten skinned-up playing with others. Her playmates thought it was just her stoical Indian nature, but it was something more than that. It was control of the sort that Dyani had become well-known for exhibiting in the Washington Greys, an expression of what others thought was iron will and an Amerindian heritage. Actually, it was far more than that.

Then she called out via tacomm, *Biotech! Biotech! Mustang Leader here! Identing my beacon! Dillon is down! And I'm hit!*

Her tacomm call had an electric effect upon the Washington Greys who were about to put tail between legs and bug out to Amran and safety.

Without waiting for orders from Jerry, Kitsy snapped to her company, *Stilettos all, reverse your front! Acquire the tagged beacons of Mustang Leader and the Leopards! Acquire the ten IR targets of their adversaries! Close on them with marching fire! Assassins, give us overhead covering fire with anything you can spare from targets on the train!*

The train is almost past the Assassins, was the response from Hassan. *We'll cross the tracks and join you, Adonica!*

Negatory, negatory, Assassins! This is Alleycat Leader! Maintain your positions, provide covering overhead fire, and watch your minus-x from the south. Goddammit, Clinton, don't go out there and get yourself whanged! Two wounded in this fracas is already enough! Jerry was trying to remain cool and in charge…and doing a reasonable job of doing so in spite of the fact that he was kicking himself in the ass for calling in an artillery salvo at extreme range. He should have known, he told himself, that the dispersion would probably be great enough to endanger his northern scouting force. He wasn't concerned about what he'd report to Curt; he was seriously worried about Dyani and Dillon.

Yeah, Hassan, stay the hell where you are and try to keep those Yemarks pinned down, Kitsy added. *We've got biotechs with us.*

Everyone in the Greys knew by now that the Yemeni guerrillas and the Yemarks paid absolutely no attention whatsoever to the white tabard with its red crosses front and rear that was worn by the biotechs. Guerrillas and terrorists played by their own rules, not the Geneva Convention and the other "civilized rules of war" generally adhered to by all national armed forces. A human target was a human target, and they fired on it. They also slaughtered wounded when they found them.

Biotech Sergeant Juanita Gomez had been the first to learn that the Yemarks paid no attention to the red cross tabard. She'd been hit when she went to succor Lieutenant Hal Clock who'd caught an old .303 Enfield round at close range. Biotech sergeants Bailey Ann Miles and Robert Vickers had been next. Both would have been dead had it not been for Curt's insistence that even the biotechs wear body armor. As it was, both were still recovering from wound traumas made with soft-pointed self-cast Yemeni lead bullets. Body armor did a good job of stopping metal-jacketed rounds, but was somewhat less protective against soft-points which had a tendency to spread on impact and deliver the kinetic energy over a wider area of armor. The result was usually a massive, nasty bruise accompanied by broken bones, torn ligaments, split muscle sheaths, and often massive destructive damage to muscle tissue.

As a result, the Greys fought with a little more motivation when one of them got wounded out at the FEBA.

Like the French Foreign Legion - which had never roboticized - the Greys never left their wounded on the battlefield, even in retreat. It went without saying that *the Washington Greys never abandon their own.*

And even though the Greys were out at the end of a long and tenuous airlifted logistics pipeline in Yemen, in a situation like this they didn't conserve ammo.

The volume of fire that went into the Yemark positions that had pinned down Dyani and the Leopards was incredible. It was sudden and it was concentrated. They had targets that were well enough defined to shoot at without hitting their own troops.

And they didn't just lay fire on the enemy. Adonica Sweet and her Stilettos began advancing up the hill to the south.

Jerry figured it was time to activate the surgical precision of a tacair strike as well now that Saucy Cans fire wouldn't make the air over the enemy so unhealthy for Harpies. *Harrier Leader, pick up the designated enemy targets now on the tactical data bus. Please take them out. And send two of your Harpies against the bastards who are coming down the rail line intent on flanking us. We'll cover the rail line itself with ground fire from here, but we'll need your help to get the bastards who are sneaking off into the puckerbrush in hopes of bushwhacking us.*

Alleycat, it's about time you called in the professionals, was the quiet reply from Captain Paul Hands, the tacair flight leader. He was in strong contrast to his squadron commander, Major Cal Worsham, whose loud, gravely voice was a communications medium for some of the ripest vulgarity ever heard in the Greys. But he was an aerodyne driver, and everyone knew what that meant. *Consider it done, and let us know if we may be of other valuable service to you down there in the sand and dirt.*

As the Stilettos and their warbots moved up the hill, firing as they went and with fire from the Assassins going over their heads, two Harpy attack aerodynes popped up over a ridge to the south, climbed and rolled inverted, then came in steeply on their attack run. When they added the ripping roar of their M300A 25-millimeter autocannons to the din already created by the fire from the other 25-millimeters on the Mary Anns, the 7.62-millimeter machineguns on the Jeeps, and the 7.62-millimeter fire from the Novias carried by the Sierra Charlies, it was a fire concentration not likely to be survivable.

"Goddammit all to hell!" Lieutenant Colonel Curt Carson swore loudly as he heard all this and watched the action develop on the tactical display inside his OCV. He wanted to be out there. He almost called for an airlift to take him there…except it was all involved in the operation already. He had to sit and watch.

Furthermore, it was out of his control now.

Jerry, Kitsy, Adonica, and Hassan had taken over and were running things. Curt was inwardly happy with the teamwork that was apparent in the operation. But it was also apparent that none of his subordinates were as cool as they were trying to put on.

The rules of engagement had gone away. He knew he'd have to reprimand Jerry for allowing it to happen, but he would have done the same thing.

And not just because Dyani Motega had been wounded, either.

He and Dyani had reached their mutual understanding about this sort of thing after Battle Mountain.

But that didn't mean he could be as coolly detached about it as Jerry was trying to be.

And as Kitsy Clinton wasn't.

Or Adonica Sweet, for that matter.

One of their own had been hurt.

Rudyard Kipling hadn't had to write about women in combat, but he'd been right about the female of the species.

Chapter Five

It was, in the vernacular of the Washington Greys, a real sheep screw.

And it threatened to get even more complex, difficult, and deadly, Curt saw from his vantage point in the regimental OCV.

Cougar, I'll cover your minus-x from here, Jerry told Kitsy who was advancing under marching fire up the rocky slopes toward the spot where Dyani and the Leopard contingent were taking and giving fire.

Alleycat, this is Leopard Leader, came the call from Captain Patrick Lufkin on the north. *We're tracking the Yemarks on this side and along the tracks uphill. They seem to be slowing down or breaking off their advance.*

What the hell? Jerry wanted to know.

Back in the OCV, Curt had a bigger picture. It was obvious to him that Jerry had his hands full with a fire fight and was on the verge of information overload. With all the data available to modern battlefield commanders, it was easy to get overcommunicated to the point where it became difficult to categorize the massive flow of incoming information and assign priorities to it. It was far easier for actual warbot brainies, troops who operated warbots by remote NE control with a lot of assistance from megacomputers such as Georgie, the divisional computer stashed under a mountainside in faraway Diamond Point, Arizona.

So, Curt decided it was time he stepped into the picture to relieve information overload on Jerry and coordinate a combined arms operation.

Alleycat, this is Grey Head. Keep it up, and I'll give you a hand from here coordinating some Saucy Cans fire and Harpy strikes against the targets the Assassins and Lufkin are watching. Concentrate your efforts on Mustang Leader and the Leopards on the south side of the tracks. I'll handle combined arms against the rest.

Colonel, I can take care of this, Jerry started to insist.

Alleycat, you've got your hands full there, Curt reminded him. *You can't do everything.*

Clinton has the south assault well under control, I haven't lost situational awareness, Colonel.

Curt knew Jerry had lost it and didn't realize it. The ASSAULTCO commander had broken tacomm communications protocol without knowing it. Jerry was close to the edge of over-communication. *I don't doubt that, Alleycat. But you've got another platoon arid a scouting contingent to watch out for as well. Plus, a couple of Harpies overhead.* Curt didn't want to clobber Jerry at this point. Jerry was doing a good job, but he'd never handled a complex close-in short-term fight like this which involved coordination of so many elements. *Support Clinton's assault. I'll cover your minus-x. That's what I'm here for.*

Uh, yessir.

"Colonel, my standard regulation EW spectrum sweep is picking up some spurious radiation that looks like old Mark Four tacomm skipping," Edie Sampson cut in verbally from her C3I console where she was doing her job of watching for possible enemy electronic warfare countermeasures. Initially, this had seemed like a make-work job that was unnecessary in Yemen because the regiment was fighting rather primitive guerrilla bands. But apparently all that had suddenly changed.

"Could be spurious stuff from the Yemen army in Sana'a. They could be inbound to take over the hot pursuit we're not allowed to do. So nail it down," Curt told her, his mind on other matters at the moment. His regiment was possibly violating the rules of engagement. Kitsy Clinton was indeed carrying out something akin to hot pursuit in forging up the slopes under marching fire to succor Dyani and the Leopards up there with her.

Henry Kester swung around and looked over Edie's shoulder. "Damn if it don't look like tacomm stuff. And from the way those Yemarks are behaving out there, I bet they got better communication than they've had in past ambushes. See if Grady can match the skip pattern with any of the patterns we used to use. Or see if it matches any of the Royal Yemen horse artillery stuff." Henry didn't exactly like the Royal Yemen Army or its leaders. He didn't say so, but it was apparent in his oblique references to the RYA as a bunch of obsolete amateurs who really didn't like to fight.

"Grady," Edie instructed the regimental computer as she did her electronic magic and designated the frequencies appearing on her displays, "note and record the skipping tacomm-like frequencies I'm tagging for you. Compare the skip pattern with previously used patterns of old Mark Four tacomms. Report your analysis."

"I see the pattern. I am analyzing the pattern. I have an analysis. But I cannot compare it against the Mark Four system. The memory cells containing data on the Mark Four tacomm system were removed in the recent upgrading," the computer replied.

"Damn tech weenies!" Edie muttered.

"Easy does it, Sergeant. Remember, you're a regimental-level tech-weenie now yourself," Henry reminded her gently. "See if you can get a patch through to Georgie."

"Hell, Henry, you mean 'Edie does it,' I'm always doing something for the free world. I'd like to see the free world do something for me for a change!" Edie's redhead's classic short temper was evident in her retort. But she got busy doing her job in spite of it. She'd have time later to cause Henry Kester to regret those words.

Curt was getting really worried about Jerry's apparent neglect of his minus-x. It seemed to the regimental commander that a hell of a lot of Yemark targets were out there in Jerry's rear. But the ASSAULTCO commander didn't seem to mind. Other than putting Hassan and Lufkin to passively watching these, Jerry was concentrating all his attention and efforts on assaulting the Yemarks in the south who'd attacked Dyani and the Leopard contingent. Curt knew that both Dyani and Dillon were wounded. He didn't know how badly. This jerked him around a great deal inside. But he couldn't let it show.

Jerry, Kitsy, and Adonica apparently weren't about to sublimate that concern. Their warbots and troops were forging up the rocky hillside with almost zealous frenzy, expending ammo liberally against any target they could spot.

Adonica made no bones about it. *Dyani, hang on! I'm coming!*

What do you mean. 'I'? We're on our way, Dyani! Kitsy's thought slammed out over the tacomm practically on top of Adonica's.

Good. I'm not badly nicked. I can return some of the fire when I can get a make on the sensor, was Dyani's reply. *Dillon's pretty bad. Lots of bleeding. Allan, we need you fast.*

I'm coming, Captain! But not as fast as I'd like. I don't want to get whanged myself. These Yemarks use the red cross on my tabard as an aiming point.

So take it off, Kitsy told him.

He can't. Geneva Convention, Jerry reminded her.

Geneva Convention be damned! It makes him a target for, these bastards! Kitsy snapped back.

Okay, Dyani, I can see you and Dillon, Adonica put in. Then she ordered her Jeep, *Stiletto One, give me covering suppressive fire. Lots of it. Knock out that incoming stuff at its source.*

Roger. I am tracking incoming rounds and returning fire to the source of those rounds, her Jeep replied, its micrometer radar picking up the Yemark bullets in flight and its computer quickly working a trajectory solution backward to the bullets' sources, using three sequential bullet vectors as basic data. Guided by this computer solution, the Jeep aimed its 7.62-millimeter machinegun and selectively put a round at each source, tracking its outbound trajectory and impact point, comparing that against the desired impact point, and then correcting for the second round. In between those two rounds, it had relaxation time to fire against three other targets. If the rounds didn't result in a cessation of fire from a source, its program put a ten-round burst into the target at a rate of 3,000 rounds per second, which was almost like a concentrated shotgun blast.

When Adonica and Biotech Sergeant Allan Williams reached Dyani and Dillon, Dyani's Jeep, Crazy Horse, reported, *Mustang Leader, I'm out of ammo. My port IR sensor has also taken incoming and is inop.*

Crazy Horse, stand down and make a small target. Scorpion will relieve...I hope.

You bet!

Dillon's taken a major chunk of shrapnel in the back, Allan Williams observed, beginning his work on the fallen first sergeant. *I'll need medivac transport ASAP if I can get this bleeding stopped.*

Mustang Bio, Alleycat will get a Chippie over to you as soon as the enemy fire is suppressed. If you can hold for about five minutes, this is going to be over pretty quickly. Jerry told him, then gave a surprising order. *Cougar, lift your fire behind the Yemark unit. Give them an avenue of escape.*

What the hell, Jerry? Do you want me to let these bastards get away? Kitsy was flushed with the heat of combat, her primary goal at the moment being to cleanly and quickly annihilate the Yemarks who'd done such grievous harm to her friends.

They want to get the hell out of here now anyway, Jerry told her. *Give them the chance.*

And let them regroup for another assault? Or come back to bushwhack us again?

They won't. Jerry told her confidently. *And we can keep them from bushwhacking us again.*

Kitsy was upset. Yemark bullets were zipping past her as she dodged from rock to rock up the slope, firing her Novia at whatever target she could spot. *Dammit, do you know something I don't know?*

Yes. And I'll tell you about it once this sheep screw is over. Right now, please do as I ask.

*Dammit, it had better be good! We've just about got these Yemarks by the short hairs where it hurts...*Kitsy began. Her tacomm transmission was interrupted by a nonneuroelectronic signal as she took a heavy .303 soft-point Enfield round in her left side, knocking the wind from her temporarily. She was knocked slightly backward by the momentum of the impact, then fell to her knees as a wave of pain washed over her. *I'm hit*, she managed to gasp.

I'm coming! was the call from her biotech sergeant, Ginny Bowles.

Alleycat, Leopard Leader here. We spot some movement among the Yemarks to the north.

Moving away, I'll bet.

Yes sir. How did you know?

Call it battlefield experience coming to the fore. Jerry told him.

Should we give them a little fire to hurry them a tad?

Negatory! They're through for the day.

I think we should watch them to make sure of that. Alleycat.

Agreed, but don't devote a lot of effort to it. I want you to lay a little fire over the heads of the Cougars up the hill to the south. Bracket both sides of the Yemark positions up there. Encourage them to get the hell out of there by giving them the distinct impression that we've got them targeted...which we do.

Adonica was checking Dyani who was crouched, her Novia still at the ready, but her back arched in reaction to having been hit. "Dy, I don't see any blood. Where were you hit?"

Without removing her right hand from her Novia at her shoulder or turning her view from the Yemarks up the hill, Dyani reached around with her left hand and gently touched her left waist just below her rib cage. "Right there, Princess. Took a piece of shrapnel."

"Okay, I see now where your cammies are torn," Adonica replied, looking over Dyani's torso. "My God, Dyani, how come you're still standing? That chunk of shrapnel is partly embedded in your body armor! And it's about twenty millimeters across! That must hurt like hell!"

"It did. It doesn't now."

"Dy, you don't have to be stoical forever. We're here and we've got you covered."

"Good." Dyani seemed to suddenly relax a little bit. She lowered her Novia and her shoulders slumped a bit.

"You're white as a ghost!" Adonica suddenly said. "Here, lie down!"

"I'm fine," Dyani insisted. "I've got it under control. I..."

She slumped completely, then fell over on her right side. Her breathing became shallow and her eyes glazed over. She'd passed out cold, but she'd done so while trying to maintain the charade that she was in total control of herself. But the situation had passed beyond the stage where sheer will power, and iron self-control could prevail.

Ginny, get the hell over here ASAP! Dyani's gone into shock! Adonica called frantically as she began to do what was necessary to alleviate Dyani's condition.

Coming as fast as I can! I'm working on Captain Clinton at the moment.

This is Stiletto Papa Two! I've just taken a hit on the body armor, too, but I'm standing, came the sudden report from Platoon Sergeant Jim Elliott. *Body armor stops the old British three-oh-three stuff okay, but them lead bullets pack a real punch. I'll have a welt for a week.*

We've got to have more biotechs in the field with us under these conditions, Adonica remarked partly to herself and partly for the benefit of Jerry Allen.

Where the hell we gonna get 'em. Captain? was the wry comment from Kitsy's first sergeant, Carol Head. *We're losing bots to wadi mines and Sierra Charlies to wounds faster than we can fix either.*

Curt Carson heard it back in the OCV. "Dammit, we can't maintain this injury rate!" he exploded. "Four Sierra Charlies hit this morning plus two wounded earlier when the mine went off under the Jeep. Twelve Sierra Charlies temporarily out of action."

"Nearly ten percent of our manpower, Colonel," Henry remarked after making a quick mental calculation.

"Yeah," Curt agreed. "A unit was once considered to be in deep slime once twenty percent of its personnel were out of action."

"At the rate we're going, it won't be very long before the Washington Greys are on the real short end," observed the regimental sergeant major.

"Well, some of the four can be back in action quickly...I hope." Kitsy and Dyani, primarily, he told himself.

"Jim Elliott can probably be back tomorrow with a big bruise where he got hit."

Curt didn't exactly want to send those walking wounded back into action right away; they could get hit again near the original bruise, and that could cause real damage according to Major Ruth Gydesen, his regimental medical officer. So, he shook his head. "No, I won't force anyone back into action right away after they've been whanged with one of those Yemeni lead anchors. Henry, we've got to play fast and raunchy with the T-O now in order to keep our stationary and mobile forces with any sort of balance."

"We can cover some Sierra Charlie losses with warbots," Edie Sampson pointed out. "We've run multiple bots in the field before. Just takes a little extra attention..."

"Which is kinda difficult when you're bein' ambushed by God knows how many Yemarks," Henry reminded her. "This kind of war ain't no place for a professional soldier. The amateur competition is too great..."

Curt noticed something on the tactical display.

So did Major Jerry Allen out where the action was taking place.

It made Jerry feel very good.

It astounded Curt.

The report came in from Captain Pat Lufkin, *Alleycat, Leopard Leader here. We're getting indications both on IR sensors and by visual that the Yemark targets north of the railway are withdrawing.*

Roger, Leopard Leader. Alleycat has been expecting it, Jerry replied cooly.

And the Yemarks to the south have stopped firing and are withdrawing, Adonica reported. What the hell, Jerry? *You got a crystal ball in your kit?*

Negatory. How's Dyani?

Conscious again. Al hit her with some painkiller over her strong objections. No bleeding. But a frightful big bruise where a chunk of Saucy Cans shrapnel nearly penetrated her body armor on her left side above her hip.

In the fleshy part, I hope.

Major, Captain Motega has damned few fleshy parts except where it counts. And she's definitely got it where it counts, too. Other than that, she's nearly all muscle, Adonica pointed out.

Well, we're going to be able to compare notes, Kitsy Clinton's "voice" cut in via tacomm. *I got that .303 round in the left side just above my hip. But I guarantee you, there's a lot less of me there than in Dy's case.*

Look at it this way, Captain, Sergeant Carol Head told her, *you're a lot smaller target to hit.*

Back in the OCV, Curt sensed the sudden shift of the tacomm traffic from combat-centered to light, almost humorous repartee. The reason was obvious. The enemy Yemarks were withdrawing. Just like Jerry had forecast.

Curt felt a lot better. Both Kitsy and Dyani were going to be all right. He was concerned about Dillon. But with the fire fight over, the Chippewas could come in for air evac pickup. Dillon would be in the regimental biotech vehicles within a few minutes. If necessary, he could be quickly air-lifted to the divisional medical unit in Sana'a.

Alleycats all, this is Alleycat Leader. Regroup for recovery.

You don't want us to chase them. Major? That was Lieutenant Hassan Mahmud of Hassan's Assassins. *Gee, we didn't get the chance to do much of anything but sit on our asses here and give a little fire support.*

We don't chase them. Period. That's an order. Regroup for recovery. I want us to be back in Amran before chow time at noon.

Roger! Recovery!

That gave Curt the chance to satisfy his curiosity. He switched to command net and called, *Alleycat, this is Grey Head. Nice work! Now, would you care to confide in me exactly how and why you were, able to predict that the Yemarks would break off their attack and begin to withdraw?*

Certainly. Grey Head, Jerry replied. *The answer is simple: Qat?*

What?

Qat.

Explain.

Jerry Allen had an encyclopedic memory. He remembered what other people would consider trivia. *Sir, Yemen used to be one of the world's finest producers of coffee. Yemeni Mocha was always considered the best available coffee.*

What the hell has that got to do with this?

The Yemeni began to cultivate a plant called qat whose leaves have narcotic effects when chewed, Jerry went on. *Qat cultivation replaced coffee production in Yemen because qat brought quicker returns. Now every man in Yemen knocks off work before noon in time to get to a qat-chewing party. Ever notice how quiet and peaceful this place becomes in the afternoon?*

Yeah, now that you mention it.

Have we ever had any terrorism incidents or guerrilla attacks in the afternoon?

Nope. Not a one in four months. I thought it might be because they take the Yemen version of the Mexican siesta. You think it's because all the Yemeni men are laying around chewing their cuds of qat and getting spaced-out every afternoon?

Yes, sir. Hassan pointed it out to me, and I remembered the Yemeni qat situation then. These guys are morning warriors.

Major, get your ass and your unit back here. I think you've just stumbled onto something that's going to change the way we operate in Yemen...and it may mean that we can pull this sucker out of the fire after all!

Chapter Six

"I followed everything on the tac displays and all of you were very good at passing along information via tacomm," Curt told the officers and senior NCOs of TACBATT grouped around him in the large upper room of the Yemeni building that was part of their casern in the little town of Amran. He sat on the edge of the table and looked around. He was glad to see so many of them there after the deadly fight that morning. But he was dismayed and angered because of the ones who weren't there due to wounds and injuries incurred during the fight.

"You did a fine job of turning a potential disaster into merely a debacle," he went on, anxious to help them overcome some of their disgust at a job they obviously didn't feel had been well done. "The screwup wasn't your fault. I intend for us to learn from what happened. The mission had at least two major problems, maybe more. First of all, we're saddled by some of the most miserable ROEs we've ever labored under. I'm going to see General Hettrick in Sana'a tomorrow at oh-nine-hundred, and I intend to make some very strong arguments for a modification of those ROEs. Captain Clinton, you have something you wish to say, as if I didn't expect it?"

Kitsy stood up. It was obvious as she did so that her left side was very sore. Major Ruth Gydesen had checked her over for internal injuries and had given her a clean bill of health save for the bruise. She'd also put Kitsy on noncombat status for forty-eight hours, much to Kitsy's disgust.

Kitsy felt a little better now…but not much. She'd had a hot shower and donned a clean khaki shirt and shorts because it was just too hot in Amran for cammies, even at three thousand meters elevation. Kitsy always looked like a squeaky-clean teenager about-to graduate from high school ROTC. However, Curt now detected a weary look in her eyes. In fact, many Greys in the room had the same weary look. They'd all been in Yemen too long under too much strain, trying to carry out an impossible mission with a Sierra Charlie doctrine that had been designed to accomplish something else.

A Sierra Charlie unit was a fast, mobile, maneuverable, shock outfit best qualified to carry out the mission of the old horse cavalry or something like the old Special Forces of the last century before warbots took over and dominated U.S. Army doctrines. Now the Greys and the other Sierra Charlies of the Iron Fist were strapped into a defensive situation; they had to guard the railroad and leave it to the Royal Yemen Army to pursue the terrorists and guerrillas. The RYA wasn't doing so well at that. And the Sierra Charlies weren't doing such a good job on their assignment, either.

"Battleaxe knows that the Seventeenth Iron Fist Division and the Washington Greys aren't defensive patrol troops," Kitsy began, using the combat code name of Major General Belinda Hettrick. "We learned that in Iraq during the war with the Kurds. But the Pentagon apparently didn't. I don't want to be accused of criticizing higher command, Colonel, but we're mismatched for this job in Yemen under the ROEs they've laid on us. I've been doing some thinking about this and talking with some of the other Greys. I believe I might have a few concepts that could allow us to change things and still overtly follow the ROEs. I request I be allowed to discuss some of these ideas with the regimental staff and present you with a report of what comes out of the exercise."

Kitsy might have looked like a Girl Scout camp counselor, but she was a graduate of the United States Military Academy in the top 10 percent of her class. A veteran of five campaigns, she wore the white-piped ribbon of the Purple Heart, plus that of the Bronze Star, the Silver Star, and the Combat Warbot Badge, although she'd never been a warbot brainy. The army had decided to award the badge to Sierra Charlies who direct-commanded warbots in the field in actual combat simply because they had no other badge yet; the 17th Iron Fist was the only Sierra Charlie division in the army, and the Greys had been the first Robot Infantry Sierra Charlie regiment.

"Care to give me a hint about what you've got in mind, Captain?"

Curt asked.

"Yes, sir, provided you realize that it has a lot of rough edges on it yet," she told him. "It's based on the fact that we're no longer up against Yemeni guerrillas and Yemeni Marxists with primitive weapons. We've got to start treating the Yemarks as real, serious, sophisticated enemies, not ignorant and undisciplined guerrillas who come out of the hills occasionally to harass our ass. Their purpose is to chase our tails out of Yemen by making things too expensive for us."

"Just like 'Nam," Captain Pat Lufkin muttered. "It's primarily a psych war. They'll keep on harassing us until your government and the news media get tired or scared of the losses and the frightful expenditures for a purpose not well-understood..."

"Not like Viet Nam at all," Jerry objected. "They haven't been able to initiate biological warfare with drugs here. The personnel in the Iron Fist have gone through basic warbot training." Everyone knew what he meant.

In order to command warbots by remote neuroelectronic linkage where a computer read your nerve impulses and converted them into warbot commands, and then fed sensor data from warbots back into your nervous system and brain through your skin, you had to have all your neurons straight and all your major peccadillos, internal inconsistencies, ego problems, and hangups well rationalized, and be able to get yourself totally under control. Occasionally, a ringer slipped through, but a warbot brainy with any kind of a mental problem was very quickly eliminated; usually, the warbot brainy did it to himself or herself. Warbot brainies had to live with themselves as they really were and with others around them as well. Warbot brainies and Sierra Charlies were often considered to be supercool, super-rational, superhuman machines like the warbots they commanded. The warbot brainies of the twenty-first century American army knew better; being super-soldiers was the professional side of their lives, and each of them had a personal life that was rigorously kept separate from their jobs. The Sierra Charlies were perhaps even more people-oriented than the warbot brainies since interaction between them on the battlefield was so important; Sierra Charlies got shot at and could actually be killed in combat.

"Lots of difference, Captain...I think because I wasn't around for 'Nam, although maybe Sergeant Major Kester might have some better insights," regimental chief of staff Joan Ward told him, the last part being said rather lightly because Henry Kester was the "old soldier" of the outfit; the younger Greys could kid him about it, and Henry always took it as if he was a grumpy old curmudgeon, which he wasn't. Even Henry had been born after Viet Nam was over, and by the time he was old enough to enlist the rough edges of that fracas had worn off those who'd been through it and were still around to talk about it. "But I agree with Kitsy: We've got to start thinking of the Yemarks differently."

"During the past several weeks, I've seen some amazing changes in the way the Yemarks operate," said regimental operations officer, Major Hensley Atkinson. "Now they're organized. They seem to be well led."

"And they've gotten substantial out-country support from somewhere," Kitsy put in. "For example, now they've got tactical communications devices like this one." She suddenly held up something that looked like a U.S. tacomm brick. "I took it off the sonofabitch who shot me in the side...after I blew his balls off and sent him to paradise where he'll have a hell of a time dallying with the houris as a result."

"Aha! I suspected they had something like this," Regimental Technical Sergeant Edie Sampson said and stood up. Reaching out her hand, she asked, "Captain, may I have a look at that, please? I have a record of the frequency skipping program that I guessed was coming from some sort of tacomm-like system being used by the Yemarks. I can probably gin-up some neat countermeasures if that thing isn't too complex."

"Certainly. That's why I brought it back," Kitsy said, passing the brick-like device to Edie. "And I suspect you'll be able to jam the hell out of it."

"Yeah. Looks like a Mark Four tacomm, but it isn't. No

neuroelectronic interfaces. My guess is that someone captured some of our old stuff and proceeded to copy what they could," Edie observed as she checked the Yemark tacomm brick carefully.

"Soviet?" Curt asked Edie.

She shook her red curls. "No, sir. Laotian."

"What?" Henry Kester obviously didn't believe that.

"Doesn't surprise me a bit. The Chinese have been gearing up Laos for a lot of low-tech microelectronics production, Henry," Jerry Allen told him. "They're moving a lot of medium tech high-production stuff out-country to make room for higher tech production in the PRC where families have run the show for a couple of millennia."

"Well, that sure explains a lot of what was going on out there today," Lieutenant Hassan Mahmud remarked. "I've never known Arabic-speaking people to be as organized as those Yemarks were out there. Not without modern communications. Left to themselves, it's every man for himself. Every man's out to show he's a bigger hero than the next one, and that he can get into paradise early. But I sort of figured that someone was running that show today. Now I know for sure."

It was the sort of insightful remark one would expect from "Hassan the Assassin," who hated his nickname but had been saddled with it since he'd joined the Greys. Raised as a nomadic hill boy in eastern Iran, he'd been rescued from poverty and worse by Curt and the Greys, who'd seen to his American education. He learned fast and prospered well under American biotechnology and freedom; now he was one of the staunchest of the young officers of the Washington Greys. He'd also gotten the reputation of being a real ladies' man. And Curt knew that reputation was more than idle rumor.

"Okay," Curt broke in, getting the postcombat critique back on the track, "we blew it in general, but we saved our asses. And now it's becoming more and more clear why the Yemarks behaved as they did. They had tactical battlefield communications, and we didn't know it, and because of that wadi mine under the bot this morning, we also know that someone is feeding them advanced technology munitions."

Slang terms get started and picked up very rapidly in a combat unit like the Washington Greys. The mine plastered under the Jeep that morning had been designed to blast downward and outward, converting any rocks and gravel under the bot into low-velocity shrapnel. If the mine were triggered in the stony bed of a typical dry Yemeni dry stream valley known as a wadi, it was even more effective. The Greys did a lot of maneuvering in the wadis because it was easy to move bots and vehicles very fast in such washes.

"Not only that, Colonel, but those Yemarks today were shooting something like a Chinese or Soviet A-99 submachinegun-carbine at us," Adonica added. She was an expert in small arms. When the Greys had first encountered her as their "native guide" on Trinidad, she'd been carrying an ancient Ruger Mini-14 in perfect condition. She knew how to shoot it and she still had it although she now considered it too ineffective in comparison to the 7.62-millimeter Novia with its caseless ammo.

"Yeah, I heard that stuff going past me. Sounded like the A-99," was the remark of Battalion Sergeant Major Nick Gerard.

"Oh, Colonel, just so happens that I managed to acquire one of those today from a Yemeni who will have no further use for it because I shot first," said Canadian Captain Patrick Lufkin who stood up and raised an A-99 above his head for them to see. "Sergeant Major Kester, I understand you're the small arms expert in this regiment. Here you are." And he handed the gun to Henry.

"On the basis of the tacomm and the A-99, I'd say it was a reasonably successful operation from the viewpoint of getting some better G-2 on the enemy," Jerry observed quietly.

Curt let the flicker of a smile play over one corner of his mouth. Tired or weary, the Washington Greys were responding in their usual disciplined if somewhat informal manner to this critique. Curt wasn't standing in front of them to tell them what their orders were or how he felt they performed during the fight; he was playing the role of manager, moderator, or interlocutor in the usual exchange of ideas and reports from professional warriors. The Washington Greys were a unique military team that would have seemed highly improbable a hundred years before, and totally impossible during the Civil War. In the first place, all of them were professionals and volunteers in a twenty-first century American army that provided a much-needed place for people who always will be warriors. Too few societies provide a viable and useful outlet for such people; those like the United States who did discovered that it helped stabilize things because the "loose cannons" were in a situation where they had purpose.

"Cheap weapon," Henry mused with distaste, turning it over in his hands after he'd checked the action and made sure it was clear. He thought to himself that he'd better teach a few things about personal firearms to the Canadian officer who'd come to the Greys from a Canadian Army warbot unit to learn the new Sierra Charlie doctrine and operations. "Don't know if it's Chinese or even Burmese. Maybe even Mongolian. Whoever made it had absolutely no pride of craftsmanship. No manufacture or proof marks on it. But, hell, why should they be proud of this junky crap? They're turning out guns there in Asia like they made fireworks for two thousand years - punch out the parts in primitive backyard shops, then send them to the regional factory for assembly."

"This is good data," Curt agreed. "I want to take that brick and the A-99 with me tomorrow. I want Battleaxe to see them. She'll go hyperbolic when she realizes her troops aren't up against primitive hill people with old Enfield rifles and AK-47s. Maybe we'll get some revisions in the ROEs...But don't count on it."

He turned to Jerry, "However, Major Allen, it was your astute observation of the Yemeni customs that saved the day this morning. And you're absolutely right. The Yemeni don't hassle us in the afternoon; they're off somewhere having their daily qat chew. And they don't hassle us at night because they're all mellow by then and want to be with their women. Got any ideas for changes in our tactics as a result of your discoveries, Major?"

"Not a bad way to fight a war," Kitsy Clinton said in sotto voce. "Fight in the morning, get high in the afternoon, then spend the evening romantically involved..."

"Not if you want to win the war," Adonica reminded her.

"But the Yemarks must want to win," Joan Ward insisted. "Someone must be backing them to create all this trouble. They seem to want to stop the railroad. Someone must want that iron ore."

"Who the hell owns it now?" Nick Gerard asked.

"The Yemen Royal Republic," Jerry replied.

"Which means Queen Arwa Bint Muhammed al-Badr," Hassan observed.

"The deal is between the YRR and the Ferron Corporation," Curt added. "Ferron pays the YRR a royalty of x-dollars per ton shipped from al-Luhaya."

"Ferron Corporation? A multinational? Maybe I'd better have my Phoenix broker check that stock," Jerry mused. "And find out who the hell really owns Ferron Corporation."

"So why the hell are we here if the United States has no stake in the mine or the ore?" Pat Lufkin wanted to know.

"Matter of fact, no one's ever explained clearly to me why we're here in the first place," Nick Gerard added.

"I've told you all that I've been told by Battleaxe, and she always tells everything she knows about an operation like this," Curt said. Then he repeated what he'd told the Greys several times before. "The United States has a mutual aid-and-trade agreement with the YRR. The Queen asked for help. The former President responded first with military aid, which didn't alleviate the situation. So, the Queen then asked for direct military assistance in the form of troops..."

"And that fell into line with the former President's policy of supporting friends. So, he said yes and sent us over in the final months of his lame duck administration," Hensley Atkinson added.

Major Joan Ward quickly put in, "Since this has become a general strategic discussion, I'd like to remind everyone of the great underlying principle upon which our country was founded: Money Talks. I've learned it's helpful to ask the question, 'Who's going to do what to whom and who's going to get paid for it?' Don't get me wrong; this isn't a criticism of our former commander in chief. Or our current one. But, Colonel, I think I reflect the sentiments of many of the Greys here and out in the field when I continue to ask the question, 'Why are we *really* here?' I've heard a lot of explanations, most of them apparently intended to maintain the morale of the troops. But something seems to be missing. The first inconsistency seems to lie in the fact that I can't for the life of me see a national security issue involved in protecting a mine and a railroad that's sending iron ore off to Madagascar to be turned into steel...for whom?"

"That's exactly what's bugging me, too," Nick Gerard added.

A muted chorus of assent went up in the room.

"We go where we're ordered to go and do what we're ordered to do within the bounds of the various international conventions pertaining to armed conflict and the federal laws and policies applicable to our actions," Major Hensley Atkinson, regimental S-3, added. "Sometimes we aren't told for any number of good reasons...or even bad reasons. But I do agree that it helps our morale and motivation if we do know. Certainly, sitting around like this wondering why we've had comrades wounded or injured in the process...Well, it doesn't help much."

"I'll ask Battleaxe for additional clarification of this mission's rationale. I'll get the best answer I can," Curt promised them because he, too, really wasn't really very happy with what he'd been told. A sudden silence fell over the group. Sensing that the group was tired and had shot their bolt when it came to a postcombat briefing, Curt looked around and asked, "In the meantime, any other observations, comments, critiques, bitches, sniveling, or requests? No? That's unusual. I figured this to go on for a couple of more hours. Okay, that means I've got some time to visit the wounded and injured. But don't think that you can go off and log some sack time. Kitsy, get to work on your new concepts. Jerry, you and Hassan give Kitsy a hand because both of you speak

Arabic and know how the Arabic mind works. Adonica, work with Henry on that captured assault rifle; let's see if you can discover who made it. Edie, I want the best tech evaluation you can give me about that Yemark tacomm unit. And, oh, yes, I decree a Stand-to at eighteen-hundred hours tonight. Time those of us not out with the Saucy Cans units let off a little steam."

Chapter Seven

"I want out of here!"

"Dyani, Major Ruth wants to keep you under observation until tomorrow morning," Curt told Captain Dyani Motega who was sitting cross-legged on a cot in the building that had been set up as a regimental hospital.

"But I'm not wounded," Dyani complained. "No bleeding. No broken skin. Just this big bruise on my left side," She lifted a corner of the white cotton infirmary gown to reveal an ugly blue and red splotch just above her waist.

"Does it hurt?" Curt wanted to know.

"Not now," Dyani shook her head, her heavy black hair falling down her back. She pulled the cotton gown back down.

"It must have hurt like hell when Al Williams brought you in here, didn't it?" To Curt, a bruise that large and ugly would give him a problem for several days even after the application of colloidal gel salve. Curt was hard as nails, and the impact of even a soft lead bullet against his body armor would have produced far more subcutaneous trauma and micro-hemorrhaging. Dyani had very little fat on her trim body, but still her female muscles were not quite as firm as Curt's.

Curt's remark caused Dyani to pause for a moment. Then she admitted with some hesitation and even some chagrin, "I don't remember."

Curt sat down on the edge of the bed next to her. He could see that she was very upset about something, and this was highly unusual for the disciplined Dyani Motega. "According to Ruth, you were in deep shock when the air evac Chippie brought you in this morning."

Dyani looked down as though she was ashamed of some-thing.

After a few moments, she admitted in a low voice, "Kida, I lost myself this morning."

This confused Curt. "Lost *what*, Deer Arrow?"

"Myself. My control," she admitted reluctantly. "Yes, it hurt when I got hit. But I know how to control pain. Something happened when Al showed up with Adonica."

"You relaxed. You knew you were in good hands then," Curt suggested.

Dyani shook her head. "No, I lost control. Then I don't remember what happened. I...just...went away. I just ceased to be," Dyani stammered, searching very hard for words to describe what had happened to her. She finally looked at him with almost a plaintive expression. "Kida, that should not have happened. I was taught to handle pain. I was taught how to control myself. And I have simply never been without existence, without awareness, without consciousness of myself. I...I think I panicked. *I should not have behaved as I did!* I'm ashamed of myself..."

"Ashamed of yourself?" Curt could hardly believe his ears. But there were many things about Dyani Motega that were hard to believe. "My God, woman, I've seen strong men fall screaming and yelling when they got nicked far less than you did!"

"They weren't me. They didn't have the training my father gave me," Dyani tried to explain.

Curt took her face gently in his hands and raised her head, so she was looking at him. "Deer Arrow, you were badly hurt out there. We all tend to react in unsuspected ways when we're hurt."

"But I've been injured before. In Kurdistan."

"You were different then. You were younger. You didn't have the burdens of company command on your shoulders. Dyani, believe me, you have absolutely nothing to be ashamed of." Curt tried to sound as sincere and convincing as he felt. Often, of late, it was difficult for him to show his emotions. He'd learned the hard way what happened to him when he let his emotions for this woman dominate his professional life as a warrior. So, he'd had to learn from Dyani something of the technique she used to maintain her legendary and almost stoic self-control. It hadn't been easy for either of them; Dyani had done it for so long that it was almost instinctual for her, and in teaching Curt she'd had to rigorize what she did naturally. Dyani had an incredible inner reservoir of steel discipline that came from her upbringing and from her heritage as a full-blooded Crow Indian. She was a true warrior woman, one of the few that Curt had ever known. Other ladies in the Washington Greys were warriors, too, but not with the intensity of Dyani Motega who was intense in everything she did.

"I need you to tell me that very quietly and very privately," she admitted to him in a low voice that was filled with longing. "I don't need to stay here. I need to prove to you and to myself that I have my control back again."

She reached up and took both his hands in hers. "I have no clout with the regimental medical officer. But you're the regimental commander. Tell Major Gydesen that you want me released on your responsibility. I want to be with you tonight, Kida. And you need me." That was indeed Dyani Motega talking. She was always straightforward, unambiguous, and without guile.

But Curt realized that she had indeed lost some of her control. She had never come close to pleading with him before; she had just gone ahead and been Dyani Motega. So, he knew then that she'd been shaken to the core of her being.

She was also recovering from shock. And it was more than mere physical shock.

He folded her into his arms and held her. "Deer Arrow, you know that I can't overrule a decision of my chief medical officer. I spoke with Ruth before I came. She understands what happened to you today. And now I think I do, too. You're still in shock. And Ruth had to load you up with some medicine and wire you up as well in order to pull you through the physical trauma. She doesn't want to let you out of her surveillance for another eight to ten hours. That's why you're still wired up."

Dyani swept one hand over the flush sensor pads on her neck and shoulders. "I don't want artificial help. I don't want bioelectronic therapy. I can do it myself. And you can help me more than all this technology…"

"Ruth says she wants you to have a good night's sleep. You wouldn't get that if you left here with me…"

"Yes."

"Deer Arrow, you need the rest. You really do. There's always tomorrow."

She shook her head where it was nestled against his shoulder. "No, not always. You could get hurt or killed tomorrow…"

He pushed her away from him and looked at her. "Do you remember Sanctuary?" he asked, reminding her of the last campaign where they'd both been in jeopardy from a religious cult that had been based near Battle Mountain, Nevada. Curt had managed to escape from the clutches of the mad prophet leader, but Dyani hadn't. Curt had gone through hell for a day until he fought his way into the cult's sanctuary and met Dyani fighting her way out. "You told me then that we had to keep our priorities straight. We spent a lot of time afterwards working on the problem and coming up with solutions, didn't we? Do you still believe we did it right?"

She didn't say anything, but she nodded with her soulful eyes. Dyani could say things with her eyes that others wasted time putting into words.

"Then this is one of those times when we *must* follow the agreements we made with one another," he reminded her. "This morning, you were hurt worse than you thought. It wasn't a permanent physical injury, certainly nothing that would warrant keeping you in the regimental infirmary overnight. But because you're Dyani Motega with everything that Dyani Motega is and believes in, you've been shaken up mentally far more than physically. Now, tell me, what have you always advised me to do when I got my neurons tied in knots over some difficult decision or problem? Sleep on it, you told me. A different perspective comes with the dawn, you taught me. I'm asking you to follow your own advice."

"I don't want my mind messed up with drugs or neuroelectronic programming."

"I think you need all the help you can get."

"You're all the help I need. Get up and close that door. Then come back over here to me."

Curt found it impossible to argue with Dyani even when Dyani was as upset and emotionally taut as she was that afternoon. It was a warm afternoon even in the heights of the al-Hijaz Mountains of Yemen at three thousand meters elevation.

When he left, Dyani had relaxed and he could tell that some of Doctor Ruth's ministrations were beginning to take effect. Dyani had been fighting them just as she'd fought off the pain of being hit by the piece of shrapnel that morning. In fact, she fell asleep before he left. The charge from the incredible emotional high she'd been through had been discharged. He could see it in her face.

Curt didn't want to leave. He fought his own emotions which told him he should never leave the presence of this woman ever again. Physically, she was stunning, but inwardly she was even more beautiful to him. They were both warriors; they needed no excuses to be or do whatever they wanted when they were together.

But they had both agreed that they had warrior jobs to do. That duty, honor, and country came first because that was the warrior ethic. That someday they would grow tired of fighting and a more tranquil family life together would then be possible. But not while either of them was likely to be killed or maimed in their professional work.

It was time to get over to the Stand-to, so Curt went briefly to his quarters, took a shower, shaved, and put on a fresh khaki shirt and a pair of slacks.

One of the traditions of the Washington Greys was the Club. Membership was about as exclusive as a rainstorm...providing you were or had been a Washington Grey. Everywhere the Greys had gone and established themselves in any sort of a temporary casern, they'd found a place for the Club. Somehow, Captain Harriet Dearborn, the supply officer, always managed to find extra rations and Class 6 supplies. It was a place for the Greys to relax in an unofficial social atmosphere in an off-duty status, a place where gripes and bitches could be freely aired, and where a judicious remark made to a superior might lead to a pass or even a leave. It was even more informal than Curt's briefings, and he'd kept those informal because previous regimental commanders had done so. The Greys were a disciplined team. The awesome power to apply physical force with arms and warbots wasn't something that could be handed to warriors who didn't have a high level of discipline. Personal manners accounted for a lot, but that didn't mean that warriors had to be stiff-necked Prussian-like prudes. When the Washington Greys relaxed and had fun, they usually tackled it with the same intensity as their fighting.

Curt was very careful to be exactly on time - not early and not late. Part of the craft of leadership is being dependable and trustworthy, doing what you say you'll do when you say you're going to do it. Although Curt knew that RHIP and used those privileges, those perks weren't something to be taken for granted; they had to be earned, and they came with a very high price.

He made sure he went around to greet everyone and to say a few words to each Grey. He listened to the gripes and bitches - mostly about having to follow the "goddammned ROEs." He proposed the typical toasts to those who couldn't be there because they were wounded, injured, in the infirmary, or out in the field on duty.

He also paid close attention to the scuttlebutt circulating in what was known as Rumor Control. Occasionally, he picked up a tidbit before it was officially brought to his attention. That wasn't often, but it happened that evening.

BIOTECO's head nurse, petite Captain Helen Devlin, remarked offhandedly to him, "Colonel, I don't know whether you were told or not, but your toast to the absent Greys missed four people out of AIRMAINCO and VETECO..."

Curt looked around, then brought his eyes back to Helen who was nice to look at. She'd been his biotech when the Greys were a regular warbot outfit, so she knew him in more than an official capacity. As a nurse, she knew things about him that other ladies of the Greys didn't. "So many Greys are out in the field tonight on those damned guard details that I probably missed noting them. We're sort of spread out here in Yemen."

"They aren't out in the field. They're in the infirmary tonight," Helen advised him quietly.

Curt raised his eyebrows. "Oh? Someone wounded and I don't know about it?"

"Not exactly," she told him. There was a note of seriousness as well as humor in her voice. "I suspect you'll catch it on Major Ruth's morning medical report tomorrow."

"Catch what?"

"Well, not what the four NCOs caught. They checked in about seventeen hundred just before I came off duty but after you left Dyani's room," Helen admitted. "Seems that things have been both so tense and boring here in Camp Disaster that four techies went out on the town last night and played rather loose and free with the local maids. A number of us ladies are rather ripped off about it because they certainly didn't have to wander afield; we were around, after all."

Curt sighed. "Okay, Helen, what's going on?"

"They picked up some good cases of VD."

"Oh, for God's sake...!"

"No, certainly not for His sake. They'll be out of action for a few days...As I said, the ladies of the Greys aren't very happy. I wouldn't want to guess what their revenge is likely to be. I suspect it will be somewhat rougher than whatever you do to them."

Curt decided he wouldn't worry about it until he got the formal, official report and had a chance to talk to both Doctor Ruth and the four NCOs. But it concerned him. It was a sign that morale was starting to slip. Badly. Even with a two-to-one ratio of men to women in the regiment, the ladies felt there was no excuse for any of the men to venture afield. However, some of the men never felt that way, preferring to occasionally have a little local adventure.

So, he knew he was going to have to institute some refresher briefings about personal hygiene. He'd probably talk to his adjutant, Major Pappy Gratton, about it tomorrow. Yemen was still a thousand years behind the rest of the world. It had been a poor country until the discovery of the iron ore deposits. Only about twenty percent of the population was literate, which nearly matched the percentage of the Yemeni who were urbanized. And the country had less than fifty hospitals. Medically and from the standpoint of sanitation and hygiene, the place was a cesspool. No wonder Yemeni life expectancy was less than fifty years.

But, as General Hettrick had often remarked, the Washington Greys were rarely sent to the garden spots of the world...

Kitsy bounced up to him with two drinks in her hands. "Colonel, I thought you should try a Canadian concoction that Captain Pat Lufkin just introduced in order to add some interest and spice to the land of Sheba," she bubbled, handing him one of the glasses.

Curt looked at the brownish milky liquid. "What's in it? Or should I ask?"

"Canadian whiskey laced with moose milk," Kitsy replied, but Curt could tell from the tone of her voice that she was kidding him.

So he went along with it. "So, what's unusual about that?"

Captain Pat Lufkin, who was seated nearby, heard the conversation and got up to add his bit to the explanation. "Colonel, it's several things. First of all, one must understand the difficulty of preparing this delicacy."

"Preparing it?" Curt decided to play the straight man.

"Yes, sir."

"First, you must find a moose," Kitsy snickered.

"Which is not difficult in some parts of Canada. One goes into the woods carrying a rifle loaded with tranquilizing darts, a milk bottle, and a guide with a moose call," Lufkin explained. "The guide is very important. He stands on one side of a clearing and blows the moose call, making a sound like a moose in rut. He hopes a female moose hears it. If a female moose does indeed hear it, she comes tearing into the clearing, whereupon you plug her with a dart and milk her."

"Suppose it's a bull moose," Curt asked.

"If it's a bull moose, you abort the mission. But not before you tranquilize the bull moose. Otherwise, the bull moose will rape the guide," Lufkin said with an absolutely straight face.

Curt knew when he'd been had, so he reached for the drink in Kitsy's hand. "So what's this concoction called?"

"A What-a-way," Kitsy told him.

Curt looked reproachfully at her. "Kitsy, I've been whanged as the straight man once tonight. And once is all the colonel will stand still for."

"After drinking two of these, you won't be standing still. You will find yourself on the floor looking up and telling yourself, 'What-a-way to go!'"

Curt took a sip. It wasn't bad. But it's hard to mess up good Canadian whiskey. "I can think of better ways to go," Curt told her.

"So, can I," Kitsy popped back. "Want to finish this experiment, or shall we search for that better way?"

"Not during Stand-to."

"Well, a girl can hope."

"Keep hoping," he told her.

"I intend to do more than that…in my own inimitable way," Kitsy promised.

Several hours later, Curt told her, "Your way is indeed inimitable. Always has been."

"Of course. And it's gotten better," Kitsy murmured. "After all, I've had the chance to do some additional programming on those nanochips the biotechs installed in my neck to hot-wire my spinal column."

"You were fine the way you were," Curt said.

"Maybe, but a gal's got to do what she can to remain competitive...and things have definitely gotten very competitive. Since I'm going to have to live with being Number Two, I'd better be a damned good Number Two. And take advantage of opportunities like tonight...in spite of everything."

"I'm surprised you can do anything. That bruise where you took the Enfield round looks pretty bad," Curt remarked.

"Does it match Dyani's?"

"Same place. But she took a bigger piece of metal and from our own guns."

"Well, our wounds may match, but since my neck got hot-wired some of my other techniques can't be matched. Let me give you an example." She did some things that Curt didn't recall she could do.

"Ain't science wonderful?" she finally whispered.

"Orgasmic!" was all that Curt could say.

Chapter Eight

"General, I don't like to lose!" Lieutenant Colonel Curt Carson said vehemently after Belinda Hettrick had motioned him to take a seat alongside her terminal desk.

The commanding general of the 17th Iron Fist Division and of the Yemen Expeditionary Force waved her hand over her terminal controls and cleared the screens. It was apparent to Curt that the lady was feeling harried. He could see it in the lines in her face and by her actions. She had a pile of problems with all four regiments that needed her attention, but she knew she had to take a few minutes to talk privately with one of her regimental commanders. It was not only her method of command, but she also knew that Curt Carson was her best field commander. She'd watched him grow and mature under her command in the Washington Greys; now he led the Washington Greys. When Curt Carson wanted to talk, Belinda Hettrick was ready to listen and would make time to do so if possible.

"Colonel Wilkinson, this is Battleaxe," she told her comm set. "I'm not to be disturbed for the next thirty minutes unless some contractor starts moving this place down to Hell where it belongs." Then she turned to Curt and replied as casually as he'd been forceful, "No one likes to lose unless one is a loser to start with."

"Well, I'm not a loser."

"I know that."

"But I'm losing, General."

Hettrick also knew that, but she didn't admit it. Instead, she asked, "Tell me what's happened to lead you to that conclusion."

"Sixteen of my Greys have been wounded or are currently out of action on a temporary basis," Curt began his litany of problems commonly called "sniveling" but not actually a snivel. "That's eleven point seven percent of my force. That weakens me considerably because the Sierra Charlie human-to-warbot mix ratio is a lot higher than in a regular RI regiment, and all our warbot and Sierra Charlie regiments are only a fraction of the size they used to be. Furthermore, at the present rate of attrition, my unit strength will be down by more than twenty percent in a week. At which point, I'm in deep slime."

"Some of your wounded will be coming back to combat level," Hettrick pointed out.

"But I'm also getting short-botted," Curt added. "I lost two Jeeps yesterday, and I've got three more out of action along with one LAMVA with its Saucy Cans gun, and the current tactical plan requires immediate operational fire cover for any attack on the railroad. Four of my Mary Anns are out. All of my damaged warbots actually require Level Four repair, which we can't do here because we don't have anything better than Level Three repair in the division. But Ellwood Otis and his crew are working eighteen-hour days patching them back together by cannibalizing one Jeep and a Mary Ann for parts that don't seem to get here via the Aerospace Farce airlift into Sana'a."

"How's your ammo?" Hettrick suddenly asked.

"About the same as rations. Not at the critical level yet. We haven't had that many targets to shoot at," Curt explained. "We keep getting shot at, but we have damned few solid targets to shoot back at in spite of the fact that I haven't issued any orders to spare the ammo. But everyone knows we're not living high on the hog here in beautiful Yemen..."

"We're out on the end of a very long logistics pipeline, Curt," Hettrick told him, although she didn't need to remind him of the fact. "Furthermore, the YEF has a very low priority..."

"What?" That was news to Curt.

"The messy situation in Kashmir and the bubbling blood bath in Suriname has caused Fort Fumble to restructure its overseas priorities," the general revealed. "Congress is screaming about American citizens being hassled in Burma and Peru, and pressure is being felt from the Hill all the way across the river in Fort Fumble on that one in spite of the current nonmilitary policy guidance coming out of 1600 Pennsylvania Avenue. The Albanians are starting to raise hell again on the southern flank of Europe by making noises and stirring up the Montenegrins and Macedonians. So, Greece and Yugoslavia are asking for military aid and advisors. The Albanian resurgence is causing heartburn in Italy because the major industrial heart of that country is in the Po River Valley with its major sea lane down the Adriatic open to possible Albanian interdiction."

She stopped for a moment, then sighed. "Curt, we've never stopped living in a very dangerous world, in spite of the big emphasis on economic and trade competition instead of warfare over the past forty-some years. Some people haven't moved forward out of barbarism in the way they think, and it's been only the military forces of the free world that have held those jerks in line. Otherwise, they'd be out there carrying on their usual sweet practices of piracy and extortion."

"General, you're preaching to the choir. I received my National War College certificate before we deployed to Yemen," Curt reminded her. He agreed with her assessment, and he was reminding her gently that she didn't need to expend valuable time repeating it to him.

"You're right. Well, without meaning to criticize our boss, I honestly believe that a lot of the increased tension in the world is a consequence of the fact that the new administration is having second thoughts about all the American military overseas commitments...And saying so loudly in public. Our enemies are listening and believing that maybe their chance has now arrived."

"Don't they understand the way our political system works?" Curt wondered.

"Not really. You know as well as I do that most of the world is all hot and eager to engage in the sort of tribal warfare that will allow ancient enemies to be wiped out and more power to be concentrated in the hands of a few uneducated military strong men. The only thing that kept most of them quiet during the nineteenth century was the willingness of both Britain and France to slit a few throats when necessary. And for the United States to flex its muscles and scare the shit out of them during the twentieth century. When it could do so and get away with it even under the badgering of the news media, of course," She sighed again. "Colonel, we're going to have to make do with what we've got."

"Which is a lot if we use it properly," Curt agreed. Then he added, "And, provided we can maintain the upper hand in terms of military technology. Which, by the way, I've just learned that we're not."

"So, what surprises do you have in the ditty bag you hauled in here with you," Hettrick asked, indicating the haversack Curt held.

Curt reflected that Hettrick rarely missed anything. He opened the bag and drew out the A-99 assault submachinegun. He lifted it up and handed it across the desk to her. "Look familiar, General?"

Hettrick held out her hand and took the weapon, checking to make sure that the action was open and cleared. "Soviet A-99. Chinese copy, maybe."

Curt shook his head and told her, "None of the above."

Looking it over carefully at close range, Hettrick muttered, "Not an ordinary A-99. Not exactly, at any rate. Cheap version. Real cheap. No identifying marks on it at all. What's Henry Kester have to say about it?"

"He doesn't think it was made in China. Maybe Laos or Mongolia."

"So! G-2 got some rumbling about that. But we received no heads-up alert that we might run into them here in Yemen."

"We just have. Took this off a dead Yemark yesterday. Which means someone is now supplying the Yemarks," Curt guessed. "General, this sheep screw is no longer just a matter of some Yemenis having a great dislike for the railroad that's running through their land killing their livestock and the few idiots who won't get out of its way..."

"Or their inability to collect a toll for permitting its safe passage through their lands," Hettrick added. "But this gun is a piece of junk! Does Henry want this goddamned piece of plastic crap?"

"You can send it along to your divisional G-2, General. Henry's seen all he wants to see of it. So has Captain Sweet. Both agree that it's good for about three hundred rounds - about six clips' worth - before it turns into a high-tech club or you shit-can it."

"Six clips. Nice package. Just about what a guerrilla can carry on a long-trek operation. Use it up, throw it away, and get the hell out of there unburdened so you can move fast. Nice tactics," Hettrick admitted. "But it surprises me that Laotians can get their hands on carbon matrix composite materials."

"The basic materials aren't hard to get or make, provided you can exercise any sort of robotic quality control...which they can do in Low Level nations when they have to. And the technology has been around for a quarter of a century now," Curt reminded her. "Any expertise that old that's been used that much gets disseminated by copying, even if it's classified. And even if the classification involves compartmentalized information. And here's another example." He reached into his haversack, pulled out the Yemark tacomm unit, and handed it to her.

A look of astonishment came over Hettrick's face as she turned the unit over in her hands. Then she looked up at Curt and asked, "I presume you recovered this off a Yemark, too?"

Curt nodded. "Sergeant Sampson spotted some EM emissions that looked like tacomm stuff yesterday. We confirmed this when Captain Clinton took this off a dead Yemark. We couldn't find another one..."

"One's enough..."

"Sampson has already been over it and gotten its transmission characteristics," Curt explained. "It's a primitive frequency-hop tactical communications unit. Has only one hop sequence, and it can't be recoded in the field like our current units. Resembles our old Mark Fours. We lost a few of those in Iran back when the Zahedan hostage rescue mission went to slime. I never thought the Iranians would be able to copy them."

"They didn't," Hettrick remarked. "Iranian stuff looks very Muslim; it's the way they see the world. From a gross look-see at the outsides of this unit, it has all the characteristics you see in cheap Senegalese radios made for sale in Low Level countries and the cheap electronic toys that get dumped on the market from Antioch."

"That's what Sampson thinks, too. My first-blush guess tells me the Jehorkhim Muslims probably traded some of our old Mark Fours to the Iranian government as part of a bribe to get off easy. The Iranians bartered them to Senegal or probably Tripoli in exchange for something they needed. The originals were circulated through the Low Level arms network until they ended up in a place where they could be ripped off..."

"And these cheap tacomms are probably circulating in the arms deals of the Low Level countries as super-expensive stuff you can use against low-level electronic armed forces," Hettrick finished. "Okay, to G-2 it goes. Thank you, Curt."

"General, this means we're in a whole new ball game," Curt suddenly pointed out.

"How so?"

"We've been laboring under the assumption that we're defending the railroad against relatively unsophisticated bands of Yemarks armed with ancient firearms and without any tactical battlefield communications," Curt explained. "This adds up along with the real deadly wadi mines we've been finding on our recovered warbots."

"I read your report on that this morning before you came. Why hasn't my G-2 seen one of those yet?"

"Because we haven't managed to get a wadi mine off a warbot without having it blow up in the process. The triggering mechanism is damned sophisticated, and none of us has the slightest idea of how or why it works. But the wadi mine blows when you touch the warbot. God only knows why," Curt said in exasperation.

"No, Curt, the people who made the wadi mine also know how it works. And my O-D people will find out. Just let them know the next time you recover a warbot from the field," Hettrick told him. "You've apparently come to some conclusions as a result of all this. Tell me about them."

"General, we now find ourselves facing an adversary with modern small arms, tactical communications, and advanced high explosives."

When he stopped, Hettrick prompted him, "Go on."

"I have no solid data, and this is speculation, but I now believe we're facing an enemy who's being supplied by an outside entity and also trained by same. We're no longer up against the classical Yemeni guerrilla or the Yemark terrorist." Curt hesitated a moment before he went on because he knew he would be touching a sore spot that he'd abraded before with negative results. "We're going to get greased real bad if we don't adapt our strategy to take this into account and change our tactics accordingly."

"So? Do you have any good ideas?"

"Not that I'm ready to trot out in front of the divisional commander quite yet, but we're working on it," Curt admitted. "One thing for sure, we can't go on the way we have been. Not with the ROEs strapping us into a losing game."

"We've been over this before, Colonel. I can't change the rules of engagement. They were laid on us by either Fort Fumble or the National Security Council."

"General, I would like to have a copy of the exact wording of those ROEs," Curt requested.

Hettrick knew what her regimental commander had in mind. Or she thought she did. She knew how Curt Carson tended to work when the rules and regulations prevented him from doing something military that needed to be done. "So that you can figure a way around them?"

"No, ma'am. That would be too obvious," Curt said carefully. "It would also get you in a heap of trouble after they locked me away in Leavenworth. Or somewhere just as comfy and inaccessible. Officially, I want to know the exact wording so that I can determine just how far I can go before I step in it."

"I thought so..."

"My official request will say that my troops out there taking the incoming want to know exactly what the limits are," Curt went on. "Actually, their morale is pretty damned low at the moment. I think I might be able to jack it up a little bit if they knew precisely how far they could go before getting their butts in a sling. It would also help if we had a better idea of why we're shedding our blood all over the rocks of Yemen protecting something that doesn't seem to have a damned thing to do with the security of the United States..."

"So that's it!" Hettrick snapped. "Colonel, we're a volunteer army of professionals. We go where we're ordered to go, and we fight."

"I agree. But we're more than a mercenary army," Curt pointed out. "The American soldier has always fought better when there was an understandable reason to fight. Any professional of any sort always performs better and does a better job when told why the professional is called upon to perform."

"Sometimes security precludes it, Colonel." Hettrick reminded him.

"Is this situation one of them, General?" Curt wanted to know.

Hettrick sighed. "No, it isn't. At least, not to my knowledge. No, I haven't been told why we're here. I have no information that you do not. I am not withholding any information from you," she told him sincerely and adamantly. Then, with a moment's hesitation, knowing that this conversation would go no farther, she continued, "But, yes, I agree with you. It would help if we knew why we're here, especially since this seemed to start out as a rather straightforward mission very much like the Persian Gulf pipeline patrol..."

"Which is great for warbot units but a complete misuse of Sierra Charlies."

"Yes, but you did a good job anyway."

"Because we knew we were really there to take care of that Soviet Spetsnaz battalion," Curt said. "But why are we here, General?

From the looks of the weapon and tacomm we recovered yesterday, I now have a strong suspicion that another outside power is involved. Maybe we were sent here in anticipation that this would happen..."

Hettrick thought about this remark for a long moment before she finally replied, "You may be right. And that's not a standard put-off, Curt. I see that you remember what I tried to teach you..."

"I try to look behind the obvious," Curt admitted.

"That isn't exactly what I taught you," she reminded him.

"You're right. I was paraphrasing, which is a dangerous departure. In the words of the teacher, *Always look behind the headlines and try to determine who is doing what to whom and who is getting paid for it.*"

"That's better," Hettrick told him. "Now, I think the teacher will attempt to follow the teachings. I'm going to follow my own preachings and do the same thing. I have a meeting with General Qahtan this afternoon. I intend to do a little digging. First of all, I want the Royal Yemen Army to be a little more aggressive in rooting out and pursuing the Yemarks we flush out of the rocks along the railroad. Now that you've captured a foreign rifle and a tacomm and had people hurt by advanced explosives, I think that information may shake him up a little bit. And maybe I'll learn something I didn't know."

"If General Qahtan knows anything more than we do..."

"Colonel Carson, you've served in this part of the world as I have. You know very well that information is an extremely valuable commodity, and the tendency is to tell someone only what they need to know in order to get them to do what you want them to do," Hettrick said, then paused. "Come to think of it, that's exactly the way the whole damned world is run."

"You taught me that, too," Curt reminded her, then quoted in the ancient Latin language, "*Nescieis, mi fili, quantilla sapienta regitur mundus.*"

"Ah, yes! 'You'll never know, my son, with what little knowledge the world is run?' Well, I intend to apply another aphorism, the one about not letting the bastards grind me down. I suggest you do the same."

Chapter Nine

As Curt was leaving the bull pen where the 17th Iron Fist Division staff was at work, he was hailed by his combat code name, "Grey Head! Stand and be recognized!" It was a tough, low-pitched, almost whispery female voice he'd heard many times before in the old South Barracks at West Point, especially during his fourth-class year when he'd roomed there. The voice belonged to one of his former next door roomies.

"Good morning, Blue Maxie," Curt responded, using the combat call code of Colonel Maxine Frances Cashier, commanding officer of the 7th Robot Infantry (Special Combat) Regiment, the Cottonbalers, who came charging up to him.

"Charging" was the only term that came to Curt's mind. Maxine Frances Cashier charged hard at anything and everything she did. The short, stocky, but physically fit woman approached him at full operational speed and stopped only a half meter from him.

"What the hell are you doing here, Curt?" Blue Maxie demanded to know. The woman was demanding. She demanded a lot from her subordinates, more from her compatriots, and an impossible level of performance from herself. She'd always been that way. And she could get away with demanding because, like Curt, she never demanded of her subordinates more than what she was willing to do herself. She was the same way socially. It helped that Maxine Cashier was an attractive woman even though she wore her blonde hair in a male high-and-tight white sidewall cut. In spite of that or perhaps to inform the world that she was, after all, a woman, she wore makeup. Not a lot. A little lip gloss. Some rouge. But, unlike many other women in combat assignments, she wore it. Curt could never remember seeing Maxie Cashier without makeup, even at West Point where even in her plebe year she'd quietly informed the upper classmen that army regulations and West Point tradition said absolutely nothing about cosmetics. Furthermore, she informed them, only the Rumanian Army had specifically banned the use of cosmetics by its officers in 1916.

"Probably the same thing you're doing here, Maxie," Curt retorted, then fired back at her in the same vein, "So what the hell are you doing here?"

Maxie checked her watch then gestured toward an empty room. It didn't have a door that could be closed behind them. Few rooms in Yemen had doors. With no air conditioning systems, the Yemenis depended upon natural air conditioning in the form of free air movement through doors and windows. However, the Iron Fist Division staffers had supplemented this with large floor fans to ensure air movement. It was possible to endure the high temperatures of Yemen if you had air movement because the air was so dry. At least in the mountainous regions.

Maxie Cashier sat down and removed her blue Sierra Charlie tam. "Thank God it's cooler up here in Sana'a!" she exclaimed. "We're trapped down in that goddamned valley at Al-Mawr with coastal humidity to match the temperature! You've got it easy, Curt!"

"Maybe, but none of us has it that easy," Curt reminded her. "I take it you're here because you're taking casualties and warbot damage, too. And you needed to snivel about it to Battleaxe. Right?"

"Right! Goddamned Yemarks are cutting us to bits! And we're stuck in the middle of nowhere. You've got it a hell of a lot easier in Amran. At least it's a town." Maxie's low, throaty voice caused her some problems commanding a company at West Point, but like her other shortcomings, she'd overcome it and could, when called upon, bellow a parade ground command with the best of them. Right then, she didn't have to do it. And Curt remembered that her voice held a certain amount of sexual promise which wasn't often obvious in her actions...except when she wanted to act that way. God save the mark when she did, Curt recalled. Maxie had a way of getting what she wanted and making others enjoy doing it.

"That causes other problems," Curt said without saying what those problems were.

Cashier knew. "That's what I hear. Four NCOs down with VD..."

"Rumor Control?"

"Yeah. You confirm it?"

Curt nodded. "Four of them."

"So, what are you going to do about it?"

"I'm so shorthanded that I can't confine them to quarters. Wouldn't work anyhow."

"I'd boot their asses out of the regiment if they were in my Cottonbalers."

"I suspect you would. But you've got a slightly different leadership style than I do, Maxie. You always have," Curt reminded her.

"So, what are you going to do?" she repeated her question.

"Education."

"My God, not those awful VD videotapes! They'd scare the hell out of anyone! As I recall, they made some of my plebes impotent for a couple of months…"

"I seriously doubt that, Maxie. Plebes are young animals in rut most of the time…if you recall," Curt corrected her. "And those tapes were designed to scare the shit out of young people and force them to use their brains instead of their gonads. No, I'm not going to dust those tapes off and show them to the troops, Maxie. Most of the Greys would laugh at them and consider them the best comic relief they've had in months. After all, my Greys are adults just like your Cottonballs."

"We're the Cottonbalers. And if anyone other than you had used that term, he'd catch it right in the chops. So, what are you going to do?" she asked for a third time.

"As I told you, education."

"Oh, really? How?"

"The ladies of the Greys will take care of the education, Maxie. They're more than capable of doing so. When they get through, the gentlemen of the Greys, commissioned and noncommissioned, will have had the course, I guarantee you! In the meantime, as their beloved regimental commander, I will regale them with the sort of fatherly advice their colonel is expected to dish out. They'll listen, but it will be the ladies who take care of things."

"But that isn't why you're here sniveling to Battleaxe," Cashier observed. "I know why you're here, so come clean with me, Curt. You and the Greys are taking the same sort of shit that I am. I heard about the train riders and your little skirmish with them. And that your people captured some interesting stuff as a result."

Curt nodded. "We did. Took some more casualties and warbots losses, too."

"Well, can you tell me what you reported to Battleaxe? Or am I going to have to inveigle it out of you in my classical and effective manner? Hell's great balls of fire, if I'm going to be facing the same weaponry, I damned well want to know about it!"

"Okay. What I tell you may cause you to modify your snivel to reinforce mine. Then maybe we'll get the goddamned ROEs changed." He gave her a brief rundown of his meeting with Hettrick and the information on the as-sault rifles and comm gear that had been captured.

"A-99s? And tacomms?"

"Yup." Curt nodded.

"Okay, it makes sense now. That's why we got creamed yesterday morning when the up-train went through Dead-man's Curve and the Tunnel," she muttered. "Damn, it was such a neat and surgical response to an attack on the train, and I for sure thought we had them by the short hairs until we got ambushed ourselves while mounting our assault. The Yemark bastards had communications to coordinate their movements throughout the whole operation!"

"Well, if it will make you feel any better, Maxie, we're working on a revised tactical plan as a result of that skirmish," Curt told her. "Jerry Allen thinks he's got a handle on something that will reduce the intensity of the Yemark assaults."

"That smart-ass plebe was always a literal fountainhead of information. Him and his damned encyclopedic memory! Could never catch the bastard on any glitch in plebe knowledge. Once he heard it the first time, he remembered it forever. Furthermore, he could talk fast, and he got so good at Arabic that he'd reply in Arabic and toss in some references to the Koran in the bargain. Always a hundred-and-fifty percent response from Allen. In everything, by the way. So, what the hell is he up to now?" Maxie Cashier wanted to know.

"Well, he's using that encyclopedic memory to its full extent right now. And his Arabic - which our regimental Baluchi claims he speaks with a terrible American accent - means that he knows and understands how these people think. He's working on improved tactics with Hassan the Assassin..."

"Aha! The youngster from Zahedan that you and Hettrick brought back from there. The kid who caused such a flap because he turned out to be so goddamned smart he really didn't have to study very hard, which gave him more time to play with the girls!"

"He's no kid any longer, Maxie."

She smiled knowingly. "I know! I know! Handsome devil! Some of my ladies have very green brass. They envy your ladies."

"Would the ladies of the Cottonbalers include the commanding officer?" Curt asked with a smile.

"Goddammit, Carson, the ladies of the Cottonbalers include all the ladies of the regiment!" She didn't crack a smile, but Curt knew from experience that she was taking it rather lightly because she knew him very well. But she went on in quasi-serious tones, "Or, if you were suddenly implying that I wasn't a lady, I might do something very unladylike right here and now! But, let's not waste time. I've got an appointment with Battleaxe in a few minutes. Curt, I want my staffers to work with your people in developing this new tactical."

"No problem," Curt replied easily. "We're all in deep slime here in Yemen. One of these days, I'll find out why we're here in the first place taking incoming that should be going in the direction of the Royal Yemen Army..."

"Shit! Those idiots couldn't fight their way out of a garbage bag! They're pretty good when it comes to pulling off ambushes of their own, or taking baksheesh to eliminate hassling you," the commanding officer of the Cottonbalers muttered darkly. It was obvious that she thought even less of the Yemeni than Curt. "But, yeah, us rugged individualists gotta stick together."

"Especially since we're all being shot at, and the incoming rounds aren't labelled for either the Cottonbalers or the Greys," Curt pointed out.

"But you've got it easier up here in the highlands, Curt," Maxie reminded him again. "I'm sitting in a goddamned hell hole down there in Al-Mawr. I'm not going to put up with this ROE shit a hell of a lot longer. And my Cottonbalers won't either. I'm coming up on the point where my Cottonbalers will fire on any bunch of Yemeni sheepherders who look even slightly suspicious…and you know damned good and well that all of those Yemeni bastards carry rifles. I'll pretend to reconnoiter, then reinforce the reconnaissance, and finally attack."

"Don't do it, Maxie. That's classic Patton. In fact, I think you quoted him. Won't work. Battleaxe knows that scheme."

"Yeah, you, bastard, you taught it to her!" Cashier complained.

Curt nodded with a smile. "That I did. Tell you what: Allen and Hassan are supposed to lay their plan on me this afternoon. It could be full of holes."

"I doubt that," Maxie said, then recalled, "Allen was always a good tactician. Damned near as good as you."

"Agreed, and I've taught him a thing or two over the years. But, just in case, any first cut at a tactical plan could be full of holes. So, let me scrub it through a red team session tonight. I'll let some blood flow, and as soon as I have a reasonably workable proposal, Maxie-probably tomorrow I'll call you, Rick Salley, and Jim Ricketts on the teleconference net…" Curt promised.

"Hell, don't waste your time with Ricketts," Cashier interrupted vehemently. It was apparent that she didn't like the regimental commander of The Regulars. "He's been sitting on his ass down there with his Regulars at al-Zuhra on the coastal plains. His regiment hasn't taken any losses."

"Well, the Regulars haven't been attacked," Curt pointed out. "The Yemarks seem to keep to the hills and apparently don't like to operate out on the coastal plains..."

"But Ricketts hasn't moved his troops out of garrison," Cashier said, drawing Curt's attention to the fact that the division's newest Sierra Charlie regiment was still a green combat outfit and seemed to be acting that way. "He's sitting there guarding a part of the railroad that hasn't been attacked yet. We could sure as hell use his Sierra Charlies and warbots up where we are!"

"Maxie, he's strapped by the same ROEs that we are," Curt reminded her. "He just happens to be in a noncombat zone right at the moment."

"So Battleaxe should move him up here where he's needed."

"And expose that end of the railroad and the ship loading facilities to an expanded Yemark guerrilla operation? By the way, I think that's the sort of thing we're probably in for as a result of the Yemarks getting an improved arsenal and better tactical communications," Curt guessed. "No, I think we should get the ROEs changed..."

"Amen to that!" Maxie interrupted.

"But if we can't get the ROEs changed because of the fact that they were given to Hettrick by a disembodied voice from on high, then we should develop a strategy and some tactical plans that function within the letter of the ROEs and make use of the enemy's weaknesses," Curt finished.

"Enemy weaknesses? Hell, with new firearms and tacomms, they've eliminated most of the weaknesses we were trying to exploit!" Cashier pointed out.

"And we weren't doing so damned good doing that, were we? Or we wouldn't be taking such high losses, would we?" Curt fired at her.

"Okay, Curt, you've got a number of good points. And you always were a whiz at tactical stuff," Cashier admitted with a sigh. "But what weaknesses have you discovered that you think I've overlooked?"

"I'll tell you if they're real weaknesses when I see the proposal from Allen and Hassan," Curt told her. "I'll bet Allen has in mind exploiting cultural factors that can be turned into Yemark weaknesses."

"Cultural factors? What the hell? Such as?"

"Have you analyzed your operational profiles lately?"

"Daily. Hourly, if necessary. I try to stay current on what's happening. What part of the profile do you mean?"

"I checked mine when Allen and Hassan called it to my attention. When do the Yemark attacks occur? What time of day?"

Maxie Cashier thought about that for a second while she ran her hand through her short-cropped blonde hair. Then she replied, "Morning, usually. After sunrise, mostly. Best time to mount an attack or an operation, of course. So, what else is new?"

Curt sighed. "Ask a stupid question, get a straight answer. Especially from you, Maxie. I should have asked at what time the Yemark assaults start, how long they last, and what's the latest time of day when they've initiated an attack?"

"We usually spend the afternoons mopping up by recovering our own injured and our disabled bots. You know me. I like to leave a clean battlefield. Makes it a lot easier to fight the second time, especially when I'm fighting on the same ground over and over again." Maxie banged her fist on the table. "Dammit, I don't like having to pay for the same ground twice! Especially when it's lousy ground to fight on in the first place! One of these days, we'll fight a war in a convenient place..."

"There never was a convenient place to fight, especially when the enemy starts it," Curt recalled Admiral Arleigh Burke's statement.

"Okay, Curt, what the hell are you getting at?" she wanted to know.

"We've made the classic mistake of believing that the enemy is just like us and thinks the same way we do," Curt explained. "He doesn't. He's got his own lifestyle. In spite of conducting a guerrilla war against us, the Yemarks haven't given up their way of life."

"Which is?"

"You've studied the Yemen culture?"

"Yeah. It's part of the business of having to fight them. Know your enemy."

"Ever tried to get something done in the afternoon in Yemen?"

"Hell, Curt, we're stuck all alone out in the middle of the boonies at Al-Mawr," she again reminded him unnecessarily. "We haven't had the time or the opportunity to get into the 'big cities' around here and partake of the local frivolities. I can't say that I want my Cottonbalers to have that dubious opportunity anyway. Look what happened to four of your Greys!"

"Agreed! If this place isn't the armpit of the earth, it runs a close second to Rwanda and other such juicy places," Curt admitted, then returned to the subject matter. "Then you certainly must know what Yemeni males do in the afternoon."

"Uh, sure. It's a druggie culture. They go to qat parties and get high."

"And, dear lady, we do what their religion forbids. We imbibe ethanol, often to excess, which makes us vulnerable as hell on Friday and Saturday nights and especially Sunday morning. Although the armed forces learned that lesson the hard way at Pearl Harbor," Curt reminded her. "The imperial Japanese knew our shortcomings there and made their war plan accordingly. So, we're going to do the same thing with the Yemeni, and especially with the Yemarks."

"But we can't attack them," Maxie reminded him. "So, what the hell good is that knowhow?"

"Maxie, I'm surprised that you don't remember what Captain Ned Vaughan tried to pound into our heads in Basic Tactics class. 'Often the obvious is unworkable and the workable is obscure. It's the hallmark of a good tactician to unscrew the unscrutible, obviate the obvious, eschew the unworkable, turn the obscure into the secure, and make the enemy quit fighting.' "

"Yeah, I remember. Who wouldn't remember all those twenty-dollar words? How the hell are you going to do all that?"

"I think I know, but I'm letting my subordinates figure it out. They need the practice, and I'm trying to train my own replacements. As Captain Vaughan himself also used to say, 'The simple proof is left to the student as an exercise.' "

"You want your star, don't you?"

Curt thought about that for a moment. "I don't know, Maxie. If it comes, it comes when it comes. In the meantime, I'm a combat soldier who doesn't like even the administrative sheep shit I have to handle as a regimental commander, but I do it because I've got to be the best regimental commander that I can be. It also means being a leader, whatever the hell that is, because the experts haven't managed to reduce it to a computer algorithm yet. It also means continuing the tradition because the Washington Greys existed long before I was born and will still be around long after I'm gone. Carlisle trained up Hettrick who trained up me. So, I've got to bring along the next regimental commander, regardless of whether or not I get a star or retire to tend my flower garden."

"Got anyone in mind?"

"Yes, but I'm not sure who will manage to cut it. Too many variables, Maxie. Which adds spice to the process."

Chapter Ten

As he stepped out of the door of the 17th Iron Fist Division headquarters building in the old or "native" quarters of beautiful downtown Sana'a, Curt saw that his M92 Personal Transportation Vehicle, his "trike," was gone. So, he queried the M33A2 General Purpose Warbot Jeep standing guard at the doorway, "Did you see anyone take the trike that was parked in space seven?"

"Yes, sir," the warbot replied.

"Why didn't you stop him?" Curt asked, angry.

"I am programmed for sentry duty to prevent unauthorized persons from entering this casern. I am not programmed to prevent people from using vehicles, sir."

"Well, did you report it?"

"I am not programmed to do that, sir."

Curt knew that a warbot had a human equivalent IQ of about the ambient temperature in Celsius, even with Mod 7/11 AI installed. It was necessary to be very specific in questioning it. But he unconsciously treated the warbot like a human being. This was becoming fairly common among the Greys as they grew more familiar with their warbots having Mod 7/11 AI and began to count on them more as stupid grunt infantrymen. Besides, Curt was angry and upset. This incident was to him just another irritant in this goddamned Yemen episode which was turning out to be one goddamned sheep screw after another, he told himself. He was so angry at the moment that he neglected to quiz the warbot further. And he automatically assumed that some Yemeni had stolen the trike, even under the surveillance of a Jeep that hadn't been given a specific order to guard it and report if anyone moved it from where Curt had parked it.

"Shit!" Curt muttered under his breath.

"I am not programmed to do that, sir," the Jeep replied.

"Okay, report the missing trike to the MPs and have them issue a stolen military vehicle report to the local RYA military police. Then connect me to the motor pool officer." Curt snapped out two orders. He was going to need transportation back to his regimental headquarters in Amran forty-six kilometers to the northwest.

"Missing military vehicle reported to the MPs and the local regiment of the Royal Yemen Army," the Jeep reported dutifully, having communicated by various links through the local ultracomputer to the Yemeni phone messenger in less time than it takes to think about it. "A comm patch through to the motor pool officer has been made. The line is ringing. You may use my audio transducers to communicate."

The voice of a young lady came from the Jeep. "Iron Fist Motor Pool, Lieutenant Jennifer Robertson, officer of the day, speaking. How may I help you?"

"This is Colonel Carson, commanding officer of the Washington Greys," Curt identified himself. "I have to get back to my headquarters in Amran. Please arrange for a trike, or other personal vehicle to be assigned to me and brought around to the front gate of the casern. I parked my assigned trike out front here a few hours ago, and it's been stolen."

"Sir, that vehicle wasn't stolen. I had one of my motor pool sergeants move it to the secure parking lot to keep it from being stolen or booby-trapped," the young woman's voice told him. "Would you like me to have it delivered around front for you?"

"Thank you. Please do so, Lieutenant," Curt said with relief. With losses due to combat and accelerated wear and tear, the regiment was becoming short on vehicles. His VETECO people could barely keep up with the situation. For some reason, the sand in Yemen was especially abrasive. He'd been told by the VETECO commander, Major Fred Benteen, that the local sand was a finely divided form of an especially hard type of silicon carbide with many sharp edges and points to its crystalline structure. If the Yemenis had ever decided to export their sand, it would make an excellent industrial abrasive. However, insofar as Curt was concerned, it was just another wonderful reason why the U.S. Army shouldn't be in Yemen. The sand got into lubricants, so-called "sealed" bearings, and other moving parts which then quickly ground themselves far out of tolerance.

When a trike showed up, Curt quickly checked its fender number to confirm it was his, thanked the sergeant who'd brought it around, hitched his Novia over his shoulder, mounted up, and took off down the street toward Amran.

He almost got to the outskirts of Sana'a when two old surplussed American ACVs bearing RYA markings pulled up, one positioning itself ahead of him and the other behind him. The top hatch of the lead ACV opened up, a RYA soldier's head and shoulders appeared in the hatch, and an old Hornet, submachinegun was aimed at him. The Yemeni soldier shouted something in Arabic.

Curt yelled back, "I don't speak your language!" But when the lead ACV stopped, he stopped. He wasn't about to argue with a man pointing a nine-millimeter Hornet pointblank at him. Curt wasn't wearing body armor.

But when he did stop, he was immediately surrounded by armed RYA soldiers toting Hornets. They'd erupted from the lead and following ACV. They motioned Curt to get off the trike.

Curt complied, asking, "Where's your commanding officer? Does anyone speak English?"

He was met with a stream of Arabic. An RYA sergeant came up with a hard copy in his hand, checked the trike's fender number against something on the sheet, nodded, and indicated to Curt that he should follow him into the lead ACV.

Curt immediately knew what had happened and mentally kicked himself. He'd told the Iron Fist Jeep to report the loss of his vehicle, which it had done. But he hadn't cancelled that order when Lieutenant Robertson informed him that his trike hadn't been stolen, only moved into a secure parking area. Naturally, the RYA spotted him and ran him down.

But before he could key his helmet tacomm and report this to either the Iron Fist casern or his own tacomm center in Amran, the RYA sergeant reached up, unsnapped the chin-strap from Curt's helmet, and pulled it from his head. Someone else pulled the Novia off his shoulder.

That left nothing for Curt to do but follow instructions and do as he was told until he was taken to some RYA officer who spoke English.

That wasn't a pleasant interlude, however. For a change, the RYA troopers were doing as they were told. Maybe they were having their own form of sadistic fun with one of the hated yet loved American soldiers who were in their homeland protecting the railroad but, under orders, not interfering with or protecting Yemeni. The "protection" of Yemeni was the job of the RYA, and they usually did it on the basis of most "protection" rackets. One was "protected" if "protection" was paid for with a little baksheesh. So, the RYA soldiers didn't ask for his military ID. They assumed he was some sort of American thief or even a spy dressed in American army clothing. The RYA personnel weren't known for their intelligence. Curt now began to share the belief of some of the Greys that the American warbots with 7/11 AI were far smarter than the ordinary RYA soldier.

He was kicked into the Royal Yemen Army ACV, made to lie face-down on the metal floor and taken over a very rough road to somewhere while two Yemeni soldiers stood there with their feet on his back and the muzzles of their American Hornet SMGs hard against the back of his skull.

When the ACV halted, he was jerked to his feet and paraded out of the ACV into a building that was apparently still in Sana'a. Curt told himself it seemed to be an RYA casern although he couldn't read the Arabic script flowing across the top of the main gate.

Although Curt was larger and heavier than the Yemeni soldiers who prodded him through the gate and into the building, he held his temper. Sooner or later, he'd be brought before an officer who spoke English. Trying to get rough with these armed Yemenis while he was disarmed wouldn't be diplomatic, nor would it contribute to him gaining his freedom. They had his trike, too. He wouldn't get very far. In his mind Curt knew that the time for violent action hadn't yet come. In a few minutes, he'd get this straightened put.

And he was right. He was hauled up before an RYA colonel seated behind a desk. The officer was a relatively young man with a long, thin face and the deep, dark eyes of a Yemeni. Curt knew he was a colonel because of the British-style crown and two pips on his shoulder boards. Either the young man was a military genius or had excellent political or palace connections to have attained such a high rank at such an apparently young age.

The RYA colonel recognized Curt's silver oak leaves at once and suspected that his soldiers might have brought in someone who was actually a high-ranking American army officer, not an ordinary vehicle thief or a disguised terrorist. The young colonel had seen no huge American terrorists because terrorists were always other Yemeni or perhaps Arabs. So, he barked a sharp order to the three soldiers and the sergeant convoying Curt, whereupon they lowered their Hornet SMGs. The sergeant reluctantly handed Curt his combat helmet but did not yet offer to return the Novia.

The Yemeni colonel stood up. "Colonel, I am Colonel Salem bin Hassayn Rubaya, commanding officer of the Fourth Guards Regiment, the Royal Yemen Army," he introduced himself. He wore his British-style uniform (a legacy of the century-old British colonial period) with the usual Yemeni *dhuma* in a plain leather scabbard at his waist. The uniform, together with his British accent, told Curt the man had been educated out-country. "I realize that under the Geneva convention, I may ask for only your name, rank, and place of birth. But I suspect we have made somewhat of an error in detaining you, so may I inquire as to your American YEF unit, please?"

Curt saw no reason to further provoke the situation, so while he slowly reached into the pocket of his cammies for his ID case, he carefully answered, "I'm Lieutenant Colonel Curt C. Carson. May I show you my military identification, Colonel?"

"Commander of the Third Robot Infantry Special Combat Regiment in Amran, of course," Colonel Salem replied easily, reaching out to take Curt's ID. After a quick look at the ID card Salem handed it back to Curt and snapped an order to the RYA soldiers.

A chair appeared for Curt. The three soldiers and the Royal Yemen Army NCO quickly left the room. Apparently, Salem wasn't worried. In the first place, in common with other Yemeni buildings, the room had no door, and several RYA soldiers and officers - the regimental staff, Curt surmised - could be seen in the next room. The Yemeni colonel apparently felt he was safe with Curt. So, he indicated the chair and told Curt, "Please sit down, Colonel. I'm sorry that we have to meet under these circumstances since we're both on the same side in this current squabble. Would you care to tell me what you were doing riding a vehicle that was just reported stolen?"

"Sure," Curt said without any rancor in his voice. He knew that if he played this right, he'd have a "gimme" on this YEF colonel which he could hopefully collect at some future time if things went to slime and he needed YEF support. "It's my own personal trike. I left the YEF casern and discovered it wasn't where I'd parked it on the street. Therefore, I assumed it had been stolen and reported it as missing through one of our sentry warbots. But our motor pool watch officer had actually removed it to a secure parking lot and told me about it when I requested another vehicle to take me back to Amran. However, I forgot to cancel the stolen vehicle report. I must have assumed that either the warbot saw me get my vehicle back or that the motor pool OOD had called the MPs. Of course, the warbot didn't do anything because I didn't give it an order. And the officer didn't know I'd reported it missing. Looking back on the situation, it was my mistake, and I paid for it. If you'll call Major Ward, my COS, you'll find that I am who I am and that the trike is mine."

Salem laughed heartily as if he had something on Curt. Which he did. He went on, "Aha! Well, I've noted that the American troops tend to treat their warbots as fellow soldiers when warbots are actually quite stupid!"

"Afraid that was the case here, Colonel," Curt admitted. When word of this got back to the Greys through Rumor Control, some of the Greys would have a little fun at their colonel's expense, but the

Yemeni colonel was already enjoying it in a nonadversarial manner.

Curt was playing this cool and easy because, in spite of being roughed up by the RYA soldiers on the way over, he was now making a good, working-level contact with a contemporary in the Royal Yemen Army. To date, the official American policy had been to keep the two armies apart. The role of the Americans was to protect the railroad since the RYA didn't appear to have the manpower or the training to do it. It was the role of the RYA to act as internal police and take action against guerrillas and terrorists, a role which was denied the Americans under the existing ROEs. The diplomats and politicians saw no reason why the two armies should get together. They even viewed a joint working arrangement as a potential troublemaker. American military history had shown a tendency for American troops to be looked upon as "friendly invaders" even when they'd come to help the locals with additional military force. The ghosts of Korea, Viet Nam, Grenada, Panama, and other "friendly forces" help wars of the last century still lingered in the halls of Foggy Bottom, which always seemed to be fifty years behind the power curve anyway. And in some of the five corners of the Pentagon where civil servants continued to play their unique role in running the military because they had the sort of job longevity that the military side of the house rarely enjoyed.

"So, the laugh is on me," Curt went on. "I discovered that your RYA troops were very efficient indeed. And that they can play rough when they want to."

This caused a flash of concern to come over the young Yemeni colonel's face. "Were you mistreated during the time you were apprehended and brought here, Colonel?"

"I was roughed up, but no worse than many of our American civil police forces would treat a suspected car thief."

To his relief, Salem realized that this American colonel wasn't going to lodge an official complaint against his troops, which would have caused him to be called on the carpet at RYA headquarters and perhaps even result in a black mark on his record. So, he relaxed. "My apologies if you felt you were mistreated, Colonel. However, now that you're here and we've met - albeit under these somewhat strange, unusual, and strained circumstances - I hope you'll allow me to show amends by inviting you to lunch."

It was nearing high noon, it would take about an hour to get things unraveled and return to Amran, and Curt was hungry. It had been a busy morning. "I accept with pleasure, Colonel."

"Excellent! We do get some good meals in my outfit. I see to that," Salem told Curt proudly. Then he added almost apologetically, "But I'm afraid I won't be able to invite you to a qat party this afternoon. The Fourth Guards Regiment is a very old and proud outfit, Colonel Carson. And we're highly disciplined. In spite of our Yemeni customs, I believe the Fourth Guards should be ready to do its job at any time...And it's patently impossible to be combat-sharp while chewing qat. My men bitch and snivel about it when they first join the Fourth Guards, but then they realize that they're on top of everything while the rest of their contemporaries are out of the loop with their chaw..."

"The lack of qat doesn't bother me a bit, Colonel Salem," Curt admitted. "We don't use it in the Washington Greys, either. We learned how to get our heads on straight and keep them straight when we were trained as warbot soldiers. And for the same reason we don't use other drugs..."

"Except alcohol."

"Except alcohol," Curt admitted, "which I realize is prohibited to you by the Koran. However, as one of my officers theorizes, 'the sum of all vices is constant.' We all have our own social vices, depending on our culture."

"That we do! Your officer is right! And I grew used to imbibing a little alcohol on regimental guest nights. It helped us break up the furniture."

"You speak and act somewhat like a British officer, Colonel," Curt observed.

Salem looked proud. "I am a graduate of Sandhurst and spent three years as an exchange subaltern in the Cold-stream Guards, sir!"

"I should have suspected as much," Curt told him with the respect of another professional. "Well, sir, if your Fourth Guards grow weary of staying in casern in Sana'a, perhaps we can develop some sort of joint or combined operations because we're not allowed to go after the Yemarks or other terrorists."

Salem looked pensive for a moment as he suddenly realized that perhaps he could forge an interesting and unofficial operational plan with this American colonel. He, too, had been chafing at the restrictions placed on him by the Yemen defense minister, General Qahten ash-Shabbi. Salem really didn't like or trust Qahten, believing that the man's ultimate goal might well be the overthrow of the royal family and the seizure of the reins of government in a coup d'état. It had happened many times before in Yemen history. And conditions were growing unstable enough that it could easily happen again. Salem was an avowed royalist. And he had his sights set on the Defense Minister's portfolio himself. After all, he was a young and ambitious officer with connections in the palace. Qahtan could still get him if he stepped out of line, but perhaps he could make some plans with this Colonel Carson that wouldn't step over the line.

Curt had the same thing in mind, but he just wanted to start winning for a change and then be ordered the hell out of this country before he lost too many people and too much equipment.

Both men unconsciously realized they were in an unusual position thanks to a stupid warbot, a well-meaning motor pool officer, and an overly zealous military police patrol.

"Let's talk, Colonel," Salem agreed and rose to his feet. "And let's forget the army mess for a change. I know a very good restaurant down the street where we can talk frankly in private."

Chapter Eleven

"Colonel, our report will be given in full staff study format," Major Jerry Allen announced as he stepped to the front of the briefing room. He took the pointer in his hands and faced his commanding officer and the rest of the officers and NCOs of the Washington Greys.

"Why the formality, Jerry?" Curt wanted to know. "We usually develop our plans in an informal atmosphere."

"As we got into the depth and details of the proposed operation, Captain Clinton pointed out that it encompassed the entire Yemen Expeditionary Force and perhaps the Royal Yemen Army as well," Jerry explained carefully. "We felt that informality works well for the Greys because we're a closely knit team. We've been on many missions as a regiment. We screw up occasionally as we did during the recent train riders episode. However, by and large, we know one another well enough that we can anticipate combat reactions. But we've never operated as an integral part of the Iron Fist Division except at Battle Mountain. That turned out to be a walk-through not requiring extremely close combat coordination. We believe that our proposed plan will require such close cooperation. Therefore, we chose to present it in formal terms so that, if approved, it can be taken directly topside."

That made sense to Curt. He was pleased that his subordinates were beginning to think in terms of regimental and divisional operations rather than merely company level tactics. It had taken Curt some time to learn how to do this satisfactorily. He still wasn't sure that he had it dead nuts himself. The things learned at the company level tended to remain predominant when an officer moved up to field grade and command. It took time to expand one's thinking processes.

Generations of his forebears could have told him this. The army command and staff schools should have stressed it to a greater degree than they had. But the twenty first century army was still a warbot army where officers and NCOs lay on their backs on comfortable couches in the rear area and fought their warbots by remote linkage at the FEBA. Command under those circumstances was a lot different from that in a Sierra Charlie outfit, as Curt and the other Greys had learned the hard way. The big problem with the warbot brainies was they didn't think they could be physically killed in combat because none of them had ever been. The Sierra Charlies of the Washington Greys knew differently. Their Role of Honor was tragically long and included the names of many comrades who had paid the ultimate liability premium of their contracts.

"'Very well, Major. Continue, please," Curt told him.

Jerry did so.

Using a silent command given by a belt tacomm transmitter, Jerry instructed Grady, the regimental computer, to display a topographical map of northern Yemen behind him.

"The mission of the YEF and the Iron Fist Division is to protect the Amran and Red Sea Railroad as an asset in which American interests have a large stake," Jerry began. "We shall not dwell on the policy rationales for this because that is well beyond our scope of responsibilities...although many of us would like some clarification of this at some time in the future. Furthermore, the rules of engagement under which we operate require that we take no offensive action and maintain a defensive posture in protecting the railroad. This has demanded that we operate in a reactive mode although we're configured and trained to operate in a proactive manner. Operating as we have been in the reactive mode, we're absorbing losses in hardware and jellyware that could render us ineffective if present loss rates continue. We can anticipate no additional level of logistical or personnel support to replace the hardware and jellyware because of the Vietnam syndrome. We've been told to do the job with what we've got.

The scene behind him changed to show a typical turbaned Yemeni hillsman with a scabbarded *jambiya* dagger at his waist and a long Enfield bolt-action .303 rifle in his hands.

"Thus far we have assumed our adversary to be the classical Yemeni. These people have been fighting in the hills for centuries. They don't like outsiders. The British had trouble with them before they withdrew from the Near East. Everyone has had trouble with them. They're like the Afghans in that regard. They've never really been conquered by anyone, including the Romans and the Islamic caliphate. However, the typical Yemeni tribesman really isn't our problem because our adversary has changed."

The visual of the Yemeni hillsman metamorphosed. A tacomm brick appeared in one hand, the ancient Enfield rifle became a modern Soviet/Chinese A-99 submachinegun, and a bandolier of A-99 clips appeared around his waist and shoulders. On the ground next to him appeared the pancake shape of a wadi mine. "Our adversary has been rearmed with modern weapons by an outside adversary, probably Nation X which is intent upon capturing the Jebel Miswar iron mine and the Amran and Red Sea Railroad for its own use."

The shape of a rocket tube launcher appeared to the other side of the Yemark's image.

"We should anticipate that the Yemarks will also be provided with something like a Soviet SA-77 *Ossah* or Wasp Baby SAM or the export version of our M100A Smart Fart. They will need these in order to counter our tacair capability which, when we can use it, devastates them.

"In short, we face a new adversary. Therefore, we must adapt our tactics to handle the changed nature of the adversary. We cannot continue to absorb the losses we're taking defending against the old adversary, much less the increased loss rate that is the likely consequence of the new weapons he possesses.

"Therefore, the problem comes down to utilizing our resources more effectively and also exploiting the weaknesses of the adversary. And our adversary does have a weakness..."

"The pattern of the assaults on the railroad show two interesting features. First of all, none of the attacks seem to have been concentrated on destroying the mine or the railroad, only to disrupt operations and thus impact the profitability of the activity. An ancillary purpose seems to involve killing, wounding, or frightening railroad personnel so that they either quit or refuse to operate the trains. That's difficult because the railroad is automated. However, someone must still monitor the robotic railway and carry out much of the maintenance and repair of the rolling stock, right of way, and signaling system. Robots can't do it all. The reason for this particular pattern seems to lie in the fact that whoever is backing the guerrillas and terrorists wants to see that mine and railroad abandoned as nonprofitable and fall into their hands intact.

"Secondly, the pattern of attacks shows a clear trend. All have taken place between dawn and noon. Nothing in the afternoon. Nothing in the evening. Nothing at night before dawn. We believe the reason for this very distinct time pattern lies in the cultural heritage of the Yemeni and in their particular lifestyle which includes a weakness that can be exploited quite easily..."

The image of a small evergreen tree about five meters tall appeared on the screen. The visual pickup zoomed in on the green leaves.

"The weakness of our adversaries is the chewing of the leaves of the plant, *Catha edulis*, or *qat*, by every Yemeni male from the age of puberty up," Jerry went on, displaying his encyclopedic knowledge. "Qat is a stimulant like amphetamines. Its use is so ubiquitous in Yemen that the old coffee plantations that once produced Mocha coffee, probably the best coffee in the world, have given way to the cultivation of qat trees such as the one shown. Qat chewing is habit-forming...and the Yemeni men all have the habit. You're not a man in Yemen unless you chew a cud of qat every afternoon. Qat contains the substance d-norisoephedrine whose effects include elevation of the blood pressure, anorexia, insomnia, increased optimism, decreased subjective fatigue, and paranoid psychosis. The Yemeni also claim it enhances sexual drive and potency. I understand that's a bunch of bot flush. Not that I can attest to that from my own experience of course..."

Jerry paused to let this information sink in.

"What do you think the Yemenis believe it does for them?" Curt wanted to know.

It was Lieutenant Hassan Ben Mahmud who answered, "Colonel, they believe it increases their endurance and potency, raises their spirits, increases mutual understanding, and intensifies their communication with Allah. In my own experience, it makes qat-chewers initially more talkative, but they end up after a couple of hours in an introverted and depressed state of mind. We could take on a qat-chewing Yemark unit at sunset and blow their lips off, sir."

"As I recall from history, although I wasn't there to confirm it in spite of popular belief," muttered Regimental Sergeant Major Henry Kester, "the Viet Cong resorted to similar tactics if their intelligence indicated that a bunch of grunts had gotten high on pot or other drugs. My uncle told me that Americans found it damned hard to fight back effectively when they were stoned out of their gourds, as he put it. First time our army had ever come up against effective chemical warfare."

"Major Allen, what's your recommendation?" Curt wanted to know.

"Sir, it's our recommendation that we create some time shifting that will take advantage of this Yemeni habit. We recommend that the railroad management be contacted and convinced to make a six-hour shift in the train schedules. Then the trains will make their two daily runs in the early predawn hours when the Yemeni are spaced-out on qat or zonked out with real fatigue, and in the afternoon when they're first getting bombed on qat. Comments, critique, and criticism, Colonel?" Jerry finished.

It wasn't a bad plan, Curt had to admit. But he had a couple of questions. "What do you expect the Yemarks to do in the morning hours if they no longer have trains to attack?"

"Sir, because they want to discourage the mine and railroad workers, once they figure out what's going on, within a few days they'll begin to mount attacks on our caserns and on the railway operational buildings," Jerry snapped back without hesitation. "We can defend those because the defensible facility isn't in motion like a train. We'll utilize our warbot firepower to hold their assaults and create massive casualties while we deploy Sierra Charlies into their rear by airlift. These are classical Sierra Charlie tactics. Furthermore, they don't in any way contradict the rules of engagement..."

"As the ROEs now stand," Curt reminded him, "that could change."

"When we're winning and doing our job, Colonel?" was Kitsy Clinton's input. "Is the Pentagon and the National Security Council interested to the point where they'd try to micromanage our operation to that level of detail, sir?"

"I don't know what the COS, Joint Chiefs, or the National Security Council are likely to do. And I refuse to try to second-guess them," Curt said. "But I like this plan because it turns a no-win situation into at least an even shot at surviving. When in a defensive situation, the best a commander can do is not to lose."

Recalling his meeting and luncheon with Colonel Salem earlier that day, Curt knew that the proposed plan would work very well with a joint operational strategy involving the RYA. At least, it could be tested with Salem's 4th Guards Regiment. He felt he could trust Salem. He wasn't sure what General Qhatan might do, if he did anything at all. Curt didn't want to become embroiled in local Yemen politics. A military assistance unit and its commanders shouldn't get tangled up in such things. Leave that to the spooks and striped pants people," Curt decided.

"Do you believe this plan can be sold to Battleaxe and especially to Colonels Salley, Cashier, and Ricketts?" he asked.

"Sir, I don't know the other colonels that well. But if I know Battleaxe as I think I do, having served under her when she was regimental commander, I suspect she'll sign off on it," Jerry replied candidly.

But Curt knew Jerry remembered Belinda Hettrick as a regimental commander. With stars on her shoulders, she thought differently now, just as Curt thought differently with a collar bearing a silver oak leaf replacing the silver railroad tracks of a captain he'd once worn.

However, he was not one to blunt the enthusiasm of his subordinates. And they were enthusiastic about this plan. He could sense it around him. If he backed this and took it up the line, it would help to have this sort of enthusiasm supporting it. Hettrick would think carefully before nixing a good ops plan which came up from below and was truly the work of gung-ho people who would have to go out and make it happen.

So, he asked carefully, "If I support this plan, will you be willing and ready to lay it in front of Salley, Cashier, and Ricketts...and then in front of Battleaxe?"

"Yes, sir!" Jerry snapped.

Curt looked around and asked. "How about the rest of you? Captain Clinton?"

"Sir, I'm getting sick and tired of sitting around and getting creamed every time we react to a Yemeni attack," Kitsy flashed back.

"Captain Motega?" Curt asked his reconnaissance company commander.

"Sir, General Crook wasn't saddled with our ROEs during the Plains Indian Wars, but he took the action to the adversary," Dyani pointed out. "His contemporaries sat in their fortifications and were nearly starved out by the Indians. That is not a one-to-one analogy to our situation. But it makes more sense than what we're doing now. It will allow us to do the job we were told to do without disobeying the ROEs."

"Major Frazier?"

"Colonel, you know damned good and well I was trained by an aggressive man," Russ Frazier told him, referring to Major Marty Kelly, now with Rick Salley's Wolfhounds stationed down at the Huth power station. "The current situation is not to my liking, sir. I support the revised ops plan."

"Lieutenant Hall?"

Larry Hall, commander of the GUNCO currently stationed at strategic points along the railroad to provide artillery support, answered simply, "Sir, I'm deployed in secure fortifications at the moment. I can hold off Yemark assaults. But I don't like to be separated from the main body of the regiment. My job is to provide on-the-spot artillery support for active Sierra Charlies. My LAMVAs haven't turned a wheel in weeks. We just sit there and pot away at unseen targets way over the hill and hope to hell we don't hit the rest of the Greys in the process. And it isn't doing a damned bit of good that I can see. So, I support this plan. It breaks up a no-win situation."

"Major Worsham?" Curt hardly needed to ask his tactical air commander, but protocol and respect required that he do so anyway.

"I don't see *how* or *where* this affects the Warhawks," Worsham growled. "But Allen's *suggestion* that the Yemarks might have Wasps bothers the living *shit* out of me! We've taken *enough* Golden BBs here in this gawdforsaken place *already,* and I don't like the *idea* that I'm losing *people* or *aerodynes* to these fucking Yemark bastards *without* being able to shoot back!" This was just Cal Worsham. All the Greys knew him and his foul mouth. He might offend some ladies of other regiments, but the ladies of the Greys took him as he was, a virile and vibrant macho type who was very good to have hovering over you in a fracas...or at other times. He was a fighter. And he was an aerodyne driver. That excused his behavior.

"Major, I'm surprised that you haven't seen what I considered the obvious," was Captain Dyani Motega's quiet observation. Dyani was also a warrior, but she was a woman of action, not words.

"What the *hell* are you *talking* about, Dy?"

"Someone is going to have to airlift Sierra Charlies into the Yemark minus-x while our warbots have them pinned down by fire," Dyani pointed out. "And the Sierra Charlies will require tactical air support from minus-x because the Saucy Cans will be busy in plus-x."

"Besides," Captain Adonica Sweet told him sweetly, "your aerodyne drivers are certainly capable of spoofing *Ossahs*. They've done it before. And that gives them a ground target to squash."

Captain Paul Hands merely nodded. "We can dodge 'em. And back-track 'em to their launchers. Which we can then scrub vigorously. Major, it's better than sitting up there cutting holes in the sky and being nothing but big targets."

"There have been times lately," added Captain Tim Timm of the airlift company, "that I thought we all had big targets painted on the aerodyne bellies just to draw fire. Right now, we just hang around waiting to see how a fight develops before we haul anything in for a vertical envelopment. I like this new plan, Major. It gives us something definite to do: We'll take Sierra Charlies around behind the Yemarks so they can be nasty. If we don't have to carry a lot of warbots, that will make the Chippies light and bouncy."

"My *aerodyne* idiots will buy it, so I *suppose* I'll have to," Worsham grumbled.

"Major Atkinson," Curt asked his S-3 operations staffer, "do you have any suggestions or critique of the proposed plan?"

Hensley Atkinson shook her blonde curls. "No, sir. You shouldn't ask me, sir."

"Why not?"

"I helped Allen and Clinton put this thing together from the ops standpoint."

"Oh?"

"Yes, sir. And the rest of your staff was involved, too." She smiled wanly. "If I look a little bushed, Colonel, it's because all of us worked late last night on it and got up at oh-dark-thirty this morning to put the finishing touches on it."

"All of you?"

She nodded again. "Yes, sir. All of us."

"And you let me waste time asking each of you if you'd buy off on it?"

"Yes, sir. As Major Allen mentioned when he began, this was to be a formal staff ops briefing."

"Sorry that it degenerated into our usual informal session of playing cerebral popcorn, Colonel," Jerry apologized.

Curt shook his head slowly. Damn, he was proud of these people! And he told them so. "Damn, I'm proud of you people! Now, don't balloon your egos. We've got to polish this slightly, run it past the other regimental commanders, then take it upstairs to Battleaxe. It's still got rough edges on it. And we have to figure out how it works with Salley over at the Huth power plant and Cashier down in the wadi gorge and Ricketts out on the coastal plains."

"We've already worked on that, Colonel," Kitsy told him. "We've been talking with their staffers on the coordination net."

"'Well, you missed one important factor. I've made excellent contact with the commanding officer of the RYA's Fourth Guards Regiment. We can count on them to cooperate with us on this and do the sort of things to the Yemarks that we can't because of the ROEs," Curt told them and checked his watch. "Captain Dearborn, when chow time rolls around in a couple of hours, please see to it that all of us have some MREs here. We'll scrub and polish this thing until it shines, and we'll run it past Battleaxe tomorrow morning..." He paused, then added, "By the way, Battleaxe knows it's coming. So, we'd better make it good! You know that lady is fair and square, but she won't sign off on anything that is half-assed. Let's get to work!"

A lot of smiles turned on around the room. Insofar as the Washington Greys were concerned, it was great to be planning a winning strategy again.

Chapter Twelve

"All I can say, Carson, is that your ops plan had better be damned good! I gave up my beauty sleep to shag my ass up here," Colonel Maxine Cashier growled.

"Maxie, in your case, I can honestly tell you that your loss of beauty sleep won't matter," Colonel Rick Salley of the Wolfhounds replied easily. This was a meeting among equals. Formality other than that required for common good manners wasn't necessary.

Cashier started to bristle. She wasn't one to suffer even friendly insults from colleagues. But Salley, being a southern gentleman, quickly sensed her hostile response and went on smoothly, "Let me rephrase that, please. A true lady rarely needs beauty sleep. That would amount to gilding the lily, as it were."

"Damned good thing you qualified that, Rick," Maxie said with just a tad less venom in her tone of voice.

"Yeah, I think she might let you live, Salley," was the comment from Colonel James B. Ricketts, commander of the Regulars, the 6th Robot Infantry (Special Combat) Regiment. "As for me, it's just a great and glorious pleasure to get up here in the hills to dry out and cool off."

"Can't be any worse in al-Zuhra than it is in al-Mawr, Jim," Cashier retorted. "We're down in the goddamned canyon. At least you can see the Yemarks coming at you down there on the coastal plains."

"Except they don't come at us," Ricketts muttered darkly. "My Regulars keep getting the reports of your actions up in these hills while we just sit around and watch the trains go past."

"Godawmighty, Jim, are you sniveling about *not* getting shot at?" Cashier asked incredulously.

"To some extent, yes," Ricketts admitted stiffly. He was the new boy on the block. The Regulars were the most recent Robot Infantry regiment to convert to the Sierra Charlie doctrine where officers and NCOs fought in the field alongside their warbots, not from comfortable couches in the FEBA where they ran the warbots by remote control. Turning warbot brainies into Sierra Charlies was, as Regimental Sergeant Major Henry Kester was fond of saying, like taking kids playing video games and turning them into adults who knew they could get killed doing the real thing. "We've trained hard since we converted to Sierra Charlies, and we've seen no action. Curt, what the hell did the Greys have to do to get so much combat during your train-up?"

"Oh, nothing special," Curt replied. "We just stood there looking available, I guess. I think the high brass decided to give us an early chance to kill or be killed. I suspect they figured that was the quickest way to find out if the Sierra Charlies were a good thing or not. So, they put us on the parapet to see if we could survive when someone shot at us. Then after Trinidad and Namibia, the Greys got 'volunteered' for a lot of nasty jobs because we were a known entity." Curt knew he had to allow a few minutes for shop talk and socializing before he called this early morning meeting of the regimental commanders to order in a conference room of the Sana'a headquarters of the YEF. Their purpose in getting together face-to-face was to give the final scrub to the new ops plan before taking it to Hettrick. Teleconferencing was useful if circumstances made it difficult for commanders to actually meet, but teleconferencing was a poor substitute for the interpersonal face-to-face give-and-take that went on in any actual conference where warm bodies were present and body language was used.

Curt also knew he had to handle this meeting very carefully because he wore only a silver oak leaf and was junior to all three full bird colonels. However, the other three respected Curt because he and the Washington Greys had shed blood in writing the Sierra Charlie book.

But Colonel Maxie Cashier was having none of the socializing. She took her tacomm from her belt and set it on the table before her so that she could grab it fast if someone in the Cottonbalers wanted to talk to her from their casern at al-Mawr down in the deep canyon of the Wadi Mawr through which the Amran and Red Sea Railroad wound its way down out of the mountains to the Red Sea. "Let's get down to business. My second in command is good, but I don't like to be away from the Cottonbalers any longer than I have to, especially in this deadly environment."

"Agreed," Rick Salley echoed. "Mornings are active times around the power plant at Huth. That's when we get the most hassle from Yemarks."

"Exactly what do they try to do to you around the power plant, Rick?" Curt wanted to know.

"Just lurk under cover up in the hills and shoot at anything that moves," Salley replied, baring his left arm which bore an ugly black and blue welt on its biceps. "I took one of their low-powered Enfield .303 the other day. Hurts like hell, by the way, but body armor saved my ass." He rolled down his sleeve again and went on, "The Yemarks haven't done anything to the incoming natural gas line from Ma'rib. It's underground, and they don't have the time to dig for it. They tangled with the fifty KV power line between the power plant and the track...once. We had fried Yemarks all over the place when the fireworks stopped. So, they've taken to ambushing patrols and sniping. Those guys are crazy! And I haven't got the slightest idea what they've got in mind for us this morning. But it will be dirty, that's for certain."

"Hold that thought, Rick," Curt told him, getting to his feet, "because you've hit upon one of the factors that will allow us to take this war to the Yemarks instead of waiting until they decide to cream us."

"How the hell can we do that? We're restricted to defense, period. You've got something in mind that gets around the ROEs?" Cashier wanted to know.

"I think so," Curt told her. He turned on the holoprojector and rapidly stroked the keypad to direct Grady, the regimental computer of the Washington Greys, to project the visual elements of his briefing. "But it isn't totally ours. My people worked with your staffers and officers to make sure that we didn't incorporate any details that might have been deadly to you in your particular situation."

"I heard about this at Stand-to last night," Ricketts announced. "I told them to go ahead. Couldn't see what harm would be done. But it must have been an all-nighter, Curt. My staff was hazy on the details when I asked my COS about it this morning."

"Mine, too," Salley added. "I hope you've got all the kinks worked out, Curt."

"I think we do. We didn't have a Stand-to last night. We did indeed do an all-nighter on this so the four of us could scrub it this morning," Curt admitted.

It hadn't really been an all-night planning affair. Things had broken up about midnight, much to Curt's relief. He was worried about wearing his people down before they had the chance to put the plan into effect.

And he'd needed to reassure Dyani that her loss of personal control as a result of being injured was only a bit of temporary stress trauma. It's always a rough go when a person first realizes that there are some situations in which tight personal control of emotions can't be maintained. It has to do, Curt theorized, with suddenly recognizing the fact that no one is immortal or immune to injury. He'd been through it himself, and he'd watched his young subordinates encounter it, too. He couldn't actually say that it had been easy to get Dyani through it, but it had ended most pleasantly. Dyani was a very strong person.

Using the visuals generated by Grady, Curt ran the three colonels through the proposed ops plan. Then he waited for the typical "critique, criticism, and comment."

He wasn't disappointed because these came quickly.

"The Yemarks are likely to catch on to this pretty fast," Rick Salley observed. "They'll be waiting for the vertical envelopment once they get caught by it a couple of times. So how do I get my Chippies out there in the Yemark minus-x without having one of those big aerodynes take the Golden BB? They're pretty big targets, you know."

"You've got tacair support?" Curt asked unnecessarily.

"Damned right! And those people are chomping at the bit to lay ordnance on the Yemarks!"

"It's their chance to do it," Curt pointed out. "Let your Harpy drivers provide ground strike cover for your Chippies. As a matter of fact, scramble the Harpies first because you'll have targets for them right off the bat. The Harpies can help keep the Yemarks' heads down while your Chippies deploy into the minus-x."

"How can you be so sure that the Yemarks will shift their focus from the trains to the caserns?" Ricketts wanted to know. He hadn't been in the thick of it up in the hills, so he was shooting from the hip on this.

"Because they can't attack the trains. Our caserns are the only targets they've got unless they go after the Yemeni population. Which they won't because they're probably part of the local populace themselves. And shooting at the neighborhood doesn't make them any friends. So, they'll come after us." Curt paused for a moment to let that sink in, then went on. "That puts us in a position where we can strike back within an offensive defensive set of ROEs. The Yemarks attack us. We let them waste men and ammo on our defenses. Then, perfectly within the rules of engagement, we counterattack. After all, they started it and we didn't provoke it."

"Nice theory," Ricketts said. "I don't know whether or not that position will withstand the flak that might come from Fort Fumble on the Potomac."

"Scroom!" Maxie Cashier exploded. "Those staff stooges and terminal twerps back at the Pentagon Video Games Company aren't taking hard-jacketed incoming! Jim, we either discourage these Yemark bastards from hitting us, or all of us will be going home in body bags before this is over!"

"I believe the commanding officer of the Cottonbalers exaggerates," Salley broke in.

"Oh? How's your loss rate been holding up, Rick?" Maxie fired back at him with venom. She didn't like having her elbow joggled.

"Hold it! Hold it!" Curt attempted to break up the confrontation. Maxie Cashier was a tough one to handle. Curt knew she'd come up through the ranks by being one tough fighter. Some of the ladies of the Greys maintained she had iron ovaries, the closest female counterpart to brass balls they could think of. Rick Salley, as Curt knew from Battle Mountain, was a serious, professional leader of warriors. Jim Ricketts, on the other hand, always acted like he'd forgotten to wear his body armor; he was super-cautious almost to the point of being wimpish. Curt honestly hoped that the man would come through in the pinch, but he didn't know at that point.

In fact, Curt was counting on all three of them coming through when the going went to slime. He also realized that, in spite of his lesser rank, he was going to have to assume the leadership role because he'd seen more combat than any of them.

Unless, of course, Major General Belinda Hettrick either zeroed-out the ops plan or stepped up to lead in her own way...which Curt knew was formidable and effective. Whether or not a general officer was correct in leading troops like a field officer was a point that she'd leave for later debate and critique.

"Let's save the tiger juice for the Yemarks," Curt went on easily. "Anything else?"

"Ammo and chow," Cashier said.

"What about them?"

"This plan is fire-intensive," she pointed out. "We'll be hosing a lot of jackets out into the rocks. How's the log air?"

Curt shrugged. "No problems that I know of. The Aerospace Force trash haulers keep up their regular schedule. We should continue to be fat on ammo and MREs."

"When do the Aerospace Force log air flight usually arrive?" Cashier continued her line of questioning.

"I don't know," Curt admitted.

"We should try to get them to schedule their arrivals in the afternoon," she suggested, "when the Yemarks are chewing qat. Then we can transfer the loads to our Chippies and make the final delivery at night. Might as well take full advantage of this qat interlude every day. Might hold down potential aerodyne losses."

"Sounds like a winner," Salley remarked.

"We'll have to work that through Iron Fist headquarters staff," Curt said, making a note on his pocket keypad, "in the same way we'll have to interface with the railroad ops people to get them to change their schedules."

"Have we missed anything?" Salley wondered.

Ricketts shook his head. "I don't think so. But I'm not really affected that much by this new plan. Just a minor change in my Chippie log flights."

"You may be affected more than you think, Jim," Cashier put in quickly. "I'm beginning to wonder how the Yemarks are really going to react when the trains don't run as usual and we sit there in our caserns waiting for them to attack. I wonder if we aren't projecting our own military way of thinking into their heads. First of all, will they be willing to temporarily give up their qat chewing afternoons to continue to harass the trains? Are we sure they'll come after our caserns? Can we be certain of where and how they'll redirect their aggressive efforts? Remember, they've got modern assault weapons now along with tactical communications, maybe some rockets, maybe some other stuff we don't know about yet."

"Like what?" Ricketts asked.

"If they're being supplied and supported by Nation X outside Yemen, how likely are they to get mortars, real mines, and other assorted weapons that we know several nations have been exporting to guerrilla groups in the past few years?" Maxie Cashier asked rhetorically.

"We don't know. At least, my S-2 doesn't know," Curt replied. "We have to run this as usual. With the best intelligence data we can get, although that may be skimpy, incomplete, and sometimes erroneous. With the hardware and jellyware we've got on hand.

With the assumption that logistics will be able to maintain its supply flow. And with the foreknowledge that we'll probably have to change the plan to meet the challenge of the Yemark response to it. Now, have we overlooked anything?"

The other three thought for a moment, then all of them shook their heads.

"Then are we ready to run this past Battleaxe?" Curt went on.

"That's not really necessary," a new voice put in.

Major General Belinda Hettrick walked through the open door of the conference room followed by her chief of staff, Colonel Joanne Wilkinson, and her prime staff officers. Curt knew all of them, especially Lieutenant Colonel Ellie Aarts who was an old Washington Grey and had been hauled upstairs by Hettrick to be her G-2.

All four regimental commanders rose to their feet at once.

Hettrick strode around the table to the far end where the breeze was blowing through an open window. "As you were," she snapped and sat down. Her staff pulled up chairs and sat behind her.

Breaking the awkward silence that ensued, Hettrick went on, "These Yemeni buildings have no doors. I could hear you all over this floor. So, I wasn't eavesdropping." She put her tacomm brick on the table, folded her hands, and observed, "Well, are you ready for me or not?"

Curt looked at the other three. Seeing no response from them, he turned back to the general. "Ma'am, if you heard our discussion, what more do you want to know?"

"The whole damned thing, front to back, with all the details," Hettrick told him. "And you'd better not leave out one damned thing or my ever-watchful staffers will be all over you like a rug."

"How much of the plan do you want to hear over again, General?" Maxie Cashier asked.

"I just told you, I want to hear all of it," Hettrick snapped, then explained, "If I'm going to have to defend this plan someday soon, I need to hear it all just in case I might have missed something. If I didn't miss it, I'll hear it twice, which will tattoo it on my brain."

"We put it together like a textbook case, General. It's very straightforward as ops plans go," Rick Salley tried to point out.

"The hell it is!" Hettrick told them flatly. "You're asking for a major change in tactics. This is going to affect the entire YEF strategy. But I wouldn't be sitting here if I didn't agree with you. We can't continue to sit on our asses, and let the Yemarks cut us to pieces with their new weaponry. And they could be getting other stuff, too. Time will tell. One thing for sure: We aren't going to get a change in our ROEs. So, we have to come up with something that gets around them."

"We suspected that, General. Which is why we had to come up with something which would allow us to do something with the existing ROEs," Ricketts tried to explain.

"Hell, I know that," Hettrick said. "You people are good commanders. You obey orders. You also study those orders carefully to figure out their limitations and how far you can go within the orders and the ROEs." Hettrick was complimenting them, although it didn't sound like a compliment the way she said it. It sounded like a statement of fact. "And right from the start let me say that I think Carson's idea is great. It's time we began to exploit the enemy's weakness. And his qat-chewing habit is certainly a weakness!"

"It wasn't my idea, General," Curt explained. "The credit goes to Major Allen and Lieutenant Hassan."

"I suspected that. I also got the word through Rumor Control. A commander isn't worth a damn who doesn't listen to Rumor Control and try to sort the rice grains from the rat droppings. The only thing I want to know is why you didn't let me in on it sooner?" Hettrick's tone wasn't reprimanding but factual.

"We didn't want to run an unscrubbed half-assed plan by you and waste your time," Curt admitted.

"That hasn't stopped you in the past, Carson! But I'm glad you listened to me when I tried to tell you not to undertake vast operations with a half-vast plan," the commanding general of the Iron Fist Division told him. "So you don't have to be defensive with me. But you'd damned well better have the whole thing thought out totally, or you'll sure as hell get comment, criticism, and critique from me...and not necessarily in that order! So, what are you waiting for? Lay it on me!"

Chapter Thirteen

"What a mess!" Captain Kitsy Clinton exclaimed as they got out of the ACV in the headquarters area of the Jebel Miswar iron ore mine on the steep mountainside west of Amran.

The whole side of the mountain had been torn away by the enormous excavation; it was a gaping open pit mine. The mountain was formed of hematite. The mine was a huge hole in the ground so large that massive trucks appeared to be toy size as they moved slowly up spiraling roads cut into the sides of the pit, carrying cubic meters of reddish ore up to the loading terminus of the Amran and Red Sea Railroad at the edge of the crater.

Kitsy was referring to the scramble of equipment strewn around, the piles of raw dirt, and the constant haze of reddish dust that hung in the hot, dry air like some sort of a terrestrial-born fog.

"I take it you've never been over to Morenci in Arizona," Curt observed. "Or over to the new hole at Komelik."

"Terrible!" Kitsy complained. "Why do people have to tear up the landscape like this?"

"Because industrial people are messy," Dyani remarked quietly.

"And because the world's civilization is built upon iron for structural purposes and copper for energy transmission," Jerry Allen reminded her. "We're shifting to non-polluting renewable energy sources like hydrogen, but we'll always need primary metals. And we have to get those out of the ground."

Curt had brought along a few of his trusted subordinates - Kitsy because she was a comer, Jerry because of his fluency in Arabic plus his general knowledge, Hassan because he could think Arabic, and Dyani because she observed and remembered everything. "Be that as it may, Major, we're here to protect all this because Americans are working here..."

"And because American money is invested here, too," Kitsy added.

"I'm not so sure. We don't really know who owns Ferron Corporation. It's a multinational. I suspect many interests are involved," Jerry said.

"But Americans are making it go. Americans work hard everywhere," Hassan observed, looking around. "Americans, Germans, Japanese, Chinese - all are obsessed with the work ethic. This mine couldn't operate without the Americans who are here." It was not said with distaste. Hassan himself was a hard worker. He wasn't like many of his countrymen who preferred to get along with as little work as they could do, leaving most of the hard labor to women who had grown too old to be good bed partners.

"We're early," Curt observed. "Might as well take a few minutes and watch the action. No one will want to talk to us before the morning train leaves."

The ore train was just getting ready to depart. The three hulking 6,000-horsepower electric locomotives sat quietly at the head end, their pantographs in contact with the 50,000-volt overhead catenary. The single, powerful laser cat's eye headlamp on the lead engine now merely projected its red beam forward; when the train started to move, that beam would swing in a figure eight pattern to provide a warning. And the engines were painted in bright international orange so they could be seen. This didn't stop some Yemenis from challenging these behemoths, and many Yemeni herdsmen and a lot of Yemeni sheep had been killed on the right of way.

The train was getting ready to make the 2,300-meter descent along the 250-kilometer right of way to the Red Sea. Rather than dissipate the energy of a 100,000-ton descending train into heating brake discs and pads, these engines used dynamic braking. Their electric motors operated as generators to feed power into the catenary. The engines of the empty up-train from al-Luhaya would use this energy to help them climb the long grade up from the sea. Additional energy to overcome losses was provided by the electric power plant at Huth which generated this electrical power from natural and flare gases piped over from the oil fields at Ma'rib.

The Amran and Red Sea Railroad was a robot railroad, of course. And it was instrumented to detect something that hadn't been done properly in making up the train. But, as Curt and the other Greys knew all too well, one places trust in an automatic machine only at dire peril. Robots can't detect what they haven't been programmed to detect, even with advanced artificial intelligence. The human eyeball backed by the human brain was still ascendant.

Turbaned Yemeni brakemen were working down the line of a hundred loaded side-dump ore cars, checking couplings and brakes. In some ways, these departure checks appeared to be a disorganized sheep screw accompanied by lots of shouting and running around. It was easy to tell who the American supervisors were; they hurriedly moved everywhere with portable communications bricks in hand. And they wore the legendary pukka pith helmets usually associated with British troops during the Indian Raj.

At 0800 sharp, whistles were blown. The air horn on the lead locomotive blared its discordant sounds through the hot, dry, dusty morning air. Men leaped off the train as it slowly began to move away from the loading facilities at the mine head, writhing through the switches of the marshalling yards onto the main line down to al-Lu-haya. It was a commonplace occurrence at the Jebel Mis-war mine, but the Greys had been so busy they hadn't really taken the time to train-watch.

Kitsy watched with fascination. She finally muttered, "Trains are fascinating. They're so...masculine!" Of course, she was echoing the feelings of almost two hundred years of avid rail buffs.

"Estrogen rush," Jerry remarked.

"You'll pay for that...sir," Kitsy fired back. They were officially on duty, so military protocol reigned.

As the two-kilometer train pulled out, the Yemeni brakemen seemed to disappear, leaving only the American and British supervisors to watch it depart.

"Time to get to work," Curt said reminding them of the purpose of their visit to the Amran train yard.

"With all due respect, it seems to me that this job is something that the Iron Fist staff should take care of," Jerry observed. "We're guarding only the upper terminus of this rail line."

"Which is why it's our job to talk to the super," Kitsy told him. "We're the closest military unit. The Washington Greys are the ones the superintendent and the mine director see all the time. Don't forget something the Army has learned the hard way over the past hundred years or so: Keep the contact with the civil authorities at the lowest possible command level and call in the high brass only for ceremonial occasions or to solve the really bitchy problems."

Right up front, Curt thought that getting the railroad to change its train schedules was going to be one of those really bitchy problems Kitsy mentioned.

He wasn't far from being right in his assessment.

The Chief of Operations of the Amran and Red Sea Railroad, John Toreva, was a short, rotund man with a round face. He was also somewhat short-tempered, responding as though the whole damned world wasn't going the way he personally wanted it to go. He sat in his corner office whose double-paned tinted windows looked out over the great train yard stretched out below and the huge open pit Jebel Miswar Mine behind it. When Curt broached the subject of their meeting with him, he exploded.

"You want me to do what?"

"Mr. Toreva, we believe that if you reschedule your trains the Yemark attacks on them will stop," Curt told him again. "It will also allow us to get the Yemark guerrilla activities under control. After all, it's our job here to see to it that your operations are not impacted by terrorism and guerrilla operations."

"Impacted! And you don't think that shifting my schedules by six hours isn't going to impact my operations? Jesus, things were a hell of a lot better before you army guys showed up," Toreva steamed, deliberately ignoring Kitsy and Dyani. The man seemed to look right through the two women as if they weren't there at all. Curt didn't know how Kitsy and Dyani would take this, but he had faith in their good manners...if Toreva didn't take his apparently chauvinistic behavior too far. "Sure, we've always had a few run-ins with the locals, but no more so than we used to have when I was assistant super for the Black Mesa and Lake Powell Railroad back on the Navaho nation in Arizona. The dumb Yemenis continue to ignore the right of way, and we end up paying for a lot of sheep. That's cheap. Occasionally, we mangle a local who doesn't get out of the way. Hell, even robotic controls can't stop a heavy ore train fast enough to avoid hitting them! No one ever heard of safety rules in this goddammed place. Fortunately, they haven't learned about lawyers and tort liability claims yet, either. So, all we have to do is cough up a little baksheesh to keep the Yemeni government types quiet..."

"The Yemeni were shooting at you before we got here," Jerry pointed out.

Toreva shrugged. "Yeah, but what the hell could they do to a robot train with no humans aboard?"

"De-rail it," Jerry told him.

This stopped Toreva for a moment. "Yeah, they did try to bust the rails a couple of times before we started monitoring with video sensors and before we started using continuously welded rails bonded to concrete ties. But busting up our right of way takes some brains and a knowledge of technology...which these dumb Yemeni don't seem to have much of in the first place."

"We have reason to believe that those dumb Yemeni are getting some pretty advanced weaponry all of a sudden," Curt revealed. "I wouldn't be surprised if they had tube rockets and very sophisticated explosives within a matter of weeks. We've already caught them with modern disposable assault rifles and some pretty advanced mines."

Toreva shrugged again. "Worst that can happen is to put the railroad down for a day or so. If they start blowing up the right of way, that's easy to fix fast. I just put my maintenance crews out of the line pronto. And that's where we're going to need protection by the army..."

"Suppose they go after your locomotives?" Jerry wanted to know.

"They have. I've got two bull-noses in the shop right now where some Yemeni screwed up the pantographs. Stopped the train for a couple of hours until we got a repair crew there and pulled fried Yemeni out of the pantographs. They don't know a damned thing about high-voltage electricity. Fifty-thousand volts AC does a very quick job. Faster than a microwave oven..."

This brought up a side subject that was bothering Curt, and this was an opportunity to broach it. So he asked, "We had a similar problem yesterday. Some Yemeni guerrilla boarded the down-train and were shooting up our outposts as they went past them."

"Yeah, I heard about it. You people got your jollies shooting at them, but my trains got through."

"So just how did those Yenieni get aboard a moving train? Did they board it here in the yard before it began to move?" Curt wanted to know. This had bothered him ever since it had happened. One does not easily board a train moving along at fifty klicks.

Toreva shook his head. "I may be just an old railroad boomer, Colonel, but I got better security than that! The line goes through Thilla Cut on an upgrade about ten klicks northeast of here. A loaded train usually slows to about ten klicks per hour climbing the grade up to the cut. It's no problem boarding a train going ten klicks per. Yeah, occasionally you miss and end up under the wheels. That's why I don't let my men do that. But I don't give a rip if some Yemeni gets killed doing it. One less I have to worry about. But it makes the rails slick for a few minutes."

"So you do indeed have to worry about the Yemeni?" Jerry caught the implied problem in Toreva's voice. From his name and appearance, Jerry guessed, Toreva was a full-blooded Navaho Indian. The man's reference to his service on the Black Mesa and Lake Powell Railroad, another robotic railroad that ran through the Navaho Indian reservation in northern Arizona, made sense, too. If you're going to operate a robot railroad, hire people who have long experience doing it elsewhere.

Toreva sighed. "You want to know what my worry with the Yemeni is? I'll tell you what my worry with the Yemeni is! It ain't their goddamned guerrilla attacks and attempts at terrorism. They're amateurs at that. Naw, it's the Yemenis who are supposed to be working for me."

"How many Yemenis work here?" Jerry asked.

"About half of them," Toreva replied brusquely, then went on, "First off, they have absolutely no idea of punctuality whatsoever! I'm lucky if I can get enough of them here to get the train rolling every morning! And it's even tougher to get the up-train positioned to load in the afternoon and to roll it at night down the hill! If they're not orbiting on qat, they've got another excuse or four. One guy will send word through a relative at the last minute that he's got a bad toe; the guy I'm thinking about always has some cockamamie excuse, but he's got enough brains to pay a native doctor to give him a medical certificate that he has gout. Another young guy has six wives because he's making enough money here to support all of them, so he sends in a series of excuses with great regularity. Hell, I know the Yemenis take on a lot more matrimonial adventures than we do, but I'll be damned if I know how he can keep six women happy at once. I got enough trouble with one!"

He sighed. Curt let him go on and get his bitches off his chest because it was apparent that Toreva wanted someone to talk to other than the mine boss who apparently didn't understand or didn't want to. "Another man has more damned family than you could count. I can understand that. I got more relatives in Tuba City than I care to talk about. But this guy buries one of them at least once a month. At least, he produces a death certificate and goes off to a funeral, he says. On top of all the personal excuses, these Yemeni are Muslims with more religious excuses than I ever knew existed...and it ain't exactly politic to interfere in those cases. Even when they're here, I can always find a bunch of them over in some corner of the shop or engine house that they've converted into a mosque. Hell, I, caught one guy asleep on his prayer rug the other day when he was supposed to be cleaning up the rectifier bay on Engine Number Nine. I got him back to work real fast. And what does he do? Shows up in my office two hours later asking for a raise...Jeez, if I wanted to work around people as lazy as that, I'd go back to Window Rock."

"The problems of management are always difficult," Curt commiserated with him.

"Mr. Toreva, I think our proposed rescheduling of the trains may help you," Jerry suddenly remarked as he got a bright idea. "Suppose you shift schedules by six hours. This means that your people can load and unload the trains in the morning. They'll be rolling in the afternoon when the Yemeni tend to engage in their national pastime. Then you'll be loading and unloading the next set of trains in the relative cool of the evening hours."

"Yeah, if I can get the Yemeni to give up their women and come in then," Toreva pointed out.

"Suppose you were to outfit some of the empty space in the buildings around here in a super luxurious manner so your Yemeni employees could enjoy their qat and women without having to leave the premises?" Hassan suggested, knowing full well that Muslim men, like men everywhere, always took the easy way out. Furthermore, Hassan knew how the mind of Middle Eastern man worked...and it really wasn't that much different from the way it worked almost everywhere else in the world except in the postindustrial countries where you couldn't survive very long without working your butt off. "And suppose you were to cut a deal with one of the madams in Amran to open a subsidiary here - with carefully controlled hours of operation, of course."

This appeared to shock Toreva. "You want me to open a qat parlor and a whorehouse out here?"

"I believe that was the gist of my suggestion, sir."

Curt told himself that he should have expected this sort of suggestion from the ladies' man of the Washington Greys who had been brought up in the different culture of a Muslim nation. But Toreva shook his head. "Dammit, it's against company policy! It has to be! I think..."

"Seems to me," Jerry added, "that company policy basically tells you to keep the railroad running so the board of directors can report a profit to the stockholders every quarter. Anything more complicated than that is probably window dressing or turf protection. I'll bet your boss doesn't micromanage you. He only expects results. And I'll also bet he doesn't give a damn how you get them."

"Your American and European stockholders won't let their sense of morality stand in the way of pragmatic profitability," Dyani added.

John Toreva looked more closely at her. Attired in cammies her hair pinned up under her blue Sierra Charlie tam, Dyani didn't look like an Indian woman to Toreva. Dyani had not allowed herself to grow fat like many Navaho women Toreva had known. As a result, she was an extremely beautiful woman even in battle dress. This was unusual, so Toreva asked a question that was one word: "Apache?"

Dyani sat straight, looked him in the eye, and proudly said, "Crow."

"You approve?"

"That's not for me to say. But if it works and if it squares with the Yemeni morals, it will help us do our job of helping you do your job," she told him in her usual forthright manner.

Toreva thought about this for a moment, then said, "May not be a bad idea. Sure as hell, it will keep the Yemeni employees happy." Then he admitted, "And that's getting to be a problem these days with all the guerrilla and terrorist activities."

He reached out and punched up a call number on his speakerphone set. A Yemeni-accented voice announced, "Jebel Miswar Mining Company, chief engineer's office."

"John Toreva here. Lemme speak to Walter Cory."

"Cory," came another voice from the phone. "John, did the down-train get off okay just now?"

"Right on the tick, Walt. Hey, I've got Colonel Carson and some of his people here from the YEF operation. They've got some good ideas on how to stop this god-damned hassle we're getting from guerrillas and terrorists. But it's going to require some rescheduling on your part and mine." He went on to explain the proposed plan to the man who ran the mine.

"They think they're running this operation?" was the chief engineer's immediate reaction. "Dammit, that means my people have to shift time as well. Or everything they do will be out of phase with the trains!"

"Think about it, Walt," Toreva urged him, by this time obviously sold on the plan himself. "We can make the shift tonight if we want to by delaying everything six hours. It's not going to screw up the ship-loading procedure at Al-Luhaya. The *Ferron Valiant* can lie at the loading wharf and the ship-workers can make those repairs to the outer hull the skipper's been bitching about not having time to fix. The ships can easily make the change because they don't move that fast."

"Uh, yeah, but that will put us twenty kilotons behind schedule," Cory objected.

"What does Ferron really care about, Walt?" Toreva asked rhetorically. "Only that the ore arrives in Madagascar on a regular schedule, that's what. Which means that the *Ferron Valiant* adds three knots to its cruise to make up the slack time. I can make the change here. It's no sweat for the ships. You ought to be able to change shifts without too much trouble. Especially when you explain to your Yemenis that the company's going to offer them some new perks."

"New perks?"

Toreva explained Hassan's suggestion.

Strangely, Chief Engineer Walt Cory didn't object. "I can do that. Sounds okay to me. Just don't tell my wife what we're doing for our employees, okay?"

"Should we let her set up a wives' auxiliary?" Toreva was half-joking.

Cory wasn't. "Not only no, but hell no! I should have let her stay in Iowa where she could be active with her church group. John, you know damned good and well she's completely monocultural. She's totally out of place here." The man sighed. "She thinks it's bad enough we've got the mixed-gender army here to help us."

"I'll agree with her on that one," Curt Carson muttered.

Chapter Fourteen

"This is the first decent Stand-to we've had for weeks! Months!" Lieutenant Colonel Joan Ward observed with effervescent pleasure as she looked around the casern room that had been appropriated and fitted out as the Club - not an O-Club or an NCO-Club, but *the* Club, there being only one Club in the Washington Greys.

"That's because our colonel decided to substitute mass, concentration of forces, and maneuver in place of having us sit on our buns out there waiting to shoot and be shot at. I'm damned glad to get my troops and guns out of the boonies. It was only a matter of time before the Yemarks decided to concentrate on taking us out one at a time. You're absolutely right. The man is a tactical genius," was the remark of Lieutenant Larry Hall, commander of the regimental artillery company, GUNCO. Or, more familiarly, "Hall's Hellcats."

"I second that, but it wasn't totally the colonel's doing," said Major Hensley Atkinson, regimental ops staffer, the "housemother" of the outfit. "Jerry, Kitsy, and Hassan were the primary authors and instigators."

"But the colonel sold it to Battleaxe, and that took some tactical maneuvering," Major Russ Frazier added. "Got around the goddamned ROEs! Orgasmic! Defense is the shits."

"No, Russ, cholera holds that title," Major Ruth Gydesen, the regimental medical officer, reminded him. "And we've got enough of that and other nasty little things running rampant in this country."

It was a typical Washington Greys Stand-to, the weekly get-together at the Club at the invitation of the regimental commander, with the first round of drinks on him. Attendance was obligatory, but presence was not. One could show up, be seen by the colonel, and leave when Stand-to was over. Few Greys ever left. Nor was it required that a Grey patronize the bar. Most did, the consumption of ethanol being one of the few vices permissible when faced with operations utilizing neuroelectronic linkage, even "soft" linkage.

Stand-to was a time to be informal. It was an old army tradition that had been staunchly maintained by the Greys wherever they might be in a dangerous world that never stopped fighting. People are social animals, and there isn't a culture in the world where people don't like to get together with friends to talk.

"Speaking of nasty diseases running rampant in Yemen," Lieutenant Larry Hall said, "I think the colonel did an admirable job during his little lecture this afternoon, don't you?"

Joan Ward laughed. "The 'Love Parade'? Rumor Control hints that the fabulous Third Herd Sextet intends to premiere a new ditty honoring that occasion tonight."

"Bloody well ought to! Time we had a little humor and recreation for a change! This bloody place is a bloody hell!" growled Captain Peter Freeman, the long-faced exchange officer from the British Army who proudly wore the badge of the 51st Highlanders. He was one of the few officers left in the roboticized British Army who had steadfastly remained a non-warbot artillery man and wore parachutist's wings as well. As an exchange officer who was with the Greys to learn something about the mixed warbot-human combat doctrine of the Sierra Charlies, he'd been posted to Hall's GUNCO where he commanded "Freeman's Fusileers" with its four LAMVAs mounting 75-millimeter Saucy Cans multirole guns.

"But isn't it a hell of a lot better place than sitting around out at Dih Bin," Hensley Atkinson told him. The two of them seemed to get along famously. Hensley looked and acted very much like a British nanny, which, as the operations officer who ran things with the firm, no-nonsense hand of a British housekeeper, in a way she was. "At least, you'd *better* say so! Or go sit at another table tonight!"

Freeman's favorite and most used word appeared to be "bloody." Except for that endearing trait and a penchant for warm alcoholic beverages - he preferred to get four to six beers at the start of a Stand-to and allow them to come to room temperature while he started off with warm Irish whiskey, no ice, please - he was a personable chap who'd become well-liked by the Greys. "Ducks, even Sana'a is no bloody paradise! Not even a decent place to go on a bloody pass!"

"Depends on the company you go on pass with, Peter," she remarked.

He looked at her. "Another problem. You bloody well butcher our common tongue! That's the sort of errant nonsense up with which I will not put, to quote one of us Brits. But I'm bloody well growing to appreciate you Yanks with your mixed-gender forces!"

"You don't handle the language so well yourself, old chap," Hensley retorted with a smile.

"And you'd better watch your Highlanders' slang, Peter!" Joan Ward warned him. "Or you're likely to be graced with a ditty of your own by the Third Herd Sextet!"

"So? I see I should bloody well teach you a few of our British Army ditties," Freeman volunteered and began:

"For it's whiskey, whiskey, whiskey,
That makes you feel so frisky,
In the Corps, in the Corps,
And it's beer, beer, beer,
That makes you feel so queer,
In the King's Own Royal Rifle Corps.
My eyes are dim, I cannot see,
I have not brought my specs with me!
I have...not...brought...my...specs...with...me!"

"We sang that one at West Point," Colonel Curt Carson remarked, joining the group. At a Stand-to, it was one of his responsibilities to try to talk with everyone there, and he was making the rounds. "But the words were slightly different. You cleaned it up, Captain. Bowdlerized it."

Freeman started to rise from his seat, but Curt put a hand on his shoulder. "As you were and stand at ease, Captain! At our Stand-to's, it's not necessary to observe formal protocol. Sort of like regimental guest night...except we don't bust up the furniture because it's sort of hard to replace it in Yemen."

"Yes, sir. But with all the informality that is generally the case in the Washington Greys, I get the distinct impression you Yanks tend to treat fighting as a bloody party," Freeman observed.

"Well, I'm not sure that the British Army doesn't and didn't," Curt replied easily. Then he reminded the Britisher of some very British military history. "It seems to me I recall reading about an incident at Port Said during the Suez affair. Something about a mess sergeant demanding priority above ammo and other supplies for off-loading the officers' champagne and mess silver..."

Freeman suddenly realized that the regimental commander was more than just a boorish Yank; he was an educated boorish Yank. But he replied with a smile, "Colonel, that wasn't the Fifty-first Highlanders! That was Her Majesty's Lifeguards. And they know how to campaign, sir!"

Curt laughed and told his companions, "Ladies, I see you're making our exchange officer feel at home in the Greys. I commend your fine sense of hospitality!"

Hensley managed to look innocent. "Colonel, our hospitality often knows no bounds..."

"Yes," was all that Curt had time to respond with.

Captain Elwood Otis, nominally the chief of the Warbot Technical Company whose job it was to keep the warbots running when Level One maintenance at the platoon and company level couldn't, stood up on a chair. He was holding an electronic accordion. Ranged around him were the other members of the Third Herd Sextet - Sergeants Jamie Jay Younger, Joe Jim Watson, Betty Joe Trumble, Mariette Ireland, and Christine Burgess - backed up by two M33A Jeep warbots. "People! People!" Otis tried calling out above the crowd noise. He was unsuccessful.

"*Quiet!*" When Regimental Sergeant Major Henry Kester used his parade ground voice, it shook the walls. Everyone shut up.

"In response to the outstanding and educational lecture we had the honor to attend this afternoon, the Third Herd Sextet would like to introduce a new Stand-to song into the repertory. It was composed in haste but with taste by several ladies of the Washington Greys who have asked to remain anonymous because they don't need any further encouragement...but they feel that some of their male counterparts do. This composition is entitled, *Mars Amatoria,*" Otis announced. Then he turned and raised his hand to give the downbeat.

The Greys didn't have a full regimental band, nor did they have a regimental orchestra. It would have been difficult to carry around musical instruments anyway. But electronics provided them with small, compact musical instruments whose sounds were virtually indistinguishable from the real, classical musical instruments. In addition, the two Jeeps had been programmed to provide additional musical accompaniment.

The Colonel he was worried and was very ill at ease,
He was haunted by the specter of venereal disease.
For four Sierra Charlies was the tale he had to tell
Had lain with local women and loved not wisely but too well.
It was plain that copulation was a tonic for the bored,
But the male Sierra Charlies were but Innocents Abroad;
So ere they take their pleasure with amateur or whore
They must learn the way from officers who've trod that path before.
No kind of doubt existed in the lieutenant colonel's head
That the best Sierra Charlies who knew a brothel from a bed
Were his adjutant and officers who were above the rest,
For the higher-ranking officers loved better than the best.
But the colonel and adjutant were not a bit dismayed,
And so they gave the orders for a Unit Love Parade
Where the adjutant by numbers showed exactly how it's done,
How not to be a casualty and still have lots of fun.
The adjutant with care explained, using visual aids,
That refreshment horizontal must be made with cleaner maids.
He showed male Sierra Charlies how to love according to the rules
And after digging in to take precautions with their tools.
And now the colonel's happy and perfectly at ease;
No longer is he troubled with venereal disease.
The lady Greys, their problems solved, are cooing like a dove
So they gave the Cross of Venus to their commandant of love.

Soldiers of any age and era sing. Sometimes, their songs aren't exactly the sort heard in polite society in spite of the "New Millennium Realism." But this wasn't polite society; it was the Club of the Washington Greys, and if any outsider didn't like it, anyone in the room would have told said outsider to fold it until it was all corners and put it someplace indecent where it would hurt. The Club broke out into a pandemonium of applause, cheers, and laughter.

"I say!" Peter Freeman observed as Curt roared. "You Greys fight hard and play just as hard!"

"We learned it from you, Peter," Joan Ward told him and mimicked him. "This bloody place needs bloody laughter. Sure as hell the bloody Yemeni don't know how to laugh worth a bloody damn! Or fight, either. Except they're just as nasty as some professionals in some ways..."

Major Pappy Gratton, the regimental adjutant, stood up with a broad grin on his face and roared, "You're all on report!"

Curt followed suit. "Yeah! Report to the showers! You were off-key! But a credit to your unit! Bartender, drinks on me for the Third Herd Sextet!"

It was going to be a raucous evening at the Club.

It was indeed. And after Stand-to as well. Curt had no idea how raucous it could get.

He expected that Major Cal Worsham would be raucous. He and his flyboys and flygirls always were. But Cal pressed a drink into Curt's hand although Curt already had one in his other hand, then laid a hand on Curt's shoulder and advised the regimental commander, "Colonel, *damn* your hide, but you are *indeed* a square shooter! You're going to give us a chance to *really* exhibit that we've got *more* than mere air superiority here. Hell, man, we've got *air supremacy!* And I want to tell you something that *maybe* you didn't already know, being as how you're a *West Pointer* with dirt between your toes and all. But *all* of us what have *wings* know damned good and well that *no* campaign has *ever* been won *without* air superiority! And we've got it!"

Cal set the partly empty drink glass down and concentrated on the full one Cal had just handed him. He liked his air boss although the man was just about as rough as carborundum dust. "Napoleon and Grant would have been delighted to know that, Cal."

"Aw, I mean not since the *aeroplane* came along, that is!" Worsham corrected himself. "Now we're going to *stop* being on the *losing* side, you understand? The Warhawks are going up there in the wild-assed blue, and we're going to haul *people* and place *ordnance* so that we can't *possibly* lose!"

"I hope you don't suddenly run up against Soviet Wasp baby SAMs or even some of the Smart Farts our American merchants of death sold to some low-tech country," Curt warned him.

"Hell, we've dodged them *before*. We'll dodge them *again*. Then we'll grease the sonsofbitches what shot them at us!" Worsham promised.

"Don't snort your slots too full of ethanol booster, Cal, or you may not be in any condition to get one millimeter off the ground tomorrow," Curt admonished him gently. The AIRBATT was, by nature, a hard-drinking crew. But aerodyne drivers and other aviators everywhere honestly believed themselves to be superior people and always had. "How can you shoot the Yemenis if you've got a hangover?"

Worsham thought about that for a moment, then replied, "*Easy!* I just don't have to *lead* them as much! But, Colonel, you're *right!* I recall that some ace - *maybe* Pappy Boyington - once said that too many drinks could make you *shoot* at the bastards and *miss* most of the time. Don't worry. I've taught *my* aerodyne drivers to metabolize *this* stuff in a hurry. When *we* shoot, we'll *hit*."

The pressure on the Greys in the past few weeks had been intense, Curt realized. They needed this Stand-to to let off the accumulated steam. And they were doing it.

Having made his rounds, Curt repaired to a table where his closest friends, former members of the company called "Carson's Companions," named after Alexander's picked heavy Macedonian cavalry, were sitting. Jerry, Dyani, Adonica, Kitsy, Hassan, Henry, and Edie were enjoying the relaxation. Tonight, they had hauled Captain Patrick Lufkin into the group. The Canadian was holding his own quite remarkably.

"I'm getting a lot of positive feedback on your new strategy," Curt told Jerry, Kitsy, and Hassan.

"It was the obvious thing to do," was Jerry's comment.

"And I expected it," Kitsy bubbled. "We're not used to being on the defensive. We're an offensive unit."

"Right! I don't think I've ever been with a more offensive unit!" Pat Lufkin joked.

"For that, Captain, I'm going to send you out on a dawn patrol tomorrow!" Dyani told him. "But before you go to quarters to get ready, please get me another drink."

Curt was astounded. Dyani continued to amaze him as time went by and she slowly lowered her almost prim personal barriers to close informality with everyone as she'd done only with him in private since she'd become commissioned. But he'd never seen her respond to a joke by using retaliatory humor before. She didn't mean it, of course, but it was the first time she'd done such a thing. And it was the first time she'd ever had more than one drink at a Stand-to. Dyani Motega was a controlled social drinker...until that moment.

Then he realized that she'd had more than just one that night.

Something about Dyani had changed drastically since she'd been hit so badly during the train riders' skirmish.

He thought he'd worked it out of her the night before. Dyani was a female warrior, one of the best. Deep inside, she knew she could be killed, wounded, or even maimed. However, she had developed defenses against allowing those deeply private inner thoughts to influence what she badly wanted to do since childhood: Serve as a United States Army combat scout as generations of her family had done with pride and competence. But apparently something was still in there chewing Dyani to pieces. And she was no longer the cool warrior she had been.

So, he moved over next to her. And when she'd finished the drink that Pat Lufkin brought her, he said quietly to her, "It's been a long day, Deer Arrow." That was a private signal to her that it was time to leave.

Dyani caught it. But when she looked at Curt, she had the eyes of a cougar, a predator, a strong and violent stalker. "Yes, I think it is, too," she said in a voice that was almost a growl.

He knew he had to get her out of there and find out what the problem was.

It wasn't difficult. In fact, Dyani practically led him out of the Club and pulled him to his quarters.

Very few men will ever admit that a woman has raped *them*. Most men have far too much machismo to ever admit it. But Curt had bedded some very wild and exotic women in his life, including one who could honestly be called an Amazon. But even that one paled in comparison to Dyani that night.

Dyani was usually vibrant, primitive, loving, and robust. But that night, she was violent, demanding, almost barbaric. It was as though generations of civilization had suddenly been peeled away from her personality. She didn't want to talk at all, not even to murmur endearments or vocalize her joy and pleasure as she usually did. Nor would she give Curt the opportunity to do so. Curt was amazed. But he was also stronger than she. Any man in less than Curt's excellent physical condition and fully rational mental state would have been bruised, injured, or worse.

As with intense combat, it didn't last very long. It couldn't, not even with two people in as excellent condition and health as the two of them. After the first "mad minute" which might have been many times that long - Dyani finally collapsed in his arms. She didn't cry out. She didn't weep. She showed no emotion, only her silent stoicism. But as she lay there, Curt could feel her trembling against him. He said nothing. He was waiting for Dyani to break her violent silence. Only if she didn't do so would he try to get her to talk.

Dyani did. She looked at him and snuggled against him, saying in her usual private voice, "Thank you. Thank you, Kida. Did I hurt you? Are you all right?"

"You didn't hurt me, Deer Arrow," Curt told her honestly because he could never be anything but honest with this woman. But he was forced to admit, "You've worn me out before, but I've never known you to act like this. You had too much to drink. I've never seen you have more than one drink."

"Kida, I felt that I needed those extra drinks tonight."

"You *needed* them? Deer Arrow, you've never *needed* alcohol! Or anything else! So something's wrong if you needed ethanol to get rid of some inhibitions or give you confidence. My God, you're one woman who's never needed any artificial means to give you confidence. Or to enhance your attractiveness," he told her quietly with as much compassion in his voice as he could muster. "Dyani, we've always been honest with one another. Please be honest with me now. What in the world is bothering you?"

She smiled her Dyani smile, lusty and provocative now, that of a woman who deeply cares for her man. The enormous charge of emotional tension that had been within her was now drained. "Last night, you talked me through my realization that I wasn't immortal. That I could be killed. But tonight, I had to reaffirm my belief in myself."

When she paused, Curt asked, "What belief, Dyani?"

"That I was still a warrior."

"You are. Oh, believe me, you are!"

"I know that now, thanks to you. For once I conquered you openly and deliberately without guile or stealth. But I'll never have to do that again, Kida." She kissed him tenderly, then she smiled again as her developing sense of humor came back to her. "I know it's trite but thank you for being you tonight."

"Well, speaking of old and well-used lines, will you still respect me in the morning?"

"I'll show you when the sun comes up," she promised with a caress that was now extremely gentle.

Chapter Fifteen

Absolutely nothing happened early the next day. But it didn't stay that way.

Major Jerry Allen tried hard not to be wildly enthusiastic about the impact of his hypothesis concerning Yemeni behavior patterns. As a result, he ended up just being smugly proud. Hassan, however, reacted with his usual ebullience.

"Not a whisper. Not a single shot. Not even any Yemarks exposing themselves along the right of way," Jerry reported to his regimental commander when Curt convened a "howgozit" session in the OCV at 0930. "Toreva and Cory reported they shifted the schedules of the ore trains without too much heartburn. They delayed the evening run by six hours and dispatched it at oh-one-hundred. The up-train arrived at oh-six-hundred hours right on the tick."

Curt knew this and more, of course, because he'd spent the morning since reveille in his regimental combat information center. The Combat Information Center wasn't in the casern building at Amran but inside his regimental OCV parked outside. Curt didn't like the idea of having a nonmobile CIC. The Washington Greys were configured, trained, and experienced as a highly mobile fighting unit. He didn't like the defensive posture forced upon him by Washington's political and diplomatic dreaming. He wanted to remain as mobile as possible so that he could go on the offensive at the earliest opportunity. If the Yemarks and the Pentagon gave him that opportunity.

"Where are the Yemarks, then, Jerry?" Curt asked him. Although he had data that answered these questions, he wanted to make sure that his TACBATT commander did too. Redundant data kept the two of them honest. And he was also training Jerry as a potential regimental commander. Someday, someone was going to have to fill Curt's shoes just as Curt himself had to eventually step up to replace Belinda Hettrick and Wild Bill Bellamack when they'd been booted upstairs. Both of them had taught him that one cannot move up the ladder of command, responsibility, and promotion unless subordinates are ready, willing, and able to take over. The twenty-first century American Army was built upon such tried and proved management and command principles. They worked most of the time, but when they didn't work, the results were often spectacular. Curt wanted to make sure that his results weren't spectacular but stodgily successful. So he was often a stern coach and trainer. And he was especially that way this morning although he now felt a lot better about a lot of things than he had since deploying to Yemen. "They certainly must have mobilized this morning to do something. They've done so for the past month or so. They've established a pattern. They don't easily break patterns because they're far more oriented toward traditional ways of doing things than we are. So where are they? And have they withdrawn from their ambuscades? And, if so, have you spotted their withdrawal yet?"

Jerry studied Curt's tactical display for a few moments, taking in the larger scope that it provided. He saw that the regimental plot matched his own battalion plot. It had additional data blocks and callouts relating to the deployment of the other three Iron Fist regiments, plus new data. "I see that the Royal Yemen Army is providing us with tactical data now," the battalion commander noted.

Curt nodded. "One of the results of my fortunate confrontation with Colonel Salem."

"I didn't think the RYA had tac beacons and digitized tac data bases," Jerry remarked.

"They don't," Master Sergeant Edie Sampson put in. "But at least now they're feeding us voice circuit data and other analog stuff via video link. I had to kluge-up some interface hardware and Sergeant Major Kester managed to adapt some software to convert this over to our database system. What you see here, Major, is the best approximation I can give you. And some of it comes from our own recce and surveillance. By the way, Lieutenant Brown is doing an orgasmic job here. And that new Canadian exchange officer, Captain Lufkin, looks like an old Indian fighter."

"I'll tell them both," Jerry promised, silently thanking Curt for keeping Edie in the Greys and putting her where her substantial talents as a tac techie would do the most good. And, of course, there was always that master hacker, Henry Kester, who not only knew more about personal combat than anyone in the Third Herd but could also patch a piece of software or hack a code with the best. He continued to study the tac display and added, "Apparently, this shift in railway schedules caught the Yemarks totally by surprise. They don't seem to have reacted to it yet."

"They knew about it," Captain Dyani Motega put in. As the commander of the Reconnaissance Company, RECONCO, she would know and was supposed to know. She looked a lot better this morning. To Jerry, it seemed that she was again the alert, confident, and competent Dyani the Third Herd had grown to know and respect. The aftermath of being hurt so badly in the train riders' skirmish now seemed to have left her. Captain Adonica Sweet, Dyani's unofficial "sister" in the regiment (the lady Sierra Charlies had developed "sisters" just as the men had developed "buddies" and, in some cases, certain men and women had developed POSSOH relationships) hadn't said much about this today, but there hadn't been an opportunity for Adonica and Dyani to chat since breakfast. And Dyani's continuing response reaffirmed Jerry's assessment. She went on, "We scouts and spooks stick together, you know. G2-S-2 has its private channels. Got to filter a lot of data so our commanders get gems, not gravel. So we've gotten reports that the Yemen intelligence network from the railway yard reported the schedule change to whomever was doing whatever coordination there was."

"Got any line on that yet, Captain?" Curt wanted to know.

"Where the Yemark command center of gravity is? No, sir," she told him, shaking her head. As usual, her long black hair was bound and braided into a tight and very tactical coif. In some ways, she was even more exciting to Curt this way than when she let her hair down in quarters. But that was just a passing thought. Over the months, he'd learned to discipline himself and to follow Dyani's advice to keep his priorities straight. It wasn't easy when he was around such an exciting woman as Dyani turned out to be. "Even if we had that information, we probably couldn't do much about it under the existing ROEs."

"Except to attempt to interdict the movement of Yemark units," Major Russ Frazier put in with the sort of eagerness that exemplified him and his company, Frazier's Ferrets.

"Can't even do that," Captain Kitsy Clinton muttered. Then she added, "Damn this defensive posture! Don't they know that he who tries to defend all defends nothing?"

"They probably didn't read that book," Lieutenant Larry Hall surmised.

"But we *could* damned well slow the bastards up real good by making them keep their fucking *heads* down!" Major Cal Worsham growled.

"Okay, but where are the Yemarks this morning?" Curt asked again. "With nothing to assault, what are they going to do? I'm entertaining speculation here. If you were a Yemark commander, what would you be doing right now?"

After a long silence, Kitsy ventured to say, "I'd be wondering where the trains were."

"I'd have scouts checking the rail yards at Amran and al-Luhaya," Dyani added quickly. "And probably the temporary fire forts we abandoned yesterday afternoon when GUNCO was recalled. And our caserns here, at al-Mawr, Huth, and at al-Zuhra. Matter of fact, that's what I figured out a few hours ago. I should be hearing from my own patrols any time now. I may have some red meat targets for you before long."

"And as the Yemark commander, when I discovered that the trains had already gone and that the Iron Fist regiments had withdrawn, I'd be busy as all hell calling off the operations for today because something's changed," Hassan put in. "I'd try to get my units to stand fast but I'd know I couldn't. They all want to attack and get it over with before the qat party this afternoon. And I'd be doing a lot of chattering on my new tactical communications units because whoever gave them to me simply said it would be safe to use them because they couldn't be jammed or tapped."

"Which, of course, they can," Edie Sampson said. She wasn't reluctant to put her contribution in even if it meant interrupting an officer. No officer in the Third Herd would ever stomp her for neglecting protocol. At least, not at an informal "howgozit" session such as this. Edie was the Number Two techie of the Greys, and no one wanted to stifle her. On the Third Herd team, she was a valuable player. She kept the C3I going. When the slime hit the impeller, everyone counted on having good command, control, communications, and intelligence. Especially now that the Yemarks apparently had something like it.

"Are you talkin' when you should be listenin', Sergeant?" That came from the regimental sergeant major, her Number One. But it wasn't a derogatory question.

And Edie didn't take it that way because she popped right back at Henry, "Not on your stripes and rockers, Sergeant. Because I can do both and I am doing both. And I'm taping it all in the raw and in the deciphered dehopped version. Which our two resident experts in Arabic can begin translating whenever they're ready. And the hot skinny is going over the data bus to Sana'a where the Iron Fist G-2 is getting it, too."

"Where's the tape?" Hassan asked. "Give me a headset so I can snoop on them."

"I thought you'd never ask, Lieutenant. You want to snoop on the current real-time incoming comm traffic from the Yemarks?" Edie handed him a headset and punched up the circuit.

Without a word, Hassan slipped them on and became lost in listening.

"Captain Motega, anything from the birds?" Curt wanted to know, asking if Lieutenant Dale Brown's birdbot recon platoon had picked up any information in the last few minutes.

"Not yet, Colonel," she replied professionally. She did indeed feel a lot better today. As she often told Curt, he was the best medicine for her. And vice-versa. Except neither of them considered it a vice. Visceral, but not a vice. "We've got ten birdbots up right now. Lieutenant Brown is holding two in reserve JIC. I've asked him to keep a close watch on the former GUNCO installations that were abandoned yesterday. I'm monitoring the freak for the latest verbal news."

Curt knew she was and would report anything the instant she heard. "Okay, we're holding for enemy instigation of Operation Wizard Kill," Curt announced, giving a name to the activity for the first time. He was damned tired of the protocol that said all ops codes should be produced by Grady's random word circuitry; that usually produced either some really bad puns or excruciatingly funny mismatches of words. So, he'd chosen this one himself. "Are we hot to trot for point defense of our casern?"

"Affirmative. Captain Clinton has that responsibility," Jerry reported.

"Yeah, dammit. Always on the defensive," Kitsy griped.

"We'd all rather be on the assault, Captain," Jerry reminded her dispassionately. Kitsy was never one to simply sit still and wait for something to happen. Like Russ Frazier, she made things happen, except that she did it with considerably less violence and a great deal more verve. "Major Frazier will lead the airborne elements...if we deploy them."

"You good to go, Russ?" Curt asked unnecessarily.

Frazier was always good to go. "Affirmative, Colonel. We're minus-ten and holding. Sergeant Garrison is covering for Lieutenant Clock."

"How's Hal coming along?" Curt asked solicitously.

"Cleared for duty maybe tomorrow if his wound continues to heal as well as it has been," Major Ruth Gydesen replied for Russ.

"Lieutenant Hall? GUNCO?"

"AP airburst rounds are already chambered in the Saucy Cans, Colonel," Lieutenant Larry Hall snapped smartly. "We're ready to make meat." That surprised Curt a bit. Hall was a gung-ho type, but he hadn't revealed that he was especially bloodthirsty until that moment. Maybe it was just a slip of the tongue. Maybe it was just some of the defensive frustration that had gripped them all. Maybe it was the thought that the Third Herd might be able to strike back hard and surgically for a change instead of chasing will-o'-the-wisp Yemark guerrillas through the desolate, rugged mountains of Yemen.

"Major Worsham?" Curt asked his AIRBATT leader, again unnecessarily. But he had to ask each one of them. He wanted to get a verbal "good to go" commitment and he didn't want to slight anyone.

"Hands has the Harpies hot. Timm has the Chippies chitterin'," Worsham reported in a somewhat disinterested tone. He didn't remark that he would be up and driving a Chippewa airlift aerodyne if the balloon went up today. One of his Chippie drivers was still recovering from wounds and Major Gydesen wouldn't clear the man for flight yet.

The OCV, a vehicle the size of a small bus, rocked as the shock wave of an explosion hit it.

Battalion Sergeant Major Nick Gerard stuck his head into the OCV and yelled, "Limpet mine against the outer perimeter wall! Major Allen, I suggest Red Alert at once!"

Nick was almost trampled by the outrush of Washington Greys, leading him to place considerably more credence in the nickname of the regiment, the Third Herd.

"Where the hell are the scouts? The sentries?" Curt yelled as he grabbed his combat helmet and piled out the door behind Jerry.

"My scouts and birdbots are out over at the railway!" Dyani yelled back at him.

"So why didn't our perimeter security system catch it?" Curt saw the smoke, dust, and rubble where the outer wall of the casern had been demolished.

Greys and warbots were already laying guns on the gap, ready for a possible assault through the gaping hole.

It didn't come.

Cougars report! the "voice" of Kitsy Clinton came through the neuroelectronic pickups of Curt's battle helmet.

Cougar Master here! was the immediate, rapid reply from Master Sergeant Carol Head, Kitsy's first sergeant. *Cougar Leader, that mine must have been planted earlier. No one has been near the outer wall since sunrise!*

Another terrorist action! Jerry surmised.

His guess was confirmed at once as Dyani reported, *Alleycat Leader, Mustang Leader here! We have multiple ground targets around the casern. Infrared signatures indicate human beings, chemical sensors indicate they're Yemeni who haven't had a bath lately.*

No one in this godforsaken place has had a bath lately! Not enough water to float a rubber ducky around here! That was Larry Hall.

Warhawk Leader, Grey Head here, Curt snapped an order. *Get the Harriers airborne! Tell Hands and his rockbusters it's time for them to make little ones out of big ones! Take a few Yemarks out of the game while they're doing it. Soften them up! Better yet, cream them so we don't have to put the Ferrets on the ground out there!*

Grey Head, you're taking all the sport out of it for my Ferrets!

Dammit, Russ, if the Harpies can do the job, I'll be fucked if I want to risk your Sierra Charlies and warbots on the ground! We've already gotten too many wounded Greys! I don't want to get Doctor Ruth overworked! Jerry suddenly sounded very much like Curt. And it surprised Curt.

Alleycat Leader, you got anyone down because of that limpet mine? Curt asked.

Kitsy, what's the story? Jerry asked, forgetting tacomm protocol in the heat of the moment. The protocol had its uses to ensure that messages were not misunderstood, so that the sender and the intended recipient were clearly identified at the start. But Curt knew that even the most disciplined troops couldn't maintain that level of formality when things hit the impeller as they had.

Cougar First to Cougar Bio! Ginny, get the hell over here! Even Master Sergeant Carol Head, the stolid Moravian first sergeant of Kitsy's company, had a lot of urgency in his tacomm message. *Tullis looks like he took some fragments or debris from the explosion. Doesn't look like his body armor was broached, but he's out of it. And Elliott is down, maybe just from the shock wave.*

Adonica, are the Stilettos able to defend your sector with two of your sergeants out? How about your Jeeps and Mary Anns? That was Kitsy making urgent inquiries about the situation should the mine explosion be followed by a Yemark assault

The Jeeps and Mary Anns are okay. They aren't soft like people, Adonica said unnecessarily. *We're shorthanded but we're fullbotted and we can cover by multitasking. We're doubling up warbot command. We anticipated that in training. But what the hell? I don't know whether we'll get a follow-up assault or not! Some of my Mary Anns and my Jeep fired into the dust of the street. Looks like we've got some civilian casualties out there.*

Yemeni casualties?

Affirmative! Have we got any spare medics?

Negatory! Grey Techie, get on the horn to the RYA Fourth Guards. Have them alert the emergency medical teams. I'm not going to send our medics out there in the street, not while the Yemeni could be madder than hell at us for firing into them! Curt realized that he had a real problem on his hands now. He was glad he'd made good contacts with Colonel Salem. This could get sticky.

Mustang Leader, Alleycat Leader! Any hot recce data on potential assault forces yet?

Dyani reported cooly and with as much precision as she could muster on the basis of the data piling into her scout-recce data center, which was mostly in her head. *Alleycat, the Mustangs have absolutely nothing as targets around the casern. We're scanning infrared and chemical. Nothing but confused civilian street traffic and Yemeni stink. And a lot of people yelling and screaming. But nothing, absolutely nothing, that looks like any sort of organized assault. No snipers in buildings. No one in the streets armed with anything more than those short dirks.*

"What the hell was that limpet mine all about then?" Joan Ward asked.

Curt turned to his chief of staff. "Diversion. Or just plain downright terrorism. It got a couple Sierra Charlies taken temporarily out of action, and the explosion looks like it hurt far more innocent civilians out on the street."

"Clearing out the bystanders in preparation for an assault?" Joan guessed.

Curt thought about this for a quarter of a second then shook his head. "I don't think so. They would have attacked by now. And they haven't. And no sign of them. So I'll bet the limpet mine incident has a couple of real nasty motives. One was to kill a lot of civilians next to our casern - which it apparently didn't do - but our warbots fired into the confusion against what they identified as hostile targets. Maybe they were, and maybe they weren't. But we'll get blamed for all the street slaughter by the locals. Not that there's any love lost now anyway. But you're right in thinking it might keep locals away from our casern, which would indeed make it easier to assault us."

"On the other hand," she told him, continuing to speculate, "a mob of civilians in the street would tend to mask attackers during the mad minute. We've always been on the assault side of such urban fighting. It might help if we could put ourselves in the defenders' shoes for change."

"We're going to get that chance whether we like it or not," Curt reminded her. "And I'm going to have my hands full with my report to Battleaxe about this one. So I'd damned well better get all the data together in one big god-dammed hurry. This is going to be in the impeller in about an hour, and Battleaxe is the one who will have to buffer us against the Yemeni authorities..."

Grey Head, Assassin Leader here!

Go ahead, Assassin Leader. Where are you and why are you talking directly to me? Curt wanted to know. Hassan was the officer in charge of Kitsy's second platoon.

I'm with my platoon ready to defend the casern, but I'm still monitoring the Yemark tacomm, Hassan reported. Curt knew that such a powerful division of thinking processes was extremely difficult under pressure, but Hassan wasn't an ordinary officer. He was a certified genius who'd turned down offers to work with the best scientists in America in order to fulfill what he considered a moral commitment to the Washington Greys who'd rescued him from Iran years before and paid for his education.

The Yemarks have been given a recall, was Hassan's message. *Whatever they were going to do, it's been aborted for today.*

Curt sighed. "That what he thinks..." he muttered to no one in particular. Curt knew his day had hardly started.

Chapter Sixteen

Curt didn't wait for the other shoe to drop. He got in contact with Major General Belinda Hettrick at once from the privacy of his OCV.

"Battleaxe, Grey Head here. We may have a problem," he told her.

Sana'a was close enough to Amran that two-way direct lasercom video conferencing was possible. Hettrick looked harried and busy. "What happened down there, Curt?"

"We were subjected to a terrorist bomb planted on the outside of the east wall of the casern facing the street," Curt explained and reported in detail with as much information as he had in hand at the moment. "When it detonated at ten thirty-seven, it took out twenty-one meters of the wall and damaged two old buildings on both sides. My GUNCO commander estimates that it contained the equivalent of ten kilos of Comp D. Enough for a single man to carry, yet small enough to be emplaced against the wall's foundations where it would be unnoticed. We had two NCOs injured, neither one seriously. One will be back on duty later today, the other will be released for duty tomorrow once my medical officer feels confident he sustained no internal injuries. I don't know how many Yemeni civilians were injured when the bomb went off. However, the Mary Anns and Jeeps of ASSAULTCO Alpha opened fire through the breach in the wall at what their programs and AI told them were approaching unfriendlies. An unknown number of Yemeni civilian casualties have been sustained at this point. I reported the possible injuries at once to Colonel Salem of the Fourth Guards Regiment of the RYA and requested that he alert the Yemeni emergency units. Colonel Salem has done that, and Yemeni units are now in the street outside the casern wall ministering to the wounded and injured." Curt's report was concise and as complete as he could inake it with the information he had in hand at that moment. The data might have been incomplete, but he knew he had to get the report in to

Hettrick ASAP because Yemeni civilians were involved.

"How many Yemeni injured?" Hettrick wanted to know.

Curt shrugged. "I don't know. Salem hasn't reported back to me."

"Why did you contact Colonel Salem?"

"I got to know him yesterday morning when his troopers picked me up as a suspected trike thief. One of your people moved my trike to the secure parking lot after I reported to you yesterday morning. I almost got busted for taking my own trike," Curt explained briefly. "I was taken to the head-quarters of the Fourth Guards Regiment where I got to know Salem. We ended up in a very informal and unofficial agreement that we'd work together in helping maintain law and order in this sheep screw that's developing."

"Dammit, Carson, you're always handing me the nastiest problems in the world!" Hettrick told him with a hint of resignation in her voice. Curt was far from being a meek commander who did nothing but follow orders and the ROEs; he always exhibited initiative and could figure out ways to operate within his orders while stretching their weak points. "Contact with the RYA is supposed to be from the YEF level to General Qahtan."

"Yes, ma'am, but it's never hurt to have unofficial working relationships at lower levels," Curt reminded her.

She nodded. "Agreed, but that sort of thing is always supposed to be unofficial. Very unofficial. Especially in this case and in Yemen. These people are fiercely proud and don't like the idea that we were called in to 'help them' do their job of protecting and defending foreign assets in Yemen. Sort of like the Saudis in Operation Desert Shield at the start. And the Yemeni are somewhat paranoid about all of this anyway."

"Yes, General, I know that. Which is why I decided to initiate lower-level personal contact with the RYA."

"Never mind. I won't belabor the matter, and I sure as hell won't mention it topside. If Qahtan or the Queen happens to get a severe case of heartburn over it, I'll simply explain that you notified a local RYA commander at your equivalent level of command because you wanted to get medical help to injured Yemeni as quickly as possible." Then Hettrick became very serious as she went on, "But the matter of firing on civilians is another matter."

"The warbots acted according to their instructions, General," Curt reminded her. "And because of the explosion, we feared an immediate assault on our regimental casern. We took only defensive action."

"It would have been defensive if your bots had shot Yemarks coming through the breach in the wall," the general pointed out. "As it was, they shot at suspected targets. That's going to be a more difficult action to explain and justify. The Yemeni really don't trust robots, anyway. They don't like the idea that the railroad is automated; they'd like to have the jobs that would be necessary to run a nonautomated railroad."

Curt recalled his conversation with Toreva yesterday. "I suspect the Amran and Red Sea Railroad's activity would be cut by at least half if Toreva and Cory had to depend on the Yemenis to actually operate the trains. Toreva has enough trouble now just getting his Yemenis to work on a schedule. These people aren't time-bound the way we are. They don't give a damn if something gets done today or not because if it doesn't get done today, it can always be done tomorrow."

"Yeah, the rest of the world seems to operate on the manana syndrome, except the Mexicans who have had to shake if off since they became a North American trading partner," Hettrick reflected, then asked, "What happened to the Yemark assaults on your abandoned GUNCO fortifications? Did the Yemarks go after them this morning?"

"They started to," Curt told her, "but they called it off shortly before eleven hundred hours."

"Your recce must be real good."

"Sergeant Edie Sampson tapped and dehopped their tacomm traffic. Lieutenant Hassan monitored the traffic and reported the Yemarks received orders to melt back into the hills."

"That's similar to reports I got from Salley and Cashier. But they didn't have Hassan to monitor and translate for them."

"Don't they have anyone fluent in Arabic?" Curt wondered.

She shook her head. "You ought to know that Arabic isn't one of the more popular second languages at West Point. Officers have tended to concentrate on Russian, the other European languages, and Japanese with the idea that we'd be fighting in Europe or working closely with the Japanese defending COPRE interests in the western Pacific rim. You're unique in knowing Mandarin Chinese, and Allen is one of the few people who speaks Arabic. As for Hassan, well, he's unusual in the first place."

"Yeah, he is. A credit to the regiment. Both of them," Curt agreed.

Hettrick thought for a moment, then snapped, "Get your butt over here to Sana'a SAP, Colonel! And look sharp! I'm notifying General Qahtan of the terrorist assault on your casern and the Yemeni casualties as soon as we sign off. I want to meet with Queen Arwa this afternoon. In view of the deteriorating civil safety situation and the fact that the Yemarks may start targeting small groups or individual officers of the YEF, get Nancy Roberts to airlift you over here. Looks like the Yemarks will stand down for qat this afternoon as expected. So you shouldn't have to worry about action after the noon balloon any more than you've had to in past weeks. Get here in the next hour, and I'll chit for the lunch. Shag it, Curt!"

Curt shagged.

And not because of a "free lunch." He knew it wouldn't be free. It would be a working lunch during which Hettrick would work out with him the presentation they'd make to Qahtan and perhaps Queen Arwa.

The 45-kilometer flight to Sana'a was uneventful, although Curt felt a bit ostentatious and wasteful using a big Chippewa airlifter and the fuel it burned for such a short hop with only one passenger aboard. Curt felt like a general officer with his own personal aircraft. On the other hand, Hettrick was right, of course. With the suddenly changed situation caused by altering the train schedules, the Yemarks might initially attempt to strike back in other and more irrational ways. Chippies had taken some ground fire from time to time in Yemen, but not the Golden BB that did real damage. A Chippie is a very big aircraft to kill with a single small arms bullet. A Soviet Wasp or a "liberated" American Smart Fart M100 rocket was something else, and either of them could do major damage or even totally destroy a Chippie.

Cal Worsham wasn't taking any chances. With Hands Harriers already set to scramble and having been denied the opportunity to lay ordnance on Yemark units that morning, he simply laid on an escort of two armed Harpies that accompanied the Chippie at slightly lower altitude, making them a more attractive target. The Harpies were loaded with countermeasures and air-to-ground ordnance, JIC. And two other Harpies remained at Amran ready to spool up if the Yemarks made any assault on the flying Chippie.

Hettrick's lunch with Curt was private and in her office between the two of them. She went over Curt's report again. Curt had brought along video data tapes recorded from the various Mary Ann and Jeep sensors. These showed the sort of targets the warbots had evaluated as potential unfriendlies. Indeed, they did appear to be guerrillas, although later evaluation of the Yemeni casualties showed they were merely tribesmen from the hills carrying their usual ancient long- barreled Enfield, Mauser, and Springfield rifles. Those old firearms were so well-made and durable that they had lasted in the dry Yemen climate for nearly a century. But the warbots couldn't discriminate between a Yemeni guerrilla carrying an assault rifle and a Yemeni hillsman carrying an Enfield; both appeared to be armed targets. Curt had checked with both Edie and Henry, and he was convinced that there was no way that the Mod 7/11 AI in the warbots could possibly be modified to make the discrimination between the two types of armed Yemenis. Hettrick, who had motherhenned the adoption, testing, and production of the Mod 7/11 AI during her Pentagon stint holding down the OSCAR desk there, knew it, too. The two of them tried to work out a suitable way of telling the story in an unclassified manner to the Royal Yemen Army chief of staff and the ruler of Yemen, Queen Arwa Bint Muhammad al-Badr. It wasn't easy. The Yemeni royalty and high command was going to have to take a lot of it on faith.

"Do you believe they will?" Curt wanted to know as they finished lunch. "I don't know Qahtan that well, and I've never met Queen Arwa."

"The Queen, probably yes. Qahtan, maybe. Queen Arwa will follow their lead. She isn't a techie. She's a ruler," Hettrick told him. "And she's a consummate politician. After all, she had to take over the reins of power when her husband was assassinated."

"I understand that wasn't too difficult for her. The former sultan had the reputation of not playing with a full chess board," Curt recalled. "The story going around is that she was always the real brains behind her husband managing to reestablish royal rule in Yemen when the old socialist government collapsed."

Hettrick shook her head and tossed her napkin on the table. "So much for the rumors. Since I've been in Sana'a, I've gotten more or less the full story on that. It wasn't that the old joint Yemeni socialist government was weak. It's that Sultan al-Badr was stronger. The real scoop with the group is that he was bankrolled by some other very wealthy Muslim royal types in several countries who were interested in helping to finance the Jebel Miswar mining operation. American, European, and Japanese interests wouldn't join the consortium that became Ferron Corporation because the risks were too high with a socialist and so-called popular government in control here."

"Aha! Well, I'd be worried about having the mine and the railroad suddenly nationalized, too, if I had my bucks in it," Curt realized. Then he asked a question that had bugged him ever since they'd deployed to Yemen, "But who the hell are these other Muslim royal types?"

Hettrick shrugged. "Saudis. Pakistanis. Omanis. Maybe Bahrain banks. Or your Brunei family could be involved." Hettrick was referring to the fact that Curt had been awarded the Sultan's Star of Brunei years ago when they'd been there. That award had made him an ex officio member of the royal family of Brunei led by the wealthiest man in the world.

"Jeez, maybe I ought to give Alexis a call about that. Or Alzena,"

Curt mused. His former subordinate officer in the Greys, Captain Alexis Morgan, had resigned her commission to marry the sultan's son several years before. And Curt had a periodic affair going with the Sultan's daughter, Alzena, for years. Although Dyani seemed to fill most of his off-duty hours these days, he still enjoyed the exotic company of the Sultana Alzena when the two of them could manage to get together.

"You do that after we've had a chat with Queen Arwa," Hettrick suggested. "In the meantime, when I called you over here I asked that you look sharp. You're dressed in field cammies," she pointed out.

Curt was surprised. "General, we're in a fighting war here even if no one calls it that. I tried to wash up before I came, but I had little time…"

"I also said that we were going to meet with Queen Arwa and General Qahtan," Hettrick reminded him. "You're certainly not dressed for that."

"General, with all due respects," Curt began, using the usual disclaimer voiced when attempting to tell a superior officer of an error in orders or requests, "you didn't inform me that I was invited along for your royal palaver."

"Well, you are. As Patton once remarked, you should present yourself so that the Queen can see if you're really as much of a sonofabitch as she may believe at this point. Have your Class B field uniform sent over from Amran."

"Uh, I'm not so sure that Major Ward could find it in my quarters," Curt said.

"Well, Captain Clinton or Captain Motega certainly can, can't they? Get them to rustle it up and deliver it here."

"You're right, of course, but…"

"I know I'm right. You're as transparent as a busted window, Colonel. TACAMO!"

"I'm just a light colonel, ma'am," he reminded her. "I don't rate an

ADC. And I won't ask either lady to be a servant to me because they have combat unit responsibilities…"

Hettrick looked sternly at him and got to her feet. "This is a request from your commanding general, Colonel. I would like to have Captain Clinton accompany us to see Queen Arwa. Kitsy was involved in the fracas this morning. She also looks like the cute American innocent abroad. Have Kitsy get over here ASAP and bring your field Class B's with her. Don't forget: We're dealing here with people to whom image means a lot. And this is usually true of most people in the world. A soldier with a full chest of ribbons and decorations cuts more ice than the same soldier in baggy cammies with a Novia - although the latter appearance may be more intimidating to the local populace. We're not out to intimidate the Queen; we've got the unenviable job of trying to act like her police force auxiliary rather than a fighting force far more powerful than her own army. So we'd better try like hell to look as helpful as we can without giving the appearance that we are indeed an occupying military force designed to do something the Royal Yemen Army can't handle."

"Yes, ma'am. I know these people are pretty damned proud of their heritage and especially of their culture," Curt said, rising to his feet as well, "even though we look on it as being something out of the eighteenth century."

"Curt, the Yemeni may not have much, which makes them very proud of what they do have…and the Jebel Miswar mine is one of them because it's helping them build their economy," Hettrick lectured him, perhaps unnecessarily. She paused for a moment, then went on, "And their heritage is something they never forget. And you'd better not either. The ancestors of these people were very civilized. They had most of their basic needs taken care of and were trading civilized luxuries with both Egypt and the ancient Israelis back in Biblical times. Remember the fuss King David went to in order to entertain the Queen of Sheba, which was the ancient name of Yemen? So, look at it this way: This afternoon, you're going to have an audience with the modern Queen of Sheba."

Chapter Seventeen

Captain Kitsy Clinton wasn't the least intimidated about being privy to an audience with Queen Arwa or perturbed about bringing Curt's Class B uniform with her from Amran. And she looked positively smashing dressed for the occasion.

Curt often forgot that Kitsy could look like an impish, innocent, and excruciatingly cute teenager when she wished. He thought her appearance should disarm any suggestion that the Americans were the "great Satans," the "merchants of death," or other appellations given to them over the past fifty years by many Islamic demagogues and dictators.

Maybe that was part of Hettrick's basic psychology in having Kitsy present.

"Thanks, Kitsy," Curt told her when she handed him his Class B uniform. "I must say that you look like a typical hard-bitten American fighting officer with that chest full of ribbons."

Her smile twinkled her eyes. "Why, Colonel, you know it's full of more than that! But, thank you. As for the ribbons, I often wish I had one for every conflict and conquest..."

"As you were, Captain!" Curt admonished her. "Now scat while I change!" Kitsy often had the tendency to go overboard, following her general philosophy that "anything worth doing is worth over-doing."

"Sir, since your valet batman isn't here to help you, I thought I might..."

"This isn't the British Army, Captain."

"And I'm glad it isn't. So, can I be your batwoman instead?"

"Later. Maybe. Stop trying to be the comic relief. You nervous in the service or something?"

"No, sir. I've met royalty before, as you may recall," she reminded him and ducked out.

So had Curt, but he nevertheless was careful to ensure that he was neatly attired for the occasion.

The royal palace in the center of Sana'a looked very much like the hundreds of old stone and brick buildings surrounding the palace compound. It was covered with the usual ethnic Yemeni gingerbread plaster ornamentation. Ancient as it appeared to be on the outside, Curt and Kitsy discovered that this was a mere facade over an incredible interior that was extremely modern in both layout and decor. Armed sentries stood guard at the towering entrance doors to the palace complex, but they were backed up by robotic surveillance, alarm, and security systems that were artfully disguised but apparent to Curt's trained eye.

Inside, the palace was covered and air-conditioned.

"It reminds me of the sultan's palace in Brunei," Kitsy whispered to Curt as a major-domo led the three of them from the massive main entrance back into the lavish interior.

"Slightly different decoration," Curt reminded her. "More ornamentation. More Arabic and Islamic."

"But conspicuous consumption anyway," Kitsy concluded.

"In case either of you is bothered by such lavish quarters in a country that seems to be as poor as this one," Hettrick added as they walked, "please note that even in our republic the White House is lavish in comparison to the way most Americans live. I don't care how democratic a country claims it is, people like the idea that their leaders live as high on the hog as possible. Even the Soviets couldn't break out of that. The power of the national state is often maintained only by image. Now do you understand why I requested that you wear something other than cammies, Colonel?"

If the interior of the royal palace seemed out of place, Queen Arwa Bint Muhammad al-Badr was even more so.

Curt had seen her pictures around Yemen, but these had showed a typical Islamic woman whose head was covered by a black shawl so that only her facial features were seen. In those official pictures, obviously doctored by a professional with an airbrush, the Queen appeared very much like most of the women in her domain.

In person and in the privacy of her palace, Queen Arwa turned out to be a tall, lithe woman apparently of middle age who wore a bright red full skirt and a shining white blouse. Her long legs were bare, and she wore Paris-fashion dress sandals on her feet. She also wore European-style cosmetics that accentuated her large eyes and full lips. Her only concession to Islamic dress code was a filmy white silk scarf over her carefully coifed dark hair. If it had not been for that white scarf, Queen Arwa could have passed as an attractive European or American woman.

She was accompanied by her son, Prince Sultan Qadi Abdul al-Badr, who seemed to be a sallow teenager trying to grow the usual mustache and goatee of a Yemen prince. Qadi had his mother's eyes - large, deep, and dark. But they didn't flash like those of Queen Arwa. Qadi also seemed somewhat petulant. Curt decided that he'd better keep a quiet surveillance on Prince Qadi, who acted like a very spoiled young man.

The other Yemenite in the room was General Qahtan ash-Shaabi, the Queen's defense minister and head of the Royal Yemen Army. He was attired in a uniform that resembled that of the British Army in the tropics except that it was sharply pressed, immaculate, and even well-fitting on Qahtan's corpulent form. Some men are stout, but the word "corpulent" was a better term to describe the General not because of his size but because of the way he sat and moved. Curt also noticed that his general features were slightly different from most men on the Arabian Peninsula; Qahtan apparently had Eritrean Hamite ancestry, a reminder that Yemen was once part of a sprawling Ethiopian empire that had straddled the southern Red Sea.

When Hettrick, Curt, and Kitsy were introduced to Queen Arwa by the major-domo - obviously just a flunky, a super spear carrier on the household staff but one whose only power was as the Queen's personal housekeeper - Queen Arwa also surprised Curt and Kitsy when she spoke to them in excellent American English with absolutely no trace of an accent; "Welcome to my house, ladies and gentlemen! General Hettrick, it's always a pleasure to see you again. And I appreciate that you've brought along two officers of your field command this time. I've met only your staff officers, and I'm delighted to meet some of your combat officers."

"You may not be so delighted, your Majesty, when you hear what I have to report," Hettrick told her frankly, shaking the Queen's proffered hand. "May I present the commanding officer of the Third Robot Infantry Regiment, Lieutenant Colonel Curt Carson?"

Curt stepped forward, ready to salute if required but not bowing to this monarch. Americans do not bow to any royal personage. When she extended her hand, Curt did not shake it but kissed it in the continental fashion. Kitsy and Dyani had told him how exciting it was to have a man kiss their hands. "Your Majesty," Curt murmured in greeting.

But Queen Arwa left her hand extended in Curt's. For an instant, this confused Curt. Then the modern Queen of Sheba said, "The ribbon you wear on the left of the bottom row of ribbons, is that the Sultan's Star of Brunei?"

Several years before, Curt had been awarded that prestigious and expensive bejeweled decoration by the sultan of Brunei not only for his heroism during the visit of the Washington Greys to Brunei but also because the Sultana Alzena had pressed her father to do it. Congress had later approved the award, but Curt didn't wear the jewel-encrusted medallion except when full dress occasions allowed it. Thus, he wore the yellow ribbon with its black and white center stripes - the royal colors of Brunei - on the lower left position of his ribbon array because it was a foreign decoration. "Yes, ma'am, it is," he told her, looking directly at her.

Queen Arwa looked at Hettrick and remarked, "General, why didn't you tell me?" Then she returned her attention to Curt, put her hands on his shoulders, and kissed him on both cheeks in the Arab manner. "A member of the royal family of Brunei is always more than welcome here. I didn't realize until I met you just now that you're the Sultan Qirhtan Muhammad bin Qars. Welcome, Sultan. My house is your house." Queen Arwa touched her forehead and gave a little nod of a bow.

This embarrassed Curt. The award of the Sultan's Star of Brunei automatically elevated the recipient to the status of a member of the Brunei royal family. Curt could therefore indeed be addressed by the title of "sultan" because he was, in principle, a prince of the realm of the sultan of Brunei. But he could never use the title because of army regulations. He had availed himself of some of its perks. His "sister," the exotic Sultana Alzena, had discovered loopholes in army regulations prohibiting Curt from accepting gratuities. As an official adopted member of the sultan's family, Curt had accepted travel in the sultan's aircraft, for example. After investigating the matter of Curt's position as an adopted relative of the sultan, the Judge Advocate General had reluctantly concluded that Curt's acceptance of Alzena's largess and that of her father was no different from any officer accepting family gifts. At least, in their confusion over the issue and until Curt's behavior was considered definitely unethical, the Judge Advocate General decided to leave it alone with the option of acting if it got out of hand. Brunei was a staunch and loyal ally of the United States in southeast Asia, and a mutual trade and military assistance pact existed between the two richest nations on earth. This had put Curt in a very difficult position, and he tried to handle it as best he could.

However, Alzena could be very persuasive with American officials. And with Curt.

"Thank you, your Majesty, but I never use the title or my Brunei family name," Curt replied frankly. "I'm a professional American-born military officer in the Army of the United States. My family has served honorably in the American armed forces for over two hundred years. My primary task here in Yemen is to protect you and Yemen's Jebel Miswar facilities."

"In which case, you're helping protect your family's investment as well," Arwa replied.

This alerted Curt. Maybe Hettrick was right. Maybe Brunei was one of the investors in this Yemen iron ore venture. But he decided that this wasn't the time or the place to push an investigation. He'd make a few telephone calls to Bandar Seri Begawan in Brunei later.

"I'm not here for that reason or purpose, ma'am. In fact, this is the first I've known that the Sultan of Brunei is an investor in Ferron Corporation. I'm a soldier. I'm here under orders of the President of the United States. I don't question my orders. Nor do I ask my superiors why they issue those orders, even though I have the right to do so. And I'm responsible and report to General Hettrick." Curt wanted to, make it clear up front where his lines of authority and responsibility lay. He'd had to do this in the past with the Sultana Alzena to convince her that he couldn't take orders from either her father or her twin brother, the heir to the throne.

Queen Arwa looked at him strangely. This man might be defacto Islamic royalty, but he obviously didn't think like an Islamic man. If she was captivated by this tall, handsome man who was also royalty - and she was - she gave absolutely no outward indication of it.

When Hettrick introduced Kitsy to the Queen, the diminutive captain saluted because Queen Arwa didn't extend her hand. To a large extent the presence of women in the combat units of the United States Army still confused the Queen as well as her defense minister. Strict Islamic law prohibited women from serving as soldiers. In spite of Queen Arwa's American education, she still had trouble with the gender equality that had slowly and carefully developed over the past century among Americans. That she herself was the queen of an Islamic nation didn't bother her. There was ample precedent for it going back even before the Prophet's wives. And it was temporary. The throne would pass to her son, not to her daughters, who were being educated in America and might hopefully marry wealthy Islamic American businessmen. But she did remark to Kitsy, "I'm still surprised by the fact that a lovely young lady such as yourself is permitted to lead combat troops, Captain."

Kitsy had learned a lot of diplomacy since she'd joined the Washington Greys. She still didn't suffer fools, man or woman. But Queen Arwa was no fool. "We're not merely permitted to do so, Your Majesty. It is our proud right to do so."

"Yes, you Americans are obsessed with your rights. I don't

begrudge you that because you're also concerned with the rights of others...which is in turn admirable even when such rights don't exist in the societies of other people," the Queen remarked, then turned and introduced her son and her defense minister to the two Washington Greys.

Kitsy didn't respond. She believed human rights were rights, irrespective of cultures and societies. And that she would fight to bring that about if she had to. Kitsy had little tolerance for intolerance, that being part of her general outlook on life. In spite of the fact that her ancestors had been slave owners two centuries before, Kitsy was living proof that human nature could indeed change.

"What's the bad news you said you have, General Hettrick?" Arwa finally asked when they had all been seated around her conference table.

"Some Yemeni civilians were killed or wounded this morning in Amran," Hettrick reported calmly.

"They were? What were the circumstances?" Prince Qadi quickly asked, a hint of hostility in his voice.

"Someone placed a limpet mine against the street wall of the YEF casern there," Hettrick explained. "It blew a hole in the wall. Two of Colonel Carson's soldiers were injured. Captain Clinton's warbots were on duty at the time. These warbots detected armed individuals through the smoke and dust of the explosion and opened fire on them. Yemeni officials were immediately notified. As quickly as I learned about it, I called your secretary, your Majesty, and requested this personal visit."

"Colonel Carson notified Colonel Salem bin Hassan Rubaya of the Fourth Guards Regiment," General Qahtan added, a note of hostility also in his voice. "I was notified by Colonel Salem. Why was this done in this manner, crossing established lines of authority and reporting, General Hettrick?"

"Colonel Carson, tell them in the way you explained it to me," Hettrick prompted Curt.

Curt sat straight in his chair with his hands folded in his lap. "General Qahtan, Yemeni civilians had been hurt. I didn't know who. I didn't know how many. I didn't know how badly. It seemed imperative to me that the Royal Yemen Army be notified as quickly as possible so that steps could be taken to save the lives of any Yemeni civilians who might have been seriously injured either because of the limpet mine explosion or the subsequent firing of the warbots. I then immediately reported the incident to General Hettrick. To me, humanitarian considerations took precedence over protocol."

"But you and your warbots fired on innocent Yemeni civilians!" Prince Qadi pointed out with an incredulous and hostile tone to his voice. "That is a reprehensible act of willful disregard for the safety and well-being of our citizens!"

"Prince Qadi, my Mary Ann warbots were the ones that opened fire," Kitsy suddenly put in. She wasn't merely sitting straight in her chair. She was leaning forward over the table, her face strangely and intensely serious. "We're here to apologize. But after having one of those civilians plant a limpet mine against our casern wall and having the explosion injure two of my noncommissioned officers, I don't believe the injuring of Yemeni civilians was totally our fault..."

"But you shot them!" Qadi reminded her. *Too bad she's a soldier,* he thought. *She's a pretty woman. Too high-spirited for my tastes, but even the most spirited mare can be broken to the saddle.*

"My warbots did, yes. They're programmed to shoot armed people. They fired on Yemeni carrying rifles."

"Nearly all Yemeni hillmen carry rifles," Qahtan observed. "Then they're going to run the risk of being shot at when we're attacked," Kitsy said with finality.

"Were they attacking?" Qadi snapped.

Kitsy looked straight at the teenaged royal prince and told him, "Look at it this way, Prince Qadi. Yemeni have been firing at us regularly. Yemeni have been ambushing us. Then a Yemeni blows a hole in our casern wall. Through the dust, my warbots see armed men. They don't know, my troopers don't know, and I don't know whether or not these armed Yemeni are guerrillas ready to follow up the destruction of the wall with an assault through the breach. What am I supposed to do? Stand there and wait for Yemarks to pour through the wall and kill my troopers? What would *you* do?"

"I would shoot. Any Yemeni man would shoot. If I happened to kill them, it would be the will of Allah."

"But if I do it, it becomes part of a religious war? Prince Qadi, we're not here to fight for a religion or impose our ways on you. We're here because your mother asked us to come and help!" Kitsy was beginning to flush in anger now at this sallow young man who had no responsibilities and who wasn't in the service of his own country. Maybe Prince Qadi wasn't old enough to serve. On the other hand, Kitsy had fought Iraqis, Turks, and Kurds who were still children and much younger than Qadi. She didn't ask why Qadi wasn't in uniform. She guessed the young man wasn't just sallow but shallow. Maybe his mother opposed his military service. Or maybe the young man was just a coward. Kitsy didn't know and didn't care. But she rankled over being upbraided by a teenager who could have been serving his country and wasn't, perhaps because of his royal position. Kitsy didn't like Qadi.

General Hettrick said nothing. But her eyes told Kitsy to cool it.

Curt quietly laid a hand on Kitsy's arm. It was a signal she recognized at once. She sighed and sat back in her chair. She muttered something in Japanese. Curt thought he understood but didn't press the matter.

"Please excuse my subordinate's remark, your Majesty," Curt said quietly, but to the Queen, not the Prince. This called for diplomacy, and he called up everything that he could remember and that he'd learned from years of association with General Jacob Carlisle and General Belinda Hettrick. He went on philosophically, realizing that the Arabic mind was basically very philosophical and enjoyed poetic-like figures of speech. "We both have eager young people in our organizations. It's probably a good thing to have young people who are committed. It gives older and wiser heads pause to reflect upon their own behavior as well as giving them something to do in passing along wisdom to the young. I'm responsible to General Hettrick for the actions of my regiment. I've expressed my regrets to her, and I took whatever immediate action I could to alleviate possible pain and suffering of Yemeni victims of this unfortunate incident."

Hettrick added, "Therefore, the reason for this visit, Your Majesty, is to offer our formal apologies. I've notified my superiors and I'm sure you'll receive an official apology from the government of the United States."

"You've just given it," was Qahtan's reply.

"No, sir. I can't speak for my government. I'm not part of the diplomatic organization," Hettrick informed him. "That must come from our State Department or our President."

"Where is your ambassador?" Qadi wanted to know, not letting up. "He should be here today."

"He isn't here because this isn't a formal apology," Hettrick explained the niceties of diplomacy to the young man. "This is a report to Queen Arwa and her defense minister from the commander of the Yemen Expeditionary Force. And a personal apology from me and from my officers who were involved."

"I accept your apology," Arwa suddenly spoke for the first time in several minutes. She'd deliberately stood back and allowed her son and her defense minister to vent their anger. She, too, was angry, but she also understood these Americans better than her contingent. She knew they were sincere. She also knew that her country was in a state of semiwar that she couldn't handle alone. She needed American help. Unfortunate accidents such as this were certain to occur, and she was relieved to know that these Americans were compassionate enough to come to her directly about it. She could handle that. Handling her son would also be easy. Handling her defense minister and some of her enemies in the "loyal opposition" would be more difficult. But she would manage. So, she went on, "I, too, have to consider it the will of Allah. Unfortunate, but that's the way it is. None of us could have done much about it under the circumstances. Which is why I feel that it was indeed the will of

Allah. We have little time for recrimination. General Hettrick, you've initiated a new strategic plan which has altered the way in which the Yemeni Marxists and their terrorists must operate. We must devote our efforts to anticipating the preparing for their change in strategy. Don't forget: The enemy wants the Jebel Miswar mine and the railroad intact for whomever is backing them."

"Do you have any idea of who may be behind the Yemarks and terrorists, your Majesty?" Hettrick wanted to know.

"Not really. But we're fighting a new kind of war here, one in which the primary objective is the control of economic resources, not control of land or people," Queen Arwa said, revealing to Curt that the woman had real smarts. Furthermore, she was giving him better insights to exactly what was going on and why the Washington Greys were in her country. "Therefore, I suggest you let me handle the domestic side of this incident, General Hettrick. So please return to the work for which you were called to Yemen. In spite of the Royal Yemen Army, your expeditionary force is the real deterrent to those who want to take over our most precious resource."

Curt noticed the expressions on the faces of Prince Qadi and General Qahtan. He sensed that the two didn't totally agree with her. But he didn't know exactly why or how. He knew he would probably find out...the hard way.

Chapter Eighteen

"Ten days! A whole damned ten days! And not one goddamned thing has happened!" Major Russ Frazier was upset. He was a man of action. He didn't like sitting around.

He wasn't the only one. "Bloody Yemarks are a bloody pain in the bloody arse!" Frazier's feelings were echoed with a typically British viewpoint by Captain Peter Freeman who disliked American cold beer as served in the Club but was partial to Scottish whiskey. Well he should have been since he was on exchange assignment from the 51st Highlanders. "And not one bloody thing to do but sit here and wait for the bloody bastards to decide what they're going to try to do to us!"

The Club of the Washington Greys was the sort of place where anyone in the Third Herd could let off steam. Plenty of them were doing just that on that particular evening.

"Peter, old chap, we're ready for them...I think. Anyway, I wouldn't bitch about the lull if I were you," Lieutenant Colonel Joan Ward told him directly. "We were deployed here to guard the mine and the railroad. We're doing a damned good job of it at the moment because Jerry and Hassan have worked out a strategy that's been successful. No Yemark attacks on either the mine or the railroad since the trains started to run when the Yemarks were qatting about." It was a pun, and she knew it. The Greys didn't pun often, but some had had to develop the talent in self-defense against Freeman and Captain Pat Lufkin who both believed they had a better command of the English language than their American military hosts. And they used punning to try to prove it.

The Greys around the table ignored it. Freeman tried to. But Lufkin fired back with, "Yeah, and it's led to dog days..."

"Bloody place is a bloody bore," Freeman put in. "At least we could be out shooting a few of the blighters for sport."

"Pete, you remind me of another Brit I got to know off in Brunei," Adonica said. "He runs the Gurkhas there. Colonel Pain-in-the-ass. Properly, Payne-Ashwell. He didn't think it was sporting for his Gurkhas to wear body armor. So, they took a lot of casualties."

"That's not being sporty. That's being stupid," Pat Lufkin muttered.

"By the way, Pete, your bloody vernacular style of speaking could possibly lead to another ditty from the Third Herd Sextet," Joan Ward warned him. "There have been rumors..."

It was a typical evening at the Club.

Combat troops don't like to sit around. They get antsy. They fret. Especially if they know that an enemy is out there but isn't shooting at them right then because he may be developing new strategies or tactics to make life miserable again. The Greys - along with the Wolfhounds, Cottonbalers, and Regulars - felt like sitting ducks in their caserns, hamstrung by rules of engagement that didn't allow them to seek-and-destroy but only to sit on guard duty. To Sierra Charlies, that sort of mission was tailormade for regular warbot outfits who could squat on one spot - as they had in the Persian Gulf, Central Europe, and the Maghreb for more than two decades. It was definitely not the sort of military job for the aggressive Special Combat units whose tactics and doctrine depended upon speed, mobility, and shock.

But Curt was somewhat concerned for another reason.

Having made his obligatory rounds that evening, he was sitting quietly at a corner table with Dyani. And he was brooding.

Dyani couldn't help but notice. As the top scout of the regiment, she noticed nearly everything. "You've been very quiet since you finally got the Sultana Alzena on the phone. What did she have to say?" Dyani asked, although she thought she knew.

"Nothing," Curt replied morosely. He was nursing a scotch and water and munching on rather stale nacho chips. Fresh chips were hard to come by in Yemen. Sometimes, the Aerospace Force airlift didn't include any recreational food in their shipments. Sometimes the Greys got ten thousand Type 3 rations made up totally of dried fruits, microwaveable hamburgers, hard candies, and mixed vegetables. Other times, they got no rations at all but only a thousand wool blankets. It was a typical deployment operation, except that everything came in by air from Baghdad.

"Nothing?" Dyani had only a glass of bottled soda. Everyone had to push liquids in this climate just as they normally did in Arizona. Dyani, of course, rarely drank anything more alcoholic than a glass of wine when it was available which it wasn't in Yemen. As the Army had learned in many overseas deployments, "Don't drink the water!" If a country happened to have good public health services, their drinking water could still cause the usual tourist diarrhea which could knock a soldier out of action for a few days. Most of the countries in the world, especially the preindustrial ones, had little or no control over their drinking water. The results had included both dysentery and cholera, in spite of modern biotechnology. In Yemen, most of the wells were polluted by centuries of improper sanitary procedures. So YEF personnel drank bottled water.

"Alzena told me she knew nothing about any investment her father might have in Ferron Corporation," Curt muttered, swirling his glass and its contents.

"I find that difficult to understand," Dyani admitted. It was after duty hours, and she'd taken her long, black hair out of the tight bun in which she normally wore it so it would fit under her battle helmet. It now fell down over her shoulders. She now looked very much a woman rather than a combat soldier. Dyani had a natural, robust, and therefore very sensual beauty, and her close friend Adonica had taught her how to project it. When Dyani really did that in a serious way, she could stop most men in their tracks. And she could also take Curt's mind off his problems. Therefore, she was extremely careful what she did and how she did it because she, too, was a professional warrior. And, as she had admonished Curt many times, they both had to keep their priorities straight. "The Sultan's family operates like a nepotic board of directors. And Alzena is the Brunei minister of the interior. She should be aware of the Sultinate's investments."

"Maybe. Maybe not. She's got her own job to do. So, I think she's telling the truth," Curt said.

"I've spoiled you," Dyani told him.

"About women telling the truth? What's the matter, Deer Arrow? Don't you trust other people?"

"Yes, when I get to know them. I don't know very much about the Sultana Alzena...except that she seems to be good for you. And she makes no demands upon you for her sake."

Dyani's forthright approach to matters always astounded Curt. Although Dyani had answered the question before, Curt asked again, "Dyani, do you have a jealous bone in your body?"

She shook her head and smiled. "You know the answer to that one. Why waste time being jealous? You're dear to others, so you're even more dear to me. And you always come back. Kida, we long ago agreed that variety is the spice of life for both of us...I can get along with that sort of equality."

Curt sighed. "Yeah, some are more equal than others," It was a quiet joke between them. Tonight, he was glad to see that Dyani had apparently totally regained her self-control, discipline, and candor after being hurt during the train rider skirmish.

"It's necessary that you do what you do, Kida. Joan Ward is a very old and very close friend of yours. So is Major Ruth. And Helen Devlin. And Colonel Lovell. Those ladies need you, and you need them. For many different personal reasons. And I shouldn't forget Kitsy."

"Yeah, Kitsy." Curt wasn't sure exactly what was going on there. General Belinda Hettrick seemed to have some sort of understanding, but she hadn't shared it with Curt yet.

Captain Kitsy Clinton chose that moment to approach the table with Lieutenant Hassan the Assassin. "What about Kitsy, Colonel? Here I am! May we join you for a moment?"

"Sure." Curt didn't know what was going on or why Kitsy suddenly showed up with Hassan. However, he'd noticed a growing relationship between the two. He earnestly hoped that it was for real, although Hassan was somewhat younger than Kitsy. Sometimes age differential meant very little, however. Especially in the modern world with all its miracles of biotechnology.

"Hassan seems to think we're in for Big Trouble," Kitsy remarked as the two of them sat down. "I agree with him."

After the brief silence that followed, Curt asked, "What sort of trouble do you mean? Hassan?"

The young officer wasn't hesitant. In fact, in many ways he was as gung-ho as Kitsy and full of zealous enthusiasm. He'd come a long way from the slopes of Kuh-e-Taftan in eastern Iran. Now Hassan was where he wanted to be doing what he really wanted to do. Although he was a naturalized U.S. citizen and a commissioned officer mostly because of his own bright mind, strong motivation, and hard work, he never forgot who had helped him get there. "You must understand that I'm not really an Arab. I'm a Baluchi, a descendant of the ancient Transcaspian Iranians, not a Semite or an Assyrian. However, I speak Arabic and understand the Islamic way of thinking." In many ways Hassan was beginning to show some of the traits of his buddy in the Greys, Jerry Allen. Hassan was brilliant and had the disturbing trait of encyclopedic memory like Jerry. "What bothers me about what isn't happening right now is hard to explain. It's not an Arab trait to step back and contemplate the consequences of the change that Major Allen and I created by getting activities rescheduled to conflict with the Yemeni qat habit. The Yemarks should have shifted almost at once to assaults on our caserns. They didn't."

When Hassan paused, Curt prompted him with one word, "Why?"

"I don't know, Colonel."

"Speculate," Curt told him.

"It's not like them to suddenly give up an offensive operation when it appears to be producing results. They quickly change tactics when the opportunity presents itself. They try something different almost at once. The followers of Mohammed ran into a lot of roadblocks when they exploded out of Mecca and Medina in the seventh century. It was a hundred years before Charles Martel stopped them at Poitiers while the Byzantines held them in the east."

When the young officer with the bicultural outlook paused again, Curt again prompted him, "So much for the historical rationale and justification, Mister. Based on these historical analogues, have you jumped to any conclusions yet?"

"Uh, yes, sir." But Hassan was apparently hesitant to announce a conclusion he couldn't back up with solid data, only hunches. "The Yemarks and the terrorists don't seem to be calling the shots. I suspect they're being commanded or directed by outsiders who are working the strategy and issuing the orders."

"We've speculated about that one. Got any idea who might be behind the Yemarks, then?"

Hassan paused, then replied, "No, sir. But whoever are, they aren't from the Islamic world. Except for America where I had to learn the culture fast, I don't know very much about cultures other than the ones in the Mideast."

"But Islamic interests may be playing a role in the Ferron Corporation," Kitsy pointed out.

"Look, we're not here to spook out who's doing what to whom and who's getting paid for it," Curt remarked testily. "We're here because we're ordered to be here. Because we all took oaths to defend the Constitution and to follow the lawful orders of our superiors. Same reason other American and European outfits have been in the Persian Gulf for decades."

"Longer than that if you count the Brits and the French," Kitsy put in. "We got the crude oil reserves out of the hands of madmen who were behaving just like their Assyrian ancestors. They've been replaced with merchants and traders. Now we've got to do the same with another natural resource our industrial culture requires: iron."

"And we aren't the first army in history that's had to protect mineral resources such as iron. Check the Bible," Hassan advised.

"Oh, yes, I read that cover to cover along with the encyclopedia, just so I'd have a better feeling for America and Americans."

"So, Lieutenant, I asked you to speculate on who might be supporting the Yemarks in a clandestine manner based on this uncharacteristic behavior pattern," Curt pushed. "Who?"

"Not European or American. Not Islamic. Someone else," was all Hassan was willing to put forth.

"Soviets?" Kitsy guessed.

"They've got all the iron and coal they can possibly handle with their unique economic system which they can't get working real well," Curt observed. "And we haven't run into any Soviet weaponry. What we've seen thus far in limited use by the Yemarks is something even our intelligence people haven't been able to identify."

"Oriental?" Hassan wondered.

Kitsy shook her head. "We haven't seen anything that might implicate Japan. I think I know something about the Japanese, and I don't see their fingerprints on anything yet. The Japanese are working hard to integrate the resources of Sakhalin into their economy at this time." Kitsy spoke fluent Japanese and thus could think like a Japanese.

"Chinese?" was Hassan's next guess.

This time, it was Curt who shook his head because Mandarin was his second language. "Maybe. But the only Chinese weapon we've run into thus far has been the A-99 assault submachinegun. The Chinese have sold nearly a hundred million of those guns on the international market. And I see no twinge of Taoist or Confucian thought patterns here. Yeah, I detect some Sun Tzu. But, what the hell, *all* of us pay attention to *The Art of War*."

"Colonel, what I'm trying to say is that I think we should be on our guard for a drastic change in enemy plans and intentions almost immediately," Hassan warned. "Whoever is backing this nasty little for-real hostile takeover of Ferron Corporation and its capital assets has now had time to evaluate our new strategy and to develop some different tactics to counter it."

"What do you recommend, Lieutenant?"

"That we be ready for massive assaults on our caserns, perhaps as early as tomorrow at dawn, sir," Hassan replied carefully.

"Why?"

"The Yemarks have now had time to carry out careful recce of our four caserns. They know where our personnel are quartered, where are weapons and ammo are kept, and where our vehicles and aerodynes are parked," Hassan went on. Then he added almost as a second thought, "And they've also studied our own schedules and daily regimen. They know we're potentially vulnerable early in the morning; they've read about Pearl Harbor, too. And if they like their afternoon qat parties, we like our evening happy hours. They also know that we're lovers as well as fighters, and they know when we like to do each."

"Bullshit!" Kitsy exploded in an uncharacteristic display of emotion expressed in soldier vernacular. It was obvious that Kitsy was very much on edge because of the waiting. "There's no set time for either one! And all of us know that!"

"Well, they've had some opportunity to check out some of the Greys in Amran," Dyani suddenly remarked. Up to now, she'd just been listening in her normal fashion. "And what happened might have been a test of some biological warfare."

"Doctor Ruth and her gang got those four Greys back in shape in about ten days," Kitsy reminded her.

"But they required medical resources that might have been needed to assist Greys injured in combat," Dyani pointed out. "The Yemarks could be testing a form of biological warfare. Venereal disease has knocked out a lot of units in the past..."

"Along with spreading dysentery, cholera, malaria, yellow fever, scarlet fever, measles...all using personal needs and desires."

"I know something about that from history," Dyani said quietly. Then she held up her hand and added, "But that was in a different century and we've all learned a lot since then. I think. However, we should be careful here. There was really no excuse for those four NCOs to do what they did..."

It was suddenly apparent that these two women had widely different outlooks and moral standards. Both were warrior women, modern Valkyries, but each in her own way. As a warrior, Kitsy Clinton was beguiling, aggressive, and disarming because she was also a coy and provocative southern belle at heart and one who tackled everything with gusto. Dyani Motega, on the other hand, was far more primitive, stealthy, and seemingly cold-blooded when it came to doing what had to be done, including killing, but she was also candid, straightforward, and explicit when she dealt with people she liked and worked with. As a companion, Curt knew, Kitsy was enthusiastic while Dyani was lusty.

Ever since Kitsy had returned from medical leave during which Dyani and Curt had become a de facto Pair in the Third Herd, he'd been waiting for and almost dreading the inevitable confrontation between the two. He didn't know how or when or where it would come. Since he knew damned good and well, he'd be in the middle, he did nothing to accelerate or encourage it. He'd been between two women before; it wasn't a pleasant predicament, especially when he cared deeply for both. He also knew that when female furball started, he wouldn't be able to stop it except to evoke his formal powers as regimental commander...which would only delay it further.

Kitsy had also had a couple of drinks that evening that had loosened up her already unfettered inhibitions. "Some of our men don't have the sort of POSSOH you do," Kitsy observed sharply. "And there are more than two men for every woman in this outfit. Don't begrudge some of the Third Herd because they have to go afield. Just be damned glad you had the opportunity to nail your man when the competition was slack..."

"I am," Dyani admitted honestly.

"If I hadn't been in Walter Reed, it wouldn't have been so easy."

"All of us were sorry you had to spend time there, Kitsy," Dyani told her frankly. "Especially me."

"I'll bet you were! Gave you an open field for running, didn't it?"

"No. I presume you've met the Sultana Alzena. And Colonel Willa Lovell."

"Absentee adversaries! As I was!"

Dyani said nothing for a moment but merely looked steadily at Kitsy. Curt was afraid they'd suddenly go at one another tooth and claw. Kitsy had been known to fight for what she wanted. And so had Dyani. But Dyani replied slowly in her concise way, "Kitsy, you're my friend. You're my sister in arms. You're a Washington Grey and a Sierra Charlie. We've fought together, and we've both fought our personal battles to be where we are. So, I won't fight with you. I don't have to. And neither do you." She stood up and went on, "Colonel, I have the duty at oh-four-thirty. I'd like to get some sleep before I put on the OOD brassard. Will you excuse me, please?"

Curt couldn't and didn't say anything, so Dyani left.

Kitsy seemed to be stunned by what Dyani had said. Hassan put his hand gently on her arm. "Dyani's right, Kitsy. Let's go. You don't have the duty at oh-dark-thirty..." He touched his finger to his forehead and said to Curt, "Colonel..."

Curt hadn't said a word during the confrontation, but now he was wondering if perhaps he should have. He suddenly found himself sitting all alone at the table in the corner. Shaking his head slowly in bewilderment, he said aloud, "I'll never figure them out..."

But he wasn't alone very long. Captain Helen Devlin, chief nurse of the BIOTECO, slipped quietly into the chair where Dyani had been. She'd been his biotech when the Greys were a full warbot infantry outfit and had ministered to him going in and coming out of warbot command linkage. They knew one another very well. "Stop trying," she told him. "Some of us are easy to figure out. We just like being there if needed."

"Well, you always have been," Curt noted, recalling their younger days when neither of them bore the weight of their current.

responsibilities.

"Except not enough lately now that my duty station is in the biotech support van. A field biotech has a lot more personal contact."

"Are you bragging or complaining?" Curt didn't care which.

"Want to find out?"

Chapter Nineteen

At 0500 the following morning, it happened.

It was thirty minutes from the beginning of morning twilight, and the hills to the east of Amran were just becoming visible against the lightening sky.

Captain Dyani Motega had taken over as OOD with Sergeant Ed Gatewood as the Noncommissioned Officer of the Day. They were in the Combat Information Center room surrounded by visual monitors and sensor readouts from the Jeeps and Mary Anns stationed at various critical points around the casern area.

"Incoming fire! Incoming fire! This is no drill!" announced Grady, the regimental computer that was monitoring all sensors. Four Mary Anns on sentry duty had suddenly picked up the radar returns of incoming missiles. Grady integrated the data into an overall picture. "Multiple returns from multiple incoming targets! Ballistic rounds! No rocket IR signatures! High-angle trajectories! Possible eighty or one-twenty mike-mike mortar rounds! First target integration indicates mobile regimental OCV, the vehicle pool, and the aerodyne ramp!"

Fortunately, Dyani and Gatewood weren't in the mobile CIC located in Curt's OCV parked in the compound.

It took the first hit, becoming the focus of a brilliant flash and the concussion of a shock wave that broke what few windows there were in the casern compound.

The guard warbot sensors that showed their outputs on the CIC screens simultaneously displayed similar explosions taking place throughout the bot pool and the aerodyne ramp.

Dyani's first action was to slap the Red Alert signal panel. In a way, that wasn't necessary. Those first explosions brought everyone in the Washington Greys instantly awake.

"Grey Head, Grey Day!" she quickly snapped into the tacomm broadcasting on the regimental command freq to Curt with absolutely no hint of panic. "Casern is under possible mortar attack!"

"I just heard! On my way!" Curt's voice came back quickly with urgency in it but, like Dyani, also with absolutely no hint of panic.

"Red Alert! Red Alert! We're taking incoming!" Sergeant Ed Gatewood called over the PA system as well as all tacomm freqs, alerting those Greys who hadn't already been jolted out of their sleep by the explosions. Then he said quickly to Dyani, "I'm just beginning to get trajectory data from incoming radar tracks. At least twelve sources, random dispersion about the casern, average ranges four-point-three klicks! Another salvo incoming! Appears to be a six to ten rounds per minute rate! And continuing!"

"Any incoming appear to be targeted on barracks?" Dyani wanted to know.

"Negatory, negatory! Appears to be concentrated on vehicles, bots, and aerodynes. Heavy emphasis on the aerodyne ramp!" Gatewood reported after he quickly studied the in-coming data bit stream from Grady.

"Damn! They're after our tacair and airlift!" Dyani guessed. Then she toggled the YEF comm net frequency and announced, "Exped Head, this is Grey Day! Grey Base is under attack!"

"Wolf Head, so are we!"

"Cotton Head, ditto!"

"Reg Head, the same!"

"Exped Day to all Exped units! Take cover! Take cover! Get the best data you can on sources and feed it up on the data bus!" Someone in Sana'a was awake. Dyani wondered what the hell they were going to do with the data.

"Captain, they're greasing our skids! Targeting is orgasmic! They must have first-order survey data on every one of our 'dynes and vehicles!" Gatewood observed, switching the information to

Dyani's console.

Dyani took one quick look and reported to a quiet tacomm, "Grey Head, Grey Day! Prelim data from impact coordinates. Looks like we've lost eight Chippies and six Harpies! Also two Saucy Cans, about half of our spare Mary Anns, and most of the larger vehicles in the motor pool!"

At that instant, Curt dashed into the CIC. He was in combat cammies with helmet and Novia, but he hadn't had time to pull on body armor. Krisflex soft armor wouldn't stop anything except small shrapnel from incoming bursts. He hadn't been sleeping in body armor; nobody was doing that. And he didn't want to take the time to squirm into the armor at that point.

"Where the hell did the Yemarks get mortars?" was his first question.

He knew Dyani didn't have the answer, but she replied, "Probably from the same place they got their tacomms, wadi mines, and new assault rifles."

"Go now to NE tacomm," Curt quickly ordered as he assumed command of the situation and slipped into his seat before a console. He triggered his helmet switch and a corresponding console switch that would link the helmet's internal NE tacomm system remotely to the CIC system. *Hellcat Leader, are you up and on yet?* he thought to the tacomm system to the commander of his GUNCO. The neural impulses from his subvocalized thoughts were picked up by the helmet's surface sensors and computer-massaged into a verbal message which was sent to his subordinates on the frequency. NE tacomm was faster than voiced communications, and speed was important in a combat situation.

Hellcat Leader here! came Lieutenant Larry Hall's tacomm "voice" in his head. *I'm making a quick survey now, but it looks like I've lost four of my Saucy Cans in the barrage! Three from Taire's Terrors and one from Freeman's Fusileers!*

Try counter battery fire on whatever targets you can reach! Curt ordered. *Alleycat Leader, any and all available Mary Anns to commence counterfire as well!*

Grey Head, the only Mary Anns that haven't been damaged thus far in the barrage were undercover or in RTVs, Jerry reported with a sense of great urgency in his voice. *We're shagging but the bots are dragging! We need to get them powered up and on the tac data base.*

How long?

Two minutes!

Do it! Warhawk Leader, can you get anything into the air for recce and counterstrike? Curt wanted to know.

Goddammit, Grey Head, I've lost damned near all of AIRBATT! Major Cal Worsham's rough, gravely voice was even evident in his tacomm "voice," and he was so enraged that he didn't punctuate his words as usual. *They even hit the ships I had in revetments!*

Warhawk Leader, can you get anything into the air to counterstrike? Curt wanted to know.

Goddammit to hell, no! I've got a couple of 'dynes that might fly once we get the debris off them! But I can't do anything until I get the fires out! We've got fires! What we didn't lose to incoming we lost to secondary fuel fires! Or to shrapnel! We've got fuel all over the tarmac. We're foaming and misting, trying to keep it from going. We've picked up a couple of dud rounds. Look like vapor explosive stuff. God knows why it didn't work!

Curt could see on the visual sensor screens. The AIRBATT parking tarmac was a first-class disaster scene. Even though Worsham had had his aerodynes parked in random fashion, making use of buildings and revetments where possible, nearly every one of the sixteen Chippewas and AD-40C Harpy tactical assault 'dynes had been hit or suffered very close misses.

Mustang Leader, can you get any birdbots up? Curt flashed his tacomm thought to Dyani who had left the CIC for her own command post in the RECONCO OCV.

Black Hawks have all twelve of their birdbots airborne at this time, came the solid, calmly voiced reply. *Two bots per person. We're heading out to look at the places Grady indicates the rounds were fired from. Damage report: Some shrapnel damage to our birdbot control vans, but the NE equipment is functional!*

While Curt was trying to get some semblance of order into the operations, he'd been joined in the CIC by Joan Ward and Hensley Atkinson. They were quietly and quickly gathering damage reports and estimating losses.

As suddenly and as quickly as the barrage had begun, it ceased. It had lasted less than five minutes.

"They caught us sleeping," was Joan Ward's comment.

"No, they caught us totally by surprise," Curt corrected her. "We had no G-2 to indicate the Yemarks had any light artillery stuff. How the hell did they get it? And how did they move it to within five klicks of us?"

"Obviously, Colonel, the name of the game has changed," Hensley remarked unnecessarily.

"Yeah! Hensley, let Jerry's Mary Anns put a couple of rounds in on those computer-derived targets. Then check the incoming bird bot data for targeting accuracy. Jerry knows enough not to waste ammo, but there's nothing worse than an artillery ambush when it comes to loosening up trigger fingers!" Curt advised her, giving her immediate responsibility for the counterfire coordination. He was doing what a commander should do: delegate so that he could back off a tad to get the big picture.

Curt guessed that this artillery ambush wasn't just another harassment operation. It was too slick, too accurate, and apparently too well-planned.

He didn't need to tell Joan to cover him while he reported up the line. She was reliable, trustworthy, a trained and loyal member of the regimental command team.

"Battleaxe, this is Grey Head," he called on the divisional tacomm net to Hettrick in Sana'a.

"Grey Head, Battleaxe! Did you just take a lot of high-power incoming?" The commanding general of the YEF was obviously online and on top of the situation, judging by the promptness of her response.

"Affirmative! Major damage to AIRBATT, some to GUNCO, less to the rest of the ASSAULTCO gear. No reported casualties thus far!" Curt made his report short and concise.

"Okay, everyone was hit!"

"All the regiments?" Curt was surprised, but then again, he wasn't. He suspected that he'd been hit as part of some grand master plan. It was growing apparent that this was the case. Hensley Atkinson had been right. The game had changed. Radically. For the worst.

"All the units! Except us! Stand by, Grey Head. I'm having you patched into the command conference net," Hettrick's voice told him, then snapped, "Heads report!"

"Grey Head here!" Curt snapped.

"Wolf Head here!" was Rick Salley's reply.

"Cotton Head here!" Maxine Cashier's voice came through.

"Reg Head here!" was Jim Ricketts' response.

"Okay, let Battleaxe here give you all the general picture," Hettrick's voice continued. "Pull up the holomap from the command graphics net."

"We've got it!" That was Edie Sampson who had quietly and efficiently entered the CIC sometime during the fuss and assumed her responsibilities as the regimental technical sergeant.

A holographic map of central Yemen appeared in the CIC holo tank with the Sana'a and the various YEF caserns in evidence.

"Here's the situation as I've gotten it from your verbal reports and off your data nets," Hettrick went on. "All caserns were simultaneously assaulted at oh-five-hundred within a minute or two in each case. That tells me the Yemarks now have outstanding combined arms C^3 that they never had before. In addition, their intelligence data allowed them to go after critical items. First, our tacair and airlift capabilities. According to the reports from the regiments, you've lost all or nearly all your aerodynes. The secondary targets were the LAMVAs with the Saucy Cans guns; they didn't get them all, but our long-range regimental artillery capability is seriously degraded as a result. Most Mary Anns and Jeeps seem to be operable. And they didn't go after the barracks; personnel losses are practically nil, just a couple of minor scratches.

"Initial G-2 analysis indicates a major corps-level Yemark operation. Furthermore, they were able to move these large and well-organized units into Yemen and deploy them for the assault without alerting the RYA," Hettrick said with a sigh of frustration.

"General, was the RYA looking for them?" Maxine Cashier wanted to know.

"They're supposed to," Rick Salley added.

"Negatory! What they're supposed to do and what they did are two different things."

"Obviously! So, what else is new?" came the growl from Cashier.

"Apparently, their patrols didn't encounter the new Yeniark units." Hettrick was also pissed off at the lack of effective recce on the part of the Yemen army. She knew that her regiments couldn't maintain constant surveillance of the southeastern corner of the Arabian Peninsula; she didn't have the resources to do it, and Washington maintained that it was the RYA's mission. Her regimental commanders knew that, so she didn't waste time complaining to them about it or listening to their complaints, either.

And because everyone in the Pentagon "knew" that the adversaries in the Yemen operation were only small bands of guerrillas and isolated terrorists, they hadn't provided her with even hours-old satellite surveillance data - although she could request real-time reconsat data if she thought she needed it.

This was one time she figured she needed it, and in the past few minutes her request had gone up the line through her staff over her code cipher.

"We'll have to depend on our own recce efforts for a few hours," she reminded her colonels. "Get your birdbots up. As soon as you have recce data, put it online to Sana'a."

"My birdbots are up," Curt told her.

"So are mine," Maxine Cashier added. "We're in this frigging valley, and the birdbots are the only eyes I've got beyond three klicks in most spots."

"Our birdbot data is going on the line now," Salley reported.

"You'll get it when I get it, General," Ricketts said, not saying that he had just had his birdbots launched less than a minute before. Nor did he report that his Regulars were pretty badly shaken by the attack. They'd been sitting down on the hot, humid coastal plain overlooking the Red Sea, and they'd had practically no contact at all with either Yemarks or terrorists during their entire deployment in Yemen. As a result - and Ricketts was reluctant to admit it since it was basically his fault - the Regulars had gotten complacent and a little lazy. In the first place, the humid heat hadn't helped. It was tough to operate where he was. And the Regulars were a brand-new Sierra Charlie outfit. This was their first combat mission. They were green troops.

Grey Head, Mustang Leader reports no targets where Grady indicated, Dyani's NE tacomm voice sounded in Curt's head.

No targets? Did you check the whole spectrum? Curt asked. That was a dumb question on his part. Dyani was an outstanding scout and she wouldn't overlook something like that. But the sudden heat of the fight and the haze of battle didn't keep commanders from asking dumb questions any more than their subordinates.

Affirmative! But Black Hawk Four and Eight have spotted something new. It's on the visual bus now, Dyani added.

"Battleaxe, we've got some new raw data coming up on visual," Curt reported to Sana'a. "My recce leader reports it to be unusual..."

He looked over at the video screen, then commanded Edie, "Put it on the one-meter display! Can you clean up that snow?"

Edie did her magic ritual with the equipment.

What Curt saw and what was simultaneously transmitted to Sana'a as well as the three other regimental CICs was a shock.

The screen displayed a stabilized aerial view of two boxy, tracked vehicles visually camouflaged against the sandy tan background and even exhibiting some infrared stealth. Sergeant Emma Crawford in the Black Hawk bot control van was combining spectral images to provide the best possible resolution and definition of the targets.

Short-barreled guns were mounted on these two vehicles, and they were surrounded by four other vehicles either tracked or multi-wheeled, it wasn't possible to see from the high sensor angle. They were moving, increasing the range from Amran. The guns showed IR signatures indicating they'd recently been fired several times.

Not a single human being was in sight.

"Armored, self-propelled artillery!" Salley attempted to identify them.

Alleycat Leader! Curt ordered via tacomm. *Get target coordinate data from Grady's processing of the vehicles' position! Fire at will!*

Grey Head. I've got the data! Targets are beyond Mary Ann range and moving quickly out of Saucy Cans range. We won't have the Saucy Cans up and ready to fire before the targets are beyond range of even Saucy Cans rocket-boosted rounds. Jerry's report wasn't good. The enemy was going to get away without being hit.

"Edie, what the hell are they putting out in the EM spectrum?" Curt suddenly asked.

"Wait one, please," Sampson replied and did more magic things with equipment. Then she reported, "I can't see much, sir. An occasional weak signal that could be side-lobe or backscatter."

"Multiple parabolic SHF lens antennas on all of them," Maxie Cashier, the most techie of the four regimental commanders, observed. "Curt, you got EMW gear on those birdbots?"

I heard. Negatory! Objective was to obtain high spectrum scans to identify potential Saucy Cans and Mary Ann targets, Dyani replied in Curt's head. *Our birdbots with EMW and ECM gear are on the ground at the moment. All birdbotters are full-up handling the bots they've got aloft.*

"I'm taping the weak side lobe stuff from those antennas even at this range. It splatters a little bit. Primitive antenna design. Real crude stuff," Edie reported. "But Grady doesn't have the synthesis power to extract signal from the noise. Better squirt it to Georgie even though the signal will be further clobbered in long-range transmission..."

"Hold it!" Maxie Cashier suddenly snapped. "Look! Between one of the artillery vehicles and the lead vehicle!"

"What the hell did you see, Max?" Hettrick asked.

"There! Again! Intermittent. Pencil beam being scattered because of the dust being kicked up by the vehicles! Laser command and control beam! Curt, get your techies on that! You've got the first-generation data there. You might be able to extract modulation for analysis..." Cashier had turned out to be a tough combat commander when the Cottonbalers converted from Robot Infantry to Sierra Charlie, and she'd come up fast through the regiment - as Curt had done - because she was both a tough combat officer as well as a consummate techie. She'd spotted something in a relayed image that Curt and even Edie Sampson had missed.

"Edie, enlarge it! Zoom in on it!" Curt snapped at almost the same instant that Sampson anticipated his request and did so.

There was dead silence in the CIC as people's attentions were riveted on the expanded screen.

They saw the pencil-thin beam of light between vehicles, first one, then to another.

Everyone breathed the same word almost simultaneously: "Warbots!"

Chapter Twenty

"Warbots?"

"Yes, Mr. President." Retired Admiral Nelson J. Fetterman, now Secretary of Defense, replied as the tape loop picked up by Sergeant Major Edie Sampson played through on the video monitor again.

"And this happened how long ago?" the President wanted to know. It was 8:30 A.M. in Washington. Less than an hour ago, the President had read the item about the Yemark assault on the four YEF caserns in the daily intelligence briefing as he was eating breakfast in the family quarters of the White House. He'd scrambled his aides to call an emergency meeting of the National Security Council, canceling his morning's meeting schedule. This included a stand-up press conference at 10 A.M., which he knew would cause trouble almost at once.

Fetterman looked at his watch. "Anyone know what time it is now in Yemen?" he asked.

General Albert W. Murray, head of the National Intelligence Agency, touched his own watch which gave him an instant time zone answer. "It's now four o'clock in the afternoon over there, Mr. Secretary." Al Murray knew the retired admiral on a first-name basis. He also knew a great deal about the former CNO and National Security Advisor. Such inside information had helped Murray remain head of the National Intelligence Agency since the nation's intelligence agency had been reorganized and re-staffed following the massive screw-ups in Trinidad and Namibia.

"Why did it take so long to notify me of this attack on our armed forces?" the President wanted to know. He wasn't a military man or a techie. Two administrations ago, he'd been the Veep, but he hadn't been involved in the Brunei affair. He had no military experience whatsoever and paid little attention to the military situation in the world. The scion of a wealthy California family, the

President was primarily a "social scientist." He paid even less attention to modern technology which he considered to be dehumanizing.

The National Security Advisor, retired Air Force General Philip C. Glascock, put in, "It's rather complicated, Mr. President. If you'll give me five minutes, I'll pull a visual out of Tricky Dicky." He was referring to the White House megacomputer and its enormous data base which could be supplemented by networking with any government agency megacomputer.

"I think I can give a one-minute briefing on the procedure since I helped set it up," Murray interjected, not wishing to get on Glascock's downwind side but merely seeking to keep things moving in this meeting. He'd square things with Phil later. "Mr. President, the video we just saw was recorded by one of the regiments of the Yemen Expeditionary Force. It was transmitted via satellite to YEF headquarters in Sana'a which then transmitted it to Georgie, the army megacomputer in Arizona that's being used as the YEF's cybernetic support. Georgie transmitted it to Old Hickory, General Pickens' mega-cray over at the Army Chief of Staff shop, which forwarded it to Tiffany, the Joint Chiefs' silicon brain. Tiffany distributed it to the various intelligence crays, and your staff picked it off the net and included it in the morning's intelligence brief. Your staff had the data in hand by midnight. Apparently, they didn't feel that it warranted waking you."

Murray didn't add that he'd gotten the information through a clandestine tap into Old Hickory. He'd known about the Yemen attacks about an hour before it showed up in Tricky Dicky at the White House. And he'd already seen highly processed images produced and confirmed by his own NIA "national technical means." One does not remain America's top spook through three administrations without staying well ahead of the power curve. Nor by revealing everything one knows, especially if the information doesn't happen to be crucial to national security. Murray liked his job and felt he could do it better than most Washington weenies. He was also a man truly dedicated to the United States of America and didn't like to play political and diplomatic games beyond those required to stay where he was. Four years of the United States Aerospace Force Academy plus a thirty-year active military career had produced a man of dedication to true duty, personal honor, and his nation's welfare.

"I ought to be immediately advised whenever any violence is perpetrated against Americans anywhere in the world!" the President insisted, forgetting for the moment that he'd issued orders to the contrary shortly after taking office three months ago.

"Sir, if that was the case, you'd never get any sleep," his national security advisor told him.

"The Yemen operation is Lima Four, Mr. President," the Secretary of Defense reminded him.

The President was primarily absorbed in battles with Congress about revised domestic social, tax, and economic incentive programs. He'd left matters of national defense to his underlings such as General Glascock and his Secretary of Defense. "I can't follow your military jargon, Phil. Refresh my memory. What's Lima Four?"

"A level of defense response priority," the National Security Advisor reminded him. "Number One is a preemptive strike against the continental United States, the red telephone stuff. It requires approval of strategic defense activation and strategic retaliation forces. A Level Two means that a major military confrontation has been initiated by a Red Player - one of a number of potential hostile entities. Lima Two means significant numbers of our forces and those of a friendly, treaty nation are involved in armed conflict. Lima Three is triggered whenever there's major military action against major American forces involved in protecting western security or friendly treaty governments - for example, the Persian Gulf Command, the Sakhalin Police Detachment, the Maghreb Mission, and the European Stabilization Forces. Lima Four means an assault against minor American forces deployed overseas under economic and military support treaties to assist a friendly government in protecting primarily economic assets with American investment which provide significant tax income to the federal government. The Yemen Expeditionary Force is Level

Four, sir, along with the Panama Canal Patrol, the Belgrade Conventicle, and the Pakistani Punjab Support Patrol."

"Activities involving Lima Four aren't considered of significant importance to warrant anything more than an agenda item in a normal NSC meeting," Fetterman added. "They're brush fires."

The Vice President, normally only an observer in a National Security Counsel meeting except as an executive officer for the President if an NSC finding and a subsequent executive order needed wide-screen real-time overview, spoke up for the first time. "Then why are we in emergency session this morning, General?"

"Because," intoned General Edwin R. Gross, CJCS, "we believe it should have special treatment."

"This is the first time since Sakhalin that our forces have encountered hostile warbots," the Army Chief of Staff, General Jeffrey G. Pickens, put in. "This is also the first time that hostile warbots have appeared in the Middle Eastern region of operations."

Although the Chief Executive didn't understand the reason for the generals' concern, he asked, "Whose warbots are they?" As far as he knew, only the United States, some European allies, and the Soviet Union had war robots. This is what he'd been told in various security briefings. But he wasn't a military man. As the former Vice President, he'd handled only scientific assignments from his boss because he, too, had come up through the groves of academia. The Party had groomed him as a safe liberal who would stay bought. One Congressional term from a safe academic district had qualified him for the ticket as Veep. This had led four years later to the presidential nomination and subsequent election as President. The leadership of the party had been so decimated by his former boss that the party was in a panic mode. He'd won only because the ill health of the immediate past President (of the opposite party) and the subsequent decision not to run for a second term had left the opposition party in a worse leadership bind.

"The warbots haven't been identified yet, Mr. President."

The President did something he didn't normally do. He called upon General Al Murray, the chief of the National Intelligence Agency who'd played the Washington power game so well that no President thus far had been able to unseat him. In an unstable twenty-first century world, continuity of intelligence resources was crucial. Besides, the President suspected that Murray knew. Most of the White House staff did, but they could have their heads handed to them if there was any leak about the biobimbos in the basement. Thus, the President was always concerned that he or one of his administration might suddenly get a FAX or call from Murray stating simply. *Leave town at once, they've found out.* However, he stroked the NIA chief by asking, "Got any inputs about that, Al?"

Murray did. But he had nothing he felt so positive about that he'd play guessing games in this group. This administration wasn't as squeaky-clean as the previous one. Too bad the former President had had health problems that prevented him from running for a second term. The former President hadn't been corrupted by the feeling of absolute power that runs through the White House because he knew he didn't have absolute immunity. Carefully, Murray began, "Our allies have warbots, and we know something about them. We know that these aren't French warbots that Societe Anonyme de Robotique has sold to some Third World countries. They aren't Russkie robots because we've got good information on their Silver Pilgrims - primitive copies of our old, obsolete Hairy Foxes. The Japanese *may* have some warbots they've upgraded from industrial bots because they've got a robotics lab at the University of Ashikawa that's doing clandestine warbot development. But the Japanese really don't need warbots. They're a very low-profile military power. They manage to get others to do their military jobs for them. And we believe the Chinese probably got some of the old warbots we lost on Kerguelen Island about six years ago…"

It sounded like a complete intelligence briefing to the President although Murray was only reporting what everyone in the room - except the President - already knew. If the President seemed weak on national security and technology issues, that evaluation wouldn't be very far from being absolutely correct. "What's your best guess?" the President wanted to know.

"Sir, I don't guess unless I've got enough information to make a well-educated guess…" Murray began.

"All right, then! I want your speculation."

"Not even speculation, sir. I've got only a hunch."

"I want to know what your hunch is."

Murray paused before he replied, "Indo-Sino-Japanese."

"How can you justify that?" the Secretary of State huffed. Dr. Andrea M. Pruitt was a former presidential advisor who, because of her prominent position as the chief of an influential think tank affiliated with an Ivy League university, had been actively pushed on the President as the new Secretary of State because of her collectivist world view. She'd tangled with Murray before. But, in her case, Murray *really* had very solid data. Pruitt also knew that Murray knew. Although she never availed herself of the White House biobimbos, she had her own "domestic maids." So, she didn't push too hard. She couldn't afford to.

"Madam Secretary, the President asked for my hunch. A hunch cannot be justified," Murray admitted. "You'll have to be accepted as just that, for whatever it's worth."

"Not worth much…" Pruitt grumbled.

"But better than no hunch at all," Fetterman put in quickly. He'd have the DIA look into the situation. NIA and DIA were supposed to cooperate and share information. But that was an agreement that existed only on paper. Information was a valuable commodity in Washington. And, just to make sure, he'd contact some retired colleagues who'd been in Naval Intelligence because once an intelligence officer, always an intelligence officer. Sometimes, Naval Intelligence had better information than anyone else.

"How many of our soldiers killed or wounded?" was the President's next question. From his tone, it was one that he didn't want to ask and really didn't want to know the answer.

"Twenty-six," Fetterman replied.

Murray knew there had been more.

"All Army," Pickens added.

"Oh, my God!" the President breathed.

"I think it's important to understand," Vice President Hamlin put in quickly, "that over five thousand Americans live and work in Yemen in technical and managerial positions. We have about six hundred military personnel there to protect assets. Five hundred are army, the rest are Aerospace Force support troops at Sana'a International Airport which didn't get hit."' Henrietta Hamlin was the mother of a naval academy graduate, a daughter who was still in the Aerospace Force Academy, and another daughter who had become a warbot brainy captain following graduation from West Point. She had none of the aversion to the military services that her President exhibited. Furthermore, she knew something about the military as a result of her offspring. "A four percent loss rate isn't disastrous, Mr. President. And only six killed. About one percent. We lose more than that in some war games and training exercises...or in automobile accidents. The military profession expects losses when fighting starts."

"That's why we're doing what we're doing, and that's part of the unwritten unlimited liability part of our contracts," said General Willard F. Walden, Aerospace Force COS.

"Well, I don't expect it!" the President snapped, irritated. "I have to answer to the news media, Congress, and the American people in that order! It was part of my campaign platform that no Americans would be sent to fight in foreign lands!"

"Mr. President," Andrea Pruitt remarked, "everyone knows that a candidate always makes read-my-lips promises. And you didn't send troops to the Persian Gulf, Europe, the Mahgreb, or even to Yemen. They were there when you took the oath of office. Your predecessor sent the troops to Yemen." She could get away with making such a statement to the President. She, too, knew where bodies were buried.

"Andrea, my military people don't seem to be able to tell me a lot about what's going on in Yemen," the President replied. Instead of taking umbrage, he put her on the spot. "I presume you've spoken with your ambassador in Sana'a. What's his report? What's the real situation?"

"I came directly from my home to this meeting, Mr. President," the Secretary of State told him in equally direct terms, "I haven't seen what's on the departmental wires this morning. I haven't had the privilege of getting an early morning brief yet. But our ambassador to Sana'a is currently on leave in Minnesota."

"What have the reports from the embassy in Sana'a been saying? Did they anticipate this assault?" he wanted to know, not letting up on her.

"They did not anticipate this coordinated assault. They don't know who's involved. I have seen no red-flagged reports from the Sana'a pouch," she replied succinctly.

Murray knew that red-flagged reports had been sent on the State Department net and in the diplomatic pouches. They'd gotten to State but they hadn't gotten to Andrea Pruitt. As one might suspect, copies had gotten to his agency. His experts had briefed him that the situation was normal in Yemen: an ongoing low-intensity civil war mixed with another ongoing long-term series of pot-shotting by hill tribesmen accompanied by sporadic banditry. He also knew why the Yemen Expeditionary Force was *really* there.

"Get Roger in here," the President snapped. He didn't understand why his press secretary wasn't on hand anyway.

"Mr. President, Roger's up to his neck in slime," was General Glascock's comment. "This meeting of the NSC conflicted with your press conference scheduled for this morning. He told me he'd be here as soon as he could figure out a good reason for cancelling the news conference and as soon as he managed to toss some oil on the troubled waters of the news media."

"Anyone know if the media's gotten the news about Yemen yet? Are they getting ready to splash it all over the evening news?" The President needed to know what was going on here because what the news media were doing at the moment would play a major role in determining what he would do in the next hour or so. He played a very opportunistic game with the press.

"Sir, if they haven't got stringers in Sana'a, they've got crews on the way," the Chairman of the Joint Chiefs spoke up. "I got the ungarbled word from my ADC on my way over here. The news vultures are already circling over the Pentagon."

"Okay, that forces my hand," the President decided. "I promised that during my administration I'd disengage American military forces from overseas entanglements. I intimated that I'd bring them home. And I promised not to send any more troops to foreign countries. So, this is a good time to start. And Yemen is a good place to start it. We're not going to lose any vital economic resources there. But we can continue to lose equipment and lives. So..."

The President made a decision on the spot. He waited for no further information. He wasn't really accustomed to making decisions that affected or would affect hundreds of thousands or perhaps millions of people now and in the future. The decision he made was based on emotion, just like millions of other decisions made by people in powerful positions.

In the long run, he made the wrong decision.

In the short term, some of the people in the meeting room also believed with sinking hearts that he made the wrong decision.

"Bring them home," he snapped in what he thought was a decisive voice.

"Sir?" Secretary Fetterman asked.

"Bring home the Yemen Expeditionary Force," the President elaborated, then tried to explain why he'd come to that decision. He shouldn't have had to do that. The proper decision-making process would have involved first getting input from everyone in the meeting room, discussing the pros and cons, and then announcing his decision. As it was, the President's decision was a fiat. "Nelson, get them out of Yemen in the fastest possible manner with the least cost and minimum risk to your evacuation equipment and people."

General Jeffrey G. Pickens, Army COS and former commander of the Persian Gulf Command, got red in the face. "Mr. President, a withdrawal from Yemen at this time poses a serious threat to our other forces in the Persian Gulf..."

"You told me you have several divisions in the Persian Gulf area.

How will pulling one division out of a backwater like Yemen affect their military posture?" The President knew nothing at all about it, yet he felt that, as commander in chief of the armed forces, he should try to speak with some assumed authority at this point.

"For one thing, Mr. President, it will be perceived as an expression of overall weakness and lack of resolve by the people there," Pickens tried to explain. "It's going to cause Secretary Pruitt some trouble..."

"General, we can handle the diplomatic situation quite well, thank you!" Pruitt snapped. But she had never been to the Middle East; she didn't know how the people there thought. "As you recall, pulling the Marine Corps out of Beirut had no ill effects..."

"Madam Secretary, I beg to differ with you," came the quick but respectful comment from Lieutenant General Littleton T. Waller, commandant of the Marine Corps. He didn't get red in the face because he already was. But his face took on the look of a belligerent bulldog. "We had to go back later and deal with the consequences...at an enormous cost, one that we're still paying on the installment plan."

Secretary Fetterman held up his hand. It was obvious that his service chiefs didn't like what they were hearing. And they didn't approve of their commander in chiefs newly announced military policy. But he was a retired admiral, and he hadn't made it through a long military career without knowing the rules of the game. "Gentlemen!" he snapped. "I have been given a direct order by our commander in chief. I am verbally transmitting that order to you now. We'll cover with the paperwork later today. We have been told to withdraw the Yemen Expeditionary Force. We have no recourse but to do so." He would talk privately with the President later today and attempt to get the decision either reversed or delayed. But that would have to take place privately or else the President would lose considerable face and clout in his own National Security Council.

He turned back to the President and folded his hands on the table before him.

"Any further matters we should discuss?" the President asked rhetorically, realizing that he was the only one who could adjourn the meeting. When he met with impassive faces around the table, he quickly said, "Then let's turn policy into action. Meeting adjourned!"

Chapter Twenty-One

Two nights after the attack, Stand-to wasn't really a Stand-to. But the Club was the Club. It was a badly needed place to get a few moments of relaxation during a period of high intensity recovery and increased surveillance and security. The guard had been doubled. As a result, fewer Greys were in the Club. But they were there out of choice because they'd had two days of ten-in-one MRE rations. Thanks to the combined efforts of Captain Harriet Dearborn, Sergeant Manny Sanchez, and Flight Sergeant Harley Earll, the Club had a supply of nonreg rations including Class Six stuff. The fact that Sanchez was an excellent cook resulted in Club food that temporarily alleviated the age-old complaint of all soldiers everywhere and anywhere: food.

Except that Captain Peter Freeman didn't agree. He was still operating with the British Army's traditional class separation between officers and NCOs. That was something the American Army had nearly eliminated in the combat arms because officers and NCOS differed mainly in what they did and how they did it. Freeman was also used to the lovely, close-knit class-stratified society of the British Isles, and it showed.

"I can't wait to get out of this bloody place!" he groused over his warm beer.

Kitsy had had about all she could take from this Brit. She couldn't get a flicker of interest out of him. Neither could any of the other ladies of the Greys. True, Freeman was polite and mannerly in his indifferent way. But he bothered the hell out of the ladies of the Greys because he usually acted as if they simply were not there at all. Hensley Atkinson, who was only second-generation British-American, thought she understood this. She suggested that Freeman ignored ladies because he was actually afraid of them. "Peter, old chap, we're stuck here and you along with us," Kitsy told him directly. "Don't you understand? When in Rome the thing to do is to shoot Roman candles."

Freeman ignored her remark, which infuriated Kitsy even more.

"And you've been warned about your excessive use of the word 'bloody.' Too bad the Third Herd Sextet isn't all here tonight," Adonica put in. Some of the ladies were ganging up on Freeman, making themselves so obnoxious that he'd have a hell of a lot of trouble ignoring them. As many of the men of the Greys had learned very quickly after coming on board, the ladies of the Greys were not to be trifled with, much less ignored. They were very strong individuals who could also be very feminine when the time was right for that. "Rumor Control reports that at last they've got a song just for you, Peter."

"Matter of fact, they did," Pat Lufkin said, never passing up the opportunity to get a humorous dig in at the expense of the Brit. Although both men had sworn allegiance to the same sovereign, that was where their commonality ended. He turned and said to the young platoon sergeant at the next table, "Betty Jo, enough members of the Sextet here to premier your new song?"

"Well, we haven't had time to do a lot of practice," she replied with a smile, "but let's see if Captain Otis will string along with us. Jamie Jay brought his guitar. If we haven't got all of the Third Herd Sextet present, maybe we can tune up the Sierra Charlie Menage a Troi." She got up and went looking.

"Now you've done it, Pat!" Kitsy said with mock seriousness.

Curt came in just as the trio was tuning up. He joined Kitsy at her table with the others. He said nothing but he looked whipped.

"You look beat," Kitsy observed.

Curt nodded. "If it wasn't for the fact that we didn't lose any personnel - only twelve Greys superficially wounded - that artillery attack would have whipped us. Damned near all our air capability is gone. About half the Saucy Cans are out of action. And no sign of the enemy." He sighed.

"You need..." Kitsy began, noticing that Dyani hadn't accompanied him.

He looked at her. "I need some hot food and about a week's sleep...alone," Curt muttered. He would have enjoyed some companionship, but Dyani had been constantly and conscientiously carrying out her duties and responsibilities as his S-2 and the commander of the RECONCO.

"Yeah, Dyani's a slave driver," Pat Lufkin admitted. "This is the first couple of hours I've had free since the casern attack."

"Captain Motega isn't about to let another one happen like that, Captain Lufkin," Curt told him sternly. "And she can use your help. I might suggest that you get your belly full, then go back and give her a hand."

Lufkin suddenly realized that he'd stepped in it. "Uh, yes, sir. But I run the SCOUT platoon, and I'm not trained to run birdbots, Colonel."

Kitsy realized that Curt was again laboring under the burdens of command. He was a man of action. He utterly detested the orders and ROEs that restricted the Greys to a purely defensive shoot-back position. Yet he could do nothing about it. And he was upset that the Greys couldn't go on the defensive offense in response to guerrilla attacks on the casern. The game had changed. A larger and better equipped force was aligned against them...and he didn't know enough about it to do very much. However, he realized that even with the revised doctrine in Yemen, the Greys had lost too much by remaining on the defensive.

"Curt, Harriet Dearborn says the requisition for replacement aerodynes, warbot, and vehicles went out this morning. When I came off duty a few hours ago, I saw the terminal message from. Georgie confirming Harriet's request," Kitsy reminded him. "The stuff is being pulled out of ready reserves in Belgium and Bahrain."

As TACBATT commander, Jerry had seen it, too. "I expect the Aerospace Force logair operation will start funneling the stuff into Sana'a within the next twelve hours. So, we'll be fat within a week, Colonel," he added.

"I'll believe it when it gets here," Curt told them. Some of Dyani's realism had rubbed off on him. "Right now, we could hold off a frontal assault on the casern if the attackers didn't outnumber us by more than five to one."

"The Yemarks would have trouble concentrating that much manpower in the streets. and buildings around the casern," Adonica pointed out.

"Captain, fighting in an urban environment is a little different from the sort of open-field running we're good at," Curt reminded her. "Buildings allow an enemy to concentrate firepower vertically. I learned the hard way in Munsterlagen. You weren't with us in Zahedan or Windhoek…"

"But I was there in Rio Claro," Adonica reminded him of an urban battle on Trinidad when she was still a "native guide."

"So you were," Curt recalled and nodded deferentially toward her. "I stand corrected. My apologies, Adonica."

When Curt used her given name rather than her rank, she knew it was a personal apology. Colonel Curt Carson could be a brass-plated martinet when the situation required it. He was also a true leader, a commander who led by acquiescence of his subordinates, not because he threatened or insisted upon strict disciplinary protocol. "Apology accepted, Colonel. I know you've had a lot of other things on your mind in the past thirty-six hours. But we've got it under control for right now. So, sit back, get a hot one, and let's see what the remnants of the Sextet are about to reveal to their eager fans, Colonel," Adonica advised him.

"Eager fans, my bloody arse!" Freeman said.

Even under stress, members of the American military forces have always kept their sense of humor. In a way, it prevented them from becoming fanatics and zealots. Every war, every engagement, every operation or mission has given birth to a host of cartoons, jokes, and songs. In this case, the creative songsters of the Greys had come up with a ditty that poked a little fun at one of their own, albeit on exchange duty, and at the intolerable situation they found themselves.

"Ladies and gentlemen…and in some cases I am using that term quite loosely," was the announcement from Captain Elwood Otis with whom the other two members of the truncated Sextet had gathered over near the wall, "tonight you're privileged to be at the premiere of a new composition whose authors prefer to remain anonymous in order to protect the guilty. We believe it sums up our opinion of the present situation. However, in the terminology of a special member of the Greys, the composer has titled it, 'Bloody Amran' or 'Slaughter In Sheba.'"

Jamie Jay Younger ran a few chords on his guitar, and the three of them began to sing:

> *This bloody town's a bloody fuss;*
> *With a bloody train but no bloody bus;*
> *And no one cares for bloody us;*
> *No bloody sports, no bloody games;*
> *This place gives us a bloody pain.*
> *Oh, bloody! Bloody! Bloody!*

> *They raid all day and bloody night;*
> *They give all of us a bloody fright;*
> *Best bloody place is bloody bed*
> *With bloody blanket over bloody head;*
> *So they will think we're bloody dead.*
> *Oh, bloody! Bloody! Bloody!*

The room rocked with laughter. And one British Army captain suddenly realized that the joke was on him. So, he laughed, too, in order to uphold the fable of British good humor. The fact that these ruddy rebellious colonial Yanks had pulled it off on him caused him to start thinking about how he might retaliate at the proper time.

Kitsy laid a hand on Curt's arm. "You're laughing. That's better!" she told him.

"Damned few things to laugh about here," Curt said with a smile still on his face but the concerns of command still in his mind. "At least, this ditty wasn't aimed at me the way the last one was!"

"Why, Colonel, I thought that the Third Herd Sextet had done you proud, sir!" Adonica said with a smile. She was joking with him, too, trying to improve his spirits. It was a bit nonreg and it broke the cordon of discipline into which the Greys had restricted themselves since the attack on their casern.

Curt couldn't get angry with someone as good-natured and as wholesome and beautiful as the little blonde captain. He realized Kitsy was right. The situation in Amran was bothering him deeply, and he saw that he was tending toward a little too much zeal and fanaticism in his concern for his regiment.

"Colonel, relax," she went on. "I know Dyani. Right now, she's super-dedicated to preventing another surprise attack. She'll level off once she's absolutely certain that she's got her surveillance and reconnaissance systems set up to her liking. The worst thing anyone can do right now is to try to budge her from her decided course of action. That can't be done."

"Yeah, you're right about that, Adonica," Curt said. He knew Adonica and Dyani had a "sister" relationship because the two of them were so alike in many ways and so different in others. Adonica knew as Curt did that when Dyani decided duty called, the call of duty drowned out every other call.

"Manny has some good roast beef tonight, Colonel," Kitsy remarked. "It was radiation cured so it didn't spoil when the mortar rounds got the refrigerated warehouse. And he's done some magnificent things with the ten-in-one veggies."

"More army rations?" Curt replied with distaste.

"Manny did wonders with them tonight. Have faith."

"If I didn't have faith, I wouldn't eat army chow at all," Curt admitted, beginning to lighten up.

Kitsy gave her little laugh, then told him, "You've had to make decisions all day. So, let me order for you tonight. You just sit back and enjoy."

But when his dinner came, Curt didn't get the chance to eat it. Or even sample it.

He was sorry that, as the regimental commander, he had to carry a tacomm brick with him at all times, especially in the hazardous situation in which they found themselves. It put him on call every hour of the day and night. As he started to dig into the dinner the tacomm signal beeped at him.

"Dammit! I knew it! Let my guard down for a moment to relax...!" Curt growled as he picked the tacomm brick off his belt, lifted it to his face, and thumbed the switch. "Grey Head here!"

"Grey Head, this is Grey Day!" came the voice of Lieutenant Jerome "Jay" Taire, the OOD. "Signal from Battleaxe! Come to Red Alert! I say again, come to Red Alert! I am therefore sounding Red Alert. Grey Head is requested in Grey Command by Battleaxe ASAP!"

Curt stood up. "Grey Head on his way!" he snapped into the brick, returned it to his belt, and said in a loud voice to the occupants of the Club, "Red Alert! Party's over!"

"Damn!" Kitsy swore under her breath. She was just beginning to get her colonel unwound, something that might have led to something else, especially since Dyani was obsessed with casern security and recce. Kitsy had learned subtlety, but that hadn't overwhelmed her forth-right demeanor.

The reaction among the others in the Club was immediate. Each of them had a Red Alert station and duty. The result was a noisy but ordered press toward the doors. Whatever was on the tables was left there.

No one wanted a repeat of the previous morning.

Curt paid little attention to anyone else. He knew where he had to go and where he had to be and what he had to do. As he erupted out of the basement door and dashed up the steps in the cool evening air, he noticed that the casern was silent save for the sounds of Greys moving to their Red Alert stations.

He heard no gunfire.

What the hell is going on? he asked himself unnecessarily. He quickened his pace, knowing that he'd find out once he got to his CIC and talked with Battleaxe.

In the CIC, the regimental staff was already on stations, some of them looking just a tad shy of tactical because they'd come up from a deep sleep or from other recreational activities. But there was no question about the fact that they took a Red Alert seriously. No one yawned. No one acted tired or sleepy. This was much too serious. Until they found out what was transpiring, it could be a matter of life or death.

"Grey Head, Battleaxe here!" General Belinda Hettrick's tone of voice was serious and steady when Curt called. She didn't have holographic transmission up, much less video. Sometimes those broad bandwidth comm features required too many channels in a situation where everything had to be shoehorned into as much C3I as possible. "Curt, here's a quick sit-rep. The Imam Mohammed al-Badr International Airport - Hell, that name is too damned long! It's the Sana'a airport! It's under attack by unknown forces! The initial RYA reports suggest brigade strength or better."

That didn't sound very good. In fact, it looked like things were shaping up into a very shitty situation. All the YEF supplies came in via logair through the Sana'a international airport. "General, enemy strength in a night attack is always overestimated," Curt reminded her. "Is it just a raid? Or are they trying to take over the airport?"

"Too early yet to tell. I'm assuming the latter."

"Does it look like it's the same warbot-type force that clobbered us yesterday morning?"

"Yes. Warbots plus new jellyware. Soldiers, not guerrillas. Organized combat units. But the RYA hasn't identified them yet."

Curt had half-expected this.

Hettrick had given Curt a background on this because she was well aware of his expertise in tactics. She was good and she'd trained Curt, but she knew she'd trained a real genius. Hettrick wasn't a turf guard; she'd use any and all help she could get. She went on, "I've got no combat troops here in Sana'a to mount a counterattack. The RYA wants the glory of defending Sana'a. So, the Second Guards Regiment of the RYA is engaged and the Fifth Guards Regiment is being called in. But I've got to be ready when they get creamed."

"What do you need from us, General?"

"First of all, I want you to be prepared for imminent assault on your casern."

"We're ready, Battleaxe."

"And I need whatever birdbot assistance you can provide from Amran."

Curt turned to his COS. "Joan, get a reading from Dyani. How well can Dale Brown's birdbots hack it at a range of forty-five klicks?" He thought he'd be able to provide some reasonable recce data from birdbots at that range, but it was getting out there insofar as distance went, and he wanted to be certain.

"Yes, sir!" Lieutenant Colonel Joan Ward snapped.

"Could do very well, Colonel, if we could get a relay established between here and Sana'a in an ACV," Edie Sampson told him.

"Work on that scenario for right now, Edie," he told her. "But I don't know if we can spare the Sierra Charlies and warbots to protect it."

He returned to the command tacomm net. "Battleaxe, Grey Head has query out. An answer forthcoming RSN. Has the Yemark assault succeeded in taking the logair facilities yet?"

"Affirmative! And they've blown two Charlie dash twenty airlifters unloading on the ramp," Hettrick passed the bad news to him. "No report on Aerospace Force support casualties yet, but it doesn't sound good. Any chance of some tacair support if the RYA needs it?"

"I can get a brace of Harpies up," Curt told her.

"Make it so! But don't spool up those Harpies until I give you a go."

"Mission? Targets?"

"I'll tell you as soon as we get some decent recce and coordinate it with the RYA," the YEF commander replied. "Frankly, the Royal Yemen Army is a royal pain in the ass! Every one of their high command appears to have suffered a double-lobed Lebanese systolic stroke. I told General Qahtan that he now has a new armed adversary in Yemen, at least brigade strength, maybe two brigades, armed with warbots and artillery. He claims they're re-armed Yemarks!"

"He doesn't believe you?" Curt asked incredulously. "Even after we took it in the shorts yesterday at dawn?"

"The Yemeni high commander doesn't believe any external military force of that size with those weapons could have infiltrated into Yemen without him knowing about it…"

"My CWB says we're not up against Yemarks any longer," Curt told her. "This is a new outfit. They don't fight Yemark style. They attacked us at dawn from a distance and let light artillery do the job on us because we weren't expecting it. I'll bet they've regrouped and concentrated their forces to attack the Sana'a airport. Which they did at an equally unanticipated time shortly after sundown. Those are not Yemark qat-chewer tactics!"

"I know it. You know it. But my G-2 can't confirm it, and we're getting zero G-2 from Gulf Command and the Potomac. And Qahtan doesn't have any intelligence operation to speak of."

"Goddam! Obstinacy in the face of evidence! Failure of intelligence!" Curt remembered what had happened when Guderian broke through the Ardennes because Gamelin ignored both British and Swiss intelligence sources. Or what had happened with something called Operation Market Garden. "When is Queen Arwa going to sack him? After the palace is captured?"

"And replace him with who? Her dopey son? Hell, I'm not even sure Qahtan isn't wired into this somewhere," Hettrick shot back.

"Colonel, RECONCO has birdbot data on the bus," Joan interrupted him.

"Good G-2 coming at you, General," Curt told Hettrick then began to study the images and the computer-generated tactical situation plot now centered on Sana'a and the international airport. Curt was no longer a raw battalion or regimental commander. He was experienced at evaluating the computer-generated data derived from reconnaissance and presented in icon form on large unit tactical displays. What he saw, he didn't like.

"General, I think I'd better put together an evac convoy for you," Curt tacommed to Hettrick. "Those bastards almost have the airport! The RYA units look like they're pinned down…whether Qahtan will admit it or not! We may have to get you and your staff the hell and gone out of Sana'a before dawn!"

"Dammit yourself, Carson! My colors don't run!"

"Well, as my Brit exchange officer might say, better part of valor and all that, y'know!" was Curt's rejoinder. "So, relocate the YEF headquarters to Amran where the Washington Greys have something left to secure your GHQ. You're sure as hell not going to find much left of the RYA to protect you in Sana'a. Not by dawn! Not at the rate they're taking losses at the airport!"

Chapter Twenty-Two

"Goddammit, Curt, I can get my own ass out of the sling here! If I have to! When the time comes!" Hettrick asserted. "We have good G-2 now. If you can keep birdbots up and functioning, I can watch this fracas develop. And I'm calling in whatever I can get in the way, of birdbots and tacair from Rick Salley at Huth! So don't figure you're the big hero here. Don't forget: We've got the whole Iron Fist Division, not just your Greys..."

"Rick is cut up badly. So is Maxie," Curt reminded her. "And Jim Ricketts is down at the bottom of the hill..."

"Ricketts wasn't hit bad," Hettrick reported. "And he's damned near as close to me as Salley. But you're my source of intelligence right now. Keep those birdbots up and looking. Figure on getting some more birdbots from Salley..."

"General, all my birdbot operators are now linked..."

"So have Salley send some up to you. He's got a flyable Chippie."

"So do I. Or I'll have one or maybe three in about six hours once Worsham's people get them fixed," Curt's AIRBATT commander was obsessed about getting something, anything, back into the air. Without the Harpies and Chippies, he and his AIRBATT were only gravel grinders with the rest of the Greys. AIRBATT and AIRMAINCO had been hard at work for nearly thirty hours now cannibalizing 'dynes that had been written off and using the parts to fix other aerodynes that hadn't been so badly damaged during the dawn attack. Curt didn't try to joggle Worsham's elbow about this. Cal knew what he was doing. So did his people. And they were more than just slightly motivated to get as much as possible back into the air.

"I didn't think Worsham would stay grounded! Curt, do what you can to regroup, repair, and recover," Hettrick told him confidently. "We haven't lost this one yet. I know your operational status. Same for the other regiments. I've got my staff working counterattack ops plans at the moment. So, I want you to start thinking about what you can put together in terms of a quick retaliation force. By quick, I mean within the next hour. I called everyone to Red Alert, but not to defend their caserns. I'm going to kick a little butt down at Sana'a airport. I'm not going to stand by and let the frigging RYA lose it. It's critical."

"Hell, General, looks like the RYA has lost it already!" Curt advised, studying the tac display. The enemy had overrun the American logair facility and was concentrating on the control tower with its communications and air traffic radar.

"Oh no they haven't! I'm going to let the RYA retreat across it while they create enemy losses. That gives us time to get the sort of intelligence data we need to effectively counterattack. It buys us time. And it's going to take time to get the Regulars, the Cottonbalers, the Wolfhounds, and the Greys up and joined to the fight." She paused and said something off-mike to one of her staffers, then came back. "I've got a sheep screw to manage here. Continue to monitor the tac net. Get your people and warbots ready to move. By air. By ground. By camels, if you can find any this late at night. Gotta go! Battleaxe out!"

"Her combat code name is sure as hell appropriate," was Regimental Sergeant Major Henry Kester's quiet comment.

Curt checked a few displays and sensor outputs. "Edie, what's our security situation?"

"No enemy tacomm frequency activity in this area," the regimental technical sergeant reported from her position on the other side of the room. "I don't see any hostile sensor inputs, ground or air."

Deer Arrow, Grey Head! I want you to keep as many birdbots over Sana'a as you can and keep feeding me data on the bus, he called to Captain Dyani Motega, using the neuroelectronic regimental tacomm channel. *Give me a casern threat evaluation, please! Any suspicious targets within artillery range of the casern? In short, tell me what it looks like out there!*

Grey Head, Deer Arrow here! Negative threat at this time. No suspicious targets within fifteen klicks. We're getting the usual Yemeni infrared targets, mostly open cooking fires. Few chemical targets smelling like Yemeni or sweaty desert troops except in the rail yards where the up-train is arriving from the coast. Everything nominal. Dyani's report was short, clipped, concise. *I see no casern threat at this time. What was the reason for the Red Alert? The Sana'a airport fracas?*

Affirmative. Continue to maintain casern security surveillance.

*I can put SCOUT out in the neighborhood...*That was typical Dyani, wanting to put human scouts out just to make absolutely, positively certain.

Curt wanted all his Sierra Charlies ready to move by whatever, means he had available when the order came down from Battleaxe. *Negatory, negatory! I want SCOUT available for a possible Sana'a airport counterattack mission within the next hour. Put as marry birdbots as possible over Sana'a airport. And stand by to be supported by Wolfer birdbots. You're the primary source of Battleaxe intelligence at the moment,* Curt told her quickly.

He toggled off, swung around in his chair, and verbally addressed his staff in the Combat Information Center. "If you were monitoring the YEF command freak, you know that Battleaxe expects us to be able to execute a counterattack on Sana'a airport within the next hour. Start all the operational activity necessary to mount that mission. Hensley, are we going to have enough airlift to hack it, or are we going to have to go on the ground?"

"Both," she came back at once. "AIRBATT will have two Chippies ready. Best they can do. Another Chippie in four hours. Another by dawn."

"How about tacair?"

Hensley shook her head. "One Harpy. Maybe two."

"I need to know now!"

"Two!"

"I'll count, on it. The airport attackers apparently don't have tacair. If they do, they're not using it."

"Colonel, they probably don't need it," Kester pointed out. "They seem to be doing just fine without it."

"We'll keep our eyes up and open on that," Curt decided. "And as for AIRBATT, get them spooled-up. We'll use whatever Harpies we have available for Chippie cover as first priority. If we don't have any enemy counter-air, we'll use the Harpies to pound sand at the airport." A regimental tactical plan was beginning to come together in Curt's mind now that he had a mission.

Somehow, he guessed that the existing ROEs had gone down the tube in the last hour.

Preparations for a quick-reaction mission required a lot of time and effort as well as a lot of communication with the various units of the Washington Greys. What would have taken days or even weeks in earlier times could now be done in hours because of modern high-rate and super-secure communications. With lots of speed-of-light communications, tactical operations could be accelerated and, just as important, coordinated as in no previous centuries. The modern regimental comm nets were extensive and interlinked through computers serving as gateways. Digital modulation schemes, signal compression, and frequency hopping allowed a lot of information to go back and forth in the limited electromagnetic spectrum along with multiphased multitransmitter radio frequency communications operated in quasineural net mode. Optical fibers transmitted even higher bandwidth signals wherever such light cables could be used. Where fiber optics didn't go, lasercomm could if it was line-of-sight. Several military comsats were up there and being used by Edie at the moment. She had lots of comm capability.

Technology that would have been extremely difficult or even impossible fifty years before was now commonplace. Even the effects of sand and heat on electronic gear were now minimal, thanks to what had been learned in Operation Desert Shield and since. Curt didn't think much about it, nor did he have much of a sense of wonder about it. He knew that what was impossible for one generation of engineers was difficult for the next and commonplace to the third.

"Incoming aircraft," Kester announced. "Flight of two. All tickety-boo. Identified by beacon code as Wolfhound Chippies."

"Rick Salley's support," Curt muttered. "Stand by in the AIRBATT revetments to land them."

"We're ready for them," Hensley replied curtly.

"Six more targets inbound from the northwest," Kester added. "The Chippie group from the Regulars."

Things were beginning to come together. But where were Maxie Cashier's aerodynes? He raised her on the divisional tacomm channel. "Blue Maxie, Grey Head here. You going to join the party?"

It took a moment for the regimental commander of the Cottonbalers to respond. "We're coming, Curt! I wanted to wait for my full compliment of Harpies to be ready. You got room for all of us there?"

"Bring your shoehorn, Blue Maxie," Curt advised her.

"Grey Head, Battleaxe here!" came Hettrick's voice. "Keep them in the air! Mount up the Greys! Those bastards attacking Sana'a airport are making faster progress than I thought they would. We need to get Operation Sanitation on the move. Activate Operation Sanitation!" The ops code was an obvious play on the name of the Yemeni capital city. It was also obvious to Curt that Hettrick had overridden the regulation that required the divisional megacomputer, Georgie, to select an ops plan code name from random word lists.

Curt didn't need to pass along the order. His staff heard it. Curt rose and started to pull on his harness. "Joan, the show is yours here."

Joan Ward whirled to face him. "Dammit, Curt, the ops plan procedure calls for you to stay here! You're the field commander for the Operation Sanitation combined regimental combat teams!" She believed that Hettrick had made a wise choice in doing that because Curt was a tested leader, a tactical genius, and an experienced combined arms commander.

"You know damned good and well that I don't lead from the rear area, Joan," he replied quietly, donning his battle helmet and checking out the picocomputer circuitry and displays. "With our truncated forces and having to leave some units in caserns for base security, I can't afford the possibility that this thing will get out of control because of three other regimental commanders in the FEBA." He knew that once the fight got going, the 1868 observation by the French military historian, Ardant du Picq, would be validated again: "*A force engaged is out of the hands of its commander.*"

"Well, then, I'm sure as hell not going to sit on my ass here," she told him. She could do it and get away with it. She was like a sister to Curt, and they'd been through some deadly sheep screws together. So, she got up and started to prepare for combat, saying to Pappy Gratton, "Major, you're next in staff line of command. Take over here. The Colonel and I will transfer the CIC to our Chippie."

This didn't bother Pappy at all. An older man, he did an excellent job as regimental adjutant. Officially in the Army records, he was a Rated Position Code 42, Personnel Systems Management Officer. He'd been shot at and shot back along with all the other Washington Greys, but he really didn't like it. It wasn't that he was a coward. Far from it. His Purple Heart had been earned the hard way in Iraq, and he had a Bronze Star as well. Pappy was an outstanding military administrator, and he'd fight when he had to. But Operation Sanitation didn't require him to fight...yet. He would if he had to. Every Grey would. But Curt wouldn't order his staff or SERVBATT into combat unless it was absolutely necessary. SERVBATT people were the ones who usually got killed or wounded because they weren't really prepared for combat the way TACBATT troops were. That made a difference.

Curt said nothing to counter Joan's actions. If he was going out where he could take the Golden BB, he couldn't insist that she stay safely in the rear. She wasn't disobeying orders because he hadn't given her an order to remain in the CIC. He was the one who was disobeying not an order but an ops plan procedure. Hettrick would be pissed, but that was expected.

Sergeant Major Edwina Sampson stood up and began to get ready.

At which point, Kester remarked, "Where the hell you think you're goin', Sampson?"

Edie looked at Henry, the only NCO in the regiment who outranked her. He was already wearing his combat gear. "I'm going with the regimental commander, the chief of staff, and the regimental sergeant major, that's where!"

"You're supposed to be here in the CIC running C3I and EW," Henry told her.

"I've thrown the necessary patches. I can run what I need to through Grady by remote. And I'm supposed to be with the regimental commander. As I recall the overall ops plan calls for you to remain in the CIC when the going gets greasy...and it's plain you're going out to cover the Colonel's minus-x. So, get the hell off mine!" Edie Sampson was a redhead, she had a short fuse, and Kester quickly saw that this was one of those times when the fuse was burning short. "Dammit to hell; he grumbled *sotto voce*, "it's getting' so I don'' have no goddamned authority over nothin' around this outfit anymore..."

"That's because you're the regimental sergeant major," Edie reminded him.

"Why the hell don't the two of you just get married and make the fighting SOP?" Joan asked them unnecessarily. It had been known for years that the two of them were more than just very good friends.

"And make it official? Anyway, who needs it?" was Henry Kester's cryptic response.

Curt listened as he completed kitting-out. He knew it was precombat jitters relief. It meant that things were nominal, copasetic, tactical.

He wasn't particularly concerned about being where he wasn't supposed to be. It wasn't Hettrick's style to micromanage her commanders. Her job, she believed, was to let them carry out the ops plan and to be available for solving problems they couldn't in the field. In spite of all the C3I available to a regimental commander, Curt didn't feel he could really stay abreast of combat action if he wasn't out there in the middle of it. He knew Hettrick would go ballistic when she discovered he'd left his CIC. But that would be just Tango Sierra because, when she found out, he'd already be over Sana'a airport with the rest of his Sierra Charlies.

Frankly, he was just happy as all hell that the Greys were going to get the chance to do something at long last.

Kitsy wasn't. She accosted him as he was dashing across the compound toward one of the waiting Chippies. "Goddammit, Colonel, why the hell are Russ and his Ferrets getting free airline tickets to Sana'a when we've got to crawl on our tracks over fifty klicks of lousy road at night? Why...?"

Curt cut her off. "Because we haven't got enough Chippie lift. Because you've got to cover Larry's Saucy Cans. Because that's the way the ops plan was laid out. Hell, yes, it's far more dangerous than riding there in a Chippie. Hell, yes, it's going to require leadership. Hell, yes, it'll take guts to move toward the fight on the ground at night. But you know the plan. And have you forgotten? No guts, no glory..."

"Guts and glory. That's me, I guess," Kitsy sighed. "I suppose you're going to tell me to shut up and soldier?"

"Damned straight! Because I have to tell you that damned near every time anyway. Why should this mission be any different?" Curt liked the little captain's spunk and her desire to be first in the fight. She was a terrier in love and war. She never failed to snivel when she got orders that might make her late to a fracas. So, he added a little less sternly, "In case you didn't notice, Kitsy, you're commanding a short battalion of two companies. The fact that you do an orgasmic job of it will look good when I recommend you for gold oak leaves. So snap and pop. The people we're supposed to be supporting are getting their skids greased at the moment on Sana'a airport. Get your part of this dog and pony show on the goddamned road before the RYA gets wiped out and we end up with the whole fucking job!"

She smiled. She might have been pissed, but this was her colonel.

Up there leading, not sitting on his ass in the rear area. Out there taking the incoming with the rest of them. On the offensive at last. Following in the tradition set by Belinda Hettrick and Jacob Carlisle and the other former commanders of the Washington Greys stretching back to the Revolutionary War. Kitsy knew she was Number Two in a lot of areas - second in the slot behind Jerry for the next potential regimental commander, second in Curt's love life, and second in Operation Sanitation. She knew it could be worse; she could be Number Umpteen in some outfits. And sometimes, as in the past, Number Two could shine brightly enough to become Number One Point Five for a while.

The UCA-21C Chippewa Assault Transport Aerodyne was full. Sierra Charlies, Mary Anns, and Jeeps filled nearly every available cubic meter. Curt clambered up to the flight deck where Lieutenant Nancy Roberts was piloting. She'd closed the cargo doors and was spooling up to lift when he strapped in. Edie Sampson settled into the other available flight desk seat where she could watch the ECM displays.

Glancing at the clock displayed on his helmet visor, he muttered, "We're late. We're supposed to be at the point of departure in five minutes."

"No later than the Cottonballs, Colonel," Edie said, pointing at a display screen. "Those are the Cottonbaler aerodynes just coming into sensor range. They've got to climb out of the Wadi Miswar valley. Not a rapid climb rate with the ambient temperature being as high as it is."

The density altitude was having a definite effect on the Chippie in which they were riding. Curt felt and heard the turbines spooling up and felt the Chippie shake as Nancy valved slot flow for lift. But it didn't lift. She not only went to 120 percent or Military Emergency Power on the throttles, but Curt also noticed black smoke pouring out of the slots as she activated the water injection system.

The Chippie rose from the ground with great difficulty. As its landing gear cleared, Nancy's neuroelectronic "voice" announced, Positive rate! Gear up!" And she flipped the aerodyne slightly sideways to get some forward motion, aiming it down the valley toward lower ground in an attempt to supplement active lift from the turbines by velocity lift from air speed. She was good. She knew just exactly how to maneuver the big aerodyne to get the maximum performance out of it in its overloaded condition in a hot and high situation.

Debris and other parts from some nearby unoccupied Yemeni buildings that had been wasted in the earlier assault flew up past the 'dyne, blasted there by the Chippie's downwash. Nancy kept it in ground effect as long as she could while she built up air speed.

When she finally got a good, positive vertical rate established, she steered to join up with the Chippies coming in from al-Luhaya and Wadi Mawr. The Wolfhound Chippies were hovering ahead, waiting for the join-up.

On the displays and on his helmet viewer, Curt saw their active air cover, Harpies, breaking ground from Amran as well as weaving around on the periphery of the assembling aerial armada.

"On to Sana'a!" Curt said unnecessarily as the aerodynes formatted. It might have been an unnecessary order, but Curt said it because he remembered a similar war cry now nearly two centuries old, "On to Richmond!" The similarity wouldn't make some persistent rebs in the Greys very happy, but that was the least of his worries at that point. The vertical envelopment flight swung around to the southeast and moved out to initiate the counterattack against the unknown warbot forces tearing up the Sana'a international. airport.

The Americans would need that rallying cry before that night was over.

Chapter Twenty-Three

The Chippie suddenly jinked wildly, throwing Curt against the restraint harness that held him to the seat.

The threat display on the panel in front of Nancy lit up in flashing red letters:

THREAT ALERT! THREAT ALERT!
INBOUND MISSILE.
SIGNATURE: SOVIET SA-77 OSSAH.
IMMEDIATE AUTO-VASIVE ACTION TAKEN.

"Thanks for telling us in advance!" Edie bitched.

Curt heard and felt something come loose down in the cargo hold. He hoped it wasn't critical. A warbot that had pulled its strap-downs and was rattling around in a maneuvering aerodyne was worse than the proverbial loose cannon. The warbot weighed more.

The Chippie kept up its evasive maneuvers as the threat panel continued to announce additional Soviet Wasp Baby SAMs coming its way.

Warhawk Leader, Fancy Nancy here! Can you please do something about the idiots launching these Wasps? Like blow their lips off maybe?

You read my mind, Fancy Nancy! Warhawk Leader has a make on the launch sites! We're rolling in on them at this time!

Harrier Leader is with you! Warhawk, we've got so marry launch points down there that two of us will be needed to suppress them!

Goddammit, Hands, stay on CAP!

The Wolfhound Harpies have us covered for counterair, Warhawk. I'm not going to let you have all the fun.

They were well within visual range - and Wasp range - of the Sana'a international airport. The airport was a black hole against the lights of Sana'a save for the floodlit parking aprons and the lights on the various buildings and hangars. The single 3500-meter north-south runway was visible only because he couldn't see the runway lights. But he did see fires burning and the bright flashes of explosions on the tarmac and around the major buildings.

He also saw the glowing residual trails of the incoming Wasps as well as the smoke trails of those that had just missed. This was unusual. Soviet SA-77s didn't leave either a smoke trail or such an obvious glowing infrared trail. Right away, he guessed that these weren't really Soviet-made Ossahs. They had to be ripoffs. Solid propellant rocket technology was worldwide now. So was the solid-state and sensor technology that allowed an SA-77 Ossah guidance system to be mass produced for less than ten thousand dollars. That could be done by anyone who had the technology to make thirty-year-old integrated circuit chips. A lot of nations had that capability. In fact, the United States Army had to deal with some of them in order to get IC chips that were no longer in production in America or Japan.

Whoever was behind the attacking force down there - and the outfit that had clobbered the Greys a few days before - could be a new factor in the international threat equation: An emerging expansionist country just coming through the advanced industrial phase with the in-house capability to handle the technology that had created the American "smart weapons" of fifty years ago. This could put a whole new spin on the sort of brush-fire wars and "armed conflicts" of the twenty-first century. Any technology will filter down after half a century, especially when a huge smokestack industrial base isn't required to support it. Electronics was one of those technologies. Composite materials was another. So was rocket propellant chemistry.

Edie Sampson had noticed it, too. "Those aren't Russkie missiles, Colonel! Crude copies. Boy, would I like to get my hands on one of those Wasps to see who made it and how they simplified it! Preferably before someone shot it at me."

She stopped and listened intently to her helmet audio sensors which, were giving her information she hadn't patched through to Curt for fear of overloading him with data. "Uh, Colonel, now that we're closer to the action, I'm picking up the voice modulation on the enemy tacomm nets. It's very highly accented and inflected English! Sounds like pidgin English. Or broken English."

That didn't seem strange to Curt. The international language of science, technology, and military operations was Broken English. "Record it. We'll get an accent analysis when the megacomputers have some time to do it…"

The sky lit up with the flash of a nearby explosion followed by the orange light of jet fuel on fire.

Fancy Nancy, this is Red Ned! We took a Wasp! I think I can get us down! I've got enough power left to do it! I think!

A Chippie is a big target, but it's also a difficult machine to destroy. A single Wasp probably wouldn't do it unless it happened to hit a vital spot on the big ship. It had been designed and built with damage-control redundancy in mind. It had multiengine power and engine-out capability. It could stay aloft with a 50 percent power loss, but not for long when heavily loaded. Lieutenant Ned Phillips would have to find a spot to set it down…and fast.

Harrier Leader will follow you, Red Ned. I'll give you whatever cover I can!

Roger! Thanks! I need your landing lights. Mine are gone. I need to see where I'm squatting this beast, so I don't bend it any more than it already is! We'll have to abandon this mother when we touch down. I've got uncontrolled fire in two fuel cells. I've pulled all the fire bottles there.

Curt was far more concerned about the Greys aboard the flaming aerodyne that he saw slowly descending just barely under control.

Major Russ Frazier, First Sergeant Charlie Orndorff, Biotech Juanita Gomez, and all of Clock's Cavaliers were aboard. Fifty percent of Curt's assault force was in that Chippie. He quickly ran an evaluation in his head. Without Frazier and the Cavaliers, would he have enough manpower and warbot power to hold up his end of the airport assault?

Ferret Leader, Grey Head! Keep your channel open and give me continuous sit reps! Curt snapped via tacomm to Russ Frazier in the damaged aerodyne.

Grey Head, it's out of my control! Ned's gotta get this frisbee on the deck! If he gets it on the deck! In one piece. Or pieces big enough we can walk out of! Right at the moment, this situation has a very high pucker factor! Very high! Shit, we could damned well buy the farm in the next few seconds! was Russ Frazier's reply. There was no hint of panic in Russ's voice; he was a seasoned fighting man. But Curt did detect that the man was scared. Who wouldn't be, trapped inside a damaged aerodyne going down in flames with an unknown chance that the pilot could land it rather than lose it and crash?

Curt was rapidly coming to a conclusion he didn't appreciate. Operation Sanitation, in common with damned near everything else that had happened in Yemen, looked like it was turning out to be one of those missions where everything went wrong. Things had been bad to start with, and they were continually getting worse. What made him mad as hell was the fact that most of it was beyond their control. They'd been hampered by highly restrictive ROEs. As Sierra Charlies, they were mismatched to the whole Yemen operation from the beginning. They'd had very bad G-2 from the very top. And they weren't prepared to encounter the sort of high-tech weapons systems that had very suddenly appeared on the Yemen scene.

But orders were orders, and orders had to be carried out.

Maybe he could save it. Maybe the Greys could pull it through.

Maybe there was no chance.

But Curt had to try. He knew the Greys would try. They didn't run from a fight. They never had. The regimental colors were topped by dozens of streamers, but the colors had never been cased in black. A black burgee had been flown on numerous occasions, placed there by the Greys themselves and later removed as a result of their superior performance and their honorable and devoted dedication to duty.

These were the dark thoughts that ran through Curt's mind, ones he carefully screened from any possible transmission to the troops via the NE tacomm unit in his helmet.

Now is the time for real leadership, he told himself.

Wolf Head, Grey Head here! One of my Chippies with about half my force is going down! We need to patch that hole in the counterattack! he flashed via tacomm to Colonel Rick Salley who was also out there somewhere in a Wolfhound Chippewa.

Grey Head, Wolf Head is tight already! Do my best to cover. What flank were your disabled forces covering in the assault?

The tactical plan called for the YEF to approach the airport from the west and land on the RYA's right, creating a flanking attack from the air. The concept was to retake the terminal and control center on the west side of the runway and hold it while the GUNCO and Clinton's Cougars moved up behind the YEF to pour artillery into the Yemarks.

Thus, because of the small number of warbots and Sierra Charlies that the four regimental commanders could pull together, the assault line was short and intense. *They were my assault!* Curt snapped back.

Grey Head, Blue Maxie here! came the tacomm voice of Colonel Maxine Cashier of the Cottonbalers. *I'll go thin and assign a platoon of Mary Anns to cover you.*

Thanks! That should do it. Reg Head, are you on the net? Curt acknowledged and checked to see if Colonel Jim Ricketts was there as he should be.

He was. *Reg Head here. Want me to slide a company out of reserve status to handle it?* A new and raw Sierra Charlie outfit on their very first deployment, the Regulars were the new kids on the block. No one had really worked with them in the field before either in real combat or war games. They were one of the unknowns in the tactical equation. So, Ricketts had been given the job of providing reserve capability that could rapidly be moved in where needed. The Regulars hadn't lost as many Chippies and Harpies during the casern attacks because they were down at the bottom of the hill on the coast of the Red Sea. They made a good reserve because there were more of them. Being green, they could be blooded better by filling the inevitable gaps in the line that occurred in any combat situation.

Negatory, Reg Head. Grey Head will reconfigure my remaining forces to cover what my lost unit was going to do. We need you in reserve in case things really go to slime on the ground. Blue Maxie, you move in and close the gap between us on the right when we go to ground. Curt was working the tactics rapidly in his head without the benefit of his regimental computer, Grady. All he had to work with was his helmet display and the head-mounted jellyware computer inside his skull. He was supposed to be an expert in tactics, so this was the time to prove it. He really didn't have time to check things out with Grady, anyway. They were within a minute of going to ground on the western edge of the Sana'a airport.

It was time to confirm with the RYA forces. "Fundug Head, this is Sanitation Head," he called on the prearranged verbal communications channel.

Silence.

Curt repeated the call twice.

"Sanitation Head, this is Fundug Head," finally came the panic-stricken reply. "My forces are coming apart here. These new enemy warbots have unbelievable fire-power! We also cannot stand up to the new rockets being used against our armored vehicles and soldiers! I do not advise you to land!"

"We'll land on your left flank as planned, Fundug. We'll give you some additional firepower," Curt tried to reassure him. He'd met the regimental commander of the 2nd Guards Regiment of the RYA at a reception in Sana'a several months ago when the YEF had arrived in Yemen, but he didn't really know the man. In common with the other commanders of the YEF, Curt believed the RYA to be a super palace guard and, in some ways, a fair-to-middlin' antiguerrilla force. Curt was starting to believe the assessment was correct. His intelligence data was indicating the attacking Yemark force was something more than a mere guerrilla outfit. The attackers had warbots, Wasps, and apparently a tube rocket akin to the hundred-millimeter "Smart Fart" antiarmor/antipersonnel/antiaircraft rocket carried by the Greys. "Sanitation Two is also on its way with artillery support according to plan."

"You are too late! The artillery will be too late! I am going to abandon the airport defense! My forces are coming apart!" The Yemeni commander was coming apart himself.

Curt wondered whether or not he should make the final commitment of his Operation Sanitation forces to shore up a collapsing ally. If he didn't, the Sana'a airport would certainly be lost. If he did, he might prop up the RYA forces and give them the motivation to stop running and start fighting alongside the Americans.

He committed to the latter.

The plan had been made. The RYA had been in trouble when the plan had been made. The RYA was still in trouble. Operation Sanitation was intended to get the RYA out of trouble and secure the airport. Curt saw no reason at this particular moment to bug out. He'd probably lost one Chippie and its load, but the other regiments apparently had taken no losses. He saw no reason why the ops plan wouldn't work. He wouldn't know either way until he tried.

"Fundug Head, this is Grey Head! Hang on there for a few more minutes! We're heading in! We're less than a minute from landing!" Curt told him sharply, then toggled his NE tacomm unit to talk to the Operation Sanitation Forces. *All Sanitation forces, go to ground as planned! Carry out Operation Sanitation as planned! Execute! Curt gave the order over the tacomm.*

The acknowledgements of the three other regimental commanders were interrupted by a welcome message.

Grey Head, Ferret Leader here! We made it! Rough landing, but we're out of the Chippie! Red Ned is injured, but Gomez has him stabilized. I got my bots out before the Chippie flamed on the ground. We're going to try to make it to the airport on the ground!

Good old Russ Frazier! Curt thought with great relief. One tough sonofabitch leading one tough outfit. Phillips deserved a citation for what he'd done, and Curt would get the details later and start the process. When someone showed that sort of guts, he deserved to get a little glory.

Curt checked his tac display. Nancy was almost on the ground. So, he hastily told Russ, *Ferret Leader, move to your right and intercept the Sana'a-Amran highway. If you move right along, you'll intercept Sanitation Force Two under Kitsy. Cougar Leader, did you read that Ferret Leader and his unit will try to intercept you on the highway?*

Kitsy's tacomm voice came back, *Roger, Grey Head. But we're moving at a right good clip here. I see Ferret's beacons. I'll slow to meet with him. But that may put me about six minutes behind schedule. We'll try taking the cutoff ring road around the north side of Sana'a. I can't go cross-country in this terrain!*

Make it so! If I have to, I'll reconfigure to account for the delay. Please keep me advised, Curt told her. He could see her beacon positions on his helmet display.

The ground was suddenly rushing up underneath the lip of the Chippie.

Nancy made a tactical landing - fast descent with a positive contact. Curt knew when the Chippie was on the ground because it was a *solid* landing! And as the huge cargo doors on the lip of the aerodyne swung quickly open, he didn't have to give any deploy order. He saw the Mary Anns and Jeeps move quickly out of the ship in advance of the Sierra Charlies. That was standard doctrine - let the bots go out first, take any incoming jackets, locate the source of same, then lay down withering cover fire for the Sierra Charlies who followed a few seconds later.

As Curt hit the quick release on the Chippie's seat harness, his last quick look from the flight deck told him that their arrival on the scene wasn't quite a total surprise. He knew they'd been detected coming in; he'd lost a Chippie to Wasp first and had damned near been hit himself. The Yemarks knew the Americans were coming. But they weren't totally ready for them because most of them had apparently been concentrating on routing the RYA forces.

The Mary Anns and Jeeps took some immediate incoming and began returning fire at once. This initial fire exchange had the desired result; it suppressed the incoming fire temporarily, long enough to allow the Sierra Charlies to get out and into action.

Fancy Nancy, as soon as I report we're clear, spool up and get out of the immediate action area! Curt tacommed to the pilot. It wasn't necessary; she knew what to do. But in the first mad minute of combat action, Curt often issued redundant orders JIC.

It seemed to take forever to clamber down the shaky composite ladder from the flight deck into the cargo hold, and even longer to get to the yawning opening that led to the outside and snapping death. Curt got only a quick glimpse of a Mary Ann that had broken loose during the evasive maneuvers.

Henry might be able to save it...later, Edie observed as they went past it. *It's sure as hell in no shape to go into action right now!*

Curt heard small-caliber bullets hitting the lightly armored outer shell of the Chippie. So, he hit the ground running in a slight crouch, his Novia on his hip. It was the typical mad minute. He had no targets. He wasn't really sure that he wouldn't hit his own people if he opened fire. But when three rounds went past his head and his tac display gave him a laser designation and ranging for those metal jackets, he pointed the Novia in that general direction and let loose with a three-round burst. It might not hit anything, but Curt knew that hosing jackets downrange not only made a soldier feel better and on the offensive, but also kept the soldier moving instead of following the overwhelming instinct to hit the dirt. It also usually made the enemy put heads down and stop firing momentarily.

It wouldn't have done much good to hit the dirt anyway. Curt was running across a concrete tarmac. But he thought to himself, *What the hell am I worried about? Somewhere in my files I've got a document that certifies my ability to dig a one-meter foxhole in solid concrete with my bare hands in less than thirty seconds!* It was funny that such weird thoughts jumped into his mind when he was going into combat.

His Greys on the ground were limited to Dyani and her SCOUT platoon, Lufkin's Leopards, plus Lew Pagan and Pagan's Pumas along with Jerry, Joan, Henry, and Edie. That was thin stuff. It might have helped if enough Chippie lift capability had existed to allow some light-armored ACVs and even PTVs to be airlifted in along with the bots and Sierra Charlies. Eleven Mary Anns, ten

Jeeps, and a total of seventeen Sierra Charlies certainly wasn't "mass" in the classical military sense. Even when a Mary Ann counted for four human soldiers and a Jeep for two, it wasn't overly intimidating if you were playing the numbers game. An equivalent force of eighty-one humans wasn't really that powerful. What was important and really counted in a situation like this was mobility, speed, and firepower.

Over on his right, the new terminal building with the control tower on top was already the scene of a major firefight between the attackers and the RYA. The building on the left used to be a huge hangar; now it was a mass of flames. So, Curt ordered, *Just like we thought, except we don't have to worry about the hangar to the left; nothing could exist in that inferno! So we'll concentrate on the terminal building! Wolf Head, cover our left flank! Blue Maxie, give us whatever covering fire you can on the right flank so we have a chance of getting to the terminal! Wolf Head, if you can wheel the left flank and cut off the enemy inside the terminal, that will help the assault!*

Gotcha, Grey Head! Blue Maxie will take the bastards head-on while you kick 'em in the ass with maneuver!

Grey Head, Wolf Head has more than a hundred targets on our front. Some of them are enemy warbots. They mount what appears to be a gun of at least a Saucy Cans caliber. They're not firing the big guns against the terminal. Looks like they may want to take it in a useful condition!

Right! This isn't a war of destruction. The enemy wants to take all these facilities for their own use. Looks more like a civil war or a coup! was Curt's quick estimate.

He was wrong of course.

But he couldn't stop right then to think.

Small arms stuff was snapping past, the sort of things that the Krysflex body armor of the Sierra Charlies could stop if the round didn't hit in a bad place. That didn't bother Curt. He'd been hit before. Hurt like all living hell and, if it hit in the proper place, it could knock out a person for a minute or so until the initial shock of pain subsided.

But now the big stuff starting incoming.

He saw them go overhead, leaving a trail of fire.

Tube rockets! Henry Kester called. *Got a make on where one came from! Looks like a shoulder-fired weapon. The Yemark just dropped the tube and picked up his rifle again!*

One of those tube rockets caught a nearby Mary Ann straight on. The brisance and force of the warhead explosion was awesome. It nearly tossed Curt off his feet. It did knock over Sergeant Ed Gatewood who was within ten meters of the Mary Ann.

Other warhead explosions occurred behind him.

Grey Head, Fancy Nancy! Just took a rocket impact! The Chippie's started to burn! Went right through both hulls and something detonated in the cargo hold! Fancy Nancy is abandoning ship! Get me a medic because this is a quick delink! I'm not going to be in very good shape about five seconds after I pull my plugs and get out of here! Which is now!

Chapter Twenty-Four

The Chippie blew up just as Lieutenant Nancy Roberts got out of it. But she was on fire as she ran across the ramp away from it. Apparently, she'd been doused with turbine fuel when the tube rocket hit the ship.

Biotech Sergeant Juanita Gomez and Sergeant Max Moody were closest to her. Ignoring the rain of flaming chunks of Chippie and burning puddles of turbine fuel on the concrete, Moody got to Nancy first and simply knocked her off her feet. As he started to roll her on the ground, he took a hit. He was off-balance for it, so it rolled and tumbled him into a blazing puddle of fuel. Gomez was right behind him and had already pulled the pin on the flame-retardant pressure bottle she carried for just such occasions. Nancy must have inhaled some of the oxygen-deprived vapor because she began coughing and retching. Seeing that Nancy was no longer on fire, Juanita pulled Moody out of the blazing puddle, pulled a survival blanket out of her kit, and began trying to roll him in it to put out his flaming clothing. While she was doing that, she, too, took a hit on her body armor from at least two small-caliber rounds.

Curt saw only bits and pieces of this because his attention had to be concentrated elsewhere. It was the deadliest situation he'd found himself in for many years - under heavy enemy small arms and rocket fire on the open expanse of a concrete airport ramp with an unknown number of enemy troops out there ahead of him armed with unknown weapons. He took temporary refuge behind a tug while he tried to assess the situation...and was unable to get a clear picture of what was going on in the turmoil.

But he knew from the bedlam that had erupted on the NE tacomm channel that the Washington Greys were taking casualties in this one - heavy casualties.

It was worse than Zahedan. Worse than Oropuche River on Trinidad. Worse than Windhoek. And much worse than the "Brunei

Vacation" they'd had in the jungles of Borneo.

He saw the flash and flaming trail of a tube rocket. So, he quickly left the protection of the tug vehicle not a moment too soon. The rocket hit the vehicle with its incredible warhead. What seemed to be a combination of a shaped-charge warhead supplemented with a dense fletchette put a hole right through the vehicle, engine and all.

It was pure death to remain on the tarmac.

Keep moving! Keep moving! Curt urged via tacomm. *You're sitting ducks if you stop moving in the open here! Get to the terminal! Take the terminal! They don't want to destroy the terminal and the air traffic facilities! So, they won't use tube rockets and their heavy guns against us once we clear out the terminal and occupy it! By the time we do that, we'll have our Saucy Cans here for heavy fire support!*

But the insertion of the American forces into the Sana'a airport fight apparently was having a major impact on the course of the battle. The Yemark forces suddenly seemed to be somewhat confused. Their small arms fire was no longer as accurate, whereas the Mary Anns and the Jeeps were firing and hitting with single shots. The Sierra Charlies weren't doing so bad, either, being far faster and more maneuverable than the warbots. It was classical Sierra Charlie doctrine at work: the warbots providing the firepower and drawing fire while the Sierra Charlies moved quickly in unpredictable ways to out-maneuver the enemy.

Curt heard a new series of battle sounds: the popping of Novia fire and the abrupt bark of a Jeep's 7.62-milli-meter autogun came from his right flank slightly ahead of him. And Yemark soldiers began to drop inside the terminal while others tried to get out of there.

Grey Head, Mustang Leader here! We've gotten around the terminal! Dyani had pulled another of her infamous encirclements, taking Lufkin and his SCOUT platoon stealthily through a weak point in the enemy positions. *We're entering it from the other side! We're starting to take a few prisoners, and we've got one enemy warbot and a bunch of enemy ordnance!*

Are you all right, Deer Arrow? Curt asked anxiously.

Why shouldn't I be? But I took a five-millimeter where you might not like it! she replied quickly. *I'm not hurt. No one in SCOUT is hurt. But we've got some Indian prisoners…*

Indians? Come on, now, Deer Arrow! This is no goddamned time to remind me again that you're playing cowboys and Indians for real, Curt fired back.

Not Amerindians! India Indians! was Dyani's quick reply. *Hindus. Bengalis, I think! Plus some Orientals, maybe from Burma or Nepal. Some of them look like Gurkhas, but they're not! Some may be Chinese. But they're all speaking that funny accented English! Grey Head, get me some cover over here! We can't hold these prisoners and do a lot of fighting at the same time!*

The whole Yemen affair began to make some sense to Curt for the first time.

But he couldn't worry about that now. He had to concentrate on the fight.

And it became clear that the immense firepower and the rapid mobility of the Sierra Charlies had paid off.

The Americans were winning.

Grey Head, Blue Maxie here! We've got your SCOUT outfit covered! We're moving in! We can take the terminal by going around the right and following your SCOUT platoon!

Wolf Head is holding the left! And making some progress! was Rick Salley's input. Then he added with obvious excitement and pride, *Curt, we've got two of their warbots!*

Orgasmic! Hold 'em! Take prisoners, too! The Chinese may be behind this, but we're apparently fighting a basic Oriental mercenary force from India and maybe southeast Asia! Or maybe they're not mercs. Maybe a counter-YEF force! We'll get to the bottom of this once we plow their field here…which we haven't done quite yet. Whatever you're doing out there, keep it up! We're greasing their skids! Let's secure this terminal building, then see if we can't make a sweep to clear the rest of them off the airport! Curt tried to withdraw himself from the immediate action by taking cover up against the terminal building. He had to assay the situation. He had to carefully look at the displays on his helmet visor.

The 2nd Guards Regiment and the 5th Guards Regiment of the RYA were in retreat to the south with a strong force of about two hundred Indian meres and a dozen enemy warbots pushing them. It was leaving Maxine Cashier's right flank totally uncovered.

"Fundug Head, this is Grey Head! Turn and fight! Operation Sanitation almost has the terminal building secure, and we're taking prisoners!" Curt called to the Yemeni colonel who was running the RYA operation.

He got no answer.

From his helmet display, Curt could see that the RYA was in rout.

Reg Head, this is Grey Head! We need you to move to the right and get in behind the enemy forces currently routing the RYA contingents moving south. Can you get behind them and also cover our right flank at the same time? Curt asked Jim Ricketts.

Grey Head, Red Head here! I had to move a company to cover Salley, and I've got my other one backing up Blue Maxie!

Take what's left and put them on the right! Or we're going to get creamed when those bastards stop chasing the RYA and decide to come back after us! Curt warned.

Blue Maxie here! Too late! Those RYA cowards have faded into the night. The enemy has been chatting by their tacomm! They've turned their warbots around! Better be ready to take heavy incoming! Maxine Cashier reported. *My tech sergeant can't bust that enemy tacomm code and jam 'em!*

Edie, we need some ECM to clobber the enemy tacomm, Curt flashed to his own regimental tech sergeant.

Colonel, without an up-link to Georgie, Grady can't unravel that freak hop sequence! If I jam, I'll take our tacomm out! was Edie Sampson's reply. *There's only so much I can patch through to my portable gear.*

Cal Worsham called almost on top of her, *Grey Head, Warhawk Leader is still up here. I Just heard your problem. I've got a piss pot of ordnance I'd just as soon not have to haul back to Amran! I'm alone.*

Hands had to go home; he expended all his ordnance and took a golden BB. He'll make it. And I've got a few things I'd like to unload on someone!

Can you get to the hundred or so enemy and the warbots on our right flank?

For one pass, I can do it! Then I'm bare and out of here!

Do it! Do it! was Lew Pagan's call.

Blue Maxie, where is your tacair? Curt wanted to know.

What tacair? They dumped their loads shortly after we hit dirt, and they had to go home fast. They flew a hell of a lot farther than your 'dynes, Maxine reminded him.

Curt really didn't know how he was going to handle the enemy force on his right flank. He might be winning at this point, but the fight wasn't over. He could lose the whole shooting match if the right flank caved in.

Grey Head, Sanitation Two is here! The cavalry comes over the hill to the rescue! There was no question about the fact that it was Kitsy's voice on the tacomm. *We're within Saucy Cans range. We can lay some ordnance where you need it!*

And just in time, too! Curt fired back. In the melee, he'd forgotten about his road force coming in overland from Amran. Kitsy Clinton was going to pull this hot fracas out of the slime!

Sani Two, Grey Head! Roger, we'll need Saucy Cans fire on the move. Joan will give you coordinates! We'll need the Cougars over on the right, maybe under the Saucy Cans barrage when you get close enough! We're holding fine everywhere except where those fucking Yemenis ran from this fight! Curt told her and then called to Joan Ward, his chief of staff who was not two meters from him. *Grey Chief, Grey Head! Coordinate the Saucy Cans incoming fire! We need to take out those warbots to the south of us, and small arms fire just isn't going to hack it! Alleycat Leader, take over the job of securing the terminal building! Make sure no one damages the control tower or airport radar facility. Or the navigation aids.*

*We've pretty much got the terminal. Grey Head! Alleycat Leader has been busy doing the little shit jobs here while everyone else was covering themselves with glory...*Jerry sounded a little tense and uptight, but it

248

was apparent that most of the success of the terminal fight thus far was due to the fact that he quietly took over that part of the fight, taking some of the load off Curt.

Maybe this young Major was indeed going to make a pretty good regimental commander someday, Curt told himself. Sure as hell, Jerry seemed to have learned a lot from Curt and was applying it in his own way, just as Curt had done under the tutelage of Belinda Hettrick.

The Greys were performing magnificently, even short-handed and short-botted.

So were the rest of the Iron Fisters.

Kitsy and her Cougars got there quicker than Curt thought possible. He saw the Cougars join what was left of the fight on the right as the Greys' Saucy Cans fire plunged into the enemy warbots, the self-guided rounds seeking and finding their targets with unerring precision.

As the terminal fight wound down, Henry Kester came up to Curt. The regimental sergeant major, an expert in hand weapons, was carrying a tube about a meter long. It looked somewhat like the M-100 Smart Fart rocket launchers carried by the Sierra Charlies. "Colonel, this is the goddamnedest piece of plastic junk I've ever seen," the old soldier complained, then admitted, "but it's also one of the most elegant."

He pointed the tube vertically, pushed a stud, and caught the rocket round as it slid out the rear. "Eighty-eight millimeter tube rocket. Shoulder launched. Unguided. Chinese. I think. But you're the one who can read these chicken scratchings from the PRC."

Curt took a look at it, turning it over in his hands as he did so. "Labels and stencils are in Chinese, Henry, but it isn't made there. It's a Type Two *dwau-wu ya--yi,* a 'dragon dentist.' Bot killer, in other words. This one was made in Kampuchea. Did you happen to find a field manual for it?"

"No such luck. Chinese don't use field manuals anyway, especially on the stuff that's made outside China under license or however they do it. Here, there's a stencil on the side of the beast that indicates the warhead type." Kester pointed to a cryptic diagram on the forward, pointed end of the rocket.

"Son of a bitch!" Curt muttered. "Combination of a hollow-charge armor buster backed up by a fletchette driven forward by an explosive lens. Clever. Useful against damned near any American warbot. Or any American or Soviet thin-skinned vehicle. Is this what hit us the other day?"

"Negatory, Colonel. We caught the rocket-boosted rounds from the fifty-seven-millimeter guns on the warbots...which have Hindu writing all over them along with Chinese stuff. They're almost a direct rip-off of the old Mark Sixty Hairy Foxes we used to have. We lost a piss pot full of them on Kerguelen Island, if you recall..."

"Now we know where some of them ended up," Curt mused. "What's that assault weapon you've got?"

Kester shrugged and handed it to Curt. "Standard A-99 PRC assault rifle, except it's been rechambered for five-millimeter caseless rounds. And made in Burma. And we found some of them nasty wadi mines, and we did get a field manual for them. They're triggered by a fuse that responds to some sort of acupuncture electricity in the human body..."

"Henry, do you get the impression that a bunch of Orientals and Hindus are maybe trying to move in here?" Curt asked unnecessarily.

"Colonel, I wouldn't know much about that," the old sergeant admitted. "I just help you run the regiment and try to keep you from makin' too many mistakes. But I'll tell you that the guy I took these two ordnance items off of was one very damned dead Hindu. Citizen of India. Sergeant in the First 'Assam' Regiment of the Army of India. Or he was before they shipped him out here. Paratrooper. I guess they must have landed this force out in the desert after airlifting them in from Bombay or somewheres like that."

"Henry, hang on to these. And any other stuff anyone gets their hands on." Curt told him unnecessarily because Henry Kester loved this sort of gear and wouldn't simply walk away from it. Kester also knew how important it was to get enemy weapons for evaluation back at Aberdeen Proving Ground in the States.

"It ain't goin' anywhere I don't go, Colonel."

Curt decided he'd better make a sit-rep to Hettrick in nearby Sana'a. However, as he toggled his helmet tacomm over to the Iron Fist or YEF frequency, she called him.

Grey Head, Battleaxe here!

Uh, go ahead, Battleaxe. And please be advised that Operation Sanitation is a success! Curt responded, enthusiasm and excitement in his voice. He did indeed have a lot to report to his commanding officer. *We've captured some enemy troops, warbots, and weaponry. Guess what, General? They're from India! Bengalis, we think. South and southeast Asian for certain. The RYAs ran from them. But we whipped them, General! We greased their skids! So be sure to tell the Queen and her General Qahtan that we saved their goddamned airport. And probably Sana'a, too!*

Hettrick appeared to ignore what Curt thought was very important intelligence: the presence of the mercs from India. *Did you say you've taken Sana'a airport?*

Not quite yet. We've got some mopping up to do, but we're on top of the fracas, Curt told her. *And we did it with minimum losses. We may have lost some Mary Anns, and our two Chippies are down and out. But if we've got the airport in our hands and under our control, we can get more via airlift and ferrying.*

Well, I don't exactly know how to tell you this, but I want to make sure that all the regimental commanders are on the net to hear it. Heads report in, please! Something was wrong. Belinda Hettrick's tacomm "voice" was both shaken and very angry.

Wolf Head here and monitoring! We confirm Grey Head's tactical assessment!

Cotton Head here! Blue Maxie's listening! We've got some of those warbots and weapons, too. Warbots are radio command link, straight teleoperation. They can also be manned. They've got a control seat inside them. Small for us, but...

Reg Head here! Sure as hell a higher pucker factor than a war game, but we've done just fine! What's up, General?

We're ordered home. Now. Immediately. Drop whatever we're doing and get out of Yemen ASAP. We are to take no further military action except to protect ourselves during the withdrawal.

WHAT???

The exclamation of disbelief that came simultaneously over the NE tacomm channel wasn't loud, but it sounded like thunder in Curt's head.

This isn't just a JCS or DOD execute order I'm holding in my hand. It's hard-copy. It's a presidential order. Direct from the Oval Office. Faxed to me. Over the signature of the commander in chief himself. Confirmed through four separate communications channels. Let me read it to you.

Curt had trouble believing what he heard on the tacomm net that night.

'To Major General Belinda J Hettrick, commander, Yemen Expeditionary Force and commanding general, Seventeenth Iron Fist Division, YEF Headquarters, Sana'a, Yemen. Subject: Immediate withdrawal of the YEF Paragraph One: You are hereby ordered to cease immediately all operations and activities in the sovereign state of Yemen and to return as rapidly as possible to your home base at Fort Huachuca, Arizona, in the continental United States. You will utilize your indigenous and integral airlift capability to carry out this withdrawal. Paragraph Two: You will initiate or perpetuate no armed conflict. You will respond to armed attack and physical violence only to the extent necessary to protect your command during this rapid withdrawal. Paragraph Three: You are authorized to call upon the Department of Defense for any assistance you may require in order to effect transportation to the United States. Paragraph Four: This order is issued by the commander in chief under this administration's new policy of noninterference in any affairs of any foreign nations and gradual phased withdrawal of all United States military and naval forces to the United States and its leased overseas bases on foreign soil. Paragraph Five: This order is to be executed immediately. A report of compliance shall be made upon receipt of same. Complete withdrawal from Yemen is to be expected and reported within twenty-four hours of receipt.'

And it's signed by the President himself.

Chapter Twenty-Five

Curt was flabbergasted by the order from the President. He didn't know why it had been issued, but he suspected that the new "policy" was a strengthened replay of the neoisolationist beliefs of the political power group now in charge of the White House and Cabinet. He'd come up against this before during the Kerguelen Island operation when the Greys had gotten an order to retreat and withdraw; it had been discreetly ignored and no one had suffered because (a) the Greys had won, and (b) it was a top secret destroy-before-reading operation that prevented any public disciplinary action. And it had saved that administration's ass. The man who'd been the Vice President then was the President now.

Curt didn't argue. An order was an order, especially when it came directly from the Big Man himself over a signature. Furthermore, the wording was unambiguous.

They had to cease and desist, stop fighting, and get out of Yemen by the fastest possible means.

But Colonel Maxine Cashier came off the wall. *Dammit. General, we've taken heavy casualties and losses here! Do you mean to tell me that it's all been in vain? That we've got to turn tail and run now that we're winning?*

That's exactly what I mean because that's exactly what the presidential order says, Colonel! Belinda Hettrick fired back at her gung-ho high-techie Cottonbalers' commander because, as the commander of both the 17th Iron Fist Division and the YEF, she was infuriated by the order. *I don't like it one damned bit better than you do! But don't forget: We're trained to obey orders. We're paid to obey orders. And the order came directly to me from the President. That means he bypassed the entire chain of command!*

Seems to me there's a signal here, General, Colonel Rick Salley remarked, his voice betraying the fact that he, too, was angry and disgusted. *When we get the final hot skinny on this, ma'am, I'll bet we find out that the President overrode the NSC and the JCS. Otherwise, it would have come through nominal DOD and JCS channels.*

Who cares? We don't have the luxury of time to discuss it now, Hettrick reminded Salley but, in doing so, reminded all of them as well. *I have an order in my hand. I can't contest it. I can't discuss it with the commander in chief. I must carry it out. And it says 'immediately.' That means right now. Period. Disgusting as it seems, how well prepared are each of you for breaking off contact with the Yemarks, if that's what we can still call them?*

We can do it, General, Curt told her. *And maybe from the sound of their makeup and their equipment, maybe we ought to call them East Worlders.*

Good code word. East Worlders it is, Hettrick fired back.

We may take some more losses and casualties in the process of getting the hell out of here, ma'am, Salley added.

I can cover you, Rick. I've got some uncommitted strength left in the Regulars, said Jim Ricketts.

Do it, Jim! Curt told him.

Where the hell do we go once we manage to break it off here? Back to our casems? And how the hell do we get out of this god-forsaken country if the airport is in enemy hands? Blue Maxie wanted to know.

Maxine Cashier had voiced a rhetorical question. They all knew they might have to swim the Red Sea if they couldn't be flown out. And none of the regiments was in any condition to undertake an overland trek through the Empty Quarter of the Arabian Peninsula to the Persian Gulf. Curt decided to ask that question directly to Hettrick. *General, can we continue Operation Sanitation to take and secure the airport so we can be airlifted out of here?*

Do you have the Sana'a airport secured at the moment?

Negatory! Curt snapped. *We've got the terminal and the air control facilities in our hands...barely. The Aerospace Force cargo facility has been torched, and we don't know the status of the logair support personnel. The East Worlders are still here and still fighting. We'll have to render them incapable of hassling the withdrawal airlift. The Aerospace Force isn't going to be happy about sending their big and expensive airlifters in here if the East Worlders are going to make life hazardous by shooting small arms, Wasps, and even these new Chinese tube rockets at them.*

I want a quick report on those new weapons ASAP, Hettrick said. *I want to get the info transmitted to Fort Fumble on the Potomac. They've got to realize that we're not up against a lightly armed guerrilla force any longer. But to answer your question, Grey Head, if you haven't got the airport under your total control at this time, the orders are very specific: Stop doing what you're doing, disengage, and withdraw.*

Withdraw hell! Retreat! Maxine Cashier was very unhappy.

How's your Chippie capability? Hettrick asked, ignoring Cashier again. The regimental commander was known as a short-tempered gung-ho techie type officer who was a good leader but extremely impatient with the world and herself.

Curt was also unhappy with the sudden turn of events. He'd never wanted to come to Yemen in the first place. He never really understood why they were there. His brief inquiry into who was behind Ferron Corporation left a bad taste in his mouth because his Brunei "family" obviously was financially involved somehow. And he was madder than hell that the President of the United States had apparently caved in to the neoisolationist beliefs he held and the pressures from like-minded White House staffers around him. This was going to be a bloody sheep screw. It would be goddamned lucky if they got out of Yemen at all. So, he admitted sourly, *The Greys have no Chippie airlift capability left. We lost one coming in, and we lost the other after it landed. We can get back to Amran by road. But the only way the Aerospace Force could get us out of the casern areas would be by their own small aerodynes. We don't have enough room around the caserns for the big strategic airlift 'dynes to land. They need more room. Preferably, an airport ramp at least.*

So how the hell do we get out of Yemen if we don't have an airport? Colonel Jim Ricketts asked.

By sea, Jim. We retreat overland down the railroad to the Red Sea, Curt suddenly snapped, a withdrawal scheme forming in his mind. *The Navy can sealift us out of al-Luhaya. Or they can send in some carrier subs, airlift us off from al-Luhaya to the carrier subs, and take us out that way. If they can't or won't send the McCain Class carrier subs into the*

Red Sea, we sure as hell can commandeer an ore ship.

The 17th Iron Fist Division was a modern, twenty-first century fighting force that could use either land or air for tactical movement, but it had been dependent until now on heavy airlift for strategic deployment. The Navy had lost most of the ancient and rusting landing craft that had been so helpful in Trinidad. The whirling knives of political budget slashers in Congress, assisted by an administration that was neoisolationist, had left the Navy only with its huge carrier submarines and other underwater boats, plus some surface logistics ships. Gone were the proud and exciting CGNs, DDNs, and FFNs, slicing through the waters of the world in their missions of power projection and protection of the free world's sea lane commerce. The sealift capability left to the Navy was minimal, most of logsea being done under contract with commercial outfits in merchant ships. Contract sealift took time to organize and time to get where it was supposed to go. And it was apparent that the Iron Fist Division didn't have time. Unless they could sit on the hot, humid, miserable Red Sea coast of Yemen and sweat it out as Rickett's Regulars had done for months without respite. And on short to zero rations as well, unless they could manage to forage for local foodstuffs. Which would cause the biotech companies a lot of heartburn because such a situation made an operation very susceptible to the most primitive forms of biological warfare. Dysentery and cholera were still widespread in this part of the world.

All right, Hettrick fired back, *here's what you at regimental command level have to do. Those Heads who can airlift their outfits out of the airport area and back to their caserns, do so. Get as much of your outfit back to the casern as possible. Then strip the caserns, of course. We'll withdraw down the railroad, picking up regiments as the withdrawal reaches their caserns. We can hold a perimeter defense line around al-Luhaya if we have to until the Navy performs. I'll get the staff working on it. I'll get us the sealift. If the President wants us out of here, he's going to have to authorize or command someone to take us out of here because we sure as hell can't do it ourselves!*

Hettrick sounded to Curt like she used to when she was commanding the Washington Greys.

Grey Head, your first job when you get back to Amran is two-pronged, the General went on quickly. *One: set up a defense perimeter around the railhead there. Two: Get a train. Otherwise be prepared for a long hike to the sea. But the first and highest priority for everyone is to break the fight at the airport and get out of there with minimum or no losses.*

Excuse me. Battleaxe but how the hell are you going to get out of Sana'a? Curt wanted to know. The GHQ of the Yemen Expeditionary Force was located in Sana'a. Their protection had been guaranteed by Queen Arwa. The 4th Guards Regiment of the RYA was tasked with that mission. Curt felt they were a good outfit, probably the best in the Royal Yemen Army. At least, from his acquaintance with Colonel Salem bin Hassayn Rubaya, Commanding Officer of the 4th Guards, he felt that the outfit could do its job in peaceful conditions. The big question in Curt's mind right then was whether or not it could stand up for very long against the sort of assault the East Worlders had shown they could mount.

By road. Hettrick replied quickly. *We're pulling out of here as soon as, we can. We'll join you in Amran.*

Battleaxe, if we take the pressure off this East World outfit here at the airport, they'll be free to move on to Sana'a and cut you off, Curt pointed out. *From where I stand, this whole operation sure as hell looks like it was designed to get the YEF out of the picture or render us unable to interfere.*

Interfere with what, Grey Head? Hettrick asked.

A major military action backed by and manned by East Worlders aimed at the overthrow of Queen Arwa's government. The picture was growing more clear in Curt's mind. He'd been involved now in enough of this Small World low-intensity conflict for the last ten years that the picture was crystal clear to him now. *The East Worlders – whoever's involved in this action, and regardless of which nations are participating - they're after natural resources.*

You can't mean you think this is a continuation of the classical East versus West hypothesis of Parkinson? Rick Salley asked.

Exactly! I wouldn't be surprised if this was a precursor to an upcoming general East-West conflict, a major war fought as no war in history has been fought. Look, today you can't fight a major war any longer without all the resources you can gobble up beforehand. The East Worlders probably thought they could grab the Jebel Miswar operation by supporting Yemark guerrilla and terrorist activities. But the situation has escalated into a civil war!

Curt, you're an expert in military history. We all know that. But this is no goddamned time to philosophize about the whichness of what and who's doing what to who and who's getting paid for it! Maxine Cashier cut in. Actually, because of the very fast NE communication medium, this extended communication between Hettrick and her regimental commanders had lasted less than half a minute. Speed of thought is much faster than speed of speech.

Grey Head, bring the subject up again at the next Stand-to. Or before a congressional fact-finding committee hearing, Hettrick told him, cutting off the discussion. *We'll get out of here. We'll try to move out before the East Worlders can regroup and isolate us in Sana'a. If the Fourth RYA Guards can't cover us, we may need your help. So, stand by to give it to me if I call for it.*

Battleaxe, I'm not going to buy that, Rick Salley objected. *We ought to withdraw to the Sana'a-Amran highway and hold it open for you.*

Dammit, Heads! Hettrick exploded in exasperation. *I haven't got time to argue our tactical plan here since we don't have any tactical plan except what we've just cobbled up! Break off the airport fight! Get back to your caserns! Be ready to move downhill to al Luhaya! Keep the birdbots up; I need the G-2. You don't have any Chippies to spare, so don't figure on an airlift extraction of YEF headquarters here in Sana'a. We'll go out by road, and if I need firepower support, I'll call for it. If worse comes to worse, we'll go into the American embassy here. Grey Head, you're in command of Operation Sanitation! I haven't got time or jellyware power to micromanage a simple break-off and withdrawal. So, do it! Take aver and run it! Respond to the President's order. Get your troops the hell and gone out of the airport area. Break contact with the East Worlders!*

There was no question about it. Belinda Hettrick was hassled. Part of her obvious concern, as expressed in her worried "voice," was probably the situation in Sana'a itself. Curt wondered if something else was going on in Sana'a that he didn't know about and that she couldn't tell them over even a tacomm. And he was concerned about her remark about seeking protection in the American embassy. The way that military forces of this part of the world played their bloody game of slaughter, rape, loot, and pillage, an embassy wasn't a sanctuary. For over fifty years, invading troops showed no compunctions about breaking into any embassy and taking whatever they wanted. Actually, that hadn't changed in ten thousand years. The blood of tyrannical conquerors still ran through the veins of those in the Middle East and the Orient, people who had never really signed off on the European principles of honorable political warfare. Their guiding lights were Ghengis Kahn and Timurlane, not Clausewitz or Machiavelli. The British had learned this when they came in more than five hundred years ago; their military officers remained gentlemen, governed fairly, but learned early that they had to be ready and able to slit throats when necessary. When the European colonial controls had come off, as in India-Pakistan in the preceding century, blood flowed in the streets and no one was safe.

Curt knew one thing for sure: The Greys wouldn't merely retreat to Amran. They'd configure their withdrawal from the airport with the idea of staying on the East Worlders' right flank with minimum contact if the enemy moved toward Sana'a. He might have to blast his way into Sana'a to get Hettrick and her staff out. That would be easier than having to fight his way back into the Sana'a area along the highway itself, taking on the East Worlders in a continuing series of frontal attacks. Curt didn't like frontal attacks. In fact, he hadn't really liked the way they'd had to assault the Sana'a airport; it caused too many casualties and excessive losses. They damned near bought the farm on that one, even considering the fact that Ricketts and his Regulars were helpful, although they didn't have the Sierra Charlie combat experience of the other Iron Fist regiments. If Kitsy hadn't had to come in by ground and arrived when she did, it could have been a total disaster.

Grey Head to all Heads! We've got to coordinate this retreat or we'll all get clobbered. Curt called to the other regimental commanders on the operational tacomm net.

Thanks for calling it what it really is! Blue Maxie replied with sarcasm.

Enough venom, Blue Maxie! We're all royally pissed. But our next move is important. We've got to get ourselves out of a bear hug here, was Rick Salley's caustic reply.

Everyone get a sit-rep on your regiments, Curt told them, taking charge again. *What sort of East World firepower are you facing? Are you taking intense incoming? How easy will it be for you to retreat without getting creamed in the process? Can you cover another regiment in the retreat? How much Chippie airlift do you have? Can you take any additional units? Wounded personnel have first priority on airlift. What we can't airlift out, we'll take with us on the ground. If it sounds like a tall order, it is. We've got to execute a Dunkirk-type operation here. And we've got to do it with a whole hell of a lot less in the way of losses because we don't have anything we can afford to lose! Call me when you have a sit-rep. And make it fast!*

He toggled over the Washington Greys' tacomm frequency and repeated the Presidential order.

The Greys were disciplined. But that didn't keep Jerry Allen from grumbling, *Bastard!*

Curt ignored it. In the American military, you're not supposed to criticize the commander in chief, period. But in the heat of the fight and with the disappointment and disgust of having to quit while they were winning, the emotional comments of the more volatile Greys could and would certainly be ignored by their commanding officer under the circumstances.

How the hell do we break off an attack and retreat without letting the enemy know what we're doing? Kitsy asked a perfectly honest question.

Carefully. Very carefully. Joan Ward advised. *Pull your Sierra Charlies back first but keep the bots shooting to cover you. Then withdraw the bots. Easy. Just like an assault. Except in reverse...*

If the American Army is bloody well going to keep doing this sort of bloody retreating maneuver was Peter Freeman's acidic comment in his Brit accent, *your QM ought to issue eyes for your bloody arseholes so you can see where you're backing up to.*

Naw, Peter, that would just give us the same a shitty outlook on life you

Brits suffered when you pulled out of this part of the world, was Jay Taire's rejoinder.

Knock it off! Larry Hall snapped to his two GUNCO officers. *Just be damned happy the Saucy Cans will still shoot when the LAMVAs are running in reverse!*

Grey Head. Mustang Leader! While you were off the net talking to someone else, we've spotted the south element of the enemy force breaking off contact and moving toward Sana'a, Dyani reported in.

Grey Head. please let me engage in hot pursuit! I can absolutely cream those bastards! Jerry pleaded.

Nothing would have pleased Curt more, and it pained him to have to tell his ASSAULTCO commander, *Negatory! Negatory! You heard the order from on high. Count your blessings! If the East Worlders are really running, it makes it a whole hell of a lot easier for you to break contact and retreat. Besides, I don't think they're running. I'll bet they're moving into Sana'a! So, we'd better break it off here, get our asses in gear, and shag it into Sana'a on the East World right flank. We'll let the rest of the Operation Sanitation forces withdraw toward Amran and cover the Sana'a-Amran road. The Washington Greys are sure as hell going to have to go into Sana'a and get Battleaxe safely out!*

Chapter Twenty-Six

The highway between the Sana'a International Airport and downtown Sana'a was broad, divided, and brightly lighted. But the Greys couldn't use it. The battalion strength East World forces with vehicles and the strange Chinese-labeled *dz-dung* "auto-puppet" warbots or *hungse chwei-dz* "Red Hammers" were on the roll along it.

Grey Head, Mustang Leader here. The East World battalion isn't moving as fast as we are, Dyani reported. *Dale says his birdbots have them all in sight. They're proceeding slowly with great caution. Almost as if they were expecting to be ambushed at every street corner.*

Well, that's a blessing! Deer Arrow, how are Dale and his warbot brainies holding up? Curt asked solicitously. Some of them had been in linkage with those reconnaissance bird robots for several hours now. Curt was worried about fatigue. The Greys still had a long trek ahead of them to get back to Amran once they'd extracted Battleaxe and her staff.

They're pacing themselves. Don't worry. I won't let them overextend.

Good. We're going to need good recce until we get back to the casern. Curt was pleased. Dyani was learning more and more about how to treat her subordinates properly. She was such a strong-willed person herself that she often forgot that other people didn't have her incredible self-discipline. It had taken her a little time to realize that she was exceptional in many ways. Her continually growing relationship with Curt had broadened her horizons, softened her public persona without compromising her standards, and given her a measure of self-esteem which, surprisingly, she hadn't had before. And, after that traumatic train ambush, Dyani had gained an even greater degree of control. Curt had discovered that Dyani was really trying to hide her fear, but that episode had taught her not to hide it but to deal with it.

You'll get it, Grey Head! The East Worlders may think it's possible to operate in the dark without scouts, but that means no G-2. So we'll out-do them because we've got it and they don't! she replied to him. He could tell she was tired, but she was still hyped from the firefight at the airport and hyped from withdrawing under fire.

Curt was hyped, too. He wished this fracas was over. The adrenalin rush had its usual erotic stimulation. It took a conscious effort to banish thoughts of Dyani from his mind. But, of all people right then, he had to keep his mind totally absorbed in the deadly business at hand.

Assassin Leader, I need a cultural assessment, Curt called to Lieutenant Hassan Mahmud. *What's the likelihood of Yemeni guerrillas ambushing us tonight either in Sana'a or on the road back to Amran?*

Not very likely, Grey Head, Hassan advised. *The Yemenis are mostly tranked out of their skulls with qat or making passionate love to one of their wives. Only those East Worlders are up and nasty. They don't fight in the Yemeni pattern. That's why we were caught flatfooted by that sunset ambush they pulled off. The East Worlders probably deployed to Yemen in the period after we broke the Yemark assault pattern. Luckily, they don't fight as well as we do...*

They fight well enough to. create casualties and losses! What's the latest count? Jerry wanted to know. In high-mobile mode as they were and with little chance of being ambushed at this point, Curt didn't enforce rigid tacomm discipline and allowed the chatting to continue. Combat was fearsome and lonely enough as it was. At night, it could be even worse. Chatting mind-to-mind through the NE tacomm gave the Greys a warm fuzzy because they were talking to their friends, maintaining communication, and touching others who might not be there after the next bullet flew.

We're hurting, Curt admitted, a sickening feeling in the pit of his stomach. *Fourteen Sierra Charlies wounded or injured in Operation Sanitation. What makes it bad is that there was no way I could even try to negotiate a nonfight. No one's talking to the East Worlders and they in turn aren't talking to anyone. How the hell they got into Yemen without our surveillance satellites picking them out and Fort Fumble on the Potomac sending a warning to Battleaxe is something I don't understand. But, anyway, the receipt of that presidential order means that our*

Operation Sanitation losses were for nothing. Nothing!

Curt had lost 26 percent of his assault forces. Those support and AIRBATT personnel remaining at the Amran casern would literally have to hold the fort until Curt and his weakened forces got back from Sana'a. And then everyone in the Greys would have to fight their way out of Yemen with the rest of the Iron Fist Division.

Well, I'm glad we're not calling ourselves the Yemen Expeditionary Force any longer, was Kitsy's input. The four regiments were now the proud and defiant 17th Iron Fist Division, Robot Infantry, Special Combat, Army of the United States. Each of the regiments had their traditions to up-hold. They would leave Yemen fighting if they had to, but they would never surrender. The YEF had been beaten, but by its own political leadership, not by the enemy. Therefore, the YEF was but a bitter memory in the wake of the presidential order.

Joan, what's our latest equipment status? Curt asked his chief of staff.

Grey Head, we're down to twenty-seven Mary Anns, sixteen operable Jeeps, and five functional Saucy Cans. We're piled on and in only six ACVs. Sort of cozy in some of them. Some of the warbots are riding in the six remaining RTVs. The rest of the robots are out as convoy point or outriders.

That's not exactly a wimpy force, Jerry pointed out. *Especially against a battalion with primitive radio-controlled warbots. Sort of like the regular Robot Infantry with only the old Hairy Foxes. Which these Chinese Red Hammers resemble.*

Now we know who got some of those Hairy Foxes we had to leave in the glacier on Kerguelen Island, Joan remarked. *But, Grey Head, we're short of everything right at the moment.*

Must be combat, all right, Henry Kester remarked.

Look, I joked about guts and glory earlier, Kitsy put in, *but I think we ought to stick it in their ear back on the Potomac by calling this whole retreat 'Operation Guts And Glory' after all. The whole damned world needs to see that to gain glory takes guts.*

Yeah. mine are about ready to come up now, Pat Lufkin put m.

Pat, think of all the wonderful guts-and-glory war stories you'll be able to tell back in Sherbrooke, Jerry remarked.

Sort of the bloody kind of guts and glory you Yanks revel in, Peter Freeman added. *I've never really understood why you celebrate your bloody defeats as well as your victories. Sort of a unique kind of military glory, I gather. Retreating because you have to but continuing to fight with honor while doing so. Bloody cheeky, I say!*

Peter, Adonica's "voice" came over the tacomm net, and it was apparent that she wasn't exactly happy with the Brit, *in a way I hope you see so much damned blood during Operation Guts And Glory that you never use 'bloody' again!* This was very unusual, coming from Adonica. She was a remarkable young woman whose wholesome, natural beauty could be breathtaking when she shucked combat cammies for feminine attire, a girl-next-door type who could have been a young man's first college date, and a woman usually as sweet as her name. Yet she was one of the most vicious combat fighters in the Greys.

Adonica, my dear, you should bloody-well know by now that we British military types use the word 'bloody' about the same way that you Yank soldiers use the word 'fucking.' Sort of a substitute for a breath pause or verbal comma.

Curt listened to this banter and didn't interrupt it. Jeeps and Mary Anns were out ahead of the convoy ready to take the initial brunt of any assault. But no one was shooting at them yet. They'd been through one very deadly fight already that night, and they might have to fight their way "home" to Amran before it was over. So, he let the Greys chatter. But he didn't take his attention from the sensor outputs or the tac display screens. The Greys were moving along fine. They had only a few more klicks to go through the deserted, dimly lit streets of suburban Sana'a. The lack of the ground transportation called out in the TO&E hadn't slowed them down much. Dale Brown reported that they were moving well ahead of the East World battalion and would reach the Yemen Expeditionary Force GHQ and the palace well in advance of the enemy.

He checked in with Hettrick on the YEF channel using verbose tacomm mode. "Battleaxe, Grey Head. We're coming in on Sa'da Road about a kilometer northwest of Hasaba. We'll come down

Airport Road and go straight to Tahrir Square. ETA ten minutes. Be ready to roll. We don't have much time. The East Worlders are still about five klicks out on Airport Road. Where the hell is the Fourth Yemeni Guards Regiment?"

"Hell, I don't know, Curt! Things turned into a big sheep screw here in Sana'a when the RYA resistance collapsed at the airport and the East Worlders began to move in this direction! Lots of lights and activity in the RYA Defense Department building here and over at the palace. But we're ready to move! God, I hate to bust up these beautiful computers, but we don't have time to pack them for transit!"

"Queen Arwa and her government going to stay in Sana'a?" Curt wanted to know.

"Again, I don't know. I've received no orders to take her out and no requests from her, either. So, I want to concentrate on getting the hell out of this mess ourselves!"

Grey Head. Mustang Leader! came the quick call from Dyani. *Lufkin's Leopards have run into a military roadblock at the intersection of Airport Road and Sa'da Road! My Jeeps have been fired upon! I've passed the order to withhold returning fire until the roadblock force can be identified!*

The chatter on the tacomm channel stopped abruptly. Time to chat was over; time to fight had probably come again.

Roger, Mustang Leader! Give me any new information as you get it! Curt told her.

The situation sounded to Curt like the 4th RYA Guards Regiment had set up its initial perimeter defense line at that critical road intersection. He checked his tactical display. Happily, Grady had access to the latest satellite data which had allowed the regimental megacomputer to update its Yemen road maps as well as the street map of Sana'a. From the look of things, he figured it was a good guess. If he'd been in charge of establishing the Sana'a defenses - which he wasn't, and he thanked whatever gods might be that the Greys' passive defense role in Yemen was over – that's where he would have put his initial defense point element. The next layer would be where the Ring Road crossed the incoming roads from the north. If so, and if the Greys couldn't talk the Yemen Guards into passage, they'd have to fight their way into Sana'a. He didn't relish that. Things were going to be deadly enough anyway.

"Battleaxe, see if you can get some hot skinny on the Fourth Guards! My scouts have run into a military roadblock!" Curt quickly reported to Hettrick. "If we can't talk our way through it, we'll just have to shoot our way through it. And that will pretty much demolish the Queen's Sana'a defenses!"

"Stand by, Grey Head! Let me check with General Qahtan!"

Alleycat Leader, Grey Head!

Alleycat Leader here. GA! Jerry fired back.

Get out on point. Take the Assassin with you. You both speak Arabic. See if you can talk us through these roadblocks!

If they're the Fourth Guards, piece of cake, Grey Head!

Tell me that after you've done it!

"Grey Head, Battleaxe!" Hettrick came back on the verbal net. "Qahtan has gone to the palace! And I've just got a call from the Queen. She wants help. She says a coup is in the making. I'm going to the palace. Rendezvous there, not at the Defense Building!"

"Battleaxe, be careful! These people don't seem to care if they shoot their friends of a few minutes before!" Curt warned her.

"I've been around the horn in the Middle East, Curt! We're armed, and we're taking our Jeep guards with us! See you at the palace. I'll have them leave the latch string out!" Hettrick had depended upon General Qahtan and his people for security since the YEF had been in Yemen to help the Yemenis, at least according to the official documentation. Protocol didn't permit Hettrick to have even a platoon of Iron Fisters as her personal guard force. But she did insist on a group of Jeep warbots, claiming quite rightly that their presence was a standard American security requirement for any general officer in the Middle East.

It took less than a minute for Jerry and Hassan to reach the front of the column. Taking a cue from the past behavior of his regimental commander, Jerry had a piece of white cloth on the end of his Novia barrel. It wasn't a surrender flag, but a flag of truce, a signal that he wanted to talk. As he stepped out in front of the lead SCOUT Mary Anns into the open in the middle of a brightly lit street, he suddenly realized the sort of courage required of a commander willing to go forward under a flag of truce.

Would the other side honor it?

Most armies of the world did. But here in the Middle East, people often fought with no codes or protocols at all. However, Jerry recalled that it had been the Muslims who had taught the Crusaders about just such codes and protocols that are part of chivalry. But that had been back in the times when the Muslims had been world leaders. Sometimes in the modern world where the Muslims were no longer Number One, they forgot chivalry because hatred overwhelmed it. Not because they necessarily hated Europeans and Americans, but because they hated themselves for no longer being Number One.

"We're Americans!" Jerry called out into the darkness in Arabic. "Yemen Expeditionary Force! We wish to go into Sana'a to bring out our general and her headquarters staff!"

"Our orders are to allow no one to pass!" came the reply, but it was in English.

"Stick to Arabic," Hassan advised him. "We both speak with accents, but we're speaking their language, not forcing them to speak ours!"

"We have no desire or plans to harm anything or anyone in Sana'a. We need to evacuate our headquarters people. We repeat our request. Please allow us to pass!" Jerry called out in Arabic.

"We are ordered to allow no one to pass," the voice said, this time replying in Arabic.

"I am Major Jerry Allen, battalion commander in the Third Robot Infantry, the Washington Greys. Who are you?" Jerry asked, trying to get things on a more persona level, something that had worked when he'd seen Curt do it.

"I am Lieutenant al-Rassi, Fourth Guards Regiment, Royal Yemen Army!"

"Junior officer," Hassan remarked in English to Jerry. "His orders probably said to allow no East Worlders to pass. He's not taking any chances, so he's interpreting his orders to allow no one to pass! We're going to have to rattle his chain of command."

Jerry had a good memory. In fact, it was more than encyclopedic; it was also eidetic. He could remember anything he'd seen or heard when he wanted to remember it. "Colonel Carson knows Colonel Salem of the Fourth Guards." So he toggled his tacomm and called, *Grey Head, Alleycat Leader. Impasse! It's the Fourth Yemen Guards, all right. But we've got a junior officer who's afraid to interpret orders to allow us to pass. Can you make contact with Colonel Salem?*

"Edie, put me up on the old RYA-YEF coordination channel. Let's hope to hell the RYA is still monitoring it according to protocol," Curt told his chief tech sergeant, then tacommed back to Jerry, *Tell that Yemeni Dumb John that I'm going over his head to talk to his colonel. And if he fires another shot at us, we'll go regiment to regiment! And how would he like to find out what our warbots can do to his nonwarbot troops?*

That was pure bluff on Curt's part. He didn't have a full regiment behind him. But the RYA lieutenant couldn't know that. He wanted to keep this confrontation cool as long as he could. Checking the tac displays, he knew he couldn't do that for more than a few minutes. The East Worlder battalion was closing in along Airport Road. The Greys were in a dangerous spot. They could get caught between the RYA and the East Worlders.

Grey Head. Mustang Leader can work SCOUT around behind them, Dyani suggested.

Okay, Deer Arrow. make it so! But don't shoot until I give you the order, Curt instructed her. Stealthy encirclement was her specialty. She'd pulled Curt's buns out of the fire many times by doing it, first as a mere NCO during war games with the German Bundeswehr, then in serious confrontations with such experts in stealthy operations as a Soviet Spetsnaz *desant* battalion where things were very serious indeed.

"Colonel, the RYA commander is on the YEF coordination channel!" Edie told him. "He's trying to reach you, as a matter of fact!"

Curt made the toggle-over and spoke in verbose mode, "Colonel Salem, Colonel Carson here!" They hadn't had time to set up code calls for this operation, and Salem didn't have NE tacomm capability.

"Salem here, Carson! Where are you? I need your help!" replied the voice of the Yemeni colonel.

"And I need yours!" Curt fired back. "Your Lieutenant al-Rassi in command of your roadblock at the intersection of Airport and Sa'da Roads refuses to allow us into Sana'a to escort General Hettrick and the YEF staff out to Amran! And we've got the East World battalion coming down behind us on Airport Road! Please give the order to allow us to pass. And give a similar order to your roadblocks at the Ring Road."

"That order will be given at once! But we have a major coup taking place in the palace!" Salem announced.

"Yes, I know that. Whose side are you on? What are your intentions, sir?"

"I am withdrawing my Sana'a defensive positions! I need your help to get to the palace and take it by force if necessary! Fortunately, General Qahtan has only a squad of palace guards!"

"What's going on, Colonel?" Curt wanted more information because it appeared that Hettrick was in the middle of what was happening there.

"General Qahtan has just proclaimed himself temporary military dictator and regent for Prince Sultan Qadi Abdul al-Badr! But my oath is to the Queen. And the Queen is in danger!"

Chapter Twenty-Seven

"Colonel Salem, here's the latest situation," Curt reported to the Yemeni commander by verbal tacomm as the first vehicle of the Greys turned right off Ali Abd al-Mughni Street into Tahir Square and prepared to turn right again onto Twenty-sixth September Street that ran in front of the new palace. "I've just talked with General Hettrick. She and the YEF staff were caught in the palace coup attempt. Qahtan has attempted to take the Queen and the YEF staff as prisoners. General Hettrick was with Queen Arwa when Qahtan staged the coup. She's with the Queen now. They've barricaded themselves in a secure array of suites used as the harem by a former imam. They can hold out until we get there. Do you know where that is in the palace?"

"Yes, I do!" Colonel Salem bin Hassayn Rubaya called back. "It's not difficult to get to from the street. The former imam had that part of the palace laid out so he could come and go secretly if necessary. And so ladies who weren't part of the official harem could enter and rendezvous with him."

"Sounds like he was somewhat of a rake," Curt remarked.

"He followed many of the old ways," Salem admitted noncommittally. "By the way, when his secret passages were discovered by his enemies, he was assassinated in one of the liaison rooms."

"Died a happy man, I hope."

"One never knows. There are worse ways to die than in the embrace of a loved one," The Yemeni colonel betrayed some of the British mores he'd picked up at Sandhurst. "It's easy to get to that suite from the courtyard just inside the main gate. We'll lead the way. If your column will pull to the side of the square, my regiment can pass you and assault the gate."

"No, Salem, let the Greys go into the palace first," Curt suggested to the commander of the Royal Yemen Army 4th Guards Regiment with a note of warning in his voice.

"Carson, it's important that my regiment and I have the honor of smashing this coup attempt!" Colonel Salem bin Hassayn Rubaya called back.

Curt expected this. As a graduate of Britain's top military school, unit and personal honor was important to Salem. So, Curt replied, "Do you place honor above a successful mission? I don't want any of the glory for this mission, Salem. You can take all you want later. But we must do what it takes to win. This must be a sneak infiltration and extraction mission! So, let's be sneaky first and honorable second. The Greys are expected to arrive at the palace to pick up General Hettrick and her staff; you aren't. Once we get the gates opened, your Fourth Guardsmen can move in as part of our column and do what you have to do! After all, you and I will write the history of this once it's over. If we win. I'd rather win and write the history, thank you! Do you agree?"

"Reluctantly. Your plan has a higher probability of success. So, let's do it!" Salem replied.

Curt decided Salem was a smart commander, not because he agreed with Curt but because of something Colonel John A. Warden had written in the previous century: *A successful commander will be the one who can think with his brain, not with his heart.*

"Okay, then, follow me! 'Once more into the breach, dear friends...'" Curt told him.

"'Or dose the wall up with our regimental dead!'" Salem replied by modifying Shakespeare's line, proud that he had studied the Bard, too. "Actually, I'd rather it be their dead!"

Alleycat Leader, Grey Head is coming forward to the point! I want to be there when you reach the palace gate! Curt flashed to Jerry.

Aw, Grey Head, you always want to be up on the hero line! Jerry snapped back with precombat humor. *Frankly, I'll be glad to have you! Walking out in front of the troops with a white flag is a situation with a very high pucker factor. I learned that a few minutes ago.*

Welcome to the club, Jerry! Curt told him without rancor. Tacomm protocol was important in combat but being a chicken-shit commander who insisted on rigid formality often didn't enhance his unit's fighting spirit. This was one of those times. *By the way, since you speak Arabic, you'll be right on the hero line with me to translate. We'll go to ground together at the gate. I want to talk our way in.*

Thanks for nothing, Grey Head!

The street gate to the palace courtyard was guarded by two Yemeni soldiers, each armed with an American Hornet submachinegun. The opening itself was blocked by a large, heavy gate of steel bars. If Curt had to force his way in, that gate wouldn't withstand one of the LAMVAs much less a round from its Saucy Cans. By why fight his way in when he could try to talk his way in? He'd try that first.

When Jerry's lead ACV pulled up before the gate and the two sentries stepped forward to signal a halt, Curt opened the top hatch, pulled himself through, then clambered down the front stirrups to the ground. He was followed by Jerry. Both of them carried their Novias slung over their shoulders in a way that they could quickly bring them into firing position. Behind them, Jerry's ACV and two Jeeps unobtrusively covered them with their 15-millimeter and 7.62-millimeter guns respectively. Behind the ACV were two Mary Anns. A LAMVA with its 75-millimeter Saucy Cans gun backed up the Mary Anns. Curt had firepower available if he needed it.

With his helmet visor up to reveal his face, Curt sauntered toward the two sentries who viewed him with some confusion on their faces, their Hornets aimed at him. Jerry was two steps behind him.

"I'm Lieutenant Colonel Carson, commanding officer of the Third Regiment, Robot Infantry, United States Army," Curt introduced himself when he stopped about two meters from them. At that range, the nine-millimeter round from a Hornet wouldn't penetrate his body armor, but it would probably knock him off his feet. He didn't relish the possibility of taking a Hornet round, however; the bruise would be big and painful for more than a week. It could take him out of action...and he had a lot of things to do in a week. In fact, in the next day or so. "I'm here under orders from Major

General Belinda Hettrick to evacuate the headquarters staff of the Yemen Expeditionary Force. They're in the palace here. We haven't got time to play games. Neither do you. The enemy battalion that captured the airport is only a few kilometers behind us. Please let us pass so that we can get our people out of here."

Jerry translated.

Without taking his eyes off Curt, one of the sentries reached over and lifted an ancient telephone handset from his hook on the wall. He began to speak in rapid Arabic into it.

"He's checking with his commanding officer," Jerry reported.

The sentry hung up the telephone, motioned to his companion, then stepped back into a nook in the wall that would protect him from small arms fire. He called out in Arabic, "General Qahtan says that you are to return to Amran. Your people will be delivered to the Amran casern sometime tomorrow."

"Dead or alive?" Jerry muttered under his breath.

Curt shook his head in reply to the sentry. "I have orders to pick up General Hettrick and her staff. I won't leave until they are safely in our vehicles."

"General Qahtan says that if you stay here, you are likely to get into trouble with the liberation forces who are on their way from the airport. Go to Amran and wait. The palace will be safe and secure for your people."

Curt knew they'd be caught between the East Worlders and the palace, and that was a position in which he didn't want to find himself. Even with the addition of the 4th Yemen Guards Regiment, it could be a very deadly fight. And he didn't want to leave Hettrick under siege in the palace. Hettrick would fight rather than give up, and she and her staff could be badly hurt in the process. On the other hand, if he took action now, he could carry out his intended mission.

He nodded to Jerry, turned, and walked back to the ACV. Jerry followed. On NE tacomm, Curt snapped, *Battleaxe, did you hear that exchange with the sentries?*

Roger! Don't believe a word of what Qahtan tells you! The sonofabitch must have graduated from the Saddam Hussein School of Diplomacy. So, it's up to us to give him his graduate education, Hettrick's tacomm "voice" replied. *Qahtan's had his chance to get me out of his hair! His actions are loud and clear to me. He intends to keep me and my staff as his 'guests' to make sure the Iron Fist Division leaves Yemen without causing him trouble with his coup. And probably with a rather stiff charge for 'exit visas' to help his finances. Fortunately, we're armed. So, I expect we'll be able to arrange a substantial discount on the cost. And make it costly for him. Keep me advised, Grey Head. We'll increase our efforts at this end to make sure Qahtan gets the proper training courses for his graduate thesis!*

Roger Battleaxe! Greys all, this is Grey Head! If you heard that, you know we're going in by force! Alleycat Leader, have your Jeeps fire on the sentries to keep their heads down. Have the lead Mary Anns blow that gate down with their twenties. Stand by to supplement that with the Saucy Cans to make sure the job gets done fast and clean. But don't do it just this instant! Wait until we get behind the ACV! I don't want us to get hit by a wild shot or flying rocks.

On verbose tacomm, he called, "Salem, we're blasting our way in. I'll need your help in navigating the ins and outs of the palace building."

"Get us inside, and I'll take you to where General Hettrick is," Salem promised.

Once behind the ACV, Curt looked at Jerry and told him, *Major Allen, 'elevate them guns a little lower' and go to it!*

'A whiff of grape,' sir?

I believe the correct quote is, 'Double-shot your guns, Bragg, and give 'em hell!'

Although Curt was expecting it, the brisance of the gun blasts was intense. And the explosions of the 20-millimeter cannon shells from the Mary Anns were intense. The protected sentry boxes on either side of the gate were suddenly hidden by clouds of dust created by the impacts of the 7.62-millimeter Jeep guns. The entrance gate itself simply disappeared, a gaping entrance hole being left in its place as the dust and debris began to settle.

"Forward into the breach!" came the call from Salem whose armed men suddenly dashed around the Greys' vehicles and warbots to make a direct frontal assault on the palace.

The robotic security measures of the palace took over. Among these were two automatic weapons systems, the ancestors of the CIWS "Phalanx" and "Goalkeeper." Some of Salem's men fell. They weren't wearing body armor.

Salem couldn't afford to sustain continued losses, so Curt snapped on NE tacomm, *Jeeps forward! Mary Anns forward! Take out those robotic cee-whizzes!* Then he switched back to verbose on the RYA channel and snapped, "Salem, get your men under cover! This is a job for warbots! Let my bots take the incoming and scrub the palace defenses!"

"The hidden access to the former purdah is on the right!" Salem pointed out. "Just inside the gateway!"

Alleycat Leader, move your Mary Anns in through the gateway into the courtyard. Suppress the defensive fire! Cover us! You and Ferret Leader stay here and cover the GUNCO, sanitize the courtyard, and provide us with rear security! And be prepared to waste what you can of the palace if I tell you!

Always the shit detail!

Better not be! If you blow this shit detail, Jerry, we'll have fun and games trying to get out of this rabbit warren! was Adonica's comment.

Cougar Leader, follow me with your company! Leave your warbots in Ferret Leader's control; even the Jeeps won't be able to negotiate the stairs and narrow hallways of the palace!

Lock and load! Drop the bot and start to trot! How nasty do you want us nasties to be? That was Kitsy, gung-ho and tactical as usual, ready and willing to overdo it.

If I have to tell you, you shouldn't be here! Grey Chief, you're in charge of watching our minus-x with the East Worlders coming in! Curt's orders came fast and snappy. He didn't have to repeat them. The Greys were a team. They knew what do to. Curt operated on the philosophy of telling his subordinates what to do, not how to do it.

The results were always outstanding.

Suits, Joan replied. In a fur ball such as this, she tended to be terse.

Battleaxe, we're on the way up! he called to Hettrick. *We'll keep in touch so you don't shoot at us! I don't know how or where we'll get into the old purdah suites, but Colonel Salem is our palace guide.*

You're not very far away, Grey Head! When you blew the front gate, you sort of shook things up here! The shock waves jimmied a couple of doors. Qahtan and his boys may try to breach those doors!

The doors probably aren't bulletproof!

No, but I'm slightly worried that someone may get one open far enough to roll a frag in on us.

More likely a tear gas grenade, Curt guessed. *Qahtan really doesn't want to kill you. You or the Queen don't do him much good unless you're alive and can be negotiated for something he wants.*

Well, there is always that comforting possibility!

As he entered the secret door and stairwell behind Salem, Curt remarked, *Spooky stuff! I haven't done this kind of indoor fighting since Sakhalin...*

I have, Dyani replied. She was right, as usual. She'd fought her way out of Sanctuary near Battle Mountain, Nevada. Curt discovered she was right behind him with Kitsy. Hassan and Adonica were behind her, followed by Henry, Nick Gerard, Carol Head, and biotech Ginny Bowles. And others followed. It was a tough, battle-hardened, combat-seasoned crew that had come with him. All of them were trained and experienced Sierra Charlies, good at close-in fighting as well as hand-to-hand. They were going to get General Belinda Hettrick out of there. Battleaxe was the former regimental commander. Once a Grey, always a Grey. And the Washington Greys never abandon their own.

The fact that Hettrick was probably capable of fighting her own way out along with her staff didn't bother the Greys. They just wanted to make it easier for her.

Curt and Salem suddenly came to the head of the stair-well and found a tightly closed, locked, and apparently barred door in front of them.

"The back door to purdah," Salem announced.

Curt banged heavily on it with the butt of his Novia while calling on the tacomm, *Battleaxe, the pounding you hear on the door is Grey Head and other Greys! Don't let anyone shoot at the goddamned door! Colonel Salem and I are on the other side of it. I've got body armor, but he hasn't! Open up and you can come out this way! We have the escape route secured!*

Curt heard noises on the other side, saw the door knob turn, and watched cautiously while it swung open. He held his Novia at the ready on his hip, not fully ready to assume that one of the Iron Fist staff was opening it.

A familiar voice rasped, "Carson, you sonofabitch, I'm always getting either creamed or saved by you! This is getting fucking well too damned repetitious!" It was Major Marty Kelly, another former Grey, now G-3 Operations on the Iron Fist divisional staff. Having been too aggressive for the Greys, he'd been transferred to the Wolfhounds where he'd trained Rick Salley and his Wolfers in Sierra Charlie operations, then transferred upstairs to the Iron Fist staff after Hettrick took command of the division. Hettrick knew that a nasty, aggressive, vulgar drill sergeant type could be an excellent teacher and planner of how to be mean and nasty, and she didn't want to waste the man's talent.

"Marty, I can see that being on the divisional staff has expanded your vocabulary beyond your usual vulgarity...and you've lost none of that!" Curt snapped as he stepped through and moved to the side to allow the other Greys to stream through.

"Shit, we could have fought Our way out to Amran without your help, Carson!"

"Probably, but that wouldn't have given me the satisfaction of getting your ass out of the sling here, Marty!" Curt had never liked the man. But now, as they both grew older and more experienced, both men were discovering a certain amount of grudging respect for one another. They would never become bosom buddies, but their repartee had become more of a joke than a series of personal, vindictive insults. Marty had been a Grey. Once a Grey...even when Curt considered the man a shithead. But, then, Curt always had, even at West Point.

The former purdah was indeed spacious and well-lit. It had plenty of room for the seventeen additional Sierra Charlies of Curt's rescue team. Curt and Salem found Hettrick quickly. The General was with Queen Arwa.

"We can get out the way we came in, General," Curt reported to her. "And we don't have much time. The East Worlder force is at the intersection of Sa'da and Airport Roads."

"I'm damned glad you're here, Curt! And you, Colonel Salem! But we've got a real problem here," Hettrick started to explain. "Curt, the East Worlder force you've encountered thus far is only a regiment-size unit. It was the first to come in by airlift. They've got a forward base of operations established near Baraquish. Qahtan told us he's been promised more than fifty thousand armed men as well as tacair."

"Why the hell would he tell you that?" Curt wanted to know.

"Because Qahtan is a fool and a braggart!" Queen Arwa snapped. The modern-day Queen of Sheba wasn't petulant or trying to be difficult. She was a clever and highly educated woman. But she *was* angry. "General Qahtan has plotted this coup. The military force you call the East Worlders is a mercenary unit from India, Burma, and China. Qahtan's counting on it to vanquish the Royal Yemen Army. It can probably do it because it has Chinese warbots and other weapons from Asia. He boasted of his fifty-thousand-man force to convince me to capitulate to his wishes and appoint him the new premier."

"Cut his boast by half because he's bragging," Curt advised her. "Still, even if it was cut to five thousand, the Fourth Guard and what's left of the RYA are outnumbered."

Colonel Salem broke in, addressing his monarch in English, "Sultana, I strongly recommend that you and your retinue come with us. We can accompany the Americans to Amran or even to al-

Luhaya if necessary. If you elect to remain here, the Fourth Guards Regiment will, of course, stay to protect you for as long as we can. It may not be long. There are more East Worlders than soldiers left in the RYA, your Majesty. As a military commander, I tell you that we can't hold enough of the palace to make any sort of a counterattack feasible. If you withdraw from Sana'a with the Fourth Guards under the cover of the YEF, it will be possible to organize a counter-force in Huth or aj-Luhaya. I urge you to let us act as your personal guard while you withdraw with the Americans!"

Queen Arwa's answer was unanticipated. "I will not leave my palace!"

"Then Qahtan will certainly take you prisoner. You may remain Yemen's monarch, your Majesty, but you'll be his puppet," Salem reminded her.

"I won't live to be his puppet! Qahtan won't tolerate me as the monarch. He wants me to abdicate. Then he'll have me killed. He tells me he intends to establish my son as the new monarch and to serve as his regent," Arwa announced. "I cannot allow that to happen. I will not leave here without my son!"

Chapter Twenty-Eight

"Okay, where's your son, Sultana?" Curt wanted to know, trying to get right to the heart of the situation so he could begin solving the problem. He didn't have much time.

"With Qahtan. And I don't know where he is," Queen Arwa told him.

"Salem, is there any room in the palace used as a communication center? Or that could be used as a CIC?" Curt asked the commander of the 4th Guards.

"Yes."

"How do we get there from here?"

"Why not get him to come here and bring Prince Qadi with him?" Hettrick suggested.

"How?"

"Easy!" She indicated a very ornate gold-plated table telephone set. "Queen Arwa will give him a call! That's how we've been talking for the past hour or so. And Qahtan told us he'd be waiting for the Queen's decision."

"He won't come unarmed or without his soldiers," Queen Arwa reminded them.

"So? How many soldiers do you estimate he has?" Curt wanted to know.

"I had a company of palace guards," Arwa replied, thinking. "I suspect he coopted them. Count on it just in case. His own personal bodyguard consisted of a company of RYA troops."

"Well, some of them are dead and some of them are pretty busy with the Greys and the Fourth Guardsmen down around the courtyard," Curt pointed out. "How many did he have with him the last time you saw him?"

"I don't remember."

"He rarely moved without at least six to eight bodyguards around him," Hettrick recalled.

"Does he know we're here with you?" Curt asked.

"I don't know," Arwa told him.

"He probably won't come with more than twelve to eighteen. It's too hard to handle and control that many men for indoor combat unless he's got NE tacomm like we do. Your Majesty, give Qahtan a call and get him up here with your son. Stretch the truth if you have to. Make up a convincing story. Your life and that of your son are likely to depend on being convincing."

Queen Arwa looked at him and remarked, "I understand why you were awarded the Star of Brunei. The Sultan always appreciated thinking people who could get right at the heart of a problem."

"The Sultana Alzena was the driving force behind it, your Majesty," Curt admitted.

"Well, she is his daughter, after all. The fruit does not fall far from the tree." So saying, she picked up the telephone.

Edie Sampson stepped over and clipped a module around the telephone cord. She activated the recording unit on her backpack and threw a switch. "You'll be able to hear the conversation on tacomm, Colonel," she remarked.

When Qahtan came on the line, Arwa told him, "I want you to come to the old purdah, General. Bring my son with you. I want to cut a deal." She was more than just a royal person, a figurehead. Curt had guessed this from their first meeting. Arwa was educated in America, and she was a clever and calculating person.

"What do you want to talk about?" Qahtan asked.

"Your life."

"*My* life? Ha! Your life and your throne are in danger! Not mine!"

"I'm sure you know what's going on in the palace," Arwa told him. "The Fourth Guards Regiment and the Washington Greys are within the gates. They outnumber your bodyguard and the remnants of the palace guard company. It won't take long for them to take you prisoner, Qahtan."

"If they can do it before my new forces reach the palace from the airport!"

"They can." Her voice was as cold and calculating as a bank loan officer.

"So I ask you again: What do you want to talk about?"

"Come up here with my son and I'll tell you."

"Aha! Do you think me stupid enough to come there when you probably have a room full of armed Americans to support you?"

"So bring your bodyguard with you. I'll offer you a deal, Qahtan. It may give you what you want."

"So talk."

"No. Not by telephone. This needs to be face to face. You know that we are a culture that likes to deal face to face, close enough to feel each other's breath. And I need to see my son and know he's all right. Furthermore, I will absolutely guarantee that the Americans who are with me will not shoot or harm you unless you attempt to harm me or my son while you're here."

Qahtan apparently didn't know that Salem was there with two of his sergeants. "How many Americans are there with you?"

"General Hettrick's staff, whom you know. Plus, a small contingent from the Washington Greys. I want your pledge of honor that you will not use force while you're here. After all, it is not possible to make a deal that's reasonable and just if one side threatens the other…"

"I'll be there, but I'll have my bodyguard with me."

"And my son?"

"And your son."

When she hung up, Curt could see that she was sweating. So, he turned to his Greys and told them, "Disperse around the suite. Sling

Novias in rapid deployment mode. General, will you please ask your staff to do the same?"

"What have you got in mind, Curt?" Hettrick wanted to know.

"I don't know. I'm making this up as I go along."

"I thought so."

"But I want to be ready for any dishonesty on Qahtan's part."

"The Queen will take care of things if that occurs," Arwa said in a strange voice.

"I'll be next to you with my two sergeants as your bodyguard, your Majesty," Salem told her.

"Thank you, Colonel. That will be helpful, I'm sure." Arwa indeed gave the impression of being very much in control. She was not only a beautiful woman, but now she was magnificent. Not only did she refuse to leave her own flesh and blood in the hands of the revolutionaries, but she was ready and willing to negotiate with them for her son. Curt would not have done so. But, then, he didn't have a son yet. Would he do it for a Washington Grey? He didn't know. The Washington Greys were one big family, and they'd risked their lives for one another in the past. But Curt wondered how much stronger real blood ties might be. He hoped someday to find out. In the meantime, too bad that Yemen would probably lose Arwa temporarily as their leader. Even if she was forced to leave Sana'a, he guessed she'd be back within a few years. And that Qahtan would pay for his coup with his head.

Qahtan hadn't been far away because within a minute a loud series of knocks was heard on one of the doors. Master Sergeant Carol Head, the huge Moravian first sergeant of Clinton's Cougars, stood carefully to one side and opened it. He was out of the direct line of fire, but his imposing size was fully visible to those who walked through.

Twelve Yemeni soldiers – Qahtan's full bodyguard - rushed in and deployed themselves on either side of the door. One of them tried to push Head out of the way. But the huge man simply looked down at the little Yemeni soldier with an expression of disdain and thin-lipped caution. The Yemeni didn't repeat the push. Nearly every American man in the room was bigger than the Yemeni men who stormed in. Round One to the Greys, Curt thought.

The next Grey the bodyguard encountered was Adonica. Her beauty was almost universal, the sort that under proper circumstances could cause strong men to sob aloud. She could stop traffic when she wanted to. She projected that, plus some of her vicious but carefully controlled persona. The Yemeni bodyguard didn't even attempt to intimidate her. The reverse was true.

The other ladies of the Greys present merely reinforced what Adonica had accomplished. The Yemeni weren't accustomed to coming one-on-one in combat with women. Females had a lower but protected status in their culture. At least until they grew old and were no longer fit for bed. Round Two for the Greys, thanks to the ancient Arab code of chivalry.

The Americans held this dual advantage in the psychological war that was going on in the suite. When Qahtan walked in, he had Prince Qadi by the arm. The youngster looked both defiant and a little scared at the same time. It was apparent to Curt that Arwa's son had swallowed the bullshit Qahtan had fed him about quickly becoming the king of all the Yemenis, and this had appealed to his teenage ego and already inflated self-esteem. The thought of absolute power and immunity is always attractive to teenagers, Curt knew. Far too many American teenagers were washed out of Basic Training when those dreams suddenly came face to face with military reality. Only the committed survived, and those who were committed only to themselves and not service to their country were weeded out next. Prince Qadi had never been subjected to any sort of selection process. Every young person undergoes a trial by fire in that regard, and Qadi didn't suspect that this was one of those times. He knew something was going on that he hadn't counted on, and he was more than a little bit frightened about it.

Qahtan was carrying a Hornet SMG, but it wasn't slung; he had it in his right hand. If he fired it, that could raise a little hell and injure those in the room not wearing body armor. Curt hoped Arwa would play it cool.

She did.

"So what do you want to talk about, Sultana?" Qahtan said in Arabic.

"Are you afraid of what you might say, Qahtan? Several Americans here speak Arabic," she told him coolly in English. "They'll know what you say. Why not speak English so everyone will know? If you won't, I will. And I'll repeat what you say for their benefit anyway."

"Very well!" Qahtan snarled in English. Round Three for the good guys. "What is your proposition?"

Arwa was straightforward about it. "Return my son to me. I'll leave Sana'a with him at once. I'll take the Fourth Guards with me. You won't have any further resistance from what's left of the RYA. The palace, the government, and the capital city will be yours. I'll accompany the Americans. Their Yemeni Expeditionary Force has been ordered by their President to leave Yemen at once."

Qahtan shook his head. "No! Installing your son as your successor on the throne of Yemen as you abdicate legitimizes the new regime!"

Arwa laughed in a way that might infuriate Qahtan, but it didn't because the man apparently thought he held a pat hand. "Legitimizes it? Ha! Qahtan, this is not the world of the past! This is the twenty-first century! The local representatives of the international news media here in Sana'a are already filing their reports of the seizure of the airport and the coup! The word is out all over the world! You can't stop it! News teams will be coming in before dawn!"

"Not if we hold the airport!"

"Who needs an airport for aerodynes, Qahtan? For short ranges, who needs hypersonic and supersonic aircraft? The teams will come in from Mecca, Cairo, and Bahrain by short-range subsonic aerodynes!"

"They will not be allowed to enter Yemen until we have stabilized our internal affairs!"

"And do you know how they'll portray you to the world for doing that, Qahtan? Even the notorious Saddam Hussein tried to stroke the news media people; he failed, but he tried. If he'd been more attuned to other than his own Assyrian culture, he might have succeeded. Might as well make a clean break of it, Qahtan," Arwa told him, not budging a millimeter from where she stood and confronted him. "Give me my son, and I'll depart. This won't be the first time a royal regime has lost power in Yemen. Last time, hardly anyone noticed it because it was a clean break with no hostages. If you accede to my request, Qahtan, you'll get your prize without additional bloodshed, without losing more lives, without expending more military ammunition and equipment for which I'm sure you're paying dearly. You might as well overthrow the royal house here and set up a 'social democratic' regime again. That's been happening for more than a century in this part of the world. So, go with the flow, Qahtan. Stop playing the old game. Give me my son. We'll leave at once. And the prize is yours."

Qahtan thought about this for only a moment. He didn't yet see where Arwa had a position from which she could bargain. So, he asked, "And if I don't?"

"I leave with the Fourth Guards and the Americans. And with Yemeni assets frozen in Switzerland, Bahrain, Singapore, and Brunei. I am the only one who can order them unfrozen, Qahtan. And I have to be there in person to do it. If I leave without my son, you'll be left with no foreign exchange except what you're able to wheedle out of those East World nations who have opted to back you thus far. I'm sure they had the idea that Yemen's foreign exchange could be counted on to pay for the military support they've given you."

The scenario and its multiple outcomes were getting very complex, Curt suddenly realized. Queen Arwa was indeed smart. She'd changed the scenario from a simple takeover to a complicated play on international finance. Curt suspected that international finance had been involved in Yemen all along in the form of Ferron Corporation. But that wasn't his area of expertise. He realized that his own area of expertise, the military, had been brought into

Yemen because of it, however. He told himself he'd have to learn something about that lest he become involved in future conflicts of this sort. After all, as a member of the royal family of Brunei, he could count on good instructors.

"And if I decide not to let you leave at all?"

"Don't be absurd, Qahtan!" Arwa said with a snort. She looked at her watch. "We have an escape route. We have the combined power of the Fourth Guards and the Washington Greys. We currently control access to and from the palace. And we're pressed for time because we know where your reinforcements are and when they'll get here. So, we don't have a lot of time to haggle. We're out of here in two minutes in any event. Make a decision."

It was Prince Qadi who, seeing his dream suddenly disappear, erupted by yelling at Qahtan, "You promised me the throne! You promised! I want to be the imam of the Yemenis! It's my birthright!"

Qahtan replied quickly, "It's your birthright only if I say so! Too bad you never had a father to properly discipline you! I'm going to have to be a substitute father for you and teach you how to be a man!"

"What do you mean? I am a man! You promised to take me to my first qat party once my mother wasn't around to say no!"

"And there will be other things that I'll teach you, my Prince," Qahtan told him smoothly, trying to gloss over the rough situation in which he found himself and the decision he knew he'd have to make. It would drastically change his plans.

"You've just wasted thirty seconds," Arwa told him bluntly. "Ninety seconds and we leave!"

Curt decided the Queen had ice for blood as well as iron ovaries.

Qahtan suddenly pushed Qadi toward his mother. "Take the little snot! He's not worth the trouble! But I grant you no additional favors! No safe conduct out of Yemen! If you want out of Yemen, you'll have to fight for it!"

"Fair enough!" Queen Arwa replied, then added. "So I will! I promised that no Americans would shoot at you here. I never said that I wouldn't…"

With a smooth but sudden motion, she had a tiny automatic pistol in her hands. Yemen was the land of ancient firearms, and Curt immediately recognized the handgun as a British-made Webley 25 Hammerless Pistol, apparently a family heirloom from the days of British colonization. Curt's father had had one in his firearms collection ostensibly for Curt's mother to use as a "social purpose weapon." Curt recalled that it was none of the above.

But Queen Arwa pulled off three shots in rapid succession. They were aimed in the general direction of Qahtan. One of them hit him in the neck.

A .25-caliber (old English system where caliber was measured in decimals of an inch) bullet is no man-stopper. Mostly, it was intended to scare the hell out of an assailant. But it happened to hit Qahtan in such a way that he was pitched over backwards, blood gushing from the wound.

Qahtan's bodyguards were indeed bloodthirsty Yemeni hillmen who'd been recruited into the RYA, but they weren't used to shooting indoors or around women. And they weren't expecting the sudden action of their Queen. However, their response was immediate.

But the Greys were more immediate. They'd been in fire fights. They'd been around when people shot at one another suddenly and without warning. The sound of a Novia being fired indoors is deafening. Four shots was all it took to dispatch the four bodyguards who'd managed to respond by pointing their weapons toward Queen Arwa. Dyani, Hassan, Henry, and Edie had fired almost simultaneously.

"Drop them!" was the snarl from Kitsy.

"Right now!" snapped Adonica.

In the immediate wake of the Novia reports, the sound of two women giving those orders stunned the Yemeni bodyguard. But not before two more shots shook the windows. This time, the reports were different. One sounded like a cannon going off. The other was less energetic. Two more Yemenis went down.

Henry Kester had his Colt M1911A1 .45-caliber pistol in his hand. That was a hand cannon; hence, the sound.

Edie's hand held her favorite close-in weapon, the nine-millimeter Beretta which Curt often chided her as being a pistol that would scare more than stop. It had done both right then.

"Didn't you hear the ladies?" Kester asked the remaining Yemeni bodyguards.

"They said drop them! They meant it!" Edie added.

By that time, the remaining bodyguards still standing had dropped their Hornets or were in the process of dropping them.

Curt looked at Hettrick. "Out of here, General! Let's move it!"

"We'll take Qahtan," Hettrick decided.

"He may be dead by the time we get him down the stairs," Curt pointed out. "How many people have we got to guard him if he doesn't die? And do we want to be the ones in this war who take hostages? General, leave him! He's more trouble than he's worth!"

"Right! Queen Arwa, get your son and let's go!" Hettrick decided.

Prince Qadi stood there in shock. He'd been standing right alongside Qahtan. He'd never seen a man shot before. Nor had he been around people who actually fired the guns they carried. He'd led a very sheltered and restricted life. That was about to change.

Arwa walked over and took her son's arm. "*Qadi! Ta'ala!*"

He offered no, resistance to her. "*Aiwa, Omm...*"

Chapter Twenty-Nine

"Thank you, Kida, for giving us a night to rest," Dyani told him.

"What do you mean, rest? Who rested?" Curt replied as he got dressed. He was feeling a little better this morning.

Dyani wrapped the sheet around her and got to her feet. "To recover from postcombat adrenalin rush, then?"

"Oh, so that's what it's called?" Curt told her in muck amazement.

"No, I call it something else. So do you. And it was indeed rest. You slept hard."

"Afterwards…"

"We both did. It was a very difficult day…and night. First at the airport. Then in Sana'a. Then getting back here in the dark. Thank God the East Worlders didn't chase us. My bird-botters were exhausted. I don't think we could have kept up the recce much longer."

"We're going to need almost continual recce during this retreat down the railroad," Curt reminded her. "Can you work with the bird-botters from the Wolfhounds and Cottonbalers?"

"I can work with anyone," Dyani told him simply. She stepped up behind him and put her arms around him, drawing herself close to him. "I'm hungry."

"Hungry? After last night?"

"For food."

"I'm glad you qualified that, superwoman. So am I. Let's see what the cook managed to kill."

"Are we getting that short of rations?" Dyani asked.

"No, but l want to make sure we don't run out. Dammit, Deer Arrow! Get dressed before I forget I'm the regimental commander!

We've got work to do! I've got to convene a quick Papa and Oscar brief, then get with Battleaxe to coordinate it. And we've got to be out of Amran this afternoon! So let's move it! Duty calls!"

That was the signal. "Yes, sir! A busy day ahead, Colonel!"

And it was.

"Where do we stand?" Curt asked once his staff and officers had gathered in the Amran CIC. "Losses? Pappy?"

The older man shook his head sadly. "We've got eighteen injured or wounded out of TACBATT. The Ferrets are damned-near zeroed-out - three left. The Leopards are down to two. So are the Stilettos. The Fusileers are out of action. Basically, a third of TACBATT is scrubbed. Sorry, Colonel, but I have no morning report yet from Major Gydesen. I don't know how serious some of the injuries are. And I have no idea at this time when or if some of the wounded will be able to return to duty."

Those were the greatest losses experienced by the Washington Greys since Curt had joined the regiment fifteen years before. A few days ago, he thought it was serious that he'd temporarily lost four Sierra Charlies to venereal disease. Now he steeled himself to accept the present situation. The Washington Greys would need to restructure what was left so they'd stand a fair chance of getting down the hill to the Red Sea.

"Can we evac the wounded to the Regulars' casern at al-Zuhra?" Curt asked.

"I've been working with the other regimental adjutants on that, Colonel," Pappy Gratton replied. He was a thorough staff man and a good one. He could anticipate what would be required of him and proceed to do it with the confidence that it was the proper action. "We have no airlift left, but we've called upon the Regulars' AIRBATT for the evac. They're short of 'dynes but the Wolfhounds and Cottonbalers both are short of fuel. We're working a combined op, but that's Hensley's turf and I'll let her speak to it."

Curt turned to his ops staffer. "Major Atkinson?"

"I'm coordinating with my counterparts in the other three

regiments, sir." Atkinson was a quiet but very thorough and highly competent operational expert. Hettrick had taught her well and Curt had put the final touches on her education for the job. She had become an expert in working with the often turf-conscious staffers of the other regiments. The return of the Army to the regimental system a half a century before had had its good points and bad ones. It greatly increased unit pride and cohesiveness but at the expense of drawing lines in the turf. With the growing integration of the Iron Fist regiments into a combined Sierra Charlie force, she had learned how to skip gently over those lines. "Actually, Colonel, I had to assume the job of the head honcho since the Iron Fist staff is still out of it this morning. But when they come back online in an hour or so, we can sure as hell use their help! The Regulars got back down the hill to al-Zuhra last night and are making ready to serve as the depot area for the sealift out of here."

"Any word on the sealift?"

"Negatory, sir! That was being worked on by the Iron Fist staff."

"How about rail transport? Or are we going to have to walk out of here?" Curt wanted to know.

"Colonel, I've run up against some resistance on the part of the railroad management. They're following a 'business as usual' policy. Now they're not returning my calls." This had vexed Atkinson. But she hadn't tried to force the hand.

"Have you told them we'll commandeer the capability if they won't cooperate?" Curt asked.

"No, sir. I wanted to get willing cooperation from them first. But I may be running out of time."

"We're all running out of time. I'll look into it after this meeting," Curt vowed, deciding that he'd have to tangle assholes with John Toreva again. Maybe Hettrick could swing some clout with Walt Cory, the general manager of Ferron. He didn't waste further time on it right then. "Captain Motega, what's the security situation?"

"Colonel, birdbot surveillance recommenced at dawn," Dyani reported professionally, then admitted with her usual candor, "But it's minimal at this time. The Black Hawks were in linkage well into the night. When enough of them are rested enough to resume in an hour or so, we'll have more bots aloft. I'm also coordinating with the other regiments to schedule round-the-clock birdbot coverage until we get out of Yemen."

"Where are the East Worlders and what are they doing?" Curt asked.

"They're busy in Sana'a. Very busy. I wouldn't want to be in their shoes," Dyani said, and this was unusual because she never cut from a fight. So, it must be exceptionally bloody in the Yemen capital city today. "Looks like the usual revolutionary takeover fracas. Still some fighting in the streets."

"Yemeni still fighting? I didn't think most of the RYA could fight worth a damn!" Kitsy interrupted, then qualified her statement. "Except the Fourth Guards. They did an orgasmic job covering our minus-x coming out of Sana'a last night. I'll fight alongside them any day! But unorganized Yemeni resistance? That sounds real strange!"

"Not really," Jerry told her, drawing on his encyclopedic memory. "The Yemeni seem to sense the East Worlders are just another invading foreign force. Yemen used to be on major trade routes, so this is an old story to them. Goes back fifty centuries or more. They're fighting like they always have and like they often fought us out in the hills - armed individuals and small guerrilla groups harassing the invaders."

As Jerry paused, Dyani grasped the opportunity to carry on. "Colonel, the East Worlders occupied the palace shortly after we left. I have no report on the whereabouts or condition of General Qahtan."

"What's the situation at the airport?"

Dyani shook her head. "The East Worlder forces appear to be very busy consolidating their hold there. No international or domestic flights have operated since the original assault last night. Most of the facilities were damaged during the fight. We're watching to see what kind of reinforcements they airlift in there today."

"What about the Aerospace Force logistics support people who were there?"

It was Major Russ Frazier, looking more tired than Curt had ever seen him, who answered proudly, "We and the Wolfhounds got them out of there with us when we withdrew. The Cottonbalers took them to al-Zuhra by aerodyne. They're helping plan the evac down there."

"Good show, Russ!" Curt complimented him. The man had lost nearly all his command; he needed bucking up right then.

"Colonel, unless the East Worlders get a lot of reinforcement today, we may not have to worry about them attacking us," Jerry ventured an assessment of the situation. "I suspect they'd just as soon allow us to get out of Yemen without further assaults. They'll probably watch us closely and if it looks like we're withdrawing in good time they probably won't waste their effort pushing us. However, I wouldn't bet the farm on it. I want to maintain close surveillance on the situation."

"Well, Colonel, we can't drag our feet anyway," Captain Harriet Dearborn, S-4, put in. "We haven't had any logair shipments for the past two weeks. The supplies from the last logair flight were still at Sana'a airport when it was attacked. So we're down to three days' food and ammo plus the hundred-hour tactical reserve, some of which got wiped out when we lost vehicles during the casern assault."

"In short, we may go a little hungry getting out of here?" Kitsy asked.

"That we can live with. Lots of sheep around. You'll get to like mutton," Dearborn told her. "It's the ammo supply that worries me. And potable water. We may have to conserve drastically." Her assessment drove home the reality that any modern, organized, high-tech military force larger than a company couldn't operate without some sort of logistics "tail." The days when an army could live off the land had passed. Besides, in Yemen there wasn't much there to live off in the first place. Down at the platoon and company level, logistics was always taken for granted. But Curt had learned the hard way that logistics was a primary consideration in keeping a fighting force in shape to do any fighting at all.

"So we're out of here as fast as we can move," Curt decided. "I'll check with Battleaxe after this meeting, and I'll get our rail transportation worked out. In the meantime, our tactical order of battle has been shot to hell. We need to put together a rump TO for the rest of Operation Guts and Glory. Jerry, I want you and Joan to handle that management-task right away."

"Yes, sir!" both of them said.

"Carson, I haven't got an AIRBATT left," came the unusually quiet and subdued voice of Major Cal Worsham. Curt understood why the man was suddenly a lot less vocal and vulgar. Worsham was a flyboy without anything to fly. The man was on the ground, and that wasn't his element. The same held true for his battalion, which everyone in AIRBATT called a "squadron," an indication that they really believed themselves to be slightly different and slightly above the poor Sierra Charlies who had to fight down in the dirt. "Two Harpies. Period. My pilots and flight sergeants have nothing left to fight with. At the moment, we're a drain on the logistics. We're not good at fighting on the ground. We're not really Sierra Charlie support troops like Wade Hampton's SERVBATT who can drop their support and pick up a Novia if they have to. Sure, we'd pick up Novias and shoot it out with you if things really went to slime, but we'd be only cannon fodder."

"What do you want to do, Cal?" Curt pushed him for a suggestion, although he knew what it would be.

Worsham didn't hesitate because he'd thought it all through during a very sleepless night. "I think we can be of real help in putting together some sort of air operation with what's left of the air capability in the other regiments. I've been talking with the flyboys in the other outfits. I want to get my AIRBATT personnel down to al-Zuhra where we'll salvage what we can and maybe give the Iron Fist *some* air ops during the evac. I want to relocate AIRBATT to al-Zuhra today. But I don't want you to think that I'm leaving the rest of you in the lurch. I want to be able to put *some* Harpies and maybe even some Chippies in the air when and if needed. If we don't have some air capability, this retreat could become a slaughter. And we might never get out of Yemen. Remember what happened at Dunkirk. And Cap Bon. We've gotta be able to keep 'dynes' over you?'

"I agree," Jerry remarked. "The East Worlders have won thus far because they wiped out our tacair on the ground at the start. Just like the Yom Kippur War. I'll bet they're bringing in their own tacair capability. In the long run, they can't win without it. And if we have at least some tacair, it'll make things a whole hell of a lot harder for them. With some tacair we won't have to crawl out of Yemen with our tails between our legs if they continue to hassle us with guerrilla-style operations!"

"I'll clear it with Battleaxe. Make it so, Major Worsham!" Curt decided, agreeing tacitly with Jerry. Then he tried to buoy up the spirits of his command, "And don't think we're crawling out of Yemen with our tails between our legs. Or because we're beaten. We're leaving because we got a direct and unambiguous order from our commander in chief. And we'll do it honorably and professionally, so our butts won't be in a sling if the slime hits the impeller in Washington! Now, you have your orders or know what you have to do. Please make it so. Hassan, I want you and Captain Freeman to accompany me over to the railroad offices."

"What exactly do you want me to be prepared to do over there, sir?" Freeman asked.

"Be British. Historically, you people have been quite tolerant up to a point. Beyond that, you have no aversion to cutting a few throats," Curt explained briefly. "Hassan, I may need you to talk some sense into any Yemeni employee who might be a little reluctant to help us out."

Edie Sampson couldn't raise John Toreva on the phone, so Curt and his two officers showed up in the offices of the Amran and Red Sea Railroad without an appointment. Since it was apparent that Toreva was trying to stay the hell out of the conflict - something he really wouldn't be able to do forever - Curt believed that the time for common courtesy was past. So he simply walked through the outer offices while the Yemeni administrative employees looked on with open mouths and made no attempt to stop the three armed men.

Toreva was indeed in his office and stood up suddenly as Curt and the two men barged in.

"Mr. Toreva, we need the afternoon down-train," Curt announced, stopping before the man's desk. "Please arrange for it to be assigned to us for the purpose of evacuating American personnel and the Yemeni royal retinue down to the coast. The American military forces have received orders from the President to leave Yemen. The only way we can get out is to use the railroad to transport people and equipment down to al-Luhaya."

The Navaho's round face showed surprise, but he managed to remain impassive. "Colonel, the roads aren't very good, but you can certainly use them without anyone's permission. I don't care what Washington told you to do. They don't own this railroad. You can't just barge in here and commandeer private property for military use! It will screw up the mining schedule so badly that..."

"Toreva, I have news for you," Curt said in a voice that wasn't exactly pleasant. "You're about to get a new boss. I don't know who it will be, but you won't be working for Ferron Corporation next week at this time. You may not be working here at all. The Yemen government has fallen, and I don't know who the hell's in charge in Sana'a at the moment. But I'll bet the Ferron mining agreement is no longer valid."

"I heard something happened in Sana'a last night," Toreva remarked in an offhanded manner. He was very casual about it. "Local politics doesn't concern me here. I've got a railroad to run. I'm paid by Ferron and the railroad company, not the Sana'a politicians. Doesn't make any difference who's in charge up there. They don't know how to run a railroad."

"I say, old chap, you may have to teach them to do it with a gun at your bloody head," Freeman remarked. "Just the way some of my forebears had to teach the Indian government how to run the bloody trains there. It was not a pretty situation, believe me! Some of our supervisory chaps went out to work with the railways of India before the bloody country gained independence. And some of them never had the opportunity to return to England. I suspect you might like to see your home in America again someday, correct?"

"Hell, the Yemenis may think they're tough, but I know how to deal with them!"

"You're not dealing with the Yemenis any longer," Hassan pointed out. "Are you fluent in Chinese? Or Hindi?"

"And have you ever tried to deal with bloody Chinese mercenaries before?" Freeman asked. "I have. I was in the Seychelles. I'm bloody well lucky to be alive!"

"And you may be very lucky to be alive next week at this time, as a matter of fact," Curt added and unslung his Novia. It had a clip in it, but Curt hadn't chambered the first round. He made the move for psychological purposes. "Toreva, I haven't got time to screw around. If you won't cooperate, I'll cut you out of the loop right now."

Toreva reacted to that. It was apparent that he'd come to the instant conclusion that discretion was the better part of valor. So, he rationalized his position. "Hell, I can't do anything to stop you if I'm looking down the barrel of a gun! I'll tell Ferron I was forced to do it at gunpoint. It may screw up this afternoon's schedule, but if I'm still around after you go down the hill I can at least manage to repair the schedule damage within twenty-four hours. What do you want?"

"I'm pleased that you decided to cooperate. I need a train to transport troops and vehicles from Amran to al-Luhaya," Curt repeated.

"How the hell you gonna ride in ore cars?" Toreva asked.

"We're not," Curt told him. "The ore train won't roll this afternoon. We'll have to use other rolling stock. You've got right-of-way maintenance cars?"

"Uh, yeah. Mostly flats for carrying ballasting equipment, replacement rails, new ties, welding equipment, that sort of stuff. Couple of rail inspection cars, too."

"We'll use them," Curt decided. "Captain Freeman is my deputy in charge of assembling the train and arranging for loading ramps and such for the vehicles and warbots. Lieutenant Hassan will serve as a liaison with your Yemeni workers; he speaks the language." He looked at Freeman. "Captain, you've got your tacomm brick. Give me a call if you run into any problems. Your tacomm code is now Rail Head."

Chapter Thirty

"I've never ridden on a train before," Kitsy remarked. She almost had to shout over the sound of the wind rushing past and the squeal of steel wheel flanges on the curves of steel rail. It wasn't a comfortable ride. The coach rocked and swayed. Although the Amran and Red Sea Railroad used continuously welded steel rail laid on concrete ties, railroads had always operated with rather loose and sloppy dimensional tolerances.

Hettrick had established a temporary mobile CIC in two maintenance crew sleeping cars. Sometimes when track crews were out working on the line, they had to stay out for several days, interrupting their track work four times a day for passing trains.

"You? A southern belle who never rode the metro lines in Atlanta?" Curt asked in mock disbelief. It had been a rough morning. Finally, at about noon, Freeman and Hassan had gotten enough railway cars together to transport the remaining warbots, vehicles, and LAMVAs at Amran. The Greys had no Chippies left. The Wolfhounds, Cottonbalers, and Regulars were operating with only six Chippies and eight Harpies between them. They, too, had suffered huge losses during casern attacks and in the abortive Sana'a airport assault. Curt was still pissed off about having to quit while they were winning, thus incurring even greater losses.

On top of the shortage of aerodynes, the Iron Fist Division was growing short of ordinary expendables. Hettrick was forced to make a decision between using the available turbine fuel for the vehicles - which would be needed in any combat during the retreator the aerodynes. Georgie calculated that there wasn't enough fuel to airlift everything down to al-Zuhra by Chippie. So, the aerodynes were abandoned at Amran, Huth, and el-Mawr, but not without destroying them.

The 17th Iron Fist Division was but a shadow of its former self. More than half its bots and vehicles were destroyed or inoperable. It had been left to the Greys to gut and destroy unserviceable equipment in Amran - and there had been a lot of it. Now, the 17th Iron Fist was down to less than two regiments in terms of equipment. Fortunately, only about a third of the personnel had been wounded or injured, and ten Iron Fisters had been killed.

"Suh!" Kitsy fired back with a smile. It was hard for the Greys to smile much right then. But Kitsy tried. "I'm no city girl! My pappy retired to Owens Cross Roads, Alabama, the pyrotechnics capital of the world! And that's where I was raised…"

"That explains your consuming interest in fire and smoke," Curt told her. "Well, enjoy the train ride anyway. And learn something from this. It isn't the first time in military history that railroads have played a major part in campaigns. And don't forget the role that a railroad played in this one."

They both had a few moments to spare, and perhaps it was chance that found the two of them together in the part of the CIC car that was used for the Greys CIC on wheels, "But this is an ancient form of transportation! The nineteenth century version of the ox cart. I'll probably never get near a railroad again. But I do indeed like railroad locomotives. They're so *masculine!*"

"Kitsy, you're showing signs of becoming a very good field grade commander," Curt suddenly told her. "You're certainly aggressive, You take the initiative. You've learned to lead, and you do very well at it. You might make it to regimental command someday…"

"I'm not sure I could hack it, Curt. Or that I want it," she admitted.

"I felt the same way. I still do. That's probably what keeps me trying to do better," Curt admitted in reply. "I think you might become a very good regimental commander. But you've got to learn and respect a lot of military history first."

"History? Why?"

"So you don't refight the same battles that others did…and lose them the same way."

"And railroads are important?"

"Yes. Before the railroads were available in the nineteenth century, large military forces couldn't be mobilized, transported, maneuvered, or supplied. Didn't you Rebs learn anything from the Civil War?"

Kitsy ignored the little taunt from Curt. Her southern background and upbringing were now far in the past. Something called West Point had gotten between her and two centuries of emotion. "How about airlift? That's the modern way to do it."

"It may be the modern way to do it, but look at us right now. We haven't got any airlift capability to speak of. Without the railroad, we'd be in a heap of trouble, wouldn't we?"

"I guess that elephants were important to those Romans who studied Hannibal's campaigns," Kitsy mused.

"He couldn't have operated in Italy for all those years otherwise, even though he had damned few elephants. Mostly they were the equivalent of modern armored tank warbots. But, yeah, the Romans did study Hannibal's campaigns. But they never really studied the use of Assyrian chariots, which is one reason they could never pin down their eastern frontier. Anyway, I'm serious about the military history part, Kitsy."

"You're a pretty good teacher. How about helping me?"

"Sure! But I suggest you sign up for a war college correspondence course when we get back," Curt suggested. "And that's a serious suggestion from your commanding officer."

The forward door opened and Colonel Joanne Wilkinson, Hettrick's COS, stuck her head through. "Curt, the general's compliments and all that. Battleaxe wants to see you ASAP."

"What's up, Joanie?" Curt felt bad about Colonel Joanne Wilkinson. She'd been the Greys' COS for a long time and finally decided to take twenty-and-out because she'd seen too much combat. Hettrick had talked her into staying in and helping her run the Iron Fist Division in a staff slot where she wouldn't be in combat. It didn't work out that way. In this abortive YEF operation, everyone was being shot at. What had started out as an innocuous railway security mission had turned into the worst debacle Curt had ever been in.

Wilkinson sighed. "The East Worlders are up and moving. Intelligence and surveillance data indicate they might try to block our retreat as we come out of the Wadi Mawr canyon."

Curt did a quick mental calculation. "We'll get to al-Luhaya before they can move enough forces to do any good."

"Want to bet the farm on it?" Joanne asked rhetorically.

"No. Goddammit, those bastards don't know how to quit while they're winning!" Curt exploded as he got to his feet. "We're getting out of their hair anyway! Why the hell are they trying to stop us?"

"Maybe they're pissed that we blew up most of the materiel we had to leave behind," Kitsy suggested. "Or maybe they want to see how their warbots really stack up against ours."

Curt looked down at where she sat. "As I said a few minutes ago, you've got the makings of a good tactician and maybe even a regimental commander."

"That's the good news," Joanne went on. "I'm sure you'll be delighted to learn that the commander in chief has refused to give the Navy permission to risk having their multi-billion dollar Raborn Class carrier submarines enter the narrow waters of the Red Sea to pick us up at al-Luhaya."

That was nearly the final blow of the day for Curt. "What the hell does the Big Man expect us to do? Row boats across the Red Sea to Egypt and then float down the Nile to the Med?"

"Battleaxe has some ideas," Wilkinson told him. "That's why she wants you up front ASAP. We've got to pull a rabbit out of a hat, and damned soon!"

Queen Arwa was the only one who was with Hettrick when Curt went into Hettrick's compartment just forward of the divisional CIC. "Good afternoon, General. You appear to be in good spirits, considering the circumstances, your Majesty," Curt greeted them, trying to maintain a semblance of civilized manners in this difficult situation. Something was indeed going on for Hettrick to call him into a private meeting with the Queen. "How's your son?"

"Petulant. But I intend to put the fear of Allah in him," Arwa replied. "He needs discipline and a good education. Can you recommend a good military school in the United States?"

Curt thought about that for a moment. The teenaged Prince of Yemen was a spoiled brat, yet old enough to bolt and run from most military schools. So, Curt replied, "Any of the Honor military schools would be satisfactory. But if you want to make sure he doesn't run away I'd suggest the New Mexico Military Institute. It's in Roswell, New Mexico. That's several hundred kilometers from everywhere. And the climate is semiarid like Yemen. Tough school, too."

"Thank you. When we get out of here, I'll look into that. I now see that he's been surrounded by sycophants in Sana'a. That's no way to raise the next king. I may have to leave Yemen temporarily, Colonel Carson, but I'll be back."

"If we get out of here, which at the moment looks nebulous," Hettrick put in.

"I understand that you need a rabbit pulled out of a hat, General. I hope I can help. But I didn't bring my magic wand."

Hettrick was in no mood for even the slightest bit of humor. "Curt, we probably won't have sealift out of al-Luhaya unless we can commandeer an ore boat. I don't want to count on that."

Although Curt had already gotten the word from Wilkinson, he asked, "Where's the Navy?"

"Steaming in the Gulf of Aden," Hettrick told him. "The *McCain* and the *Cromwell* are submerged and waiting to come in and get us. A couple of escort submarines are standing by there as backup. However, the President won't approve their entry into the Red Sea."

"*What?* Why? Who advised him on that?"

"I don't know who. As to why, the best information I can get out of

Pickens in the Pentagon is that the President said no after he was briefed by the Navy. So, we're to go to al-Luhaya and await further orders."

"A great place to defend ourselves!" Curt muttered. He'd seen the terrain of the Tihamah, a narrow strip of dry coastal desert with a few fertile oases near the foothills. He'd talked to Jim Ricketts whose Regulars had been based there for four months. It was a miserable place. Hot and humid. Barren. No water. No way that the Iron Fist personnel could live off the land. Ricketts didn't have much to say about the Tihamah that was encouraging. Curt had hoped to spend as little time as possible there while they embarked on seagoing vessels.

He went on, "I've sat in on Navy briefings. Those people can be superconservative. Much more so than ours. A Navy file once told me that they were more cautious than we because the Army has never had a parade ground sink. Plus, the fact that the Navy had to snivel and give blood to get those *Raborn* Class subs. A couple of generations of admirals put their careers on the line to keep that long-term program going."

Hettrick nodded. "My assessment tells me the admirals gave the commander in chief the 'can do' plan. Then they added that no one had enough good G-2 on this East Worlder intervention to determine whether or not hostile naval forces might be involved in the close confines of the Red Sea. They might have also hedged on whether or not East World air interdiction might catch their boats on the surface with their flight decks all tied up with evac. Surveillance satellites show the East Worlders brought aerodynes and ground-pounder aircraft into Sana'a and Baraqish this morning. That puts their tacair within two hundred klicks of al-Luhaya. And there's no way to tell if the East Worlders have subs lying on the bottom offshore, just waiting."

"The East Worlders seem to have planned this reasonably well. The Navy may be right," Curt had to admit. "Stuff could be lying on the bottom out there, just waiting. Depends on how serious the East Worlders want to get. Do they want a general war, or do they want the Jebel Miswar?"

"I don't know, and I can't worry about it. My orders are to evacuate the former Yemen Expeditionary Force from Yemen," Hettrick snapped, still irritated at the order.

"Well, General, how the hell do we do that without naval support?" Curt wanted to know. "We can go only so far before we run out of land. Our bots can ford a ten-meter river, but they'll have a little trouble with the Red Sea. Our vehicles won't float worth a damn. And we certainly can't swim across that ditch!"

"Sarcasm won't feed the bulldog, Colonel," Hettrick reminded him, although she knew he was just blowing off steam prior to tackling the problem. "If the United States doesn't have either the guts or the capability to get us out of the place they sent us to, I'm not above calling on our allies for help."

Queen Arwa spoke up for the first time. "I've spoken at length with King Abdullah bin Saud in Riyadh. He's disturbed about this new foreign incursion to the south of his kingdom. I have a mutual assistance treaty with him, but he's hesitant to commit support until he knows more about the mercenary forces in Yemen."

"Your Majesty, we've captured personnel and equipment," Curt reminded her. "The mercenary troops came from India, Burma, China, southeast Asia, and maybe Korea. Their equipment was made in those countries, too."

"I told him that," Queen Arwa interrupted. "I also told him there was no indication that any Islamic nation was involved. The absence of personnel and equipment from places such as Pakistan, Singapore, and Indonesia was striking. I think we're beginning to see a new world pattern emerge here."

"East versus west?" Curt ventured to guess.

She nodded. "But in a new guise. You're aware of Parkinson's east-west piston theory of history?"

"I've studied it," Curt admitted. He felt there were a few holes in the historian's analysis, now more than a century old. "I think he was wrong when he said that Marxism would be the new religion of the Orient. That hasn't happened. Marxism still appeals to the poor nations and it's used a lot by dictators. But it never really turned into a real religion."

Arwa held up her long hand. "Ah, yes, and there you've hit upon it, Colonel. East versus west may still be a valid theory. But the religions haven't changed! I'm a modern Muslim. I have no trouble with the other religions that developed in the Middle East - Judaism and Christianity. Those religions believe in one God, too. The prophets, messiahs, and saints differ, but Islam easily embraces them in its pantheon. On the other hand, I have trouble with the religions of the Hindus, Buddhists, Taoists, and such. Those are the religious beliefs of the East Worlders, Colonel! Their contemplative religions are uniting them temporarily. Otherwise, they've accepted modern capitalism in place of Marxism, suitably adapted to their cultures."

"Are you telling me, your Majesty, that we've got a religious war starting here?" Curt wanted to know.

"No. It's the usual grab for land, resources, and wealth using military force," Arwa admitted. "Easier for adolescent cultures to grasp that concept than the one about working hard and organizing into modern market economies. However, the leaders are using the vast differences between the oriental and western religions as the ideological fulcrum. It's an old story."

Curt knew it was. But Arwa had put a modern, twenty-first century spin on it. "So does King Abdullah realize this?"'

"He's conferring with his advisors about it. I think he'll help us. But a little nudge might push him faster. I think you can provide that nudge."

"'Me?" Curt was astounded at that suggestion. "I'm just a light colonel in the United States Army, not a diplomat!"

"You are also Sultan Qahtar Mohammed ibn Qars, wearer of the Sultan's Star of Brunei and therefore a member of the royal family of Sultan Ahmad Iskander bin Muhammad Shah Rejang Brunei, ruler of Negara Darussalem Brunei," Queen Arwa reminded him.

"An honorary title and position, I assure you," Curt said.

"Perhaps. But you are known to him. He is a generous man not beyond responding to a family member's request..." Arwa began, then went on earnestly, "Colonel, please call Brunei and ask the Sultan to call King Abdullah ibn Saud," She spread her long hands. "That is all I ask."

Curt always hesitated to use the power that could be his by virtue of the award of the Sultan's Star of Brunei. He turned to Hettrick and didn't even need to voice the question. "General?"

"As you remarked a moment ago, we have direct orders to leave Yemen, Curt," she told him. "If the Navy can't support that for whatever reason, then we're expected to act in the sort of opportunistic manner of good American soldiers: Figure out a way to do it ourselves."

"I'd be acting way the hell outside my authority, General. I'm not authorized to make diplomatic contacts like that."

Hettrick smiled. "Curt, insofar as I'm concerned, it's a family matter in your case."

"Okay, a telephone call is easy," Curt acquiesced. Then he got to a matter of immediate concern. "Then what are we going to do if the East Worlders are really moving to intercept the train before we get to the coast?"

Major General Belinda Hettrick looked squarely at him and told him, "After you make that telephone call to Brunei, you're going to confer with the other regimental commanders and develop an operation plan. You, sir, are my tactical expert. I started teaching you, but you quickly outdistanced the teacher. So, I need a plan for the defense of al-Luhaya if we get there without a fight ahead of time."

"What if the East Worlders want to fight?"

"Well, you can refuse to like someone - or lend them money - but if they want to fight, you've got to oblige them," Hettrick remarked pensively. "So you should develop a plan to give those East Worlders what they want. Remember, of course, the sage advice of General Ulysses S. Grant: *'Find out where your enemy is. Get at him as soon as you can. Strike at him as hard as you can, and keep moving on.' "*

Curt thought about that and countered, "I'm going to have to pull off a von Moltke style defensive offense as well as make use of some advice from Clausewitz about making use of the given means in combat. Very well, General, where's the telephone? First things first."

Chapter Thirty-One

"Jeez, I hope this works!" Major Russ Frazier's voice came through the quiet darkness.

"Worked fine before, Russ," Curt muttered in reply. "At El Guettar. Passchendale. Bussaco. Talavera."

"I say, Colonel, you do indeed know your bloody history," Captain Peter Freeman put in, scanning the dawn horizon with his IR binoculars. "I suspect you know that it was the favorite tactic of General John Wellesley."

"The Duke of Wellington? Sure!" Curt responded. "Dyani, any signs of them yet?"

Curt was atop the ridge of Jebel Wahid, "Lonesome Mountain," an elongated foothill that reared some one thousand meters above the valley of Wadi Mawr and the railroad as it snaked out of the hills onto the open plain of the Tihamah to the west. Most of the Greys were on the western slope behind him. Curt was there because he needed to run his portion of the coming fight where he could actually see it. He didn't want to depend on remote sensors and tactical displays in a converted ACV. He wanted the direct input of such experts as Captain Dyani Motega. He wanted his most aggressive assault company leader, now without a company, at his side to assess the fight and feed him direct info. He wanted Captain Peter Freeman with him because the British exchange officer who no longer had a Saucy Cans platoon to run, was an experienced artillery officer.

The tactical plan had occurred to Curt as he'd studied the holographic topo maps of western Yemen where the railroad came out of the mountain gorge and arrowed across the Tihamah plain to Al-Luhaya.

All four regiments and the RYA 4th Guards were deployed around Jebel Wahid. The 4th Guards were at the oasis village of At Tur blocking the Haija to al-Zuhra road that snaked out of the eastern ridges.

The railway was blocked at Bani Kubayl by an ore train parked on the single-track line.

On either side of him along the ridge were emplaced eighteen LAMVAs with their multipurpose Saucy Cans 75-millimeter guns, the artillery of the Iron Fist Division.

Down the forward or eastern slope of Jebel Wahid, fifty Mary Anns were deployed in carefully prepared stealthy positions where they could be withdrawn quickly up the slope to the ridge or northwesterly along Jebel Wahid.

Some forty Mary Anns were on the right flank of the mountain between the high ground and the wadi.

A few Sierra Charlies were with the Mary Anns to command them. Mary Anns might have artificial intelligence, but they weren't smart enough to fight without human supervision.

Most of the Sierra Charlies were on the western or reverse slope of Jebel Wahid.

This tactical deployment puzzled most of the Sierra Charlies. But Curt had paid attention to what the ancient Chinese tactician, Sun Tzu, had written: *"Those skilled in war bring the enemy to the field of battle and are not brought there by him."*

Curt was going to choose the time and place for battle, not the enemy.

And he didn't like to fight on the defensive. Sierra Charlie units operate best on the offense. So, Curt had chosen to organize the coming battle as the Prussian General Helmuth von Moltke might, using the offensive defense.

The first order of business was to blunt the heavy 57-millimeter firepower of the armored Red Hammer warbots.

Hettrick had bought off on the battle plan after it had been thrashed out during the night by all five regimental commanders, their staffs, and Hettrick's staff. It was complex, so Hettrick was going to run the show from an OCV parked in the Al Mishal oasis west of Jebel Wahid.

Dyani replied to her commanding officer's question, "Negatory, Colonel! Black Hawk Leader reports continuous birdbot surveillance. We're getting an excellent real-time downlink from several overpassing recon sats. The train is approaching Ash Shahil about twenty klicks away. Should be at Bani Kubayl in thirteen minutes. The force on the road will come around the curve in about thirty-four minutes." As usual, Dyani was brief and succinct.

"The road force is running behind the train," Russ remarked. "Why did the stupid bastards split their forces?"

"Same bloody problem I had in Amran," Peter explained. "The railway has lots of bloody ore wagons, but bloody few goods or passenger wagons. I bloody well stripped the rail yard clean. Their warbot contingents had to come by road because the ore wagons wouldn't accommodate their bloody warbots. The East Worlder infantry is riding in empty ore wagons."

"Peter, one of these days, I want you to show me a bloody warbot," Russ jibed.

"Go down to the repair sheds when your maintenance chaps are checking hydraulics," Freeman replied. "In the British Army, the warbot hydraulic fluid is dyed red. Just like yours. You use the term 'bot flush.' We're a bit less graphic. It's just warbot blood to us."

Curt checked the time. The sky was getting very bright. Sunrise in four minutes. Not that it made any difference to Curt and the other Sierra Charlies, or to the warbots. Each of them were fully capable of fighting several hundred black panthers in a coal mine at midnight. And they could fight into the sun. The rising sun would be a very bright light in their organic eyes, but they had the radar, laser, and infrared eyes of their warbots and battle helmets. Their excellent sensor suites and outstanding data communications gave every Sierra Charlie a tactical battle map displayed on the helmet visor.

Russ still didn't believe the tactical plan would work. "Jeez, they'll have the sun behind them, and we'll be fully illuminated!"

"With practically no shadows to provide them with visual information on size and shape," Dyani remarked, continuing to scan the terrain.

"Hell, we don't have the foggiest fucking notion how god-damned good their sensors are!" Frazier complained.

"Hassan, Henry, and Edie went through that Chinese warbot we captured at Sana'a airport," Curt reminded him as he continued to monitor the incoming tactical data stream squirted to their helmet displays by both Georgie and Grady. "They've got the usual sensors - radar, lidar, infrared - but Edie says the accuracy and resolution both suck beyond three hundred meters. And we don't know much about their new short-range sensors."

"Is that new sensor the one they used to trigger wadi mines?"

"Yeah. Our intelligence people are going to love us for capturing one. Don't ask me how it works, but it's new. Hassan, our scientific genius, conferred with Blue Maxie about it," Curt tried to explain, not so sure that he understood it himself. "He claims the Chinese made a connection between the bioelectronics of acupuncture with something called longitudinal waves. Says it's an electrical scalar field that's been ignored for over a century. Doesn't behave like ordinary electromagnetic radiation. Don't ask me why. I'm not a scientist. Hassan is. He could have stayed at Cal Tech, but he wanted to be a Sierra Charlie."

"Oh, to be young and idealistic again!" Russ said with a sigh. "He'll learn…"

"There's the train!" Dyani interrupted them.

"Going to NE tacomm," Curt warned them and switched over to

the neuroelectronic communication system in his helmet.

Battleaxe, Grey Head here confirming that the train is comin' 'round the mountain!

Let's keep our water cool, Grey Head. I want to see what happens when they come to the parked train. All hands, our Harpies are spooling up now!

Battleaxe, Blue Maxie! How marry we got to call on if we need them?

Count on thirteen Harpies. And six Chippies, but only for medical evac! Our biggest problem is fuel reserves. So, don't call for air support unless you absolutely, positively need it! In short, I won't approve it unless you really snivel hard.

Dyani was watching as the incoming train pulled to a halt at Bani Kubayl. *Grey Head, Deer Arrow! Looks like a Chinese fire drill down there.*

Grey Head, Grey Tech here, was the call from Edie down in the main technical support ACV on the reverse slope of Jebel Wahid. *Lots of action on the East World tacomm channels.*

Are you reading their hop pattern? Curt asked. That was unnecessary. He knew that Edie was on top of it at once. But precombat jitters drove him to check it out, just to make sure.

Roger that, Grey Head! As an additional security precaution, they're not conversing in English. Sounds like Hindi. Might be Chinese.

Grey Tech, Assassin here! I can follow some Hindi! Hassan's voice came through.

If it's Chinese, I might be able to read it, Curt advised her. *Squirt it to the Assassin and Grey Head on Channel Niner-Tango-seven.*

Grey Head, it's a lot of chatter! You sure you won't get data overload?

Okay, you monitor it. Assassin, get on it. If it begins to sound like orders being given, patch me in. It would make me feel better. if I knew who's in command of this East World outfit. Grey Tech, if you hear anyone who sounds anything like someone we know, flash me.

Like General Qahtan?

You've got it, Grey Tech!

Grey Head, Alleycat Leader! Qahtan was pretty bloody when we left him in the palace! Jerry pointed out.

But Arwa hit him only once with that lady's social purpose pop gun, Curt replied. *In the neck. Lots of blood. But we don't know how much damage was done. Or how good the East Worlders' biotech is.*

I'll tell you for sure that Asian biotechnology is pretty damned good! There was no mistaking Kitsy. If the Bruneis hadn't stepped in and helped Walter Reed patch my spinal column with implanted nerve jumpers, it would have taken me a couple more months to get out of that death trap!

So Qahtan could be in the lead, Jerry went on. *He won't be the first military leader in history who led while badly wounded but alive. He's got a lot of motivation. He wants the Queen and her son. His position is sort of shaky without them.*

Salem isn't about to allow that! The Queen's in al-Luhaya in a very secure situation. Kitsy told him.

Curt allowed the chatter to go on because nothing seemed to happen for long minutes. Curt knew the troops were getting antsy. But until the East World force began to come together down there in Wadi Mawr, Curt didn't want to give away the positions of the Iron Fisters.

Then the data flow began to increase.

Secondary East World column rounding the bend on the road, Dyani reported. *They've got the Red Hammer warbots with them!*

Hold fire! Freeman advised calmly, his message as the forward artillery observer going out to the Saucy Cans commanders. *Let them all get exposed. Begin to choose and track your targets now. Load sadarm rounds with EFP! Go for the lead warbots on the first salvo, the rest on the second, and remaining warbot targets of opportunity on the third. Then stand by to load fletchette AP rounds!* In the tension of forthcoming battle, the British exchange officer's language suddenly became very terse. His usual vulgarisms disappeared. The Saucy Cans were tasked to take out the East World warbots with sense-and-destroy explosively formed armor-piercing projectiles. Then they could be shifted to a support role by air-bursting fletchettes over the East World infantry.

It was getting close to the mad minute. Curt took one last opportunity to check and double check deployment of detachments. What he saw on his helmet display looked good. A silence settled in on the tacomm channel. In the desert-like environment around him on the hill, only the sounds of dawn were heard.

Commence firing! came the call from Freeman.

The ridge line erupted with the sounds of Saucy Cans.

Curt riveted his attention on the road ten kilometers to the southeast where at least fifty warbots plus an equal number of vehicles were rolling along against the backdrop of a sharply rising bluff. There would be no rounds over-shooting; those that were high would hit the bluff nearly over the warbots and trucks.

He had to switch from visual to dust-cutter IR sensors. The road was in the dawn shadow of the bluff and suddenly became nothing, but a huge mélange of sand and dust illuminated by the bursts of the projectiles and the flashes of the EFPs hitting warbots and vehicles from above.

Russ Frazier's job was to maintain surveillance on the infantry on the train. *The East World infantry is reacting to the Saucy Cans barrage,* he reported brusquely. Looks like they're bailing out of the ore cars.

Grey Head, Grey Tech is picking up orders on the enemy tacomm. Assassin reports those are Hindu troops. He catches snatches of orders in Hindi to form up and prepare to move against the ridge line!

Mary Anns, hold fire! Curt instructed. *Don't shoot until you see the whites of their sensors. Mary Anns on the forward slope, start picking targets when the range closes to two klicks.*

Incoming! Incoming! was the cry from somewhere.

Curt heard the sound of 53-millimeter shells from the enemy warbots. They were firing at maximum range, and the small caliber shells really didn't pack much energy by the time they reached Jebel Wahid. This is just what Curt was hoping for. *Fusileer, keep the Saucy Cans firing, but choose targets carefully! You missed some warbots on the road. Get them if you can. If you can't, don't shoot at shadows! We don't have an infinite supply of ammo ourselves. And the other hand, I want the East Worlders to expend as much of their ammo as possible at long range.*

Part of the infantry force is attempting to move southwest to flank the hill! Russ reported. *They're moving parallel to the railroad!*

The rest of the infantry force is moving in open order as skirmishers toward Jebel Wahid, Dyani said. *In the open. Moving fast. Range four thousand meters and closing. A good spread about two thousand meters wide. They'll be at the base of jebel Wahid in less than thirty minutes at their present route marching rate.*

I thought for sure they'd have some sort of armored infantry vehicles, Russ remarked in amazement. *They must have left them at the top of the hill in Amran.*

They had no way to bring those vehicles on the train. So, they brought them by road. Judging from the immediate result of the Saucy Cans barrage, I suspect we've rather dinged those bloody personnel vehicles out there on the road! Obviously, they bloody well didn't expect to encounter us here! Freeman speculated. *They must have figured they were going to roll right on into al-Luhaya and engage us there. I think they had in mind sort of a replay of Dunkirk.*

Different battle. Surprisingly, that was Kitsy Clinton who made the remark. *They didn't push us when they had the chance the way Guderian went after the French and British forces. They gave us time to regroup! By the way, Grey Head, what do you think the Big Man is going to say about the fact that we set the East Worlders up for this?*

Battleaxe here has the definite opinion that we had to protect our evacuation point of al-Luhaya by defense in depth, Hettrick's voice suddenly came through. *Let's plow these bastards into Yemeni soil! Then we'll worry about the Battle of the Potomac when we get our asses safely out of here! All hands, be on the lookout for their tacair! We haven't seen it yet on sensors, but it could be coming in nap of the earth over those hills. It should take about twenty minutes for that to get here. And we don't know how much of it will be coming.*

Strangely, this battle was remarkably slow to get rolling, Curt decided. Part of it was the distances. It took time for the East Worlder infantry to move along the road as well as across the five-kilometer open plain.

Then the infantry units trying to go around the south side of Jebel Wahid ran into the Cottonbalers' Mary Anns which opened fire on them with a withering volley of 25-millimeter AP rounds.

The tacomm channels got very busy.

Battleaxe, Blue Maxie is taking heat! East World infantry has lots of Bot Killer rockets. They're taking out my Mary Anns on the right flank! Blue Maxie needs tacair! Blue Maxie needs tacair NOW! Dammit, Jess, where the hell are you now that I need you? Get your damned Harpies over us!

Warhawk Leader, Battleaxe. Be careful! The Fourth Guards scouts report Wasps being carried by that group!

Warhawk Leader can help you, Blue Maxie! Screw the Wasps! We're coming in on the deck! Call the targets, and I'll take 'em out with my twenty fives!

Worsham, those are nap-of-the-earth Wasps! Not standard Sov stuff! Watch it!

We're wild weasling it! Got six Harpies maneuvering to come out of the sun. Those of us coming in down sun will draw attention and fire!

Dammit, you're sitting ducks down sun!

Shit, it's a dirty job and someone's got to do it!

Attention, all tacair drivers! Iron Fist sensors show bandits, angels ten, one-zero-five true. Closing rate will engage you in three minutes! They are non-stealthed and IR dirty! Clay pigeons if you can break off some sand pounding and take them on!

Stupid bastards, coming in un-stealthed! What the shit? Did they think we weren't gonna be looking for the stuff they brought onto Sana'a?

The tacair situation and the impending air battle were going to have to run their courses without Curt's attention because the forward slope of Jebel Wahid began to get busy.

Colonel Rick Salley, commander of the forward slope Mary Ann force, called in as Curt saw the enemy infantry reach the ascending ground, *Battleaxe, Wolf Head is opening fire with Mary Anns! We can do our job without tacair right now. Let the 'dyne drivers take the pressure off the right flank. But can we get some overhead AP bursts from the Saucy Cans, please?*

One salvo, and then the Saucy Cans have to withdraw. Wolf Head, don't spend too damned much time engaging the enemy! Get them to expend fire on your Mary Anns, then get the hell out of there. Remember, if you can't withdraw the Mary Anns, leave them! Hettrick emphasized the orders given in the tactical plan. She knew that Salley and his Wolfhounds, trained by the aggressive Marty Kelly, would try to stop and even defeat the oncoming infantry which greatly outnumbered them. But that wasn't the plan. The enemy had to occupy the ridge line. But the enemy had to be in bad shape when it did so.

I don't like to retreat, Battleaxe, but I understand why this time. Just cut me a little slack, please. These targets are just too damned good to turn away from!

The final Saucy Cans salvo from the ridge went over Curt's head and the AP rounds burst above the East Worlders on the forward slope. It didn't have as much effect as Curt thought it would. Once in the rocks and other cover of Jebel Wahid, the enemy soldiers showed they were as good in the final assault as they had been brave in crossing kilometers of open ground under fire. They sought cover and returned the Saucy Cans and Mary Ann fire with the short-range Bot Killer rockets.

Curt saw that things were moving fast on the forward slope. *Freeman, get your Saucy Cans back down the slope! Now!*

Right-o!

Bot Killer shoulder-launched unguided rockets were taking their toll of the forward slope Mary Anns. *Wolf Head, clear out of there! Retreat!* Curt called.

Can't! Bot Killer just hit the rock alongside me. No puncture wounds from rock shards, but a fucking big piece of rock must have busted my leg!

I see him! I'm going after him! Russ Frazier snapped and called, Bio-tech! Sergeant Hale! Come on, Shelley, I'll cover us! Shelley Hale was the only bio-tech on the ridge at that time and was getting ready to withdraw with the Saucy Cans. She responded instantly.

Curt couldn't have stopped Russ even if he'd had time to order him to stay put. The situation was lethal and heated. People acted and reacted. Orders were something for peaceful times on parade grounds.

"Curt, we've got to get out of here!" Dyani suddenly broke tacomm protocol and told her colonel verbally over the din of the battle as she touched him on the shoulder. "Some of the East Worlders are only two hundred meters down the slope in front of us!"

Curt brought his Novia to his shoulder as he indicated where Russ Frazier had suddenly broken cover next to him and started down the slope toward Salley. *Deer Arrow, pick your targets! At two hundred meters, Novia fire outranges their A-99 stuff! Russ and Shelley need all the covering fire we can give them! So does Salley! We'll try to hold off those bastards until Russ and Shelley get Salley out!*

Chapter Thirty-Two

Well, I'm bloody well not going to leave the two of you up here alone! Captain Peter Freeman's voice came to Curt. *Come along, now! I've got two Saucy Cans up here! Might as well shoot from cover if you can! If you don't mind the bloody concussion of these seventy-fives!*

Curt checked his helmet tac display and saw that Peter and two LAMVAs were about twenty meters to the left of them on the ridge in a place where Russ, Shelley, and Rick Salley could still be given covering fire. *Deer Arrow, move it left with me! Marching fire!*

We're on the skyline!

So move it fast and erratic!

Right! Like I taught you! Dyani knew how to move in the open in a manner that presented the hardest possible target to hit. Generations of her Crow Indian forebears had provided her with incredible survival talent in her genes.

The Mary Anns on the forward slope were beginning to move back toward the crest. As four of them came near, Curt snapped to them via tacomm, *Mary Anns Nine, Ten, Sixteen, and Eighteen! Back up the hill. Continue firing on the enemy! Rendezvous with the two Saucy Cans vehicles! Move!*

It was like living in slow motion. Curt moved with Dyani, jinking and shooting as they went toward the LAMVAs which didn't stop firing but were putting very short-range air bursts right over the heads of the East Worlders less than two hundred meters down the forward slope. Freeman was also covering them with his Novia while Curt and Dyani tried to cover the three Greys thirty meters down the slope.

The 25-millimeter fire from the Mary Anns did a lot to make the East Worlder infantry keep their heads down. Warbots don't miss if they've got a good target, but the infantry targets tended to be many and highly mobile. Not every Mary Ann shot found a target that morning. Their covering fire probably saved Curt and Dyani.

But Curt did take a round from one of the East Worlder A-99s, but he got it squarely in the torso of his body armor. Fortunately, he wasn't inhaling when it hit or the breath would have been knocked out of him. All it did was spin him around and nearly knock him to the ground while the tough Krisflex crystalline composite fabric spread the impact energy quickly out along its surface.

But Dyani was hit then, too. Being smaller, she was knocked down. Curt nearly panicked at that point, but Dyani rolled and was on her feet again in a cat-like motion. Her expression told him that she'd been hurt by the round, but he was certain her body armor hadn't been broached.

Russ Frazier was fighting his way up the hill with Rick Salley over his shoulder in a fireman's carry. Shelley was with him, but from the pained expression on her face, Curt knew she'd been hit, too. The ladies had a tendency to bruise a bit more than the men because, although they were lean and hard, being female meant that they had a little bit more body fat, one of those gender differences than no amount of physical fitness could change.

Busted leg! The colonel can't walk on it! Cover me. Curt! I've got to get him down the reverse slope! Frazier reported as they came up on the LAMVAs.

Move it! Move it! Curt urged him!

Goddamn it, Colonel. I'm pedaling as fast as I fucking well can! Russ snapped back. Then he was gone behind the LAMVA.

Okay, let's follow them! Curt urged. *Back this sucker down the hill, Peter!*

Curt, behind us! East Worlder infantry! They must have got past while our attention was on Russ and Salley! Dyani suddenly reported, breaking tacomm protocol in the heat of the moment.

Grey Head, Alleycat Leader! We see you on the ridge line! We've got the trouble covered in your minus-x. But we may fire into you to take them out of the game!

Dammit, Jerry, open fire! We'll take their fire in our minus-x if you don't! Let me know when you've greased them! Curt ordered.

But I'll be firing into you! Jerry warned.

I signed off on your Expert Marksman medal! Dammit, shoot! And tell the other Greys to shoot! Otherwise, we'll buy the farm up here! Curt insisted, then added another tacomm channel to his transmission. *Grey Head needs some tacair support! Any Harpie driver who wants some targets, check the ridge line for my beacon which I am identing now!*

Grey Head, Battleaxe! I've got no available tacair for you! Hettrick suddenly broke in.

Curt suddenly spotted four tactical aerodynes coming in from the north, their cannon blazing.

Then what the hell is that coming along the ridge? Curt wanted to know.

Where? Oh my God! I've got them on visual now! How the hell did they get there? Must be some East World ships that worked their way in from the north!

Dyani! Peter! Move it! Break down the reverse slope! Get away from these LAMVAs right now! They're obvious targets for those enemy 'dynes! Curt told the two of them. This situation was rapidly becoming far too dangerous and deadly for Curt's liking. They were, in fact, in a real killer position. *Jerry, take out those goddamned riflemen in our minus-x! And if you've got any Smart Farts up and ready, blow the lips off those incoming aerodynes that snuck up on us!*

No Smart Farts shouldered and ready, Grey Head! We were told the enemy aerodynes are to the right over the wadi! And we didn't see these bandits until you did! Jerry fired back quickly.

But Curt then saw that the incoming aerodynes weren't firing at them or the Saucy Cans. Their explosive cannon shells were tearing up the East Worlder infantry on the forward slope.

As the nearest aerodyne went past him, it flipped its belly side toward him, apparently unafraid of the possible Golden BB.

On its bottom, he saw a round green-white-green cockade with a palm tree and two crossed scimitars in the center.

And in both English and Arabic script was written, "Royal Saudi Air Force".

Battleaxe, Alleycat Leader, everyone! Curt suddenly snapped, almost yelling aloud as well as thinking into his tacomm. *Hold fire! Those 'dynes over the ridge are Saudis!*

Curt, I told you a telephone call would do the trick, was Hettrick's comment. *Roger, everyone, do not fire on aerodynes! Too many different ones up there right now! Concentrate on ground targets! My comm people are attempting to make contact! Damn it, why didn't they tell us they were coming and give us some frequencies so we could talk to them?*

The sudden tacair attack on the forward slope had temporarily blunted the East World assault on the ridge. The small arms firing slacked off enough to allow Curt, Dyani, and Peter Freeman to back down the reverse slope, taking the Mary Anns and Saucy Cans with them.

Curt said nothing until they were well down the slope to where Jerry and the rest of the Greys waited.

It was both Kitsy and Adonica who broke cover, ran out to greet them, and showed them to protected spots behind rocks and small hillocks on the reverse slope. No one said much of anything. The battle was still in progress and the outcome hadn't been decided yet.

The enemy had one more move to make, and Curt hoped that the history books had been right. Would the East Worlders be sucked into the trap?

He hunkered down alongside Jerry and waited. He didn't have to wait long.

The East World infantry troops gained the ridge line. Through visual binoculars, Curt looked at them. They seemed to be tired. They should be, having fought their way up the forward slope under heavy fire that had taken its toll of their numbers and their ammo. Then they started down the reverse slope, their movements indicating confidence that they'd beaten the Americans, that the battle was now theirs, that they'd swing south and carry out the ultimate dream of all field commanders: a Cannae-like encirclement of the enemy force.

But they were silhouetted starkly against the dawn sky.

And they were not expecting what Curt had planned: the classic reverse slope defense.

Battleaxe, Grey Head. Looks good to go here. May we bring this furball to its gut-wrenching but glorious end, please? Curt tacommed to Hettrick.

Stand by. Wolf Head? Ready?

I'm hurtin' for certain, but the Wolfhounds are ready!

Commence firing!

A shattering volley of Novia fire erupted up the slope toward the easily discernible targets against the skyline of morning. On the flanks, Jeeps opened up with the 7.62-millimeter high-rate automatics. Other Jeeps were interspersed among the Sierra Charlies, and their fire was withering.

I'm talking to the Saudi aerodyne drivers! Stand by for them to make a helping pass on the reserve slope, then over the ridge to mop up anyone left on the forward slope, was Hettrick's call.

Battleaxe, we appreciate their help, but this turned into a turkey shoot! Curt replied, speaking now a little easier.

The reverse slope of Jebel Wahid became a slaughterhouse as the East World Hindu and Burmese infantry was totally surprised and mowed down by the Greys and Wolfhounds. Exhausted from the forward slope uphill fight, low on ammo because of the intense fire defense put up by the Mary Anns, decimated by the AP rounds from the Saucy Cans, and then with victory obviously in their hands to run into a maelstrom of death on the ridge, the East World forces began to withdraw under incredible fire. Curt estimated that more than three-fourths of the enemy force that had left the train was wiped out. He didn't yet know how badly mauled the road force was, but his tac display showed very little left over on the far right flank across the railway.

The reverse slope defense had worked. Sometimes it hadn't in the past. But this time it did because the 4th Guards had held the road. Because the Cottonbalers had held the right flank on the open plain. Because the men and women running the Saucy Cans on the ridge and the Mary Anns on the forward slope had hung on and did a job that took real guts, facing superior enemy assault forces, badly outnumbered, and knowing that they'd have to retreat over the hill in order to draw the enemy into the trap.

No guts, no glory. Curt told himself, not allowing his thought to get into the tacomm circuitry. But the glory wasn't the same thing that it used to be in the days of Napoleonic warfare when the Duke of Wellington had first used the reverse slope defense to win in a situation where he could have easily lost. The glory was made up of self-satisfaction, of having done a good job and earning one's pay, of having survived without being wounded or disfigured, of having come through for and with everyone he called his friends and, yes, even his loved ones. He realized he did indeed have affection of various sorts for all the Greys.

In spite of what he considered to be a cowardly, pacifistic order from the highest office in the land, one that could have killed them all, Curt knew the Washington Greys - and the Cottonbalers, the Wolfhounds, and even the Regulars who were holding the al-Luhaya port facilities - had beaten the living hell out of the East World mere force under far less than the best conditions. They'd taken on the Red Hammer warbots and beaten them. They'd prevailed against the Bot Killer rockets. They'd done all that they could have done and more with far less than they were supposed to have. Except that they did indeed have guts.

It was really all over suddenly except for the Cottonbalers cleaning up the mess on the right flank. But with the main enemy force decimated on the ridge and the Red Hammer warbots destroyed on the road by the 4th Guards, there really wasn't very much left for the enemy to do but to withdraw.

It was over very quickly. The Greys did not pursue. The enemy was too badly cut up to think about a counter-counterattack.

Good show, Grey Head! Good show, Wolf Head! Blue Maxie, do you need any help on the right? came the call from Hettrick.

Battleaxe, this is Wolf Chief, was the report from Salley's chief of staff. *Wolf Head needs to be evacked with a broken leg but no wounds. The*

Wolfers are in great shape!

Grey Head here! Everything's copacetic, Battleaxe, Curt responded.

Battleaxe, I might have called for tacair a few minutes ago, but you or someone did an orgasmic job of providing it when it got here! was the reply from Colonel Maxine Cashier of the Cotton-balers. *The enemy is routed. Running like hell. We'll let 'em go because they're running right into the Fourth Guards. Now that's one Yemeni outfit that knows how to fight! And they do not like these East Worlders one goddamned little bit! So I think we'll leave the contact and pursuit up to them. They need the practice because I sort of think one of these days real soon now they're going to chase these bastards right out of Yemen.*

But not right away, Blue Maxie, Curt advised her.

No, but with the Saudis taking sides, as they have, this Yemen civil war is far from over, Hettrick guessed, paused for a moment, then announced, *First the bad news. We're not going to leave any warbots or equipment here for the East Worlders to pick up. So, what's busted must be destroyed. Right here. Right now. So better get busy. Never mind the East Worlder dead. The vultures will take care of them as they always have. But the vultures don't like the taste of warbots, so bust up the busted warbots and use the back blades on the LAMVAs to doze them under. G-2 and DIA wants all the enemy stuff we can haul, even the dinged stuff So we drag that to al-Luhaya.*

In the pause, Curt heard Captain Peter Freeman say to the Canadian Captain Pat Lufkin, "Well, old chap, I suspect now we'll have to teach these bloody Yanks how to leave a properly neat British battlefield."

When Hettrick didn't immediately come back on line, Curt asked her, *And what's the good news, Battleaxe?*

I just got it this instant on the satellite link, which accounts for the delay, Hettrick admitted. *The Saudi defense minister notified me of the King's decision to assist our withdrawal by sending in two squadrons of McDonnell Douglas Sky Devil aerodynes. And the Saudi Navy will have two frigates, three cutters, a repair ship, and ten coastal patrol vessels waiting for us at al-Luhaya by sundown! Looks like we'll sleep between sheets tonight instead of on piles of hematite on an ore carrier! I don't know about the rest of you girls, but I could sure as hell use a shower after all this tearing around the countryside! Okay, go to it! The quicker we picker up, the faster we'll blast out of here. Like we were ordered to do. I'll apologize to the commander in chief for the little delay we had at Jebel Wahid! Too bad those East Worlders thought they could cut us off at the pass...*

But the Greys were not quick to leave cover, get to their feet, and expose themselves. Wounded or isolated East Worlder soldiers might still be lying doggo on the reverse slope. So, the wrap-up was slow and cautious.

Finally, about noontime, Curt called the Greys together for chow and chat. It was time to unwind. And the Greys usually did it together. Not all of them were there, of course. The wounded were in al-Luhaya under Major Ruth Gydesen's expert care. Most of the SERVBATT were also in al-Luhaya. So were the AIRBATT people because that's where the remaining aerodynes were. So, it was just the real gravel crunching combat types who gathered around the ACV that served as a temporary CIC.

Curt hurt. It was great to have body armor that would prevent small arms fire from penetrating his body, but something had to absorb the energy of an impacting bullet. The body armor helped by spreading out the energy over a wider area. But it didn't prevent bruises. His side hurt. But he hurt even where he hadn't been hit. His shoulders hurt. So did his neck. And his legs. And his feet.

Even Kitsy looked tired. And when she looked that way, some of the spunk seemed to have gone out of her. It was apparent that she could snap and pop when she had to, but it was also obvious that she'd just about had it.

"You didn't get very much sleep last night, did you?" Curt observed.

She shook her head. "No, and it wasn't because of male companionship, either. In case you're wondering, the companionship was a book. I downloaded one of Hackett's books from Georgie into my hand reader."

"That's what I thought."

"Well, you said I should start to learn something about military history," Kitsy reminded him.

"But in the middle of this? And getting ready for combat?" Curt was flabbergasted at this woman for whom he'd developed a very strong attachment over the years. She'd changed, of course, as she'd matured: But Curt was liking what he saw in her maturing process.

She looked up at him with her pixie expression. "Well, Colonel, Rule Ten was in effect. It was either read or fret. But I guarantee you that I will be doing neither tonight on our Red Sea cruise!"

"If I lift Rule Ten," Curt said, kidding her.

Someone touched his elbow. "You'd better!" was Dyani's quiet remark. She didn't need to say any more.

"And you're hurting," he observed, noting the way Dyani moved.

"Yes. But only physically. Not the way I was after that train rider ambush," Dyani admitted. "This can be treated with a little massage. Not ego stroking like before."

"Well, ladies, I hate to tell you this," Curt said with a little smile playing around the corners of his mouth. He was kidding them, but he went on, "You should know that Saudi King Abdullah is sending the royal yacht to al-Luhaya for Queen Arwa and Battleaxe. And Battleaxe has asked me to join them for the trip up the coast to Jedda..."

Kitsy looked at Dyani and said., "Dy, neither of us is bigger than he is. Either of us would have a little trouble if we resorted to physical violence."

"No, Kitsy, I wouldn't want to strike a superior officer," Dyani replied with equal mock seriousness. "I believe we should consider what we might do as a suitable alternative."

Curt thought for a moment that he'd taken his kidding too far. After all, these were ladies of the Greys. They could be vicious. Both were highly experienced veterans who had proved this. He really didn't want to incur their ire, real or humorous. "Well, I suppose I'll just have to ask Battleaxe to invite you both as well..."

Kitsy shook her head. "Sorry, Colonel, but I'll have to say no."

"Really?"

"Really! I have accepted an invitation from a dashing young officer of the Greys who speaks Arabic fluently and who's promised to show me all around Jedda and Mecca when we get there," Kitsy admitted sweetly, an impish smile on her tired face. There was only one person who qualified and was available. "Always a lady, Colonel, in spite of hell! But it was very kind of you to think of me."

"Which means, Colonel, I should also decline the invitation," Dyani put in, saying one thing in her quiet voice while her eyes said something else, "because I need to find a good masseuse to work the hurt out of my impact bruises. And I really wouldn't want to impose on your sybaritic sea voyage with the Queen of Sheba."

"Well, let me put it this way, then," Curt told her. "If I decline the invitation myself and go on one of the frigates, I have the equivalent rank of a Saudi naval captain. So, I'll have private quarters with a private hot shower. And the ship's captain could be persuaded not to hurry. It could take two nights on the Red Sea to get to Jedda..."

Dyani looked up at him. Her smile was full of relief and longing. "I've reconsidered. But only because I've always wondered about what really happened during the Arabian Nights..."

Aftermath

It was like being in a different world. Trees were everywhere, newly leafed out for spring. Some of the cherry trees were already in blossom. The ground underfoot was soft green grass, not rocky sand and barren soil. The terrain was rolling, not jagged peaks. And the buildings weren't made of mud and rock in dull shades of brown but gleaming edifices of shining white marble.

However, the shining white marble objects that bothered Curt were the endless rows and ranks and columns of identical headstones that covered Arlington National Cemetery.

"I can't find them all, Dyani," Curt admitted, shaking his head. "I didn't realize we'd lost so many of them. This place has gotten so big now that I can't even remember where my father lies."

"Or my grandfathers." Dyani herself was somewhat stunned by the expanse of final resting places for those who had honorably served their country. "We haven't got time today to search them all out, Curt. Even the ones we just lost. We're due at the hearings on the Hill in less than an hour. We'll just have to pay our respects in general to everyone."

"We lost too many people in Yemen," was Curt's quiet reply as he shook his head slowly.

"We could have lost more."

"We could have lost none."

"But that would have meant running from a responsibility we all took on," Dyani reminded him.

The soulful bugle notes of "Taps" is almost constantly heard over Arlington. The sound came to the two of them then. Quietly, Curt came to attention and saluted the field of graves. Dyani did likewise. It was the least they could do to honor their forefathers and their cherished friends who were the fallen dead of the

Washington Greys on a day that was already pressed for time.

When the bugle call was over, the two of them heard Major General Belinda Hettrick call to them, "Come along, you two! We can't be late!" Hettrick had agreed to the quick stopover at Arlington. She didn't come into the field of marble with them but took care of some of her own remembrances privately.

Back in the army limo, Curt merely said, "Thank you, General."

"Frankly, I'm glad you asked me to stop," Hettrick told them as the doors closed and the limo rolled away toward the Memorial Bridge. There was a slight emotional catch in her voice. "I discovered I needed to take care of some personal business there myself. Besides, it helped strengthen me for the day's ordeal."

"What are the senators looking for, General?" Dyani asked. She was almost totally apolitical.

"A scapegoat."

"That might include us. We retreated," Curt wasn't happy about Yemen.

"We were ordered to do so," Hettrick reminded him.

"I don't think we should have been there in the first place," Curt recalled.

"Perhaps. But, Colonel, that's your personal opinion," Hettrick told him firmly, then tweaked his memory. "I once told you that as long as you wear that uniform, you have no personal opinion. I hope you'll remember that today when you testify."

"I will, General."

"We don't know the full story. We may never know the full story. That doesn't make any difference. Within the law and the various conventions of warfare, it's our job - our duty - to go where our national leaders order us to go. And to come back when they give orders to do so, too. We aren't the first to have gone with no explanation given. Or the first to come back under orders." As the limo swung past the Viet Nam Memorial, she nodded toward the low, almost invisible monument and added, "Sometimes there are good reasons to go. Sometimes, those who go don't think so, but they go anyway."

"So who are the senators after?" Dyani wanted to know.

"The President. Congress can criticize him. Some of the senators may try to get us to do so. We can't. We must not. We don't make national or foreign policy."

"So what do we tell them? What do I say when they ask me about being in Yemen?" Curt requested guidance from her.

"Tell them the truth as you knew it and the facts as they appeared to you," Hettrick advised.

"Be a scout reporting from a patrol," Dyani told him in simple terms.

"It would have been better if Maggie MacPherson hadn't gotten hold of us after we got back," Curt mused, recalling the beautiful video news personality he'd gotten to know on Sakhalin Island. She'd devoted a whole weekly Maggie's Hour program to the Yemen affair. Curt felt she'd done a fair and truthful job of reporting and analyzing what had happened. Her interviews with the Greys at Fort Huachuca had been forthright and free of hype or bias. As a result of that program, Congress had fallen all over itself to hold hearings about what really happened. The Senate was first to the door. The House was waiting impatiently to nail to the wall the hides of those in the Executive Branch who survived the Senate hearings.

"No, Curt, she was doing her job and did it well. We may not criticize our leaders, but she can and should. When the news media does their job properly like that, they do their duty to the country! And Congress is doing the right thing in trying to bring it all out into the open so maybe a future administration doesn't make the same mistakes. They'll make mistakes, all right. But maybe they won't make them the same way."

"Frankly, this scares me more than going into combat."

"Me, too," Dyani agreed.

Hettrick smiled at them. "But just think of all the glory that will be heaped upon you! What's the matter? No guts?"

APPENDIX ONE

THE 3rd ROBOT INFANTRY REGIMENT
(SPECIAL COMBAT)
"THE WASHINGTON GREYS"
ROLE OF HONOR
FALLEN IN THE LINE OF DUTY IN YEMEN:

1st Lieutenant Harold M. Clock
Sergeant Thomas C. Cole
Sergeant Donald J. Esteban
Biotech Sergeant Juanita Gomez, P.N.
Sergeant Richard L. Knight
Sergeant Maxwell M. Moody

WOUNDED IN THE LINE OF DUTY IN YEMEN:

Flight Sergeant Zeke Braswell
1st Lieutenant Clifford B. Braxton, R.N.
Flight Sergeant Grant Brown
First Sergeant Tracy C. Dillon
Sergeant James P. Elliott
Flight Sergeant John Espee
Sergeant Louise J. Hanrahan
1st Lieutenant Mike Hart
Biotech Sergeant Wallace W. Izard, P.N.
Supply Sergeant Lawrence W. Jordan
1st Lieutenant Bruce Mark
Technical Sergeant Bailey Ann Miles
Platoon Sergeant Willa P. Miller
1st Lieutenant Gabe Neatherly
Sergeant Walter J. O'Reilly
Master Sergeant Charles L. Orndorff
1st Lieutenant Lewis C. Pagan
1st Lieutenant Ned Phillips
1st Lieutenant Harry Racey
1st Lieutenant Nancy Roberts

Flight Sergeant Sergio Tomasio
Platoon Sergeant Betty Jo Trumble
Sergeant Paul T. Tullis
Technical Sergeant Robert H. Vickers
Sergeant Joe Jim Watson
Technical Sergeant First Class Raymond G. Wolf
Sergeant Jamie J. Younger

APPENDIX TWO

ORDER OF BATTLE

3rd Robot Infantry Special Combat Regiment, the "Washington Greys":
Lieutenant Colonel Curt C. Carson, commanding officer
Headquarters Company (HEADCO) ("Carson's Companions")
Lieutenant Colonel Joan G. Ward, chief of staff
Major Patrick Gillis Gratton, regimental adjutant (S-1)
Major Hensley Atkinson (S-3)
Captain Nelson A. Crile, regimental chaplain
Master Sergeant Major Henry G. Kester, regimental sergeant major
Sergeant Major Edwina A. Sampson, regimental technical sergeant
Tactical Battalion (TACBATT) ("Allen's Alleycats"):
Major Jerry P. Allen
Battalion Sergeant Major Nicholas P. Gerard
Reconnaissance Company (RECONCO) ("Motega's Mustangs")
Captain Dyani Motega (S-2)
First Sergeant Tracy C. Dillon
Biotech Sergeant Allan J. Williams, P. N.
Scouting Platoon (SCOUT) ("Lufkin's Leopards")
Captain Patrick Lufkin, Canadian Army exchange officer
Platoon Sergeant Harlan P. Saunders
Sergeant Thomas C. Cole
Sergeant Donald J. Esteban
Birdbot Platoon (BIRD) ("Brown's Black Hawks")
1st Lieutenant Dale B. Brown
Platoon Sergeant Emma Crawford
Sergeant William J. Hull Sergeant Jacob F. Kent
Sergeant Christine Burgess
Sergeant Jennifer M. Volker
Assault Company A (ASSAULTCO Alpha) ("Clinton's Cougars")
Captain Kathleen B. Clinton
Master Sergeant First Class Carol J. Head
Biotech Sergeant Virginia Bowles, P. N.
First Platoon: ("Sweet's Stilettos")

Captain Adonica Sweet
Platoon Sergeant Charles P. Koslowski
Sergeant James P. Elliott
Sergeant Paul T. Tullis
Second Platoon: ("Hassan's Assassins")
1st Lieutenant Hassan Ben Mahmud
Platoon Sergeant Isadore Beau Greenwald
Sergeant Victor Jouillan
Sergeant Sidney Albert Johnson
Assault Company B (ASSAULTCO Bravo) ("Frazier's Ferrets")
Major Russell B. Frazier
Master Sergeant Charles L. Orndorff
Biotech Sergeant Juanita Gomez, P.N.
First Platoon: ("Clock's Cavaliers")
1st Lieutenant Harold M. Clock
Platoon Sergeant Robert Lee Garrison
Sergeant Walter J. O'Reilly
Sergeant Maxwell M. Moody
Second Platoon: ("Pagan's Pumas")
1st Lieutenant Lewis C. Pagan
Platoon Sergeant Betty Jo Trumble
Sergeant Joe Jim Watson
Sergeant Edwin W. Gatewood
Gunnery Company (GUNCO) ("Hall's Hellcats")
1st Lieutenant Lawrence W. Hall
First Sergeant Forest L. Barnes
Biotech Sergeant Shelley C. Hale, P.N.
First Platoon: ("Taire's Terrors")
2nd Lieutenant Jerome "Jay" Taire
Platoon Sergeant Andrea Carrington
Sergeant Jamie Jay Younger Sergeant Pamela S. Parkin
Second Platoon: ("Freeman's Fusileers")
Captain Peter Freeman (British Army exchange officer)
Platoon Sergeant Willa P. Miller
Sergeant Richard L. Knight
Sergeant Louise J. Hanrahan
Air Battalion (AIRBATT) ("Worsham's Warhawks")

Major Calvin J. Worsham
Battalion Sergeant Major John Adam
Tactical Air Support Company (TACAIRCO) ("Hands' Harriers")
Captain Paul Hands
1st Sergeant Clancy Thomas
1st Lieutenant Gabe Neatherly
1st Lieutenant Bruce Mark
1st Lieutenant Stacy Honey
1st Lieutenant Jay Kennedy
2nd Lieutenant Richard Cooke
Flight Sergeant Zeke Braswell
Flight Sergeant Larry Myers
Flight Sergeant Adam Adams
Flight Sergeant Grant Brown
Flight Sergeant Sharon Spence
Airlift Company (AIRLIFTCO) ("Timm's Tigers")
Captain Timothea Timm
First Sergeant Carl Bagwell
1st Lieutenant Ned Phillips
1st Lieutenant Mike Hart
1st Lieutenant Dorothy Peterson
1st Lieutenant Nancy Roberts
1st Lieutenant Harry Racey
2nd Lieutenant Jess S. Switzer
Flight Sergeant Kevin Hubbard
Flight Sergeant Jeffrey O'Connell
Flight Sergeant Barry Morris
Flight Sergeant Ann Shepherd
Flight Sergeant Robert Pritchard
Flight Sergeant Harley Earll
Flight Sergeant Sergio Tomasio
Flight Sergeant John Espee
Service Battalion (SERVBATT)
Major Wade W. Hampton
Battalion Sergeant Major Joan J. Stark
Vehicle Technical Company (VETECO)
Major Frederick W. Benteen

Technical Sergeant First Class Raymond G. Wolf
Technical Sergeant Kenneth M. Hawkins
Technical Sergeant Charles B. Slocum
Warbot Technical Company (BOTECO)
Captain Elwood S. Otis
Technical Sergeant Bailey Ann Miles
Technical Sergeant Gerald W. Mora
Technical Sergeant Loretta A. Carruthers
Technical Sergeant Robert H. Vickers
Maintenance Company (AIRMAINCO)
Captain Ron Knight
First Sergeant Rebecca Campbell
Technical Sergeant Joel Pruitt
Technical Sergeant Richard N. Germain
Technical Sergeant Douglas Bell
Technical Sergeant Pam Gordon
Technical Sergeant Clete McCoy
Technical Sergeant Carol Jensen
Logistics Company (LOGCO)
Captain Harriet F. Dearborn (S-4)
Chief Supply Sergeant Manual P. Sanchez
Supply Sergeant Mariette W. Ireland
Supply Sergeant Lawrence W. Jordan
Supply Sergeant Jamie G. Casner
Biotech Company (BIOTECO)
Major Ruth Gydesen, M.D.
Captain Denise G. Logan, M.D.
Captain Thomas E. Alvin, M.D.
Captain Larry C. McHenry, M.D.
Captain Helen Devlin, R.N.
1st Lieutenant Clifford B. Braxton, R.N.
1st Lieutenant Laurie S. Cornell, R.N.
1st Lieutenant Julia B. Clark, R.N.
1st Lieutenant William O. Molde, R.N.
Biotech Sergeant Marcela V.Jolton, P.N.
Biotech Sergeant Nellie A. Miles, P. N.
Biotech Sergeant George O. Howard, P.N.
Biotech Sergeant Wallace W. Izard, P.N.

OTHERS

Major General Belinda J. Hettrick, commanding officer, 17th "Iron Fist" Division, AUS, and the Yemen Expeditionary Force, headquarters at Sana'a, Yemen Royal Republic.

Lieutenant Colonel Joanne Wilkinson, COS, 17th Iron Fist Division, AUS.

Lieutenant Colonel Martin Kelly, G-3, 17th Iron Fist Division, AUS.

Colonel Frederick H. Salley, commanding officer, 27th Robot Infantry (Special Combat) Regiment, "The Wolfhounds," 17th Iron Fist Division, AUS.

Major Martin C. Kelly, Operations Officer, 27th Robot Infantry (Special Combat) Regiment, "The Wolfhounds," 17th Iron Fist Division, AUS.

Colonel Maxine Frances Cashier, commanding officer, 7th Robot Infantry Regiment (Special Combat), "The Cottonbalers," 17th Iron Fist Division, AUS.

Colonel James B. Ricketts, commanding officer, 6th Robot Infantry Regiment (Special Combat), "The Regulars," 17th Iron Fist Division, AUS.

The President of the United States of America.

Henrietta Hamlin, Vice President, United States of America.

Dr. Andrea M. Pruitt, Secretary of State, United States of America.

Nelson J. Fetterman, ADM, USN (Ret.) Secretary of State, United States of America.

General Philip C. Glascock, USAF (Ret.), National Security Advisor.

General Albert W. Murray, USAF (Ret.), Director, National Intelligence Agency.

General Edwin R. Gross, USAF, Chairman, Joint Chiefs of Staff.

General Jeffrey G. Pickens, JCS, COS AUS.

General Willard H. Walden, JCS, COS USAF.

Admiral Cyrus A. Read, JCS, CNO USN.

Lieutenant General Littleton T. Waller, JCS, Commandant USMC.

Queen Arwa Bint Muhammad al-Badr, ruler of Yemen Royal Republic.

General Qahtan ash-Shaabi, Yemen Defense Minister, commander in chief, the Royal Yemen Army.

Colonel Salem bin Hasayn Rubaya, Commanding Officer, 4th

Guards Regiment, the Royal Yemen Army.
John Toreva, Chief of Operations, Amran and Red Sea Railroad
Company, a subsidiary of the Ferron Corporation.
Walter G. Cory, Chief of Engineering, Jebel Miswar Mining
Company, a subsidiary of the Ferron Corporation.
Prince Sultan Qadi Abdul al-Badr, heir apparent, throne of Yemen.
King Abdullah ibn Saud, ruler of Saudi Arabia.

APPENDIX THREE

HISTORY
THE WASHINGTON GREYS
3rd ROBOT INFANTRY REGIMENT

Motto: *Primus in Acien* (First in Battle)

Symbolism: The shield of the Washington Greys' coat of arms carries the geometry of the coat of arms of George Washington with the exception that the field is light silver grey rather than white. The three stars symbolize the three states from whose militia companies the original Regiment was formed - Delaware, Maryland, and Virginia. The Roman numeral III within the laurel wreath of victory on the crest recalls the first designation of the Regiment as the 3rd Infantry in 1791 and the current designation as the 3rd Robot Infantry Regiment. The blue and yellow braid separating the shield from the crest carries the regimental colors for decorative braided piping - blue for infantry and yellow for cavalry because the Regiment contained mounted troops when it was originally constituted in 1784. Light blue and yellow are also the service arm colors of the Robot Infantry. The Regimental colors consisting of a blue flag on which the Regimental Coat of Arms is centered are affixed to a staff made of wood taken from the flagpole of the Castle of Chapultepec on 13 September 1847 capped with a silver eagle cast from Mexican silver wine goblets captured there.

Distinctive insignia: The distinctive insignia of the Regiment consists of the simple Regimental shield carrying Washington's coat of arms with three red five-pointed stars horizontally arrayed above two horizontal red bands of unequal width on a field of silver grey.

Lineage:
1784 - Constituted 4 June as the 2nd American Regiment of companies from Maryland, Delaware, and Virginia, including a unit known as Washington's Mounted Guard.
1791 - Redesignated 3 March as the 3rd Infantry, Regular Army.
1792 - Redesignated as Infantry of the 2nd Sublegion.

1815 - Consolidated May-October with the 7th and 44th Infantry to form the 1st Infantry.

1861 - Relieved from the 1st Infantry and constituted 3 May as the 2nd Battalion, 17th Infantry, Regular Army.

1869 - The 2nd Battalion of the 17th Infantry reassigned to the 5th Infantry.

1918 - Assigned 27 July to the 17th Division.

1919 - Relieved from the 17th Division.

1923 -Assigned 17 March to the 9th Division.

1927- Relieved from the 9th Division and assigned to the 5th Division.

1933 - Relieved from the 5th Division and assigned to the 9th Division.

1941 - Relieved 15 July from the 9th Division.

1942 - Assigned 10 July to the 71st Division.

1946 - Relieved from the 71st Division and inactivated 15 November at Salzburg, Austria.

1950 - Reactivated 15 July as the 33rd Infantry and assigned to the 7th Division. Adopted the name, "The Washington Greys," because of direct descent from Washington's Mounted Guard and the grey uniforms worn in 1816 due to a shortage of blue cloth.

1956 - Relieved from the 7th Division 3 April and assigned to the 20th Division.

1957 - Relieved from the 20th Division 1 July and reorganized as a parent regiment under the Combat Arms Regimental System.

2009 - Reorganized as the 3rd Robot Infantry Regiment (The Washington Greys) and assigned to the 17th Iron Fist Division (Robot Infantry).

Campaign Participation
Revolutionary War: Trenton, Princeton, Saratoga, Yorktown
War of 1812: Canada, Bladensburg, McHenry
Mexican War: Monterey, Vera Cruz, Chapultepec
Civil War: 1st Manassas, Shiloh, 2nd Manassas, Antietam, Chancelorsville, Gettysburg, Chickamauga, Wilderness, Appomattox
Indian Wars: Tippecanoe, Black Hawk, Commanches, Arizona 1876; Apaches

War with Spain: Santiago
Philippine Insurrection: Samar 1901, Samar 1902, Mindanao
World War I: Ainse-Marne, St. Mihiel, Meuse-Argonne World War II: Oran (Torch), Tunisia, Sicily, Salerno, South-ern France (Anvil), Ardennes, Rhineland, Central Europe Korean War: Inchon, UN Offensive, CCF Intervention, Chosin Reservoir, UN summer-fall Offensive, Second Korean Winter, Korean Summer-fall 1952, Third Korean Winter
Vietnam: Counteroffensive, Counteroffensive Phase II, Counteroffensive Phase III, Tet Counteroffensive, Counter-offensive Phase IV, Counteroffensive Ph se V, Counteroffen-sive Phase VI, Tet 1969 Counteroffensive, summer-fall 1969, winter-spring 1970, Sanctuary Counteroffensive, Consolidation I
Grenada: Operation Urgent Fury
Iraq: Operation Desert Storm
Sino-Soviet Conflict: Sakhalin
Saharan Expeditionary Force: Cameroons, Chad, Tibesti Petro-Fed Multinational Operation: Second Kasserine, Sfax, Basrah, Tyre, Trans-Jordanian Patrol
Panama Relief Expedition: Colon, Gatun Lock
Mittel Europa: Munsterlagen
Zahedan: Operation Squire, Operation Cyclone
Trinidad (Operation Steel Band): Oropuche River, Rio Claro, Sangre Grande
Namibia (Operation Diamond Skeleton): Swakopmund, Strijdom, Windhoek (Otojomuise)
Sonora (Operation Black Jack): Bisbee, Douglas, Rio Baba-danchic, Casa Fantasma
Kerguelen Island: Operation Tempest Frigid, Operation High Dragon
Brunei (Exercise Happy Abode): Longliku
Persian Gulf Command (Iraq): Asi, Caldiran
Sakhalin Police Detachment
Battle Mountain, Nevada: Operation Blood Siege

Decorations
Presidential Unit Award, Streamer embroidered BISBEE
Presidential Unit Award, Streamer embroidered NAMIBIA

Presidential Unit Award, Streamer embroidered TRINIDAD

Valorous Unit Award, Streamer embroidered BIHN DOUNG

Valorous Unit Award, Streamer embroidered AP BAU BANG

Valorous Unit Award, Streamer embroidered BIHN LON PROVINCE 1969

Vietnamese Cross of Gallantry with Palm, Streamer embroidered VIETNAM 1965-1970

Valorous Unit Award, Streamer embroidered SAIGON-LONG BIHN

Valorous Unit Award, Streamer embroidered PARROT'S BEAK

Valorous Unit Citation, Streamer embroidered TIBESTI

Valorous Unit Citation, Streamer embroidered MAKAROV

Valorous Unit Citation, Streamer embroidered ZAHEDAN

Presidential Unit Citation (Army), Streamer embroidered ORAN, ALGERIA

Presidential Unit Citation, Streamer embroidered SICILY

Presidential Unit Citation, Streamer embroidered SA-LERNO.

Presidential Unit Citation, Streamer embroidered BAS-TOGNE

Presidential Unit Citation, Streamer embroidered SAAR RIVER

Presidential Unit Citation (Navy), Streamer embroidered CHOSIN RESERVOIR

Presidential Unit Citation, Streamer embroidered SFAX French

Croix de Guerre with Gilt Star, World War I, Streamer embroidered AINSE-MARNE

French Croix de Guerre with Palm, Streamer embroidered ST. MIHIEL

French Croix de Guerre with Palm, Streamer embroidered KASSERINE

French Croix de Guerre with Palm, Streamer embroidered CHAMBERY

Luxembourg Croix de Guerre, Streamer embroidered LUX-EMBOURG

Cited in the Order of the Day of the Belgian Army for action in the ARDENNES

French Medaille Militaire, Fouragere (3rd Army) Republic of Korea Presidential Unit Citation, Streamer em-broidered KOREA 1950-1953

Korean Presidential Unit Citation, Streamer embroidered INCHON

Panamanian Presidential Unit Citation, Streamer embroi-dered GATUN LOCKS

German Bundestag Outstanding Unit Citation with Palm, Streamer embroidered MUNSTERLAGEN

Japanese Order of the Crysanthenum, Streamer embroidered BALUCHISTAN

Japanese Order of the Crysanthenum, Streamer embroidered GREY LOTUS

Sultan's Royal Star and Crescent of Brunei, Streamer embroidered ROYAL BRUNEI LEGION

Sultan's Royal Star and Crescent of Brunei with palm leaf, Streamer embroidered SAKHALIN POLICE DETACHMENT

State of Nevada, Governor's Award of Appreciation.

APPENDIX FOUR
GLOSSARY OF ROBOT INFANTRY TERMS AND SLANG

ACV: Airportable Command Vehicle M660.

Aerodyne: A saucer-shaped flying machine that obtains its lift from the exhaust of one or more turbine fanjet engines blowing outward over the curved upper surface of the craft from an annular segmented slot near the center of the upper surface. The aerodyne was invented by Dr. Henri M. Coanda after World War II but was not perfected until decades later because of the predominance of the rotary-winged helicopter.

Artificial Intelligence or *AI:* Very fast computer modules with large memories which can simulate some functions of human thought and decision-making processes by bringing together many apparently disconnected pieces of data, making simple evaluations of the priority of each, and making simple decisions concerning what to do, how to do it, when to do it, and what to report to the human being in control.

Beanie: A West Point term for a plebe or first-year man.

Beanette: A female beanie.

Birdbot: The M20 Aeroreconnaissance Neuroelectronic Bird Warbot used for aerial recce. Comes in shapes and sizes to resemble indigenous birds.

Biotech: A biological technologist once known in the twentieth century Army as a "medic."

Black Maria: The M 44A Assault Shotgun, the Sierra Charlie's 18.52-millimeter friend in close quarter combat.

Bohemian Brigade: War correspondents or a news media television crew.

Bot: Generalized generic slang term for "robot" which takes many forms, as warbot, reconbot, etc. See "Robot" below.

Bot flush: Since robots have no natural excrement, this term is a reference to what comes out of a highly mechanical warbot when its lubricants are changed during routine maintenance. Used by soldiers as a slang term referring to anything of a detestable nature.

Cee-pee or *CP*: Slang for "Command Post."

Check minus-x: Look behind you. In terms of coordinates, plus-x is ahead, minus-x is behind, plus-y is to the right, minus-y is left, plus-z is up, and minus-z is down.

Chippie: The UCA-21C Chippewa tactical airlift aerodyne.

CIC: Combat Information Center. May be different from a command post.

Class 6 supplies: Alcoholic beverages of high ethanol content procured through non-regulation channels; officially, only five classes of supplies exist.

Column of ducks: A convoy proceeding through terrain where they are likely to draw fire.

Creamed: Greased, beaten, conquered, overwhelmed.

CYA: Cover Your Ass. In polite company, "Cover Your Anatomy."

Downlink: A remote command or data channel from a warbot to a soldier.

FIDO: Acronym for "Fuck it; drive on!" Overcome your obstacle or problem and get on with the operation.

FIG: Foreign Internal Guardian mission, the sort of assignment army units draw to protect American interests in selected locations around the world. Great for Robot Infantry - units but not within the intended mission profiles of Sierra Charlie regiments.

Fort Fumble: Any headquarters, but especially the Pentagon when not otherwise specified.

Furball: A complex, confused fight, battle, or operation.

Gener/Ducrot: Any incompetent, lazy, fucked-up, incompetent officer who doesn't know or won't admit those short-comings. May have other commissioned officer rank to more closely describe the individual.

Go physical: To lapse into idiot mode, to operate in a combat or recon environment without neuroelectronic warbots; what the Special Combat units do all the time. See "Idiot mode" below.

Golden BB: A small caliber bullet that hits and thus creates large problems.

Greased: Beaten, conquered, overwhelmed, creamed.

Harpy: The AD-40C tactical air assault aerodyne which the Aerospace Force originally developed in the A version; the Navy flies the B version. The Office In Charge Of Stupid Names tried to get everyone to call it the "Thunder Devil," but the Harpy name stuck with the drivers and troops. The compound term "newsharpy" is also used to refer to a hyperthyroid, ego-blasted, over-achieving female news personality or reporter.

Headquarters happy: Any denizen of headquarters, regimental or higher.

Humper: Any device whose proper name a soldier can't recall at the moment.

Idiot mode: Operating in the combat environment without neuroelectronic warbots, especially operating without the benefit of computers and artificial intelligence to relieve battle load. What the warbot brainies think the Sierra Charlies do all the time. See "Go physical" above.

Intelligence: Generally considered to exist in four categories: animal, human, machine, and military.

Intelligence amplifier or *IA:* A very fast computer with a very large memory which, when linked to a human nervous system by nonintrusive neuroelectronic pickups and electrodes, serves as a very fast extension of the human brain allowing the brain to function faster, recall more data, store more data, and thus "amplify" a human being's "intelligence." (Does not imply that the army knows what "human intelligence" really is.)

Jeep: Word coined from the initials "GP" standing for "General

Purpose." Once applied to an army quarter-ton vehicle but subsequently used to refer to the Mark 33A2 General Purpose Warbot.

KIA: "Killed in action," A warbot brainy term used to describe the situation where a warbot soldier's neuroelectronic data and sensory inputs from one or more warbots is suddenly cut off, leaving the human being in a state of mental limbo. A very debilitating and mentally disturbing situation. (Different from being physically killed in action, a situation with which only Sierra Charlies find themselves threatened.)

LAMVA: The M473 Light Artillery Maneuvering Vehicle, Airportable, a robotic armored vehicle mounting a 75-millimeter Saucy Cans gun used for light artillery support of a Sierra Charlie regiment.

Linkage: The remote connection or link between a human being and one or more neuroelectronically controlled warbots. This link channel may be by means of wires, radio, laser, or optics. The actual technology of linkage is highly classified. The robot/computer sends its data directly to the human soldier's nervous system through small nonintrusive electrodes positioned on the soldier's skin. This data is coded in such a way that the soldier perceives the signals as sight, sound, feeling, or position of the robot's parts. The robot/computer also picks up commands from the soldier's nervous system that are merely "thought" by the soldier, translates them into commands a robot can understand, and monitors the robot's accomplishment of the commanded action.

Log bird: A logistics or supply aircraft.

Mary Ann: The M60A Airborne Mobile Assault Warbot which mounts a single M300 25-millimeter automatic can-non with variable fire rate. Accompanies Sierra Charlie troops in the field and provides fire support.

Mad minute: The first intense, chaotic, wild, frenzied period of a fire fight when it seems every gun in the world is being shot at you.

Mike-mike: Soldier's shorthand for "millimeter."

Novia: The 7.62-millimeter M33A3 "Ranger" Assault Rifle designed in Mexico as the M3 Novia. The Sierra Charlies still call it the Novia or "sweetheart."

Neuroelectronics or *NE:* The synthesis of electronics and computer technologies that permit a computer to detect and recognize signals from the human nervous system by means of nonintrusive skin-mounted sensors as well as to stimulate the human nervous system with computer-generated electronic signals through similar skin-mounted electrodes for the purpose of creating sensory signals in the human mind. See "Linkage" above.

OCV: Operational Command Vehicle, the command version of the M660 ACV.

Orgasmic!: A slang term that grew out of the observation, "Outstanding!" It means the same thing. Usually but not always.

POSSOH: "Person of Opposite Sex Sharing Off-duty Hours."

PTV: Personal Transport Vehicle or "trike," a three-wheeled unarmored vehicle similar to an old sidecar motorcycle capable of carrying two Sierra Charlies or one Sierra Charlie and a Jeep.

Pucker factor: The detrimental effect on the human body that results from being in an extremely hazardous situation, such as being shot at.

Robot: From the Czech word robota meaning work, especially drudgery. A device with human-like actions directed either by a computer or by a human being through a computer and a two-way command-sensor circuit. See "Linkage" and "Neuroelectronics" above.

Robot Infantry or *RI:* A combat branch of the United States Army which grew from the regular infantry with the intro-duction of robots and linkage to warfare. Replaced the regular infantry in the early twenty-first century.

RTV: Robot Transport Vehicle, now the M662 Airportable Robot Transport Vehicle (ARTV) but still called an RTV by Sierra Charlies.

Rule Ten: Slang reference to Army Regulation 601-10 which

prohibits physical contact between male and female personnel when on duty except for that required in the conduct of official business.

Rules of Engagement or *ROE:* Official restrictions on the freedom of action of a commander or soldier in his confrontation with an opponent that act to increase the probability that said commander or soldier will lose the combat, all other things being equal.

Saucy Cans: An American Army corruption of the French designation for the 75-millimeter *"soixante-quinze"* weapon mounted on the LAMVA.

Scroom!: Abbreviation for "Screw 'em!"

Sheep screw: A disorganized, embarrassing, graceless, chaotic fuck-up.

Sierra Charlie: Phonetic alphabet derivative of the initials "SC" meaning "Special Combat" soldiers trained to engage in personal field combat supported and accompanied by artificially-intelligent warbots that are voice-commanded rather than run by linkage. The ultimate weapon of World War IV

Sierra Hotel: What warbot brainies say when they can't say, "Shit hot!"

Simulator or *sim:* A device that can simulate the sensations perceived by a human being and the results of the human's responses. A simple toy computer or video game simulating the flight of an aircraft or the driving of a race car is an example of a primitive simulator.

Sit-guess: Slang for "estimate of the situation," an educated guess about your predicament.

Sit-rep: Short for "situation report" to notify your superior officer about the sheep screw you're in at the moment.

Smart Fart: The Ml00A (FG/IM-190) Anti-tank/Anti-aircraft tube-launched rocket capable of being launched off the shoulder of a Sierra Charlie. So-called because of its self-guided "smart" warhead and the sound it makes when fired.

Snake pit: Slang for the highly computerized briefing center located in most caserns and other Army posts.

Snivel: To complain about the injustice being done you.

Spasm mode: Slang for killed in action (KIA).

Spook: Slang term for either a spy or a military intelligence specialist. Also used as a verb relating to reconnaissance.

Staff stooge: Derogatory term referring to a staff officer. Also "staff weenie."

TACAMO!: "Take Charge And Move Out!"

Tacomm: A portable frequency-hopping communications transceiver system once used by rear-echelon warbot brainy troops and now generally used in very advanced and ruggedized versions by the Sierra Charlies.

Tango Sierra: Tough shit.

Tech-weenie: The derogatory term applied by combat soldiers to the scientists, engineers, and technicians who complicate life by insisting that the soldier have gadgetry that is the newest, fastest, most powerful, most accurate, and usually the most unreliable products of their fertile techie imaginations.

Third Herd, The: The 3rd Robot Infantry Regiment (Sierra Charlie), the Washington Greys (but you'd better be a Grey to use that term).

Tiger error: What happens when an eager soldier tries too hard.

Umpteen hundred: Sometime in the distant, undetermined future.

Up link: The remote command link or channel from the warbot brainy to the warbot.

Warbot: Abbreviation for "war robot," a mechanical device that is operated by or commanded by a soldier to fight in the field.

Warbot brainy: The human soldier who operates warbots through linkage, implying that the soldier is basically the brains of the warbot. Sierra Charlies remind everyone that they are definitely not warbot brainies, whom they consider to be grown-up children operating destructive video games.